Praise for *Under a Dark Sky*

"A brilliant concept, brilliantly told! . . . A novel that you simply can't put down. Populated by living, breathing characters and filled with fresh prose and sharp dialogue. . . . I guarantee this book will resonate with you. Because, let's face it, aren't we all afraid of the dark?"

—Jeffery Deaver, *New York Times* bestselling author

"Lori Rader-Day is a modern-day Agatha Christie: her mysteries are taut, her characters are real and larger than life, and her plots are relentlessly surprising. . . . There are enough breakneck twists to captivate modern readers. A dynamite late summer read!"

—Kate Moretti, *New York Times* bestselling author of *The Vanishing Year*

"An atmospheric and absorbing mystery with an intriguing cast of characters. You'll want to read this gripping novel with the lights on."

—Heather Gudenkauf, *New York Times* bestselling author of *The Weight of Silence*

"This is the kind of book you can't help but read too fast: You can't wait to find out what happened, no matter that you never want it to end."

—Elizabeth Little, author of *Dear Daughter*

"I don't know a writer who captures better the insecurities and damaged and damaging relationships of ordinary women."

—Ann Cleeves, *New York Times* bestselling author

"Splendid stuff from a master of the genre."

—Catriona McPherson, Edgar Award–nominated author of *Go to My Grave*

Praise for *The Day I Died*

"Lori Rader-Day is so ferociously talented that it kind of makes me mad. Not fair! *The Day I Died* is a terrific novel—gripping and twisty and beautifully layered. It kept me locked up and locked in from the very first word to the very last."

—Lou Berney, Edgar Award–winning author
of *The Long and Faraway Gone*

"The story is compelling, the characters interesting, and the theme of a mother's love universal." —*Mystery Scene*

"*The Day I Died* firmly establishes Lori Rader-Day as one of the most important voices currently writing mystery fiction. Her taut prose grips the reader and never lets go. . . . Rader-Day's sharp understanding of the human condition has been on display since her brilliant debut, but here, it glows and is even more jaw-dropping and insightful. You won't want to miss a sentence. Especially the last one."

—Larry D. Sweazy, award-winning author of *Where I Can See You*

"A vividly imagined and beautifully written mystery."

—Terence Faherty, Edgar Award–nominated
author of *The Quiet Woman*

"Lori Rader-Day offers readers one of the most compelling and original voices in literature today. . . . I found it beautifully written, satisfying on every level, and I couldn't help but love it. I guarantee that you will, too."

—William Kent Krueger, *New York Times* bestselling author

"Rader-Day juices her young-widow setup with enough soul-searching, menace, and dirty linen to make you think of Mary Higgins Clark with teeth bared." —*Kirkus Reviews*

the
lucky
one

Also by Lori Rader-Day

the lucky one

A Novel

LORI RADER-DAY

wm

WILLIAM MORROW
An Imprint of HarperCollinsPublishers

P.S.™ is a trademark of HarperCollins Publishers.

HarperCollins books may be purchased for educational, business, or sales promotional use. For information, please email the Special Markets Department at SPsales@harpercollins.com.

FIRST EDITION

Designed by Diahann Sturge

Feather illustration © great19 / Shutterstock Inc.

Library of Congress Cataloging-in-Publication Data has been applied for.

ISBN 978-0-06-293807-7
ISBN 978-0-06-293806-0 (hardcover library edition)

20 21 22 23 24 LSC 10 9 8 7 6 5 4 3 2 1

For my dad, Melvin Rader, who gave me a lucky life.
Also for Paula Dodson, Janie Rader, and Danny Dodson.
But, really, this one is for Jill Bryan.
This book is also dedicated to the memory of
Debra Jean Cole and Frances Annette Cole.

the
lucky
one

Audrey89: RE: RE: RE: . . . This thread is getting long and tedious already and you jerks are starting to repeat yourselves. I'm not saying we kidnap some kids, you assholes. The missing stay missing, so they can't report back. All I'm saying is WOULDN'T IT BE COOL if we understood the experience better?

MrJonesToYou: RE: RE: RE: . . . @Audrey89 This thread is not so long that I won't tell you you're an idiot.

SparkleSoo: RE: RE: RE: . . . @Audrey89 Check the Doe Pages stats before you spout garbage about the missing always staying missing. Don and Jenn have had a lot of successful matches over the years.

CooooKIES: RE: RE: RE: . . . @Audrey89 What does this have to do with the topic of this thread? I thought we were talking about the Jem Gallagher case.

LuckyOne: RE: RE: RE: . . . @Audrey89 Some of the missing don't stay missing.

JennDoePagesMOD: @MrJonesToYou Let's settle down here. Thanks for the vote of confidence @SparkleSoo, but our matches are usually to unidentified remains, so I'm not sure that's in the same spirit. We work hard for every match but that's not exactly what @Audrey89 is talking about, I think. Clarify?

SparkleSoo: RE: @JennDoePagesMOD We HAVE to count the matches to remains as wins. Otherwise, why BOTHER with all this?

CooooKIES: RE: RE: @SparkleSoo Give that despair some air!

MrJonesToYou: RE: RE: @CooooKIES You are also an idiot.

JennDoePagesMOD: RE: RE: @SparkleSoo It's easy to get frustrated. Remember our guidelines for volunteers. Take a step back, take care of yourself.

JennDoePagesMOD: RE: RE: RE: @MrJonesToYou Second warning. We allow only civil discussion here, not name-calling. Calm down or your login privileges will be revoked. @Audrey89, I have to remind you about name-calling, too.

Audrey89: RE: @JennDoePagesMOD I am only saying that we can't possibly wrap *our* minds around what the experience of the missing person is like. If you think you can, you're just watching a lot of *Law & Order*.

MrJonesToYou: RE: RE: @Audrey89 Hey. *Law & Order* is my love language.

JennDoePagesMOD: RE: RE: @Audrey89 Let's not talk down to anyone's inspiration for getting involved. Lots of people have come to the Doe Pages by way of popular culture.

LuckyOne: RE: @JennDoePagesMOD Some people are inspired to get involved by their own experience.

C0oooKIES: RE: @LuckyOne Since we're NOT talking about poor Jem Gallagher, I guess I'll bite. What experience is this? I'm sure YOUR experience outpaces everyone else's.

MrJonesToYou: Why do I hang out here? I do know REAL people. I'm starting to miss them.

Audrey89: RE: @MrJonesToYou You can log out anytime you like, buddy. Open invitation.

LuckyOne RE: @C0oooKIES *COMMENT DELETED BY AUTHOR*

C0oooKIES: RE: @LuckyOne WHAT?

Somebodyz: RE: @LuckyOne WHAT JUST HAPPENED

MrJonesToYou: RE: @LuckyOne Holy shit.

Audrey89: RE: @LuckyOne Are you serious?

C0oooKIES: RE: @LuckyOne OMG YOU HAVE TO TELL US ABOUT THIS.

Startlevision: RE: @LuckyOne What?! How old were you?

Dreaming312: RE: @LuckyOne What do you remember about it?

JealousTypist: RE: @LuckyOne When was this?

JuJuBee95: RE: @LuckyOne You were kidnapped? YOU YOUR ACTUAL SELF?

SparkleSoo: RE: @LuckyOne I smell a troll.

Slapdash: RE: @SparkleSoo Leave her alone.

JuJuBee95: RE: @LuckyOne OMGGGGG THIS IS CRAZY!!!1!

JennDoePagesMOD: Everyone, calm down. Let @LuckyOne tell her story if she wants to. Maybe @Audrey89 is right. We can learn from her experience.

CooooKIES: RE: JennDoePagesMOD: I want to hear this, but can we start a new thread? This one SHOULD HAVE BEEN about the Jem Gallagher case.

XFilesForever409: Wait. What did I miss?

Audrey89: RE: @LuckyOne Hello?

JealousTypist: RE: @Audrey89: She deleted her comment. And logged out.

SparkleSoo: Told you. Totally a troll.

CHAPTER ONE

ALICE

A dead woman looked out from the laptop resting on Alice Fine's kitchen table. The woman's skin was waxen against the metal slab. Thin shoulders, thick hair. She stared with sightless black eyes.

Alice spooned cereal into her mouth and scrolled for details. Jane Doe Anaho, 367UFNV, had been found naked in a patch of remote high desert, miles from the nearest town, named for the island wildlife refuge nearby. Discovered by hikers.

Couple of stoned kids who'll never hike again.

Alice studied the photo. Juanita Doe, maybe. They didn't know. They might never know. Race *Unk.* Unknown. Everything Unk. at the moment. That was the basic point with UIDs. They were unidentified.

The doorbell rang. Alice's attention rose slowly from the depths of open tabs. She was supposed to meet some of the other Doe Pages volunteers for lunch—another level of unknown, one she wasn't sure she was ready for—and had resorted to old study habits, cramming for an exam. It was easy to get lost in the Does, to lose time.

She reached for her cell phone. When she moved in a couple of months ago, her dad had immediately installed one of those systems that sent live video from her door to an app. Just a precaution, with all the weirdos out there. She'd met more than her fair share.

On the app, the woman in the back apartment peered into the doorbell camera. Her long gray hair had been scraped back from her face, creating a grimace that showed a crooked incisor. "Miss Fine? Is this . . . ? Can you hear me? I just need a minute of your time."

A classic line for someone who expected to have the door slammed in her face, if she could get it to open in the first place.

"I'm busy, Patricia." Patricia? Was that even the right name? *Patricia Gussin*, or something like it on the mailboxes near the back door. Alice wasn't as curious about her neighbors as they were about her.

"We're getting an action together on these new security cameras."

No sense of irony as she peered into Alice's security camera. There was no "we," no association, no association board. Only Patricia and her tinfoil-hat petitions, her keen sense for when others did as they pleased. Her emails to Rajul were legend, all caps lock and exclamation points. Rajul held no post. He had only lived in the building longer than anyone else.

Alice looked back at the dead woman, impatient for her.

"Miss Fine?"

Alice pocketed her phone and went to the door. Patricia, hearing the peephole cover open, looked up from the hallway carpet, her face stretched feral in the fish-eye. She held a clipboard. "Are you *there*?"

Alice opened the door to the chain. "What about the cameras?"

"Well, to begin with, if the cameras are for our security, why do they only point toward the *front* doors? I caught someone trying to jimmy the back door only last week."

A good point. Alice only used the back door to take out garbage and hadn't noticed. "Is the petition to place cameras at the back?"

Patricia's eyes widened. "My God, no. Are you—" She gestured at Alice with the clipboard. "Surely you're joking."

"You said someone was trying to break in—"

"No one seems to know where the video feed *goes*. They shouldn't be allowed to monitor our movements in this way."

"They who?" Alice didn't mind the security cameras. In point of fact, she liked them. Against her hip her cell phone buzzed. It made a pleasant little growl, *rnn*, whenever she got a new text.

"What was that noise?" Patricia's eyes darted overhead toward the nearest camera. She had a large, stretched freckle at her jawline.

I bet she doesn't know that's there. "Just my phone," Alice said.

"I would never carry a *tracking* device around on my person *willingly*. You're doing their job for them—"

"*Them* who? Honestly, I need to go. I'll be late to work."

"I thought you worked for your dad." Patricia peered over Alice's shoulder, as though she expected him to be there.

For a privacy nut, she was nosy enough. "Just . . . catch me this weekend. I have to go." She closed the door against Patricia's last protests, closed the peephole cover, and returned to her computer and Jane. She had started to think of the dead woman as *her* Jane.

She raised her mug, stone cold, to her lips and then put it down. She was *actually* late, not excuse-late. And it didn't matter that her dad owned the company. She was supposed to set an example. A *good* example, instead of the kind she often was.

ON THE DRIVE, she decided to cancel on the Does meet-up. By the time she pulled into the lot down the block from the site and squeezed next to Jimmy's sleek BMW, she had changed her mind back. She'd never minded not keeping up with old friends from school, busy with her mom's care, then wedding plans. Now her mother's dress hung on her closet door like something out of

Dickens, and she spent her time online with the Does. She should attend the lunch, meet some of the other volunteers in person.

Alice hurried along the fence. Above, the crane swung. She could hear a concrete mixer or two churning under that. At the gate she shaded her eyes, noted the crew up on the second deck, and waved when Gus called out a good-morning. The six-story elevator shaft at the corner of the structure-in-progress served as sentry, a ticking clock. They were at least a week behind, summer winding down around them.

The problem was, no one had the right enthusiasm for it. It was too much a letdown from their last project, a thirty-seven-story 'scraper downtown, a beacon of the south Loop, a real stunner. On this suburban garage the crew was leaner. Decimated, really, the friendships among the crew still reshaping themselves around absence. Among the crew, it seemed to Alice, everyone put in their time, heads down, hearts not into it. They had built their cathedral, their once-in-a-lifetime. From here on out, they were just putting down bricks.

She yanked open the trailer door. The air-conditioning had been set low enough to store meat. She was the meat. In the back alcove of the trailer, her dad swiveled in the chair he and JimBig King used, phone to ear, eyes narrowed.

Sorry, she mouthed, and hurried behind her desk. Five minutes late. Who else got the stink eye for five minutes? Seven, tops.

"Well, that's just not going to cut it," he said. He'd spoken into his phone, but she sensed it was meant for her, too.

Alice stowed her backpack and started her computer. Under his audience, she put effort into miming the efficiency that came so naturally to him. They were nothing alike. Where he was compact and controlled, quick, decisive, she was expansive, long-limbed. She took up space, more than women were supposed to. More than her mother, obviously, who hadn't passed down her fine bone structure, her petite debutante's body—only her tendency toward migraine. The family joke had always been that Alice was a throwback to her great-uncles on the Fine side, all tall and lanky, with nicknames like "Slim" and "Stretch." Sometimes her dad called her that, "Stretch," when he was in the mood.

He wasn't in the mood this morning.

"Well?" He held his hand over the phone mouthpiece. He was a former cop, intolerant of unanswered questions and unassigned guilt.

"Sorry," she said. "My neighbor—"

Her phone buzzed in her pocket. *Rnn. Rnn, rnn.* She reached for it and turned it off. "Sorry."

"Is that more of that John Doe nonsense? Don't bring it in here."

Her dad turned in the chair. From here she could see the scar at his jaw, a bad nick from a barber when he was young. Cataloguing the scratches and dents of people was a habit she'd picked up from her short time with the Does, so she supposed she couldn't help it anymore, bringing it into their lives. He thought it was morbid, and maybe he was right. Scars, tattoos. Crooked teeth, badly healed fractures. She was imagining the corpses they would become, the abandoned bones.

"I truly don't understand why you got involved with that." His back to her.

"You know why." She'd been trying to explain it for two months. She wasn't playing Sherlock on social media. She had a purpose. "Like, why did you want to become a police officer? You wanted to do something to help people—"

"Living people."

"It's for the living, Dad."

The people featured on the Pages were almost always dead, half the profiles for unidentified remains, and half dedicated to missing persons, most of the cases at least a decade cold. They could only hope for a match between a found body and a lost person. A match was the holy grail—to bring an end to a mystery and give closure for some weary family.

Don and Jenn, who ran the Doe Pages, called the long wait *open-ended grief*, like a sentence without punctuation, a story half told.

Grief was open-ended, though, wasn't it? *All grief, if it could be called grief at all.*

"Can't you do something else?" he said. "Stir the pot at a soup kitchen?"

"You know I can't cook." She subsisted on takeout, foraging meals in her own kitchen like a rodent. "This is the thing I can do." Maybe. She hadn't been that helpful yet, and the work was meticulous, taxing. Thankless.

"Are you going to tell me what held you up?"

Oh. "Nothing." She didn't want to get into Patricia, the petitions. He'd gotten her the apartment through a friend, someone owed a favor, a good deal, a nice place, but he'd have rather she stayed at home forever. She certainly couldn't admit to being late because of Jane Doe Anaho. "Traffic. Sorry."

She'd been apologizing a lot lately. He'd been short-tempered, ever since—

"Has Matt been in here again?" he said. Right on cue.

"No." She could feel herself blushing. "Not that I know of."

He spun in his chair, nodded toward the floor.

Alice leaned forward over her desk. Perfectly shaped boot prints led from the door to her desk, then toward the trailer's bathroom.

The fucking dust.

It paid to be Harrison Fine's daughter, to be granted the easiest job in the world and a salary she didn't earn. So little was asked. She kept the filing, answered the phones, paid vendors and payroll. Her priority task, though, was keeping the construction dust at bay inside the trailer, where visiting clients and investors seemed to expect the pristine business environment of a bank. But the guys on the crew sometimes scammed coffee or used the trailer's toilet instead of the Porta-Johns. How much did it matter, when no one was due for a visit?

Alice reached for her desk calendar, remembering as she did that they actually were expecting a visit. Uncle Jim was back from his impromptu vacation today, and he had to lead some stakeholders on a site tour, a regrets visit to pass out the excuses and apologies. He'd probably bring them inside at some point to sign paperwork and jolly them into good moods, just shoot the shit for a while. Jim King was a terrific shooter of shit, and so was her dad, Jim's right hand. *And left*, Uncle Jim always said when he had the opportunity, though it was for laughs. Everyone knew JimBig—as he was called by almost everyone—ran the show, and that Jim Junior, Jimmy, was the heir. Jimmy, who ran around the sites getting the cuffs of his suit pants dirty, so that everyone knew he was destined for better things. Harrison Fine? Harris Fine was simply the one who got things done, and, when there was something to do, so was Alice. In this way, they were exactly alike.

She got up from her desk and went to the closet in the back. Pulling out the mop, she caught a wink from her dad.

"Sorry," he said. "With Big gone, I've been— You know why I worry. I just want you to be safe."

"I do," she said. "I am." It was a balm. She'd skip the meet-up this time.

She sidled up to him and reached around his neck for a hug. He squeezed her arm while she breathed in his scent. Shaving cream, coffee, cinder block. It paid to be Harris Fine's daughter. It always had.

Then she took the mop and got down to business, even if business, this time and so often, was only dust.

CHAPTER TWO
MERRILY

Merrily Cruz walked past the women in the front office, sunglasses still on, attitude set to stun. She saw the exchanged glances. Five minutes. Not a crime. Or were they noticing the demure sweater set, the skirt that was not the right length for her or for fashion? Underneath: commando. So what? She filled that sweater out, made it *work*. If they spent more time on their jobs and less time on *her* business—

She saw the silver balloon first, like a beacon over her cubicle. "Shit."

Up the aisle to her desk, she saw the damage. Her desk was littered with candies and her chair wrapped in toilet paper, her computer monitor draped with wilted paper streamers. The star-shaped balloon, half deflated, had been tethered to the handset of her phone.

Kath rolled out from behind the pillar that separated their desks. "Happy belated!"

"Ah, thanks," Merrily murmured, slipping her sunglasses into her purse. She swiped at the toilet paper and sat down, stuffing the mess quickly into the bin under her desk. "Belated only because I took the day off."

"That's smart, though. Who wants to put up with this bullshit on your birthday? Was it *so* fun?"

Lunch and shopping down on the Mag Mile, that had been the plan. Lunch and shopping *only*, but then Mamá had talked her into going home for dinner. Merrily still thought of Port Beth, just over the state line in Indiana, as home. She wished she didn't. She wished she could set boundaries, but she had no luck there, not with her sweet mamá, alone in Port Beth, and not with any of the indulgences she'd offered in celebration.

Like the cake she'd made. Slaved over and dangled, back home in Port Beth. At least it had been worth the trip. A cake of angels and beauty itself, chocolate on top of chocolate, like a last request before execution. Merrily had passed out in a food coma in her old room and had to borrow the twinset and skirt from her mom's closet for work. Her mom *loved* it. Merrily looked like a giraffe dressed for church, but she still looked better than the women in the front office any day of the week. *Fact*.

"Shopping with my mom, and, ugh, the cake—"

"It's *so* great you two are *so* close," Kath said, her attention already back on her computer screen.

Merrily started up her computer and untied the ribbon from her phone. "Yeah." The dying balloon floated at gut-height, waiting for instruction. Finally Merrily stretched its string around the pillar and leashed it.

"Find anything cute in the tall-lady shops?"

They hadn't shopped, really, only walked up the hot street in one direction and back on the other, stopping to browse and sample air-conditioning as the whim took them. Then a pricey lunch, with a glass of chilled Prosecco. On a Wednesday, at lunchtime! Not that she was surprised. Her mom had never wanted her to move to the city, and now used every opportunity to show Merrily what fun she could be. Occasional splurges showed how far a dollar stretched when you lived below your means in Port Beth instead of in the devil's backyard. The train ride to the city was only an hour, Mamá had marveled, twice. Such a *clean* train. By the bottom of the second glass, she'd stopped suggesting Merrily commute back to the city at all. *You could get a better job.*

Merrily wouldn't argue that. "I wasn't looking for anything special," she said to Kath. She'd been careful not to let her gaze linger too long on anything. There'd been a dress, designer. She was used to keeping her mom from thinking there was anything she hadn't provided for her. She might have bought it for herself, but not in front of her mom. It was an expense she couldn't have explained, not on her salary.

Merrily slumped into her chair, feeling sorry for herself. The short skirt rode up her legs. "Did I miss anything yesterday?"

Kath rattled off a list of minor skirmishes in a hushed voice: paperwork gone wrong and hazard avoided, a snub between colleagues the rest of them had spent the day taking apart. Merrily let her go on, like a radio someone had left in an empty room. "And then this morning a couple of cops marched right into Billy's office."

Merrily pushed off from her desk and rolled into the aisle. "What? What happened?"

Kath scooted back and craned to see the corner office. There was a smear of something on her chin. "They're still in there. It was *so* early, and no one was here but me. And Billy, of course."

Code name: Billy was Mr. Williams, their manager. Or "Bills," as in dollars. Billy had hungry eyes, all the time, for advancement, for leverage. Lately, for her. What would she do if Billy finally got around to grabbing her ass? A lawsuit? Could she force a severance large enough to shut down this career theater for a while, take a trip? Buy a fucking designer dress and not care who saw how much it cost?

"Maybe they'll drag Billy through in handcuffs," she said. She'd been living in fear she'd meet Billy out in the wild.

Kath glanced her way. "You're in a mood."

Merrily reached into her purse for her cell phone. Cake hangover. Actual hangover. They'd had more wine back at the house, and she'd decided against the late train and called it a night by ten, crashing in her childhood bed. Now her birthday had come and gone, and no one beyond her mom had seemed to care. A few funny cat texts from her roommate. And now Kath and this tired balloon. She'd gotten a weird message from Rick, not his usual dorky birthday greeting. That was it. Another trip around the sun. She'd just sort of expected . . . something more, somehow.

"It's not a *mood*," Merrily said. "This is the new and improved *mature* Merrily Cruz."

Kath scoffed behind the pillar.

"I mean it," Merrily said. "I turned thirty. *Thirty*."

"A baby," Kath said. "Believe me, when you're my age . . ."

Merrily tuned out. Kath had no idea. Thirty was a *monster*. She'd been pursued by it and now here it sat in her lap, breathing its stink on her. Her age would ruin everything, if not this year, then soon. It was absolutely mind-fucking to watch the clock run out.

The door to Billy's corner office opened, cutting Kath's monologue. Merrily recoiled into her cube, face to screen, but listened. She peeked over her cube wall. Four men emerged, two in state trooper blues, hats held in front of them with both hands, the other stranger in a bad suit, plainclothes, serious as a heart attack. Billy led them, his head down. Why was his head down? It was a funeral procession. Merrily watched the parade out of the corner of her eye, losing them behind the pillar. And then she heard foot-steps.

Let it be Kath. Whatever it was, let it be Kath.

"Merrily," Mr. Williams said quietly from behind her. She turned her head. He was Mr. Proper now, Mr. Human Resources. "These gentlemen need to talk to you. Can you come with me?"

The rest of the room was still, silent.

She hadn't done anything illegal. Had she? There were gray areas, of course, but she hadn't gone as far as others. Why did she have to be the one? She'd been so careful to keep things casual. Innocent. Almost. Most of the time.

How had they tracked her *here*? Wait—

Merrily pushed back from her desk, standing on shaking legs. Billy's gaze rose with her, his eyes sweeping, flat, over the tight sweater.

"Take your stuff," he said. "Just in case."

Well, she thought. *On to plan C.*

MERRILY LED THE police officers out of the cube farm and to a meeting room near reception. Head forward, eyes avoided. Door closed. One of the uniforms stayed outside.

They were already talking to her.

Help us out with a little matter, one of them said. *Nothing to worry about.*

She listened as best she could through the rushing of blood through her ears. Her pink purse sat on the table like an internal organ ripped from her body.

Her mind raced ahead. This couldn't be about—

No, it had to be something else.

Mamá.

Merrily placed both palms on the table. What would she need to absorb? She couldn't hear that her mom had collapsed in the street or been crushed on the way to the grocery store or some other horrible suburban outcome. She couldn't. Not with her mouth still brackish from all that wine and icing.

"Miss Cruz," the guy in the suit said. He had a stern face pushed back on his neck, the flesh rolling like a bulldog's. "Are you an acquaintance of Richard Kisel?"

She looked up from her hands. "Richard—"

Rick. Of course. Of *course* Rick. "Rick was my— My mother dated him when I was really young. *Really* young. But he keeps in touch." The men exchanged glances. "Sometimes," she said.

The state trooper was closer to her age, cute, but the bulldog was doing all the talking. "When did you last hear from him?"

"Did he do something wrong?"

"See if you can remember."

"I can do better." Relief swelled in her, made her dizzy. She pulled out her phone and scrolled for Rick's last text. He usually sent her a breezy message every few months, his way of saying hello after a long silence. Merrily held out her phone, and the men hunched over it.

"Yesterday," the young cute cop breathed.

" 'Hey, kid,' " the other read from the phone. " 'It's best if I don't bother you anymore. Have a good life.' " He looked up. "Sounds like a breakup to me."

"He was like my—" She started over. "He's just a friend of my mom's who checked up on me. Don't make it gross." She looked at her nail polish, wondering how far out on that particular ledge she should go.

"This is the only method by which you communicate?"

"He's called before," she said. "But, like, once. He doesn't even text that often. I mean, yesterday was my birthday, so he would normally send— Oh, God. Is he OK?"

The men conferred through another silent look. She had asked them what he'd *done* first, then how he was. They didn't know Rick, though, or they would understand.

Rick wasn't her dad, *thank God*. Once she'd heard her mom talking on the phone to a friend about Rick's three kids, all with different mothers. A slut, if he'd been a woman. Luckily, Rick wasn't even her stepdad, because her mom had never married him. He was *like* a stepdad. Like a former stepdad. Or like . . . something. He was something to her, if she hadn't exactly figured out what. But sometimes she knew how little she was to him, and when he'd sent that weird peace-out message instead of a *happy birthday*, she'd only assumed this was one of those times. Sure it hurt. A birthday cake emoji—would it have killed him?

"Is he OK?" she said again.

"He's been reported missing by his landlord," Bulldog said.

She sat back. "Is he behind on his rent?"

The bulldog stared at her, his neck strained against his collar. "Do you have some kind of grievance against Mr. Kisel?"

How long did they have? "No, it's only— The thing you can count on with Rick is that he's going to be Rick."

"And that means?" the uniformed cop said. *Really* cute. He had a thin silver bar pinned to his uniform that read *G. Vasquez*.

"Rick Kisel watches out for himself," she said, grateful she could direct herself to this guy. She wished for a little silver bar to remind him her name was *M. Cruz*. Could they not get along? Be nice to a half-brown girl who poured one out with her *mom* for her big three-oh? "I've gone months without hearing from him before." She held out her hand for her phone. "A year."

She sounded pathetic.

The bulldog leaned back and scrolled through Rick's older messages. Merrily tried to catch Vasquez's eye. Her rights were in the process of being violated, but she was still relieved, still hoping if she behaved just so and said exactly what was expected, everything would be fine. Best behavior, and it would all turn out. Even Rick. He could be OK.

"His neighbors haven't seen him in two weeks," the bulldog said.

Merrily sighed. "But that's *Rick*. You don't know him."

"Do *you* know Rick? For instance, that he's been living under a different name in Wisconsin? Why would that be?"

Merrily's breath caught. Another name. *What did that asshole get himself into?* "Maybe I *don't* know him."

"And meanwhile, *we* don't know *you*." Her phone was pushed across the table. "Where were you yesterday evening?"

Merrily claimed her phone, frowned at it. "I thought you said he disappeared a couple of weeks ago."

Vasquez leaned in. "We were trying to get a word with you at your residence yesterday—"

"Oh!" Again, relief that answers were so readily at hand. "Yesterday I took the day off work to spend with my mom and then stayed at her house."

"Can anyone else verify that?"

"My . . . mom?"

"That's the same mom who dated Mr. Kisel?"

She got it then. All this Mr. Kisel this and that, while she and her mamá had to report their whereabouts and open up their private messages. She got it. Rick Kisel was going to ruin their lives, all over again.

CHAPTER THREE

ALICE

Alice watched the day's progress at the window behind her desk. The trailer was visitor-ready. The filing done. Payroll not due for a few more days. Outside, it all seemed like cathedral-building, while inside her tin-can office she built only piles of paperwork.

She watched until Matt's blue plaid shirt appeared near the back gate. The shirt she'd gotten him, the one that matched his eyes precisely. He should not be allowed to wear that shirt. He should not be allowed . . . lots of things.

Her dad, Uncle Jim, Jimmy, all AWOL. All somewhere being important, doing things that mattered.

She sat down, thought it over. Finally, she pulled out her laptop and opened up to the black eyes of Jane Doe Anaho, listening for footsteps on the gravel outside.

How did people come undone from all ties to lie alone in a coroner's vault? That was the real mystery. Behind this case file were hundreds—*thousands*—of profiles, all lost people one way or another. All posted to the Doe Pages in the hopes that someone would recognize a face where there was no name or, where there was a name but no body, some small detail in a report that would pull the two worlds toward one another, missing and found. A tattoo, a scar, a birthmark, evidence of an old broken bone, a piece of jewelry she always wore, the color of nail polish she favored. Anything. Anything that might bring a body back from the roadside, from the forest preserve, from the shallow grave where it was found.

Alice clicked to her Jane's police report again and combed for details. Under the section for clothing and items found alongside the body, the cops had listed one gold hoop earring, some trash that might have collected against the body in the wind or might have been hers, and a piece of orange fabric, nylon ripstop, like the material from a backpack.

Alice clicked away from the police report and navigated to the Jane's Pages profile to add that detail: *nylon, ripstop, orange.* She'd have been a hiker. Maybe visiting from a distance? European, even. An orange backpack or tent was the kind of detail that might someday lead Jane Anaho home, to be interred in the family plot. Did it really matter? Alice thought of the shady green hill where her mother was buried. It mattered. She clicked to save the update and republish the profile with her edits.

The website churned on King and Fine's bad connection, slow as a washing machine. She had turned up the AC temp, and now it was growing warm in the trailer. Alice watched the spinning wheel of the cursor, lulled.

The door opened, a knife of sunlight stabbing the floor. Alice jumped, snapped her laptop closed, and shoved it under her desk.

Uncle Jim came in. "There she is," he said, his voice larger than the space between them. He'd been gone only a couple of days, but he might as well be coming back from a three-month polar expedition. "There's my Alice in Wonderland."

Alice got up and met him for a hug. He couldn't swing her off her feet anymore, but the old nickname never failed to shrink her to fit the tiny door of childhood. He wasn't her real uncle but JimBig King and her dad could be brothers. They'd been working together so long, they were meeting in the middle like an old married couple, same steely build, same sandy hair graying to granite.

"How was Florida?" she said.

"Good, good. Just what the doctor ordered." Up close, though, he looked tired, not at all like he'd been on vacation. No tan. He'd probably fretted this site's timeline, the next project's permits, this tour he had to give.

"You didn't even go outside, did you?"

"They serve those little umbrella drinks inside, too, did you know?" He grinned. "You should have your pop take you sometime. How are things holding up here, boss?" An old joke only he found funny. She was fine with it, as long as he didn't put her in charge of anything.

"We managed without you," she said. "Now that you're back, you'll just fuck it up."

"All that fancy schooling." Uncle Jim shook his head, feigning dismay. He loved her as foulmouthed as the crew, saucy, independent. He seemed to think he'd had a hand in making her that way, and maybe he had. "I plan to. You seen Jimmy?"

"Saw his car, so he's here somewhere."

"What about your dad? I think he's hiding from me."

"He was in first thing this morning," Alice said. "He's probably out getting ready for the tour."

"Tour's canceled," Uncle Jim said.

When she didn't say anything, he looked up, then around at the trailer. "Oh, yeah, sorry. You sure did a nice job on the cleanup.

These money men, you know how they are. You can't set a clock by them. They make their own rules."

The investors spoke in Monopoly-money numbers when she bothered to listen. Mostly she didn't. The actual business of King and Fine was something best left to her dad and the Jims. When investors came to the trailer, she tried to make herself scarce. Some of them had lingering eyes the second her dad's back was turned.

For some reason, the canceled meeting nagged at her. She had nothing to take pride in beyond clean floors? Nothing to look forward to?

"I'm going out for lunch today," she said, deciding once and for all. "You want anything brought back?"

"You got a hot date, kid? Break an old man's heart."

Sometimes she was sure he meant these quips for Jimmy's sake, but she wasn't sure. There'd been a short-lived thing, kid stuff, before she got shipped off to her girls' school out West. Her dad, saving her from Jimmy King. But around Uncle Jim, she was careful, in all ways, of his feelings and his temper. "Just meeting some friends."

"That's nice." He wandered to the back and sank into the chair. He seemed frail, actually, his clothes loose like an old man's. *If he's an old man. . . .* It chilled her. He and her dad were almost the same age, had lived the same lives. Her mother had only died two years ago, which had been hard enough. *All grief is open-ended.*

She swallowed hard. "Lunch, then?"

"Nothing for me, Al, thanks, but if you see Jimmy on your way out, send him to find me. Your dad, too. Either of them, both."

"I can get Gus to call them in. Anything wrong?"

"Don't trouble Gus. It can wait. Nothing the boss can't fix when she's back from her break."

"Shouldn't take more than an afternoon, right?"

He looked up, confused. Then the smile, and everything was fine again. "That's right. That's our girl."

AT LUNCH, ALICE stepped down from the trailer just as Matt rounded the corner. They both stopped. She should have checked out the windows. The peephole first, always.

"Hey," he said. "How—how are you?"

"Fine," she said, then wished she hadn't. He'd accused her of always saying everything was fine, specifically *fine*, even when it wasn't. "Sorry."

"No need to apologize," he said.

"I didn't—that's not what I meant. You're the one—" She stopped herself and looked around. She didn't want the rest of the crew to hear her sounding so wounded. He'd broken it off out of the blue, weeks before the wedding. She'd driven out to her dad's house in the woods to rage and claw—to turn her anger and hurt over to him, hoping somehow Harris Fine would know what to do. But then she'd made the mistake of telling him about the tattoo, and then *that* had turned into a whole thing. He'd demanded to see it. *When the hell did you get that?* he'd said, missing the point entirely.

"I was just trying to be, I don't know. Supportive." Matt took a step backward. He was a couple inches shorter than she was. He'd always said he didn't mind, but now he seemed to. He'd gotten a new truck since the breakup, too, one of those extended-cab beasts. "You know I only did what you didn't have the guts to do."

"So I'm a coward, on top of everything else?" He would have told the guys, too, so she'd be a figure of pity among them. "Everything you say makes things worse."

"Come on, Al. What else can I apologize for?"

"How about for not *fucking off*? Any self-respecting man would have found a new job after jilting the boss's daughter."

Matt stared at the gravel. "And here I was feeling bad for you."

"For being deprived of you?"

"No." He looked away. "Your headaches. The fainting—it's not normal."

"You didn't break up with me because I get *migraines*." The spells came fast, without warning. She experienced them as the wings of some great black bird, the low and distant beat of wings taking flight and then sudden blackness. Her head ached now, a bad sign.

"If that's all it is. I mean, *no*. But I do think you should see someone about it."

Someone. She glared at him. "I am—I'm great. As it turns out, calling it off with you was the best way to go."

"Is that what your daddy told you to think?" He looked like he wanted to swallow the words as soon as he'd said them.

There had been doubts. Real doubts that she should marry into the crew, tangle every loose end of her life to the knot of King and Fine, to the poured-concrete kingdom that would someday be Jimmy's. All the fragile eggs in one basket. Was that all she wanted out of life? This nothing job? This nothing—

He clenched his jaw as though she might strike him.

"Thank you for reminding me you were no big loss," Alice said with forced composure. "Now, if you'll excuse me, I'm late." How many times today had she said that? *I'm late, I'm late.* She was not Alice in Wonderland. She was the white rabbit.

CHAPTER FOUR

MERRILY

At the end of her police interview, Merrily had a moment of uncertainty. There were many rules about unescorted guests roaming the premises, though if anyone could wander around without a minder, she supposed it was a state trooper. She was supposed to usher them out. She grabbed the pink purse off the table and took the elevator down with them.

In the lobby, Officer G. Vasquez held the door for her, so she stepped outside. People got smoke breaks, didn't they? So what if she didn't smoke? The others marched off, but the cute one reached into a pocket on his chest, right under that silver *G. Vasquez* bar, and handed her a card. "In case you think of something else to tell us, yeah?" Then he followed the other guys across the plaza, under the Calder sculpture that was supposed to be some kind of bird, to a waiting police cruiser parked illegally with two tires on the curb. Merrily waited to see if he would look back.

She'd given them her mom's phone number and address. Merrily dug into the horrible purse for her phone.

Her mom picked up after a single ring, her voice causing in

Merrily such a struggle of emotions that she couldn't speak. Back in the conference room, she'd been forced to consider that her sweet mother could come to harm. She'd never felt so close to the impossible, toes over the edge at the end of the world.

"Hello? Mer? Merrily, is that you?"

She cleared her throat. "Mamá. I just—Rick's missing."

"Rick who?"

"*Mamá.*"

There was a soft sigh on the other end of the phone. "What's it have to do with you or me? How'd you find out?"

"Well, he didn't text yesterday—"

"Oh, Merrily, please—"

He had, but she didn't have the heart to tell her mom that Rick's message was somehow worse than nothing.

"—and then the *police* showed up at my *office*." Merrily looked out at the cars passing along the street. She could hear the drama built into her own voice, as if she were talking to Kath about someone else's bad day. She imagined having to walk past all her coworkers on the way back to her cube, all the questions and whispers. Merrily hitched her purse strap onto her shoulder and started across the plaza. Surely a police visit about someone missing who was almost but not quite family was a good enough reason to call it a day. "It was awkward, to say the least."

"I'm sure Rick's OK," her mom said. "He's always just fine."

"Have the police ever come about him before?" He was definitely in some kind of trouble. "They said he had a different name. Who does that?"

Her mother went quiet. "What name?"

"They didn't say." She hadn't even asked. It hadn't seemed like the most important question at the time. It still didn't. "Why?"

"So are they coming to see me, is that it?"

"Put the kettle on."

"Ayyy." A long exhalation. "Why is it always Rick?"

"It's not always—" She didn't want to defend him. "You're the one who thought he was datable."

Her mom laughed. Merrily felt the sound like a hand to her cheek. "At least I came to my senses," her mom said. "Eventually. I'll go get— Oh, that's the other line, my dove. It's probably the *fuzz*."

"Best behavior, Mamá," Merrily said, and hung up. That was what her mom had always said to her, growing up. Best behavior meant putting on the public face, showing people what they wanted to see. Especially white people, even though what they wanted to see was never entirely clear. She and her mom had had to put on a lot of best behavior in Indiana, and even now in the city Merrily caught herself painting on a mild expression, watching her mouth, taking herself out of the equation. By the time she reached the L platform toward home, Merrily felt bad for herself again, for all the days of her life she'd had to pretend to be a good little girl. On the train she texted Billy to say she had a family emergency. Close enough.

At the door to her apartment, Merrily could smell bacon and smoke. The living room was filled with haze. "Justyce? You OK in there?"

"What are you doing home so early?" Justyce rounded the corner and stopped in her tracks. She did an exaggerated double take, the long braids of her hair jolting. She clicked a pair of greasy tongs in the air, her other hand reaching for her throat. "Or is it *late*? What are you wearing, my girl? Is that a—is that what they call a sweater *set*? This is the weirdest slut walk I've ever witnessed. I want details."

"I wish," Merrily said. "I had a weird day."

"Did you get *fired*?"

"I'll explain later, OK? I'm not . . . feeling that well."

"You and Mamá Cruz got your drank on," Justyce growled. "Love it."

It was easier to let it go. "Yeah, a little."

"Too much white wine," Justyce said, her voice now trilling regally, Queen of England–like.

Merrily decided not to take this as some kind of classist shot—sometimes she wasn't brown enough for Justyce—and smiled. "Eat your bacon and try not to burn the place down."

In her room she threw her mom's clothes to the floor, then scooped them into the back of her closet, closing the door as though keeping something at bay. She caught sight of her nearly naked self in the long mirror leaning against her wall and turned sideways, slid her hands down her stomach. Cake and wine. She grabbed some leggings and a sweatshirt from the floor, probably not too dirty, some clean underwear from the basket of laundry she'd never put away. She threw her hair up with a rubber band. In the mirror now stood a single woman, thirty years old, her whole life ahead of her. That's what her mom said at the birthday lunch. Her whole life, but then, that was always true. Everybody's whole life was ahead of them, however long that turned out to be. It mattered, though, if you made the most of it.

Merrily pulled the band out of her hair, changed the sweatshirt for a V-neck T-shirt, freshened her lipstick, and sat down at her desk. Maybe one of her guys would be home early, too, and she could salvage this ruin of a day.

She opened her laptop to the *plink-plink* of ChatX notifications—the sound of coins hitting the bottom of her piggy bank. Michaelangelo24 had invited her to chat.

"Hey, Mike," she said when his face showed up on the screen. Michaelangelo24 was pudgy, baby-like, but with glasses and a few days' growth of beard. In a smaller box up in the corner, her own face peered out. She had the laptop stacked onto a couple of old textbooks and the screen tilted down, so that she looked small and defenseless, someone the guys might want to protect. It didn't hurt that the angle tipped the lens the tiniest bit down the V of her neckline. She leaned forward.

"What's going on, Mer-Maid?" he said, pronouncing it wrong. Most of them did but she didn't correct them. "You're online early today."

"Yeah, it's—" Her voice choked out. She was being ridiculous and such a bore. "Sorry."

"You OK? What's happening?"

"Had a gross day, that's all. Lost my job." Once she'd said it, she realized it was true. She wouldn't go back there.

"Your . . ."

"I had an actual job, Mike, and I was pretty good at it." A lie. She had only needed to be good *enough*, so that's what she'd been.

"Layoffs? That's rough."

But she was thinking about Rick, and dammit if her eyes didn't swim.

"Don't be sad," he said.

"It's my birthday." She wiped at her eyes. "Did you bring me a present, Mike?"

He smiled. "What are you wearing there?" Mike liked bare knees—and tits, obviously, they all liked tits. She kept things clean and virginal, though. Except—thirty years old. How long could she pull this off? If he asked, she'd say she was twenty-two.

Merrily stood up and slid the leggings off under her long shirt, watching herself strip them off in the little frame of her room. Slowly, giving the man what he needed. Then she sat down and brought the computer to her lap, backward, facing the screen down her naked legs.

"Mer-Maid, you have legs for *miles*."

She stretched out, adjusted the screen so that he could see her, thighs to pedicure. "Good for you, Michael?"

"I'll drop a birthday treat into your account in a few minutes, help you out with the job sitch. Point your toes?"

She complied, thanked her lucky stars for high arches. "Thank you so much, Mike. You're a . . ." Lifesaver? Too close to reality, and no one wanted that. "An *angel*, as advertised."

Mike was already somewhere else, somewhere her legs and pointed toes had taken him. A Thursday afternoon! But really, for her it was nothing. It was like visiting the doctor—no, not quite that clinical, not even that physical. Taking a chat with one of her guys was more like waiting for the city bus. A fine way to get where you're going, but don't touch anything.

She didn't touch. She didn't perform. For some of her guys, she didn't have to do a thing. She could flick through a magazine, paint her nails. Most of her regulars didn't log in for a turn-on. They only wanted to feel as though they were in the same room with another human. They might have turned to drink or drugs, so it didn't seem that awful to her that someone might need to look at a pair of long, shapely legs. She did have good legs. She leaned over the top of the screen and nudged the volume down. Way down.

Afterward she found a nice round bonus in her ChatX account, more than she normally could count on. How many birthday parties for herself could she run online this week? Or—for other people? It always paid to think of the needs of other people, especially when their needs aligned so well with her own.

HAIR BACK UP, sweatshirt back on, Merrily wrenched open the closet again. She moved things aside, reaching to a high shelf in the back.

She'd discovered the photos in the trash one day when she was a kid, fifth grade or so. Her mom must have finally torn what was left of Rick out of their lives that week. *Eventually*, Mamá had said. Eventually took, oh, ten years or more. But that week, clothes, shoes, books, papers, every scrap of Rick in their life appeared in the bin. Merrily plucked out the photos, left the rest. What could she do with one of Rick's old leather jackets? Wear it? Not for a second. But the photos—what could it hurt?

Now she took the box to her bed and nestled in, realizing as she did that maybe she'd found the source of her problem. She didn't really remember Rick, and yet he was a figure in her life. Because he'd lived with them when she was a baby? Because they'd visited him once when she was ten? Because he texted her once in a while to say hey like some distant uncle? No, she thought of Rick as part of her life because of these stupid photos.

It didn't matter that she didn't really know him. He was as real as Michaelangelo24 or Searcher6 or any of the guys she talked to online—but in a totally different way. He was just another guy who existed entirely online.

She opened the box. Rick as a teen with a prom date, big hair on both of them. Rick as a young man with, maybe, one of his girl-friends, their faces turned toward one another. Maybe it was one of the mothers of his kids. Merrily studied the barest crescent of the woman's profile, wondering. Had he been texting his real kids all this time, too? Or was she somehow safe to talk to because she didn't require anything of him and had no claims?

Merrily pawed through it all, plucking out a photo here and there to take a closer look. Rick as an adult, with a fishing pole in his hand and a cigarette dangling from his lips. Rick as a child, a toy forgotten at his feet. On the back it said: *King Richard conquers the Dunes*. King Richard! She found herself smiling. She had always assumed that Rick was more than he was to her, but how much more might he be? Maybe he had siblings. Maybe he had kept on having kids after he'd left her mom. There could be a child army of Rick spin-offs, little scammers and liars, heartbreakers every one.

Merrily understood what she was doing. She was conflating this rando from her childhood with the man she would never know, could never know. Her own father was lost to her, long dead with no family left behind, no hints, not even a box of photos to sort through. One car accident before she was born and all she had was a name, a dead end. She'd considered doing one of those DNA spit tests to see what he might have left her, other than nothing. But it was a lot of spit. And then of course you could never unlearn what you found.

Also, her mom would *kill* her. She thought those DNA tests were a lot of begging for trouble.

In the depths of the box Merrily found remnants of her own childhood. Souvenirs, she'd called them then, but it was all trash: candy wrappers, receipts her mom had given her to draw on the backs of, paper place mats listing the kids' menu, stickers stuck to every damn thing. Early creative attempts, too, her fat-fingered crayon efforts at ABCs, then pictures and stories. She was a tiny magpie adopting bits of garbage everywhere she went, stowing them as treasure. Underneath this, she found more photos: adult Rick alongside buddies on the shore of some green water with beer cans raised; Rick as a teen, dapper for a high school dance, a scrawny self-conscious brunette at his side.

Somewhere there was a photo of her as a baby, sitting awkwardly in Rick's lap. The fact that Rick had dated a brand-new single mother had always made her feel more kindly toward him—probably more than he deserved. But he'd also kept in touch when he didn't have to. He must have been a good guy, deep down. Deep, deep, deep.

She got to the bottom of the box and reached for her phone.

Nothing from her mom, which was weird. She had texts from Kath, though, with a lot of question marks. Instead of answering her, Merrily called up Rick's messages and read a few, then tapped to send one.

Hey? she wrote. *Are you OK?*

She started to write more, but deleted that and then hit send and clicked over to social media. She rarely posted anywhere outside ChatX, but what the hell. She had a PhotoSocial login, might as well use it for the greater good. She snapped a selfie with one of Rick's dating photos and tapped out a caption. *Missing: Richard Kisel,* she wrote. Hesitated. *Stepfather.* Missing from; last seen. Wisconsin? She didn't know the details. She deleted *stepfather,* posted it.

Then she lay back among her pillows to read his old texts, time-traveling back as far as they went. His pattern *immediately* obvious. A wave of texts and then silence, again and again, months in between but always coming back, joking, playful, charming, as though they'd talked just yesterday. That was Rick. A lot of their conversation was the same: *Hey, kid, what's new, nothing much here, how's your mom.* From her: *She's talking back to the TV,* smiley face. And then a few months later, another *Hey, kid.* It was all flat, boring. Why had he bothered?

A couple of years ago when she'd finally finished her college degree a hundred semesters late, he'd sent some straight-faced messages about life. Not very Rick-like. Rick, giving advice? She'd only been embarrassed for him. He was like one of those old e-games where the electronic hamster needed occasional feeding, except that day the hamster started spouting bootstrap advice she didn't need.

Luckily the heartfelt messages quickly reverted to the standard fare: chitchat and Cubs scores, jokes and TV show references. Merrily yawned, curled around the box, and read text after text, *Hey, kid, Hey, kid,* until she started to dream. Deep, *deep* down.

JuJuBee95: So are we doing this thing, Chicagoland Metropolitan Area?

MrJonesToYou: RE: @JuJuBee95 Doing what?

JuJuBee95: RE: RE: @MrJonesToYou Do you live in Chicago?

Audrey89: RE: RE: RE: @JuJuBee95 No, he doesn't.

MrJonesToYou: RE: RE: RE: . . . @Audrey89 What do you know about it? Stalker.

JuJuBee95: OK, AS I WAS SAYING. Chicago, just a reminder that we're doing a meet-up for any interested DoeNuts, noon today, Thursday, at Marmalade's on Hiawatha in River Bend. How many should we count on?

MrJonesToYou: RE: @JuJuBee95 Oh God, that place is awful.

Audrey89: RE: RE: @MrJonesToYou He lives in ALTOONA, PENNSYLVANIA, @JuJuBee95. HE DOESN'T FUCKING KNOW.

Slapdash: RE: I'm in if you drive @JuJuBee95.

JuJuBee95: RE: RE: I got you, @Slapdash.

LuckyOne: RE: @JuJuBee95 That's near where I'm working right now. I might come.

MrJonesToYou: RE: RE: @LuckyOne Way to commit.

Dreaming312: RE: RE: RE: @MrJonesToYou Fuck off.

MrJonesToYou: RE: RE: RE: . . . Uh, Whoa. Lurker! You never post, never say a word, and then swoop in to tell people off like you own the place? @JennDoePagesMOD, can I get a ruling on this one?

Dreaming312: RE: RE: @LuckyOne What's the point of a meet-up, anyway? Don't you people have lives?

JuJuBee95: RE: @Dreaming312 Watch the "you people," dude.

JennDoePagesMOD RE: @MrJonesToYou You don't want a ruling on this one. Please have some respect. That said, @Audrey89 and @Dreaming312, please use respectful language on the boards or we'll have to unleash the disciplinary kraken. And I really don't want to do that. I'm three seasons behind on my shows, for one thing. I don't have the time. Have fun at your meet-up! What a great idea!

CHAPTER FIVE

ALICE

Alice arrived at the restaurant for the meet-up, early and unsettled from her conversation with Matt.

How was she supposed to recognize anyone? She had no idea. It was a chain place with uncomfortable booths, tin-eared circus music. No place you'd want to linger. King and Fine had built six of them in the greater Chicagoland area, not their best work.

Alice chose an empty table in a window booth overlooking the parking lot and slid in, finding the right direction to unfold her legs. After a minute of twitching, of recalling the things Matt had had the nerve to say to her, she reached for her laptop.

Jane Doe Anaho's updates hadn't fully loaded when Uncle Jim had interrupted her. When she got a Wi-Fi signal, Alice clicked to load the page again and watched the profile thumbnails redraw. In this view, all the Doe Pages profiles shuffled together, sorted by time of latest update. The missing got smiling snapshots, mug shots. The unidentified got drawings or clay reconstructions or generic avatars. Slab photos like Jane Doe Anaho's were more rare, only for a clean death—recent or preserved. While the e-cemetery built on the page, row after row, Alice reached for the menu. Maybe she'd get a Chicago hot dog, now that she wasn't starving herself into her mother's dress.

Finally, the familiar face of 367UFNV loaded, and then right after, another thumbnail, an even more recent update.

Alice felt a pinprick of resentment for her Jane, for herself, for not holding the pole position. It didn't matter. She clicked the newer profile photo to take a close look.

He was an MP, or Empty, in the Doe Pages parlance when they talked among themselves. He was an older man, someone's dad probably, standing in front of a blank white wall, his arms crossed over his slim chest, his head turned. More J.Crew catalogue than mug shot, but something about the man's face made her uneasy. She scrolled to the details.

Richard Miller. Milwaukee.

She scrolled back up to Richard Miller's photo. He seemed familiar somehow. *Last seen.* Two weeks. They'd started allowing newer missing cases onto the Pages, special favors for police districts that worked closely with the site, she presumed. Still, two weeks was pretty new. She checked the metadata. Jenn herself had added it a few minutes ago.

Movement at the window caught her attention. Two women moved across the parking lot, one dark-skinned and shining with youth, bouncing ahead, the other lumbering, a distended shadow in head-to-toe black and Converse sneakers but older, gray-haired. For some reason, Alice knew these were Doe volunteers. They just didn't make sense together any other way.

She was stashing her laptop when they appeared in the entrance. The young one spotted her at once.

"Heyyy," she said, sidling up to Alice's table. "Any chance you're LuckyOne?"

"Alice Fine. You're JuJuBee95?"

The woman sat across from Alice. "I look just like my avatar, right?" The community members used tiny pictures of cereal box characters or stills from TV shows in addition to the punny screen names. The image for JuJuBee95 was a fat yellow bumblebee. "My real name's Juby. This is Slapdash, also known as Lillian."

Lillian plopped next to Juby with a groan.

"We hoped you'd come," Juby said. "We weren't sure how many people might be in the area, but your avatar—well, we were pretty sure."

Alice used a tiny Chicago skyline, King and Fine's skyscraper front and center. She had always meant to hide behind that photo. What was she doing here?

"There was one guy we hoped wouldn't show up," Juby said, looking around the room.

"Tell her," Lillian said. Her voice was husky, wheezy.

Juby leaned over the table. "Lillian wants me to explain that she has a lung condition that keeps her from talking that much. In person. On the site, she's a freaking *demon*. We work together up Hiawatha at the hospital. Lil got me started with the Does. A year almost."

Lillian poked Juby for a menu.

"So have you made a match?" Alice said.

"Me, no," Juby said. "But Lil here is up in the leaderboards. She's got two confirmed matches."

"In fifteen years." Lillian peered at Alice through the bottom of her glasses.

Alice reached for a menu, if only to put a barrier between them. "So . . . what do you do at the hospital?"

"Oh, never mind that," Juby said. "We want to know about you. You and your *kid*napping."

"What?" Alice felt the world shrink down to a dime. Through the noise of the restaurant, she could hear the distant beat of black wings.

"How old were you? Were you on the Pages?"

"I'm guessing," Lillian said. "The internet didn't exist yet."

"But," Alice said. "I—"

"We saw your original post," Lillian said. "Before you deleted it."

"Were you on a milk carton?" Juby said.

She shouldn't have posted that night. That Audrey person had started spouting off, and Alice had been sitting at home alone with a glass of wine and laugh-track comedies streaming continuously for company. She was new to the site, new to the idea of life without Matt. She hadn't been thinking. She hadn't been thinking about *consequences*. She'd only wanted to participate in the Greek chorus of the site—contribute something, anything, to a world that seemed to be going on without her.

The responses had come fast and rude, demanding and entitled. She'd deleted her comment and slammed the laptop closed, dread ruffling at her gut. She'd told herself it would be fine. She was proud to have survived such a thing. What was the harm? Not too many people could say they'd lived to tell that tale. The girl kidnapped by the religious cult, Elizabeth something. Her. That was it, basically. And those women in Cleveland, definitely.

The Doe volunteers, though, were hangers-on, fans of a *genre*, not—what was the word? She hadn't been able to think of the right word.

She wouldn't say *victim*.

"Milk carton? No. No, it wasn't like that."

"What was it *like*?"

"I don't want to talk about it."

"What's the big deal?" Lillian said. "Jubilee could dig it up."

"I invite her to try," Alice said.

"Ohhh," she breathed. "Not in the papers. *Old* school." In her smug appreciation for how things used to be done right, she owned it all, as though she had lived centuries and guided generations. "Easier to be." Wheezing breath. "A shitty parent, then."

"My parents weren't *shitty*, thanks. My dad was a cop, and—"

Alice stopped and turned toward the window. She stared into a sunburst on a car's windshield until her eyes hurt. When she turned back, the glare burned out most of Lillian's mild smile. "I know what you're doing."

"Here for the milkshake," Lillian said.

Juby leaned over her menu. Her yearning had a wavelength that Alice could *feel*.

"Why do you want to know so badly?" Alice said.

"I don't know," Juby said. "You got away, and that's a big deal. There are *so many* missing. And we plug along, hoping for a tiny bit of information, just—something—but even when we help make an identification, the person's already a corpse."

The waitress chose that moment to appear at Alice's elbow. Alice placed her order and watched Juby while Lillian made her choice.

She knew the climbing panic of realization that so many people went missing and stayed that way. Working with the Does was swimming with your airway barely out of the water. You went under sometimes, or what were you? They had to take turns at despair. It was just Juby's turn.

"The thing I don't understand." Lillian paused to catch her breath. "Why did they tell you?"

"Who?" Alice said. "Tell me what?"

Lillian gestured to Juby.

"Your parents," Juby said dully. "Why did they tell you you were kidnapped?"

"You were a *baby*," Lillian said. "Knowing something like that. Can give you." Lillian looked Alice over again. "Certain anxieties."

"Well, I was *three*," Alice said. Tabletop psychiatry, her least favorite game. It was her lack of curiosity turned inward. "They didn't have to tell me. I remember."

They stared at her.

"You remember? You *remember* being kidnapped?" Juby said.

A series of errors had brought her here. They were all her errors. Until now the story had featured a kid none of them had known. Now she was the thing she hadn't meant to be: *interesting*.

"Only a little," she said. "Hardly anything at all."

"You could—" Lillian said.

"Then why not—" Juby began.

The waitress appeared with their drinks. Alice waited her out.

"Why not—" Juby started again.

"*Fine*," Alice said. "Fine. I'll tell you to get you off my back."

"*Fine*." Juby laughed. "Didn't you say—Alice Fine is *fine*?"

"Shush." Lillian jabbed an elbow at her. "I want to hear this."

"Like I said, there isn't much I actually remember, but . . ." Alice looked around for escape, but the chaos of the restaurant only isolated them. "When I was three years old, I was kidnapped." They leaned in. "My dad was a police officer—this was in Indiana—and he rescued me."

She reached for her iced tea, thinking how many of her stories went exactly that way. She got into a scrape. Her dad got her out.

"That's it?" Juby squeaked.

"It was only a couple of hours," Alice said.

"But you remember," Lillian huffed. "Being taken?"

Alice sat back. She remembered a sunny day, being held against her dad's warm chest and rocked, cradled. His warm hand against her back. That must have been when he retrieved her. She had the memory of feeling absolutely safe and loved.

She could also remember a stranger's arms reaching for her, remembered fighting the grasp, stiffening away. Sobbing, turning her puffy eyes from the stranger in loathing, feeling so sick and empty she hadn't known what to do. She'd clutched her favorite little scrap of comfort blanket, and probably sucked her thumb and wet her pants and all the things a scared kid would do. She'd made herself into a *fist*. She had *dared* them.

No one had needed to tell her a thing.

"I remember," she said. She saw the man's hand reaching for her, then his profile as he turned to look over his shoulder. She also still recalled a few details about the house she'd been taken to. Not the taking, not the arriving, only a dumpy couch in a dark-paneled den, the TV bright in the corner, cartoons, and a mattress on the floor in the next room. There was a baby there, too. The smell of a dirty diaper hung in the air, but she was the big girl, wearing pants but forgetting and wetting herself. She might have wet herself on purpose, mad at them all. The woman, the man, the baby the woman handed him.

Alice's memory wavered there. There was something she could almost reach—

She grasped for it. The black bird fluttered at the edges of her vision.

"Alice?" Lillian said.

She forced herself back toward their voices, the noise of the restaurant, her feet on the floor. She reached for her glass and held it. "I remember the house," Alice said when she was sure of her voice. "The inside. I couldn't give them many details or, like, an address."

The other two women seemed to be holding their breath.

"It was dirty, maybe. Definitely a mess, lots of things lying around on the floor, clothes and blankets and toys. It was a couple. And they had a baby with them."

"They kidnapped another kid?" Juby yelped.

Alice looked around. She didn't know. She'd tried to tell the adults everything she knew. Her dad had treated her memories seriously, taking notes for the police report, asking her for any little detail she recalled, descriptions, surroundings. Even much later he would ask what she could remember, when she was eight, nine, ten, when the memory of that day had long started to fade.

"They got away," she said.

"What about the baby?" Juby said.

He hadn't been able to rescue the baby. He'd been so relieved and anxious to get her home to her distraught mother, who was tissue-thin at the best of times, he'd let them get away. With the baby.

That child had worried Harris Fine into a new career. Not long after Alice had been brought home safe, he'd given up his position on the force and moved them to the Chicago area to start over. A new career for him working with JimBig King, a new house out beyond the reach of the city for her mother to make into a home. A new everything. They'd needed the new start, her dad had once explained. She'd been returned safe but, as a family, they hadn't gotten away clean. *Certain anxieties.* Alice put her hand, cool from the glass, to her forehead. Her inheritance, then: chronic migraines, fainting spells. The night terrors that worried Matt. She'd always had them. In her childhood, they'd shaken the house and brought her dad bounding down the hall to her. Always her dad.

Now she thought she understood better why he'd always been the one to come to her. Her mother slept well because she was medicated, and Harris Fine stood watch for them all, guarding them against disaster. Alice caught herself scratching the thin skin at her wrist. He guarded her still.

"It was their baby," Lillian said.

"Then why would they need another kid?" Juby asked.

"You know kids aren't kidnapped. Because they are *needed.*" Lillian turned on Alice, gathering breath to continue. "Nothing more known. About them?"

The couple who took her. A woman and man—

Alice heard the slow beating of the black wings and placed her palms on the table. The moment passed. She ignored the look that passed between Juby and Lillian.

This was why she didn't like to tell the story. People were always so much more curious than she expected, and far more demanding than they had any right to be. They wanted the darkest detail. They wanted the sights and smells and the terror, packaged and delivered. And they always expected justice, expected a closed case and a mug shot of the—

Alice's hand slid to the edge of the table and gripped.

Juby jumped. "What's wrong? What is it?"

Lillian only stared. A plate plunked onto the table in between them. Time passed, plates were placed, reassigned.

"Can I get you ladies anything else?"

"No," Lillian said, blocking the woman out with her shoulder. "You remembered something. You did."

"Oh, my God," Juby said.

"No." Alice pushed her hot dog to the side, sick. She remembered only the feeling of helplessness. Black wings unfurled, stretched. "I can't—it's not—"

"That day?" Lillian said. "The kidnappers?"

Juby sat forward, ashen and concerned. This was what friendship was. It had to be. Alice felt the branches of it reaching toward her, a way out.

"I saw—" Her throat closed up, remembering the face, turned, the arms crossed. The missing man, gone two weeks, posted among this morning's quarry on the website. "My kidnapper. I saw him this morning on the Pages. He's a *Doe*."

The black bird took flight, rushing to engulf the room, and she started to fall.

CHAPTER SIX

ALICE

Alice shuffled slowly back down the street toward the worksite. She shaded her eyes to hold her delicate head. Cars on the street rushed by, too fast.

The blackout was quick, at least, and she hadn't fallen to the floor or hit her head. She'd had worse. Juby and Lillian had wanted to call an ambulance or for her at least go back to the hospital with them. "It happens all the time," she'd said, brushing them off. "I'm fine."

Juby didn't make the Fine joke again. "All the *time*?"

She'd distracted them with her laptop and the image of the Doe.

A face among thousands. Doe profiles went way back—they had a former Civil War general who had served as Billy the Kid's lawyer, missing women even Pinkerton detectives hadn't been able to find, children who had been missing so long they could have lived full lives, having families, building communities, dying natural deaths, all under a name they didn't know was false. Sometimes Alice scrolled the site to see the scope of the thing, sifting through the profiles like a deck of cards cut one way, then another. Chronologically, to see the hair and fashions change. Geographically, to see how much more dangerous one place might be than another. To investigate how often old people went missing. How often children. The unidentified side revealed an array of crude sketches, facial reconstructions sculpted from bone, computer-generated age progressions, some of them too sleek, too robotic, real uncanny valley stuff.

In this sea of misery stood Richard Miller. That was his name.

Ordinary, Alice thought. He had been a sort of UID to her, an unidentified body in her memory, a set of hands reaching to take her. But now he was among the missing, revealed to her only by being gone.

With little effort, Lillian found a notice about his disappearance from a Milwaukee newspaper and, in it, a quote from a neighbor. The story didn't mention family, or who had reported him gone. Brown hair, brown eyes. Six-foot-five, scarring on his left upper arm.

Lillian was a long-standing researcher for the Pages; she knew how to build a case. *Are you sure this is the guy?* She sent Alice through her memories again: homesickness, the hovel, the comfort of being back in her father's arms, safe.

When Miller's image came back to her now on the street, Alice felt the gentle brush of the black wings, like a tickle at the base of her skull. She put a hand out on the hot bricks of the nearest building. Richard Miller's face was a raw nerve, a live wire that sizzled and leapt. It was him.

Alice looked up from the sidewalk to find she'd almost reached the last turn on her way back to work. Normally she enjoyed walking up to their projects, liked seeing the local view of whatever they'd been commissioned to build, liked seeing the crane rising and spinning as though they were rebuilding the world. She minced forward, her fingers trailing the wall and then gripping the corner of the building.

Above, the crane hung still, its shadow thrown at sharp angles across the unfinished façade of the project. No crew were visible in the parking decks. Below, the gate stood open to the street, and lights flashed against the fence's windscreen.

An ambulance. But she was *fine*—

Uncle Jim? *Dad.*

She ran, her laptop banging against her in the backpack with each stride. At the fence, she had to leap out of the way of the ambulance as it backed out toward her, beeping.

Then her dad stepped into view, directing the ambulance into the street. They communicated by a complex set of facial expressions: he was fine, she was fine, something bad had happened, she was late. Give him a minute.

Up on the top deck of the project, someone peered over the edge. No hard hat. Alice shaded her eyes to see which crew member had gone up without gear, but he'd already ducked out of view. Most of the guys stood around the end of the trailer, their hard hats at their feet. It had the look of a funeral. Uncle Jim crouched on the stairs to the office with Jimmy hovering, his business suit as out of place as a gorilla costume. Alice held back, catching her breath. Which group of men needed her? Whose tragedy was this? Her dad came in from the street and tucked her under his arm. He led her to the crew.

"Fellas," her dad said gently. "He's going to get the best care there is."

"Who, Dad?" she whispered.

"What *happened*?" one of the younger guys said. Brody lived at home, brought in PBJ sandwiches for lunch with the crusts cut off. The older guys tore him to pieces and loved him for taking it.

He was also willing to say whatever he was thinking so they didn't have to. They loved that, too. "He's a pro! How could he fall like that?"

"Even pros get distracted once in a while."

Alice sorted the men. None of them would look at her. "Dad?"

"Matt," one of the older guys said. "Sonofabitching Matt."

"What?" Alice said. "*No*. What—?" She heard her own voice turn horrible.

Her dad's grip on her shoulder tightened. "Let's go inside."

"His sister, Dad. We should call Lita."

"We'll do that," he said, wiping his hand across his face.

"I'll do it," she said, trying to gain command of herself in front of the crew. They'd had too many chances to see her cut down lately.

"No, I will." He glanced toward the stairs, where Uncle Jim nodded. That was it, then. Alice had watched her dad wait for the nod from JimBig for as long as she'd been alive. "Head out, guys," he said. "We'll clock you out. And be careful on the way home. If you're praying men . . ."

They filed off toward the gate silently, kicking up dust. Her dad nudged her toward the trailer, where Uncle Jim had turned dry eyes to the ground.

Jimmy folded his arms. " 'We'll clock you out'?" he mimicked. "When? An hour from now, by which time they've drunk the afternoon away? Why should we pay them to get hammered?"

"Jimmy," JimBig said.

Jimmy hadn't looked toward Alice, but she thought the performance might be for her. Look at Jim Junior, big-man-in-training, hardly ever getting close enough to the site to require a hard hat. It would mess up his hair. He had a ring across his forehead from a hat band today, though. *Well, congratulations*, Alice thought. *You work here.*

"We're ten days behind schedule," Jimmy said. "Eleven now, with—"

"Jimmy, shut it," JimBig said.

Her dad took a step closer to Jimmy. "Making the crew work on a day when one of them fell two stories—do you think they're worth a damn right now?" Next to Harris Fine, Jimmy King was taller, but scrawny, his suit shiny. "How many more accidents you want this afternoon?"

Alice wiped at her cheeks. She felt helpless at moments like this, as though she had no say in anything that happened near her. The great men, building up the structures of the world.

"Let's get on the horn," her dad said. "Matt's sister, the insurance guy, who else?"

"The police," Alice said. "Oh, I guess they're already up there."

They all looked at her.

"On the top deck?" she said. "I thought I saw—"

"I'll take that one," JimBig said, getting up. "Harris, call the family. Jimmy, you get the insurance guy's number from the office and let them know what happened. No details. Just basic stuff. You talk too much."

"What can I do?" She wanted to do something. Anything.

JimBig turned to her. "You keep our spirits up, kid, just by being you."

As usual, then. Nothing.

IN THE TRAILER, Jimmy made for her desk. She sank into the visitor's chair, abandoning her backpack at her feet. "I can find that number for you."

"No, no," Jimmy said, digging through a drawer. "You're supposed to be sitting there looking *pretty*. And how pretty you are, ugly-crying over that klutz."

"Screw you, Jimbo."

"Now, now. You had your chance."

"Get the insurance guy on the phone and ask him what 'sexual harassment' means."

"That's rich," he said. "You being the *boss* and all."

"Stop it," she said. Every sweet thing about Uncle Jim, Jimmy could ruin like a funhouse mirror. She liked to think that Jimmy was adopted, some changeling JimBig and his ex-wife had found and taken home. "The insurance papers are in the vault."

He looked up, then toward the wall with the safe in it. It wasn't much of a secret, the safe, hidden behind a framed photograph of their crowning achievement, the 1799 South Michigan Avenue high-rise. A triumph for King and Fine. *The* triumph, likely never to be repeated. Parking garages, waterfront embankments, a strip mall if they got lucky. They had always been the guys to call for usable, for practical, for *fine*. Until 1799 South Michigan, like a comet.

The grand opening invitation, printed on nice paper, was tacked to the wall by her desk.

Jimmy stood up and crossed the room. She closed in on her station while he hesitated in front of the frame.

"I know it's *there*," she said. "I told you the papers were in it."

He treated her like a scullery maid, but technically they both owned the same portion of King and Fine: one percent each. The month they'd graduated from high school, they'd come in to meet the lawyers. Uncle Jim strangely emotional, keeping a stiff lip while they signed. An inheritance, Dad had said. Her mom was seriously sick by then, and Alice had recently moved back home from Montana, cap and gown in suitcase, college deferred, to take over her care. A gap year without end. So the future had been on her dad's mind. It was an insurance policy, she supposed, handled with the unnecessary ceremony of an imperial transition. He'd only wanted her to be taken care of.

She had assumed she would be.

In another life, she'd be married, racing Matt's ambulance to the emergency room. Alice sat at her desk. Her hands were shaking. In another life, maybe she could take care of herself.

Jimmy moved the frame off the wall and stood staring at the face of the vault.

"Twenty-two right . . ." she said.

"*Hey*, what if the crew heard you?"

"Didn't you say they'd be blotto by now? And I think the insurance paperwork is safe, even if you left it out in the Porta-Johns as reading material. As *toilet* paper."

He got the safe open, pulled out two big leather-covered books, and then riffled through the rest of the contents. After a few sighs from his direction, she said, "Eight-four-seven, six-six-three . . ."

Jimmy turned, arms laden with files. "You knew the phone number the whole time?"

"I offered to get it for you. It's right here on the board. Eight-four-seven . . ."

He put the ledgers and papers back, a mess she would have to tidy up later. "Things are going to change around here one of these days," he said, giving her a scowl. "You'd better have a plan B, *boss*."

"Someday like when? When is everything going to start coming up Jimmy King?"

He wouldn't say it. "Your dad thinks he has the run of the place, but on my watch he's going to have to answer to me."

"My dad is a full partner—"

"Who do you think will have a controlling interest when— when the inevitable happens? My share plus my dad's will be enough to start running this place like an actual business. Harris's sandbox days are over."

"You're forgetting my share." Her paltry one percent.

"I'll buy your share right now. Name your price. Or we can consolidate the old-fashioned way."

She was tired, half not in the room. *If Uncle Jim heard him talk that way, or her dad?* She wasn't sure what they would think, but she didn't want them thinking it. Maybe she was just as shortsighted as Matt. She should have gotten another job by now. "Enough, Jimmy."

"Well, you'll change your mind the first time you need the cash. And you're definitely going to need cash. Consider it an open offer. The buyout, I mean."

He looked down at the phone in his hand, then at her.

"You should have written it down," she said.

"You heard your old man ask me to call. Isn't this how it works? A mess gets made and *we* clean it up?"

"I'm the one with my own mop. And how is this anyone's *mess*, if Matt fell—"

"With an investor on site? That is bad for business."

"The tour was canceled," Alice said. She repeated the number, watched him jab at his phone.

"You got bad information," he said, brushing the hard-hat halo from his hair. "Dad was giving a solo tour— Hello?"

This last he said into the phone, and bolted. He left the trailer door hanging open.

Alice went to close it and paused to survey the site, now eerily quiet. The structure-in-progress, empty in broad daylight, was a worst-case scenario scene, postapocalyptic. She sat back at her desk, numb, then stood up.

She should be with him.

She sat back down. She wasn't family. She wasn't anything.

Alice reached for the day's paperwork and mail. Then she logged into the payroll system and clocked out the entire crew for their standard time, all the while waiting for her dad or Uncle Jim or even Jimmy to come back to the trailer and make it clear that there was something to do or that there wasn't and it was time to go home.

An hour went by, two, and then she heard the chain in the gate.

She went to the door and looked through the window, just in time to see the fence clang closed. Someone pulled the chain through, fussed with the padlock.

They'd forgotten her. Distracted by the accident, probably. She had her own key, of course, no harm done, but it was galling to have been left behind. Matt was her—

But he wasn't.

As she watched, a shape appeared on the fence's screen, the thin shadow of her dad or Uncle Jim. Tough call which one. Then a second silhouette appeared, thicker, broader in the shoulder. The figures exchanged a few gestures, separated. The first hurried off toward the parking lot. In these movements, she recognized JimBig.

The other—

She scanned the fence. The other shadow had paused at the gate, standing with his squared shoulders at the gap.

Alice stepped back from the window. It was probably just the investor from Uncle Jim's tour, taking a last look at the site. Why hadn't he left when the ambulance did? And why had Uncle Jim said the tour was canceled, when it obviously hadn't been? Maybe he'd just meant that no one would be brought into the trailer, so she didn't need to tidy up. He might have said so. *Say what you mean*, Alice thought. *Mean what you say.*

She went to her desk, closed down the payroll system, backed up the day's meager work.

When she reached for her phone, she found a series of texts she'd missed since lunch, when she'd exchanged numbers with Juby. She read them in reverse order.

R u going to look for him?
Kinda weird, right?
"All the time"? That really happens all the time?
This is Juby. U get back to work OK?

Alice closed her eyes. She never should have met them. It was just more of the same unrelenting curiosity, unearned.

R u going to look for him?

Before she knew what she was doing, she'd returned to her work computer and opened up a search bar. *Richard—*

She hesitated. *Miller* had such a pedestrian quality of nothing-to-see-here. There would be hundreds of them. Thousands.

Who are you, Richard Miller? Alice thought, typing the name. *And where did you go?*

To: alice@kfconstruction.com
From: admin@topfloormgt.com
RE: RE: RSVPs for King and Fine

Oh, thanks! I'm glad to know we'll be seeing you and the Kings again. Thanks for the confirmation! I had Mr. Fine down as a yes already. Did he tell you we'll have the penthouse tenanted soon? You know I was hoping for a good-looking guy to move in!;)

Jennifer York-Niemann
Top Floor Management

CHAPTER SEVEN
MERRILY

When Merrily jolted awake from strange dreams, her mouth still tasted weird. What day was it? She looked around, dazed. She reached for her phone, peeled a photo of Rick off her arm.

She'd only been asleep a few hours. It was only the afternoon, the smell of bacon still thick in the apartment.

No texts from her mom. Weird. She also hadn't gotten any hits from her PhotoSocial post about Rick being missing, not even any messages of support. Well, that's not where she got her support, anyway.

She did have several notifications from ChatX, including one from her new favorite, the gravy train who had rolled in a couple of months ago. This guy was ideal, never bothering her for pics or time, always keeping things clean. He spent freely, could have had anyone. But he'd sit and listen to her bitch about Justyce or her mom for a half hour and then drop a few zeroes in her account. Like therapy that paid *her*.

The first time he'd contacted her for a chat, she was sure he was a cop or something. But Searcher6 was simply a lonely divorced type. Not smooth, not even that charming. Camera-shy. A message from him, though rare, was always good news for her.

Merrily smoothed her hair and logged in from her phone. His invitation was waiting. A Thursday afternoon? She accepted, and her screen filled with an image of a tranquil stretch of water, a photo Searcher supplied in place of his own live video feed. There was something freeing about broadcasting out to him without having to make eye contact. The avatar for his profile on the site was a photo of a strong jawline resting on a fist, one thumb against his chin. The fine gold hairs on his wrist made her stomach flutter. Probably a daddy complex, but she was allowed her kinks, too.

"Hey, Mer-Maid." She hadn't had to teach him to say it right. "How's your day?"

So far she'd participated in Rick-centric worrying and workplace shame and brought a grown man to his knees for quick cash. All in a day's work. With any of her other guys, she'd turn it back on them, ask them something about themselves. Like lighting a can of gasoline—she never had to ask twice. Each of her guys wanted some different relationship with her, her body, her life. Searcher's only requirement seemed to be time, but she was the one who had to fill it.

"Well, today hasn't been my favorite day ever," she said.

"Sorry to hear that. Anything you want to talk about?"

"Just family stuff. I won't bore you. I think I quit my job today."

"Must not have been much of a job if you're not sure."

"I won't miss much about it. It was getting in the way of more important duties." She winked into the camera.

"What's that?"

"What?" She peered into the video image of herself on her screen to spot what he was seeing. Near her shoulder lay one of the drawings from her childhood she'd excavated from her closet. "Oh, only evidence of my early genius."

"Show me?"

She'd drawn pictures of monsters and ponies, of princesses and dragons. Of little girls with their mothers, but never herself and her mom, exactly. Merrily held up one of the drawings for him. "A family of bears, maybe? Or porcupines? I'm not sure."

"The genius part is that it could be both."

"You understand me."

On her bed lay the scattered pictures, a workbook page with a gold star. She had not been a gold-star kind of kid, even though she tried so hard to please, to will everyone and everything around her to be OK. Best behavior, so that no one could not love her. So that no one else could leave her, she supposed.

Merrily held up a receipt from McDonald's, the back of which she had decorated with a landscape of . . . cornfields and pigs?

"Lovely," he said. "And who's that?"

One of Rick's photos rested near her elbow. It was the one with his buddies, beer cans in the air. Merrily held it up so he could see. "My stepdad on the right. My former— Well, it's complicated."

"He looks happy. Where's that taken, do you know?"

She turned the image around. Three men, Rick laughing. Green lakeshore, a dock in the background. "No idea. I think this is before he crash-landed into our lives. I wouldn't even have been born yet."

"Any more photos?"

"You finally want some show-and-tell from me, and it's old pictures of the guy my mother used to bone? Your wish."

She went through the photos one at a time: baby-faced Rick on a date; trim-waisted Rick in a kitchen drinking from a jam jar, a pack of cigarettes rolled into his sleeve, the edges of a black tattoo peeking out. She finally found the image of the two of them together, stuck to the back of another photo.

"This one is called *Awkward Father Figure*," she said. In the photograph she's a nearly bald, nearly infant blob on Rick's knee, his hands keeping her upright. He's gazing down at her in a way that is a mix of astonishment and fear. Had he loved her? For the two minutes he'd been in her life, had he thought of her as part of his family?

She saved the best for last: *King Richard conquers the Dunes!*

Searcher had gone quiet at some point. "Still there?" she said, holding the phone at her best angle. "Anything I can do for you today?"

"You do enough by just being you, Mer-Maid. You always do."

Enough might not be *enough*, though. She was out of a day job, and the fact was, he turned her on. Maybe this could be something real, or at least something more lucrative. "I just want to make sure you know that we can change things up at any time. You don't have to be shy with me or with anything you need. Or want?"

When he answered, she could tell he was smiling. "I'll keep you posted on what I need or want. Deal?"

"Deal."

After they said their goodbyes, Merrily put the photo of tiny Rick on her desk, leaned up against a speaker. She went to her ChatX account and watched as a deposit dropped. *Quite a good deal, in fact.*

CHAPTER EIGHT

ALICE

The search engine results for *Richard Miller* were vast.

Alice checked the time. Juby and Lillian were back at work. Gossiping? That's what she would be doing, if anyone here took the slightest interest in her work with the Does. Gossiping about her, probably.

She pulled out her phone.

U get back to work OK?

At least they were nice people. She hadn't known what to expect.

R u going to look for him?

She texted a reply: *How would I do that?*

The idea of searching for the guy made a nervous trill slide up her spine.

The response was immediate: a smiley face.

Then: *We thought u would never ask. Pick us up!*

Community Memorial Southwest, entrance F.
Follow the signs for the morgue.

Alice stared at the last bubble of Juby's message, waiting for a punch line. She wasn't sure which were the jokes.

Smiley face again, its tongue stuck out. *KIDDING!!!*

Alice let out a breath and watched the messages stack up with directions, her second Doe meet-up in one day.

The crew was clocked out. Couldn't she . . . ?

She clicked over to the thread of texts with her dad. He didn't use technology much, but it wasn't a bad way to get quick answers from him or to coordinate the occasional dinner. Not a bad way to check in more often, since she had her own place and didn't get out to Fell Creek as often.

Alice frowned at her phone, thumbing through their most recent texts, then finally tapped out a new one: *How did it go with Lita?*

She couldn't help thinking that she should have been the one to call. Was that him saving her again, this time from unpleasantness?

She sent: *Did you leave already?*

She couldn't just leave. She'd already disappointed him so many times today.

This was the real reason she should get a new job. Here, she was Fine's kid, the boss's literal favorite. It should have come with some slack, but it didn't. It came with high standards and no chance to match them. In a job outside King and Fine she'd be just another clock-watcher, nobody's favorite, nobody's example.

But then she'd have to get that job on her own skill and merit. Maybe if she tried, she'd find she had some.

Maybe if she tried—at anything—she could prove a few things. To Jimmy, to Matt. To herself. To her dad most of all.

Richard Miller, she thought. *After all this time.*

There was a black hole inside Harris Fine where the kidnapping episode had gone. She could feel it. It was a wound with him—the near-loss of his kid, the actual ruin of his first career. What would he give to have it solved?

He wouldn't want her messing in it. Not Doe stuff, not for him.

Her dad hadn't answered her texts.

To Juby, she sent: *Leaving now.*

Alice opened up the time sheets again and revised her clock-out to the exact time. She would be a damn good example, dimple in cheek.

ALICE WAS ON the other side of the gate putting the padlock back in place when she heard someone say her name.

Down the street, a man leaned against a parked silver car. Tanned arms, dark hair, indeterminate age behind sunglasses and a smile. She didn't know him. She turned and walked, quickly. Keys in hand, listening for footfalls behind her. When they came, she pivoted on him, brandishing her pocket pepper-spray key chain.

"Whoa, hey."

"Back off." Fight or flight. The beat of wings in her ears. She had her phone in her other hand, ready for 911.

"I just want to talk to you."

She hated the assumption that she had to allow it.

"Nope."

He nodded, glancing at the spray in her hand. "You're prepared."

She'd been taught to be, after the kidnapping. *Even if they call you paranoid.* But people didn't know she had a reason. They just wanted her attention, only a moment of her time. She'd kept moving, ignored the names she got called.

This guy was big, and probably fast. "Stay back." She hated how small her voice sounded, hated how you just had to take it, whatever people dealt out. Robocalls, back when she'd been keeping the house quiet for her mother. They'd gotten a P.O. box and a gate at the end of the long drive to keep salespeople and true believers from wandering in and hitting the doorbell anytime they wanted to.

"One question," he said.

Alice took a big step backward, spray hand out. In broad daylight? Cars drove by, no one stopped. "No." Another.

"You don't want to know?" He was a half block away now, watching her with amusement while her blood thumped in her veins. "You're not even a little bit curious?"

"Not as a rule," she said, turning.

"Where is—"

But she was running now. When she pulled out of the parking lot, the last car in the lot, he and the silver car were gone.

Alice drove toward the hospital with her gut in knots. Why were there so many whack-jobs out there? Why did they always seem to want to talk to her?

At the turn for the hospital campus, she realized her mistake. Where Juby and Lillian worked was most likely the nearest emergency room to the River Bend project site. Somewhere inside, Matt fought for his life.

He might not have made it. She should park and go in.

She pressed her hands to her eyes. There was no playbook for the role Matt had foisted on her.

Alice drove up to the front of the building, admiring the smooth circle drive, like something from a country club. She found a spot to pause and text Juby, then studied the building itself. King and Fine could do this kind of work.

The truth was she hoped they didn't. She didn't want to be anywhere near here or any hospital, and not because of Matt.

After a few minutes, Juby and Lillian emerged from a side door. Juby jumped into the backseat, and Lillian heaved herself into the front, filling the car with rustling papers and a thin wheeze. *Who needed the emergency room?*

"You're OK to drive, right?"

"I'm *fine*." A neat trick. Now she would have to entertain whatever crazy idea they had cooked up. "Where are we going?"

"Road trip," Lillian said.

"Don't get mad," Juby said. "Milwaukee?"

"Wait, really?"

"It's a short trip," Juby said. "And if we leave *now* . . ."

"Lillian," Alice said. "How did you agree to this?"

"My dance card isn't all that full," the older woman said. "Jubilee said she'd buy me dinner. Best date I've had in decades."

Juby laughed, a trilling, musical sound like a birdsong. Alice wanted to hear it again. Milwaukee?

At least it was something to do instead of another night on the couch with her laptop, the Does singing to her from their unmarked graves. Instead of the early bedtime she craved, punctuated by nightmare visions of Matt falling from the sky. This would probably be the best date Alice had had in a while, too, but she didn't say so.

CHAPTER NINE

ALICE

Milwaukee-bound.

Juby had Richard Miller's address from the newspaper mapped and her phone set to call out directions in an Australian accent. A man's voice, like a riotous good time to be had. *Turn roiight*, it said. Juby repeated every direction as though only she could hear the voice, trying out the accent for herself. The mood of the car was Juby's to direct, it seemed to Alice. They were having fun as long as Juby was.

Lillian took command of the car's entertainment. She'd done as much digging as she could with the tools she could access at work, and had come up with the same dead end as Alice: too many Richard Millers. Now Lillian rustled through sheaves of information she'd printed, highlighted, underlined. Nothing was certain. Richard Miller, even with his approximate age as a parameter, was everywhere and nowhere.

"Richard Miller, age sixty," Lillian said. "He lives in every state. In the nation."

"Another road trip?" Juby called from the backseat.

"What do you do for the hospital?" Alice said.

"Track down payments," Lillian said.

"And people who don't make 'em," Juby said. "Is it any wonder we prefer dead bodies?"

Lillian tucked away the pages into the cloth purse that hung across her chest and began a lecture on Milwaukee: geography, history, sordid details.

"Jeffrey Dahmer lived there, you know," she said.

"Who?" Juby said, and pulled a strand of her black hair across her mouth dreamily.

Alice hoped Juby was joking but didn't know. Lillian dug back into the beer barons, bootlegging, the lake. The lake lay somewhere beyond their vision—myth, until they could see it off to the east.

By the time they arrived and got out of the car, stretching, Alice felt a strange fondness for the miles they had traveled, for the dirty street the Aussie's voice had led them to. Two hours beforehand, she had not been planning anything other than a quiet night with Jane Doe Anaho's death details in front of her and macaroni and cheese from a box. And now she was in another state, somewhere she'd never been. Maybe she didn't prefer dead bodies. Juby and Lillian conferred over the address a few feet away.

Alice's phone revved in her pocket. She reached for it and saw a text from her dad. *Sorry! Got caught up and left you.*

She tapped back quickly. *News about Matt?*

She watched the bubble of her own message with dread. What if he wasn't OK? Did she want to hear it now, like this? She turned her back on the other women, waited.

Stable for now. Don't worry. Probably full recovery.

Alice let out a deep breath. *Send flowers tomorrow?* she texted. *From K&F?*

Good idea. Then: *Out of the office tomorrow, in case you forgot.*

She'd forgotten. *Sure. See you Monday.*
Last-minute . . . he wrote. *Dinner tonight with old dad?*

Can't. Out with some girlfriends.

His reply was swift and full of questions. He'd been on her to join a book club, an alumna club of her old school. Take a cooking class. He didn't really want her living too much of a life, in her opinion. He'd only meant she should stop centering her time around the Does.

Alice looked over at Juby and Lillian, their heads still together. He didn't have to know the Does *were* her friends.

She typed: *I could come over Sunday.*

See you then. Be safe.

At least he didn't ask her to text the second she arrived home.

"Alice," Juby said. "Tell Lillian we didn't come all this way just to stand out here and look at the roof needing replaced."

"What did we come? All this way to do?" Lillian huffed. "Break in?"

Alice said, "We could take a closer look, right?"

"Yesssss," Juby said, pumping a fist in the air.

Alice had been emboldened by the conversation with her dad. She wanted to give him this. They both deserved an answer.

"Which one is it?" she said.

Juby led them up to the front of a flat-faced brick building, an old house that had once been cheerful, the home of a family. Now it had four mailboxes next to the front door, and the covered porch pitched toward the street.

There were three doorbells. The other women held back at the sidewalk.

"Are we—what are we doing?" Alice said.

She listened to Lillian breathing.

"Ring the bell?" Juby's eyes were shiny, but she held her arms across herself.

They were nervous. They were number-crunchers, paper-pushers, just like her—not at all accustomed to knocking on doors to ask for dangerous men. She hadn't thought this through. "He's missing from here," Alice said. "So he won't *be* here."

Juby blinked at her. "That's a good theory."

Alice led the advance.

At the door, Juby's finger hovered over one button, then the next. "Miller," she murmured, almost a purr.

"Are you trying to divine which one it is?" Alice said.

Lillian leaned on the handrail without coming up the steps.

"It's the back one," she wheezed. "He lived in the back one."

"Well, he's not answering any doorbells, is he?" Juby said. Her finger stopped over the top bell, where a name was neatly written. "Bajaj." She pressed the button and they all went still. Juby's black hair lifted in a breeze. She turned her head toward it and closed her eyes. "Someone's making curry," she said. "Smells like my gran's."

Someone had come to the door. There was a peephole. Alice smiled in its direction until the door at her shoulder opened to the chain. The dark outline of a small elderly man stood in the opening. "What do you want?" His voice was raspy, worn.

Juby nudged Alice aside, bright smile in place. "Oh, it's your kitchen that smells so nice, hello."

The man didn't seem to know what to say to that, but Juby was worth looking at. "What about it?"

"My friend here knew the man who went missing," Juby said. "A long time ago she knew him, and she was sad to hear that he might be in trouble. Have they found him?"

Alice held her breath, waiting for the man to snap the door closed. Adventure over. Wasted trip. And then he did—the man closed the door, slid the chain, and opened it wide. He stood now in the opening, small and shriveled in a stained white tunic. The curry aroma roared out around him, almost visible. The man eyed Alice. "No, they have not, and I wonder if they will."

"Why is that, sir?" Juby said. The man's gaze dropped to her, turning affectionate. Juby had been adopted. "Do you think he's met some kind of bad end?" Alice glanced at Lillian. A low-level Australian accent had sneaked into Juby's voice.

"I'd rather he got found so he could pay me the rent he owes," the man said. "But the ones that leave me holding the bill, I don't expect they'll want to be found."

"How long did he live here?"

"A year, most. They move around a lot."

"Who moves around a lot?"

The man chewed through a few words, dispensed with them all.

"Mr. Bajaj, is it?" Juby said. "Was he a good tenant? Did he make a lot of noise?"

Bajaj wiped at one of his eyebrows, thinking. "No, no. He weren't much trouble, but he weren't much of a talker, either. They say he worked at the casino, so maybe he wanted the quiet at home."

"Did he ever have friends over? A girlfriend?"

"Not that I saw, but I didn't stand guard, if a man had a lady over." He surveyed the street up and down, exactly like a man standing guard.

Juby sighed. She wasn't having fun anymore. She glanced at the mailboxes. Alice looked over. They were labeled A, B, C, R. "Was he friendly with any of the other tenants?"

"None of them here now," he said. "They're not friendly and he was on his own at the back."

Lillian made a self-satisfied sound.

The landlord peeked over Juby's shoulder, took Lillian's measure. "Ma'am."

Lillian took her chance. "The Indian casino?"

"Indian, yeah," the man mumbled, his eyes glancing off Juby. "Not Indian, us. Indian, them. The Bingo Casino, as was. Now it's Pow Wow—something."

"Potowatomi," Lillian said. He nodded.

"What did he do there?" Alice asked.

Her voice seemed to startle them all, as though she had faded into the face of the house, out of memory.

Wear and tear on *her* car, *her* gas money. *Her* kidnapper. *Her* Doe.

The man shook his head. "He was always trying to avoid me. Always arrears. I just know he was casino. He might have owned the place, or maybe he cleaned the toilets."

If he'd owned the place, he wouldn't have lived in the back apartment of this sagging heap, but no one said this.

"What did he wear to work?" Juby said.

"I see, yes, I see," the man said. "He wore black pants, white shirt. Like he worked in the rest'rant, maybe."

All the waitstaff and busboys and dealers at the tables would wear black pants and white shirts. It would be a big place. The world was a big place, to find one man.

"Was he good?" Lillian said in her gasping way. "At anything?"

The man smoothed his eyebrow some more. "He wasn't a bad man. He doesn't deserve something bad."

He hadn't understood Lillian's broken way of talking, had missed the narrowing of scope meant to find hobbies, passions, the interests and habits that he would have packed along with him.

Something bad. The mood of the porch turned.

Alice looked among them. They had to feel sorry for Richard Miller now? She was supposed to pretend she didn't care the man she'd wanted to marry was lying in the hospital near death, and that she *did* care what happened to the man who'd snatched her?

"Why do you think something bad happened to him?" Alice demanded. "Why don't you think he just dodged the rent?"

The landlord's wrinkled brow furrowed deeper. "They said he wasn't Richard Miller at all. Sounds like a man already running."

Alice and Lillian exchanged slow glances. "Who said that, sir?" Juby asked.

"The police. The one that came after, dark clothes. I'm sorry I don't know more," he said. "He seemed . . . a decent man, when he lived here. No trouble."

"You said he wasn't friends with any of the tenants now," Juby said. "*Now.* Do you mean he used to be close to someone here?"

"He was friendly with a woman used to live here, but when she moved on, no, not like with Rebekah and her little girl."

Alice had been ready to go down the steps and leave but now pivoted back, her knees weak.

Juby stopped her with narrowed eyes. "Rebekah and her little girl?" Juby said, her voice calm and warm, a cup of milky tea for Uncle to keep him talking. "How old was this girl?"

The landlord looked uncertainly among them. "You knew him?"

"I did," Alice said.

"Why so many questions, then?"

"I knew him when I was young," she said, trying not to let her voice waver. "Like Rebekah's daughter."

"He took you?"

Alice stammered. "What?"

"He took care of you?"

The man nodded toward the street, and they all turned. The next block was flat, dotted with trees. A couple of tractor tires had been half buried in the ground, and there was a long swing set and a slide. "He watched the girl while Becki worked, some days. Took her to the park there."

Seven, he said. Rebekah's daughter was seven, maybe. No, he didn't have any contact information for Rebekah or anyone else Miller/not-Miller might have known. None of them had much to say after this, even Juby. They thanked him for his time and listened as the chain slipped back in place on the other side of the door.

Alice started down the sidewalk. *Took you.* She looked back for Juby's reaction.

Juby stood at the edge of the porch, hands twitching at the hem of her shirt. Her hair lifted in the breeze again. And then she turned back toward the door and opened the lid on the top mailbox.

"Juby," Alice hissed.

Lillian turned to see. "That's a federal offense—"

"Don't tell me, Lil," Juby hiss-whispered. "If I don't know, I can play dumb at my trial." She thumbed through the flyers and envelopes, shoved them back, and reached for the second mailbox. "Richard Miller, you're in here somewhere."

CHAPTER TEN

ALICE

In the backseat, Juby hummed over her pile of ill-gotten goods, making little noises. Lillian wouldn't ask. Alice drove.

The sun was finally setting, cooling things down. Alice was tired, and heartsick. How many little girls had been caught up in Richard Miller's snare? Her hands, on the wheel, vibrated with rage. Now she knew why her dad had needed a new job. How could he stand it? How many men like Richard Miller were there? How could anyone stand it?

Alice glanced into the rearview mirror. Juby had transferred her attention from the stolen mail and was thumbing her phone, her face lit by the screen. "Well?" Alice said.

Juby looked up, smiling wide. "Turn *roooiiiight*," the GPS voice said.

"What?" The exit appeared, and Alice turned sharply into it. They'd been heading toward the interstate to go home, but now they descended from the high road down into a subterranean area of Milwaukee's downtown, the support beams of the highway above surrounding them like trees in a strange concrete forest. "What are we doing?"

"I thought you might like to meet *Becki*," she said, holding up an envelope. "I'm sure it's not a federal offense to take junk mail—"

"It is," Lillian said.

"—or to take junk mail when you're trying to protect a young *child*."

Lillian said nothing.

"I'll hand over Becki's mail personally at the cah-seeeeee-no," Juby said. "Where she *works*. With Richard *Miller*. You're *welcome*."

"How do you know she works at the casino?" Alice said.

"Her full name was on this offer for—what is this?—lawn care? Did that squat even have a lawn? Full name goes into the phone— *beep boop*—and spits out a not-unhelpful social media presence and a photo—" Here Juby waved her phone between them. "A photo of casino Employee Day at Six Flags from the company newsletter, including one Rebekah Young with her probably- seven-year-old daughter, right there in the front."

"Is Miller in the photo?" Lillian said finally.

"Not that I can tell." Juby was engrossed with more search find- ings or put off by the tepid response to her genius.

"Turn *rooiiiight*," the phone said. "And you will *arroive* at your destination."

Alice slowed the car. The exit had dumped them in an indus- trial area, warehouses and container trucks. In the middle of it all, a spaceship had landed. The casino was a glowing blue building with its name in overlarge, brightly lit red letters across its crown. The parking lot below teemed with life, everything coated an eerie alien color.

Alice let the car idle, allowing the day to wash over her. It was getting dark. The trip home wouldn't be any shorter for the late hour, and the morning no easier. The guy had to be stopped—but why did it have to be her who tracked him down? She felt for her phone in her pocket. Her dad would know what to do, who to call.

She could turn left and put them on the highway toward home. Call it off, all of it.

But then what? She would miss this. Right now she was in the middle of this—adventure? whatever it was—but eventually it would end, and she knew she would someday look back on this night with regret and fondness. She also pined for the quiet evening she hadn't had, her stomach growling for the dinner she hadn't eaten. Her life was splitting in two, each half going a way she would never choose to go. Sometimes she wasn't sure who she was.

"I've never been to a casino before," she said, making her voice Juby-bright as she pulled into the parking lot under the large red letters. A red-letter day. But wasn't red a warning, too? She pulled up to the curb to let them out.

Inside the casino, Lillian was easily found among the lights and buzz of the casino floor, slumped at a slot machine. Beyond her, the blinking and pinging row of machines ran a quarter mile. The place reeked of smoke, old and new. Juby was gone.

"That kid," Lillian said.

"Where did she go?"

"She went to change. A twenty." Lillian took a deep breath. "Into the currency of this nation."

"Wait," Alice said, looking around. "Are we actually gambling?"

"When in Rome."

"I don't think I like to gamble," Alice said.

"Are you sure? You're taking a big risk." Lillian's face was lit green, blue, green, blue by the lights on the machine. "Looking for this guy. Is risky."

"What do you mean? You don't think he would—what do you think he would do?"

"We don't know." Lillian gazed around her, like a queen surveying her holdings. Alice had already seen a woman on a scooter, hooked to an oxygen tank. She didn't like to think someone might look at Lillian and not understand what she now knew, that Lillian was funny, sharp. Lillian was good company. "It's a risk to go looking," Lillian said. "Have you thought? If you find something? You didn't want to know?"

Here came Juby, though, hooked by the arm of a large, square-shouldered man in black pants and a white shirt—plus black jacket, black tie, and a gun in its holster at his other hip. Security. What had she tried to steal now?

But no, Juby was smiling, and so was the security guard.

"She's a golden ticket," Lillian breathed.

"Heyyyy," Juby said, beaming at the security guard like he was an award she'd been handed. "I just met Rayyan here, who says Becki's about to go on her break and we can meet her right here."

"Will you recognize her?" Alice said.

Rayyan frowned, reclaimed his arm. "I thought you said you knew her."

"I know her," Lillian said quickly. "But I don't move so fast. As you can see." She gasped to finish. "If I know Becki. She'll be moving fast."

Rayyan seemed placated, if confused. Bored. "You ladies have a good night. Rebekah should be along."

Juby saw him off with a beaming smile. The second his back was turned, she wheeled on Alice. "Could you be *cool* once in a while and not say the first thing inside your head? Good thing Lil is so fast on her feet—"

"So to speak," Lillian said.

"—or we might be waiting for Rebekah *outside*."

"Sorry," Alice said.

"Or from *jail*, I suppose, since I'm a felon now." Juby pulled her phone from her pocket, thumbed it, and held it up to Alice's face. "Future reference, *that's* what Rebekah looks like."

The crowd in the photo wore matching neon-green shirts. Juby had zoomed in on a woman in the front row, compact, even muscular. She had gold rings on every finger and straightened but short, sleek black hair. The little girl next to her was lighter-skinned, with puffs for pigtails and deep dimples. "OK, got it."

"Rebekah's your age, I'm thinking, but she's closer to my color, so we're going with Plan Juby," Juby said. "Per the usual."

It's my Doe. But Juby had a point. "OK."

"I have low blood sugar," Juby announced. "As soon as we bag this Becki babe, let's get food. I promised my gal Lil a date and she is going to have a date."

"If she's on break," Alice said, "maybe Rebekah would like a snack, too."

Juby appraised her. "That's better. Now you're thinking. You're also buying."

WHICH WAS HOW they came to be seated in an open corner of an inside café near the entrance with a woman they'd just met, an order for four expensive cheeseburgers placed.

Rebekah Young, black pants, white shirt, had been tipped off by the security guard before leaving for her break, so she hadn't been ambushed. She seemed in fact quite happy to be treated instead of eating her packed lunch in her car. It was almost ten p.m. by the time they sat down. Rebekah only had twenty-two minutes to give.

"I want to get a smoke before I go back up to the tables," she said.

"You may regret that. One day," Lillian said. "This is the lasting result. Of a rock 'n' roll lifestyle."

Rebekah might have been trying to smile at Lillian, but it came out as a sneer. Without the cheerful puff pigtails of her daughter and the colorful, matching T-shirts, Rebekah, in person, was fearsome. "They'll dock me if I'm a *minute* late. What did you want?"

Juby gave Alice a look and jumped in. "You used to live in the same building as a man named Richard Miller, right?"

Rebekah leaned back coolly from the table. She glanced toward the door. "What is this?"

"Look," Juby said. "I'm going to level with you. We are not the cops. We can't make you talk to us. *But* we have reasons for asking about Richard Miller and, actually, there are some things about him you might want to be aware—"

"Who sent you?" Rebekah stood up, her chair scraping the floor. "How in the world—"

"Now, Ms. Young," Lillian began.

"Don't Miz Young me in the place I work!" Rebekah looked frantically toward the door and another security guard there. "Shevon, where's Rayyan?"

"We really don't mean any harm," Juby said, trying the milky-tea voice she had used on the landlord.

"I don't know who put you up to this—"

"Richard Miller is a danger to your daughter," Alice said, cutting through the rising chaos. The group went quiet. Juby sat back.

Rebekah turned her wild eyes on Alice, looking her up and down. "Who are you? Are you . . . ?" She shook her head. "I've left my kid with him a million times."

"What I'm saying," Alice said, enunciating clearly, "is that it might be a bad idea to do that."

Rebekah gathered her things. "I would trust Richard Ki—I'd trust him with my daughter's life, and mine, and you know what? I did. You're the ones come digging where you don't belong. Wherever he is, leave him be. And don't lead anyone else there. Or here."

She hurried away, toward the security station.

"We're so getting kicked out of here," Juby said. She reached into her pocket and threw down four red casino chips. "Not a single dollar lost. Get the check, Alice. I've got the tip."

"Guess I'll get. A head start." Lillian dug herself out of her chair onto shaky legs. "Best date in decades."

CHAPTER ELEVEN

MERRILY

Merrily woke up the morning after she'd heard Rick was missing, and knew that she would go looking for him. Furthermore, she knew how to do it.

She dumped the box of photos and keepsakes onto her bed and sorted. They had visited him, just once, in the town he'd moved to. She had doodled her childhood away on the backs of every slip of paper that had passed through her hands, especially on trips in the car—but the fronts, the fronts of the receipts were the treasure. She dug out sixteen slips, some of them too faded to read, most from Port Bethlehem. Five of the legible ones were from places she didn't recognize. She held them aloft, paper gold: dates, times, town names. She picked up her phone, noted that her mom hadn't responded to her texts. Nothing from Rick, either. She mapped the receipts, finding that two were from towns west, toward Chicago. The other three led south out of Port Beth along the interstate toward Indianapolis. That was the trip she remembered.

When Merrily put the receipts in order by date and time, they told a story. The first was for a few bucks at a gas station, just enough to get moving. Another for a McDonald's, just a couple of dollars again, in cash, not enough for two people to eat. Merrily could nearly feel the soft bills crumpled in her hand, could imagine holding the change tightly until the pennies were warm.

She might have hit a dead end if not for the third receipt. It was for a full tank of gas purchased in a small town that Google reported was miles off the highway. A full tank of gas, twenty years ago. It was a lot of money for a woman who couldn't afford to order a cheap cheeseburger for herself. Merrily imagined her mother, young, curly hair gone fuzzy with humidity, suddenly flush with cash. Was that why they'd visited Rick in the first place? When had Rick ever been wealthy enough, or generous? They'd stopped at the same McDonald's again on the way back and feasted like kings. She didn't have that receipt, but she remembered it, remembered the feeling of throwing a little money around. Of bingeing a bit to make up for deprivation.

Merrily slipped out of the apartment with her purse and a handful of nearly burned bacon Justyce had left in the fridge. She was on the road and letting her phone tell her the way by the time she might have been sitting in her cube at work, the birthday balloon by now surely dangling from its string to the floor. The freedom was delicious, the sky perfectly blue. She passed the exit for Port Beth and hit I-65, turning south toward downstate Indiana. The cornfields, waving and green, somehow beautiful in a way she'd never noticed.

Of course, she'd not been out among them in a while. The only travel she'd done in the last few years had been between her apartment on the South Side of Chicago and her mom's house, a distance of only forty minutes in decent traffic. She'd always wanted to see the world, but had settled for such a narrow sliver.

Almost an hour later, Merrily regretted her spontaneity. There was so much *out here* out here, so much corn, so many miles. This town was much farther away than she'd realized, and the scenery so ridiculous and empty. Who would live out here? The only excitement she'd managed was stopping at the same McDonald's they'd eaten at on the original trip, an old-model restaurant untouched by time in the crook of the exit for Dora, Indiana. She used the toilet and got a Coke, headed west into the corn.

She knew the town as soon as her car sailed out of a curve and up a small rise. A sign posted along the road read Dora, population 1583. More people than she would have guessed, by the look of it. The gas station where her mom had filled the tank was easily found but no longer in service, and the rest of the town might have been closed for business, too. The certainty she'd felt driving into town rushed away. It was just a town, nothing special, nothing familiar. She'd come all this way but he wouldn't still be here, even if she found the exact house. He was missing from *Wisconsin*. What had she expected to find?

Merrily parked the car and rolled down a window for air. According to the receipts, they hadn't stayed in town more than an hour. Had they even seen Rick? She searched her memory. Yes, he'd played hide-and-seek with her, while her mom smoked a cigarette, one hip jutting out. Merrily knew that pose. It meant, *Watch your ass.*

There'd been a park, maybe, where she'd dug in a sandbox with some local kids, a trio of girls who'd competed for her attention. Maybe they'd been Rick's children! Her mom and Rick fought in quiet tones on a bench nearby.

"Can I help you find something?"

Merrily startled, dropping her Coke into her lap. "Shit shit." She leapt from the car, the crotch of her pants sodden, cold. An older woman with a dog on a leash backed out of her way and reeled in her pet. Merrily reached back into the car for napkins and pawed at herself helplessly. "What?" she said.

"I said—well, I said could I help you. But it looks like I did the opposite." The woman was a hip grandma type, with short messy white hair. She wore bright athletic shoes, fresh from a box, probably. Where did you buy such things, when there were no stores?

"I wasn't expecting anyone, I guess." Wasn't expecting anyone to bother her.

"Are you having car trouble?"

Merrily sorted the options quickly and decided to head straight in. "No, I was trying to find a house I visited once as a kid," she said. "Hey, there." She knelt down and let the dog approach her. "It's been a long time. I guess I thought I would recognize more than I do. This might be a wasted trip."

"Relative's house?"

"Yeah," she said. "He used to be my stepdad but they've been broken up for years. Rick Kisel? Richard? This would have been twenty years ago."

The woman didn't flinch. "I've lived here my whole life," she said. "It was this town?"

"Well, I thought so," Merrily said. "But I might be wrong. Was there a playground or a park here, ever?"

The woman's eyes lit up. They walked together across the street and into the neighborhood. Two blocks in, a squat, flat box of a building appeared. "The school," the woman said, but she didn't have to. Merrily had picked up the sound of children roaring in play somewhere on the other side of the building. They walked along the chain-link fence to the far side of the school grounds until they could see the source of the noise, a group of second- or third-graders racing, tagging, swinging, climbing. A group of girls sat cross-legged in the grass near the fence. As the shadows of Merrily and the woman passed over them, the girls looked up, took in Merrily's wet pants, and laughed. "Did she *pee* herself?" one of them said. Merrily would have flipped them off if not for the woman with the dog.

Merrily wasn't sure it was the right place. "Maybe," she said, and pivoted to take in the houses nearby. "This might be it. Thank you."

"Well, don't hang out near the fence too long," the woman said, gazing up at the school and then at Merrily. Her eyes dragged down Merrily's long, brown arms. "They call the deputies out for almost anything these days."

Merrily looked away. Message received. She wanted the woman to leave so she could shop the houses on the block for the right one. "I'll be fine," she said.

The woman bobbed her head and turned back the way they'd come. At the last minute, she faced the school again. "When was your friend here, again?"

Merrily swallowed a sudden lump in her throat. "Twenty years ago? I don't know how long he would have lived here. Richard Kisel? Did you know him?"

"It makes me think . . ." the woman said. Her bright shoes were already pointed away, the dog nosing down the block. "There was a fire in town about twenty years ago, and a man died—is your stepdad OK?"

"Oh, yeah," Merrily said. "I had a text from him this week."

The woman smiled, relieved. "Good, there wasn't much left of—well, the house or the man. Not enough to have something to bury, from what I hear, but then no family came forward. The town put up a stone. Anyway, I'm glad he's not the one you mean. *That* would be a difficult trip, to find a nameless grave at the end of it." The dog strained at his leash. "I guess we're off. Welcome to memory lane."

They parted ways. Merrily kept to the fence but walked on. No need to meet any deputies. She kept her head down, watching her red sandals kicking out with each step. At the end of the block, some intuition pulled her to the left, so she crossed the street and followed it. For two and a half blocks, she let memory or whatever it was drag her farther from her car.

Merrily stopped on a street lined with houses of the same post-war shapes, colors. A few had been built up or out. One house had been taken to the studs and rebuilt, but she could still see the ghost of its former style peeking out from behind a new face.

Just in front of her, though, rose a different sort of house. A Mc-Mansion, her mom would have called it. A proper giant of a house for the lot it had been built on, and closer to the sidewalk than the others. It was the kind of house whose owners would have hassled the neighbors for exceptions. The sort of house they'd started not to make as much, high ceilings making them noisy and hard to heat. Soulless, Mamá Cruz would have said, spitting a little.

Soulless, newer than the rest, and sitting in the precise spot her feet had taken her. This was the house. This was it. No. This wasn't the house. This was what had been built in its place, once the ashes cooled and the dead were removed.

She started to reach for her phone, thinking of old wiring, tinderbox attics. *Good thing you moved, dude*, she would text to him. But she didn't. She put her phone away and turned back toward her car.

ON HER DRIVE out of town, Merrily caught a glimpse of green, of white marble crosses. She turned toward the cemetery and, hungry, her pants sticky and cold, she walked the rows, reading the markers. What was the point? It wasn't Rick anyway. When she saw the headstone off on its own along the fence line, though, she went to it.

JOHN DOE, the inscription read. REST IN PEACE. And a single date, the day of the fire, she supposed. What other date could they have used?

A picket fence stood guard, and on the other side the fields began. Merrily looked out on them, less enthusiastic about corn than she had been earlier in the day. It was a lonely place. Lonelier still with no name and no one coming to mourn.

Later, Merrily sat in the drive-through of the same McDonald's. She should be miles down the road toward home but she needed one of those kid meals in her belly before she drove another mile. The worker leaned out of the first window to take her money, exact change, handed back a receipt, and waved her toward the second window and her lunch.

Merrily held the receipt.

"Pull forward, please."

The date on the *receipt*.

"Ma'am?"

The date on the nameless grave was the same as the date on the old receipt her mom had kept, Merrily's pony drawing on the back. The house where Rick lived had caught fire, and a man had died—and it had happened the same day they'd made their only visit to Rick.

Merrily pulled forward to the next window. For the first time, she wondered: Why had Rick left them? And why had he gone to that town of so few attractions? She had a hundred questions, but they all boiled down to one. *What's going on?* There was only one person she could ask.

CHAPTER TWELVE
ALICE

Friday morning, early, Alice bolted upright in her bed. She'd dreamed of black birds, whirling like vultures, converging until the sky disappeared.

She'd forgotten to send the flowers.

She launched herself toward the bathroom, the shower. In the mirror she caught sight of the tattoo that had so disappointed her dad. He never should have seen it. It was on her hip, for Matt's eyes only. Back when it had seemed like they'd last, they'd gotten them together. It was her idea to get the crows, of course, like she was reclaiming her life from them, the migraines, the nightmares. There was nothing wrong with crows. They were smart, cagey. They remembered, paid debts. Held grudges. She could have been the kind of woman drawn to starlings, attracted by the shapes of the flock in flight, the murmuration as they swarmed at dusk—but she wasn't. The crow was like a dark corner of herself, unfolded. To show who she really was.

She'd thought she'd known.

Matt didn't care about flowers, but it was the least they could do, and she could use them as a way to check in with Lita, his sister. More than that, she'd promised her dad she'd send them, and she hadn't. Instead she'd gotten caught up in searching for Richard Miller, then had to drop the other women back at their cars. By the time she arrived home to the dark, empty apartment, she had mixed feelings about the search, ranging from frustration that they hadn't learned more about Richard Miller to relief they hadn't.

Turning the key to her door the night before, she'd had the strangest feeling that she was returning to a crime scene, that something would be changed. But there was her cereal bowl in the sink, the tea bag drying on the saucer she'd left out that morning. That morning, before she'd seen Richard Miller's face on the Doe Pages. A million years in a single day.

In the shower, she imagined the day she might have spent in the hospital, another splinter of her life down a path she might have chosen.

Ten minutes before visiting hours started, Alice was waiting outside the critical care unit, a heavy and aggressively cheerful arrangement of sunflowers held against her hip. She'd texted Uncle Jim and Jimmy that she was taking care of an errand for her dad, reminding them he was out of the office for the day. Uncle Jim sent back a simple OK. As much a Luddite as her dad.

From Jimmy, for her courtesy, she received silence. Fine. She sniffed at the flowers. Sunflowers weren't fragrant, but that seemed OK.

Alice heard footsteps behind her. Lita, moving fast, a bag swinging from her shoulder. When she saw Alice, she stopped, almost skittered backward.

"What—what are you doing here?"

Alice adjusted the vase higher against her. "Just a token from King and Fine. How's he doing?"

Lita fussed with her bag. "He's—well, you can come in for a minute. But they don't allow flowers inside critical care."

"Oh." She should have remembered that. "We could put them in the family room, for everyone."

Lita turned and led her down the hall and through a door. Inside the dimmed room, a man had made a bed of three chairs, coming to rest in a series of uncomfortable shapes. He opened his eyes immediately.

"Good morning, Lanny," Lita whispered. "Any news?"

The man shook his head and closed his eyes.

Alice carefully slid the vase onto the nearest table and retreated. The room smelled of unbrushed teeth and missed showers, of time passing, of decay. She should have ordered flowers to be sent up from the gift shop. She never should have come here.

"I don't want to bother M—"

"You should see him," Lita said.

They'd been friends, but in the breakup, Alice had lost Lita as well. Lost her laugh, lost her love of books and her stories from the school where she taught first grade. Lost the context Lita provided for who Matt was, the glowing appraisal she rested upon her brother when he wasn't looking.

She missed it all. As an only child, Alice considered Matt's sister the closest thing to a sibling she'd ever known.

Alice followed Lita back to the CCU doors and through them, trying not to look too closely at anything or anyone as they made their way through the white and clinical landscape to the back corner, a room blocked by a sliding door of sterile glass. On the other side, a figure swathed in white bandages lay among white sheets, his face almost as pale. His legs were in large contraptions, wrapped to twice their size, his arms both in splints held out from his sides. Wings.

Alice felt the most keen revulsion. Pity. Then, finally, sadness. "Dad said he would make a full recovery. I'm so relieved."

Lita's eyes raked over her. "Too early to say."

"He's—" Words failed. Full recovery must be a distant dream, a hopeful thing her dad had gifted her. "What have the doctors said?"

Lita didn't answer. When Alice glanced at her, she could tell the other woman was trying to master her emotions. She braced herself. She had taken a lot of bad news over the years but it was a learned skill, earned. Not everyone had it. No one wanted it.

"You don't have to tell me. I have no right."

"I think you should hear how he's doing," Lita said. "Someone over there should hear it, and it might as well be you. Full *recovery*? Look at him."

Alice turned back to the glass. He was a pinned moth. "He broke both his legs?"

"He fell three stories, Alice," Lita said, too loud for their surroundings. Over Lita's shoulder, the nurse on duty at the central desk turned to watch. "Three. He broke everything. He is—he is in *pieces*. He went to work for Fine and King a whole man and came back . . . *this*."

King and Fine. Alice wouldn't correct her, and knew better than to apologize or accept blame. People could get hurt working construction, a fact of the business. The lawyers would sort out Matt's health bills, the company's liability if it had some. None of that was for her to decide. Between that and the breakup, she didn't quite know what she could say. "Has he been awake at all?"

Lita gaped at her. "Awake? What—no! He's in a coma. Alice, I don't think you or your—you have no idea what's happening here."

"Please," the nurse said. "Ms. Weissman, could you—"

Lita took Alice's arm and propelled her past the nurse and out of the CCU. Lita was two heads shorter, tiny as a sparrow, really, but Alice felt violence in her grip.

She would do me harm. Maybe Alice had misunderstood something about Lita. Maybe she'd gotten things wrong.

Lita Weissman force-marched Alice past the family room, out to the floor's waiting area, right up to the elevators.

"Lita, I'm so—" But she worried which words she was allowed to say. "Have the lawyers been in touch?"

"Lawyers?" Lita's face drained of color. "You don't think—no, we don't need to speak to any lawyers—"

"It's just handled that way. It's nothing to worry about."

"Did someone come to you and say he was speaking for us? Because we're not going to anyone, you understand. Tell them that. Tell Fine and King that."

"King and Fine," Alice said. "I didn't mean to accuse you of—"

"We understand each other. We'll sign whatever we need to sign." The woman's chin jutted out, but then she faltered. "I mean, I will. I'll sign whatever it is."

She hurried away. Alice stared at the elevator doors, then pushed the button. She didn't think she did understand, actually. She was definitely getting something wrong.

Three stories.

She watched the panel above the elevator count the floors as it approached.

Three stories of a parking garage, too, built tall to make way for the SUVs, panel vans, delivery trucks.

The elevator doors opened.

"Are you going down or not?" someone in the elevator snapped.

She shook her head, backed away, then thought better of it and rushed in, shouldering the closing doors. The people inside shifted to make room for her.

She sensed someone looking at her and realized she hadn't turned to face the front. She obliged and watched the floors count down, wondering. Three stories? Did it matter that someone else had said Matt had fallen only two?

CHAPTER THIRTEEN

MERRILY

Merrily drove north to Port Beth, ignoring the corn, and let herself into her mom's house. She grabbed a stained pair of sweats—too short—from her old room, found a T-shirt in the clean laundry that her mom wouldn't miss, then peeled the soda-sticky pants away and got into the shower. She let the water get scalding, thinking about a story she'd heard, the one about how a bullfrog will sit in a pot of water as it starts to boil, will sit and attend its own death without sensing the danger. How much could a person stand? Would you recognize the line when you crossed it, into harm?

The bathroom door clicked open. "Burglars don't use all the hot water," her mom called. "Back for more of my fashionable clothing?"

Merrily laughed, turned off the water.

Her mom handed a towel in, the stack of bracelets on her arm clanging together. "Why aren't you at work?"

"I'll be out in a second," Merrily said.

"That sounds not good."

"I just took a day off, Mamá. People take days off."

"Some people take more days than others," her mom said, and closed the door.

Merrily stepped out of the shower to dry off and found herself in the wide, steamy mirror over the sink. She didn't mind herself naked, the way Justyce or Kath seemed to, from how they talked about themselves. Her skin was a nice color, con leche, her mom called it. She had a slim build, lanky, long. Lucky, she considered herself, for a girl with a pear-hipped mother. Merrily wiped the mirror and leaned in, checking her face. Zits, wrinkles, both? *Thirty years old*. She toweled off, lonely for the coin sound of ChatX.

In the kitchen, her mom had made tea for them both. "Those pants make you look like a giant."

"I am a giant."

"Next to me, sure," her mom said. "So . . . day off. Another one?"

Merrily blew on the hot tea, looking past her mom out the window to the bright backyard. She had played there as a child, safe and loved. Her mom had raised her strictly but not in a straitjacket—allowed to roam, to make mistakes, to learn and discover. She wondered now if she should keep the day's activities to herself. She knew, without exactly understanding how, that by making the trip to Rick's old house, she'd caused the water around her to start to boil.

"Is Rick dead?" she said.

Her mom crossed herself with a few whispered words, bracelets chiming. "How should I know? Is that what they said? The cops—they never—"

"I don't mean now, I mean—did he die a long time ago?"

Her mom's eyes rolled upward to a spot high over Merrily's shoulder. Her mouth opened, words delayed. "Start at the beginning."

"We went to visit Rick once, a long time ago," Merrily said. "I was ten."

A spot near her mom's mouth twitched. "No."

"*Yes*." Merrily sipped her tea. "I drew pictures on the back of our McDonald's receipt. You ate some of my fries but we didn't have enough money for us both to eat."

Her mom fidgeted with the tea bag in the saucer in front of her. "I can't believe you remember that."

"We went to the playground—"

"The park."

"—the *playground* of a *school*, and you and Rick argued—"

"Talked!"

"—*argued* while I played with some kids who lived nearby. And then we filled the tank of the car and drove home."

"So?"

Merrily took a deep breath. "So this morning I went to that town."

Her mom made a sound. "No, you didn't."

Merrily would have been confused by her mom's reaction if not for the date on the receipt and the grave marker. A strange feeling came over her then, that she was near the center of something—no, not the center. She was at the edge, separated from a new world by a gap she might leap over. Sometimes she felt the presence of another universe near her own, what could have been—and it wasn't always better. She knew there were hurts she had been spared. Yes, her father had died, but he was gone before she could love him, and so her suffering was almost secondhand. In another universe, she had a father. It was fun to imagine. She felt that other world now, could almost hear the scraping sound of the two orbits dragging against one another as they met and careened away. The life she lived and the one she hadn't.

"Why did we go there?" Merrily asked.

Her mom stood, drained her mug into the sink. "To visit Rick, of course," she said. "It was a bad idea. We never did it again." Under her breath, she said, like a curse, "Impossible man."

"Did we never visit again because he was an impossible man? Or did we never go back because he wasn't there?" At the sink, her mom's back went straight. Merrily hesitated. She and her mom could talk about anything, except sometimes not, like this, when suddenly Mamá's memory went suspiciously hazy or her eyes shuttered closed. She should have gone at the topic a different way, at least, not directly to the center, stomping in like Godzilla. But it was too late. "Or did we never go back because he died in a fire that day?"

When her mom turned, she looked more curious than upset. "Who told you Rick died in a fire?"

"No one." Her defenses were up suddenly. Something in the air had turned away from danger. Merrily knew she was getting the story wrong, now that her mother was participating. "The fire happened that day, after we left—"

"So you know I didn't set it, at least," her mom said.

Jokes? "Mamá—"

"I thought Rick was texting you happy birthday balloons or monkeys—"

"*Emojis*, not monkeys."

"—and now you think he's been dead for twenty years? I don't understand how you think, Mer, I really don't. How does it make sense . . ."

Merrily recognized the signs of a conversation between one woman and herself. Now she was a kid who had been patted on the head and dismissed.

But the fire was too huge a coincidence. The only time she'd ever been taken to visit Rick since he'd left her life, and the same day someone, but apparently not Rick, had died in the same house?

She chewed on this while her mother prattled on, then broke in. "So did Rick start the fire?"

"Why would you think a thing like this?"

"You can't have it both ways, Mamá," she said. "Either Rick is a shit or he's a saint, but—"

"Watch your language," her mom said. "He is neither of those things and all of it and a lot more, and I'm tired of talking about him. There are other things two grown women can discuss than a man, surely? Are you staying to dinner? I have leftover cake. Since you're here I won't have to get out the step stool."

Merrily stood and retrieved the covered cake plate she had stowed on top of the refrigerator the day before. The plate in her hands, her stomach flipped at the thought of another gummy mouthful. The other universe whirled away from her, out of reach. She handed down the cake, listening to the music of her mom's bracelets as she raised her arms to accept the plate.

She was lonely. In this moment, here in her childhood kitchen with her beloved mother, with a trusted roommate back at her own apartment, and Kath at work . . . forget Kath. She had Searcher6 and Michaelangelo24 and the others. She had people who cared, and yet she had felt brittle and precious since the moment she'd thought they'd come to tell her something had happened to her mom. Nothing had been right since then.

She sat heavily at the table and held out a plate as her mom cut a deep slice. The cake fell onto the plate against her hand, chocolate smearing her thumb. She stuck it into her mouth to suck off the icing, her mom pleased and laughing. But the icing was too sweet. Too sweet, too much, but then also too little, and no one to ask: Was this all there was?

CHAPTER FOURTEEN

ALICE

Saturday morning, Alice woke slowly, this time a pleasant dream clutching at her, drawing her back. She squeezed her eyes shut and lingered, stretching toward it. Her mother, young and singing at the sink, long hair and barefoot, even. *You are my sunshine* . . . Pancakes on her plate, with a bacon smile—

Alice sat up, looked at the clock. She'd fallen back asleep and now the dream didn't seem as pleasant as she'd thought. Didn't they say you'd always have your memories? As though that were some kind of consolation prize? In her experience, having the warmth of old memories made not a *dent*. Most of it couldn't be salvaged, not for her.

She took her tea mug to the couch. Her backpack lay on the next cushion, her laptop inside. She didn't want to work on the Doe Pages. She'd picked up some of Juby's despair, perhaps. It was her turn down the rabbit hole. Why did they spend their time on Does when they stood such little chance of success? The possibility of a match was too tantalizing. What if they could help someone find a lost loved one? Even if the story of what had happened was lost forever, surely there was some comfort that could be had.

Of course, with her mother—

Alice reached for her computer and booted it up. There was little comfort, even if you attended the illness and then the death, and saw the casket lowered with finality. Even when you could visit a grave, the correct details chiseled firmly in place, the blows kept coming. Memories, missed moments. The relationship frozen in time, no new chances to get it right.

Alice navigated to the Doe Pages but hesitated to click into the Missing Persons profiles to see Richard Miller's face again. Richard Miller, the boogeyman of her childhood. Could she find him? Did she really want to? In order to face him? And say what, exactly? She had no complaints, really, because her life had turned out just—

Fine.

If she ever actually located Richard Miller, she could ask her dad. He would know exactly what should be done, and probably take care of it.

Alice wasn't sure she wanted him to do that. Maybe she could take care of it herself.

Of course, maybe nothing could be done. No jury would listen to an eyewitness giving thirty-year-old testimony from when she was a toddler. She'd seen enough crime TV to know that if she ever made it to the stand, they'd pick her apart. Were there statutes of limitation on kidnapping?

Was she talking herself out of it? Or into it? She felt as though she were waiting for permission to keep going. She wanted to *know.*

Curiosity, at last! Was that not a good enough reason to keep going? The great mystery of her life, solved?

Other people had suffered so much worse, of course. A man

had disappeared from their old town years back, presumed dead. Someone her dad had known, a guy with a family. *That* must be devastation: uncertainty in the face of terrible, actual, unnatural loss and the wide-open of the unknown.

When she thought about that guy and his family . . .

Well, she had at least talked herself into helping out at the Doe Pages for a little while longer.

Alice went to put her mug into the kitchen sink. On the counter near the trash lay a few of the pieces of the mail Juby had stolen from Richard Miller's neighbors. Just junk mail, but left in Alice's car to deal with. She didn't know Juby well, but this might be a very Juby thing to do.

Should she throw it away? Shred it in the trailer on Monday? She didn't want Rebekah Young's mail anywhere near her—

A new name jumped out at her from one of the envelopes, a credit card offer.

She tried out the name in a whisper: "Richard Kisel." She didn't like the sound of it, or the taste.

No one had mentioned anyone named Kisel, had they? It wasn't a name she knew, probably just another resident of the sad house in Milwaukee. She sifted through the rest of the junk mail, finding another piece for Kisel. Both addresses referenced "Apt R."

Richard Miller had lived in the back of the building, the *rear* apartment, wasn't that the phrase? *Richard*, such an unexceptional name. *Miller*? A dead end, almost invisible.

She put the mail down and went back to the couch and laptop. Alice had never moved apartments herself, but she'd heard a few stories among the guys on the crew about checks getting lost, old bills finding them years later, mail arriving for former occupants long after a home ceased to be new. Junk, mostly, but sometimes it was real mail: summonses and child support demands, desperate inquires to reconnect from past friends and distant relatives, former lovers. The trail of the lost often ended with a bad address. Some of the crew members they'd had would not be above applying for a credit card in the name of a former occupant, she knew that much.

The search engine didn't make much of Richard Kisel, but there were enough hits to troll through them for a while. Alice switched to an image search, scrolled some more. She clicked over to narrow the search by time, hovering over the options: "last year," "last month." Why not? She selected hits only from the last week, and the page that resulted was white, blank except for four results. Alice leaned in to the screen. One link was the original Doe Pages post. When she clicked through, the post had been updated to include an also-known-as. *Aka Kisel.*

"You don't say," she muttered.

He was still missing—that hadn't changed. But now he was missing from two different names, two different lives. An interesting case, then, not just your usual Empty. Alice stared at his profile, memorizing his long nose. *Lillian will have a field day with you.*

Two of the other links were news reports out of Milwaukee. Missing local man. Any information, etc.

The last result was a link to a site called PhotoSocial. When Alice clicked, she was sent to a log-in page. *No, thank you.* She didn't spend time on anything like that. She backed out and clicked on the stored cache for the result instead. Dead end. She retreated again and looked more carefully at the original link. The photo attached to the post was small, but she could see a young woman's narrow face, dark wavy hair. The snippet text underneath read *Missing: Richard Kisel. Last seen*—and then was cut off.

Alice sat back, her laptop gone loose in her hands.

Somewhere along the way, the guy had done something serious enough to slough off his entire identity, abandoning Kisel and adopting Miller. But here was someone who cared anyway. Here was someone who missed Richard Kisel.

Alice studied the young woman in the photo again. What had Lillian worried about? That she, Alice, might find something in this search that she didn't want to know?

It was Rebekah Young she thought of. Leave him where he is, and don't take anyone else there. Was that protecting Richard, or protecting others?

Richard Miller/Kisel had a lot more to him than she'd first imagined, but what made him more interesting might also make him more dangerous. Alice reached for her phone, then hesitated. She couldn't get a fix on Juby. First she was nervous, then game, and then at the casino, short-tempered and protective of the search when the stakes should have been Alice's, not Juby's. It made no sense. And yet, she didn't think she could do it alone. She didn't want to.

She texted Juby: *I'm sorry I'm so bad at this.*

She took a breath, hit send.

Then: *I need your help.*

CHAPTER FIFTEEN
ALICE

Richard *Kisel*. God, it's such a relief to be digging for an *alive* person," Juby said, thumbing her phone in the backseat of Alice's car. "With recent addresses and car registrations. If he had a social media footprint, he'd be a real live boy."

"We *hope* he's alive," Lillian said. She turned down the passenger seat visor against the Saturday afternoon glare of the Skyway. It was hot out, and they could hear Lillian better with the windows closed and the AC on. "Right, Alice?"

"Of course," Alice said. He was no good to her dead. She wanted answers, if not justice—not some kind of sick revenge. But Lillian's questioning had a way of cutting to the bone.

After she'd told Juby and Lillian about Richard Miller's alter ego, they'd had to face the fact that he might be more than missing. Richard Miller/Kisel was dragging a lot of trouble behind him, trouble they didn't understand.

She wanted the truth. It wasn't the same as wanting to get involved.

"Stand by for GPS coordinates," Juby said in a robot voice. "*Beep boop.*"

The Australian accent on her phone had been replaced by a woman's voice, which told them to keep heading in the direction they were going.

"Why did you change the voice?" Lillian said. "I miss that Australian footballer bloke."

"Got tired of some dude telling me what to do," Juby said.

"Since Thursday?" Alice said, and saw Juby shoot her a look in the rearview mirror. She had not noticed until now that Juby's usual sparkle was dimmed. "What's wrong?"

"I didn't sleep well," Juby said.

Alice wondered where the line was. There was friendship and there was whatever they were until they got to friendship. Road trip companions. Partners in crime. A scaffolding existed between one level and the next. A delicate structure, and questions were heavy—or the answers to them might be. Alice felt the chasm below them, distance they'd already climbed. It would be so easy to fall all the way back to the beginning.

"I just realized I don't know either of you well enough," she said, choosing the words, the tone, the approach. "All this craziness having to do with *me*, and I never asked—Lillian, do you have a family?"

She thought she might have zigged or zagged into a bad topic, but then Lillian picked up the thread and told them about her family of origin, sisters, a brother, waxing on a bit as best she could between pauses to catch her breath, until she said, finally, "All gone now."

"I'm so sorry." She shouldn't have brought it up.

"Nothing to be sorry for," Lillian said. "Nobody's left to ask. Never get to say their names. I like to say their names."

Juby had been silent in the back, listening, but now she leaned forward. "What are their names again, Lil?"

Parents Beatrice and Samuel, older sisters Vi and Susan, little brother Christopher. Vi was short for Violet. "That's a lovely name," Juby said. "I've always wondered what it was like to have grown up with a sister."

"Do you have a brother?" Alice said.

"He's a troll," Juby said cheerfully.

"Fuzzy-headed doll?" Lillian said.

"The kind under the bridge," the younger woman said. "He's an absolute shit. My parents' favorite, of course."

"What about you, Alice?" Lillian said.

"Only child."

"So, the *favorite*," Juby said. Alice caught her smile in the rearview. She was almost back to full wattage.

Alice said, "So much the favorite I would be embarrassed to tell you how spoiled I was."

No one said anything. Alice glanced into the backseat.

"*Was?*" Juby said.

They all laughed. "So you've met me," Alice said. "I'm sorry I'm not fit for human companionship most of the time. I was basically raised in a tower."

"A happy one," Lillian said.

It was not a question, but the other two women left room for her to answer. "Yes," she said. The sun was out, and these women were her friends. The scaffolding had held.

In the backseat, a woman's robotic voice suggested kindly they take the next exit.

RICK KISEL'S LAST known address was in Indiana, but not far from Chicago. One minute they were in the outskirts of the city, the skyline just visible in the side mirror, and the next they were in another state. Alice imagined a passport for interstate travel, the stamps she could collect this week alone. She had not traveled far, did not have a real passport. Had never thought to.

The town was not far in miles but in many ways, it was far from home. Approaching town, they'd witnessed relics of the old steel industry still hulking along the shoreline like haunted houses shaped from rust. Once they were in town, the decay was no less visible. The dwellings were small and close together, lined up behind sidewalks that needed replacing. Deeper into the town, though, the place started to pull together. Houses tidy, yards mowed. The neighbors had spent effort on flowering shrubs, window boxes, themed mailboxes. The first impression pried itself away. Now Alice saw the care that had been tended, the time, if not money. This was a proud street, a charming community. It disappointed her greatly that Kisel had lived a nice life.

"Which house is it?" Lillian said.

"That one." Juby pointed through the windshield.

Alice's chin pivoted. A fine specimen of its kind, rather nicer than even its neighbors. She could see down the side of the house into a little raised garden bed in the back, overflowing with greenery.

Carrots. The ridiculousness of their situation hit her. She might laugh. She could not laugh.

"What do we do, Jubilee?" Lillian said.

"Last known address doesn't mean he lives there, you guys," Juby said. "But we could see who does."

"We're all going," Lillian wheezed. "To the door?"

"You can stay here, Lil," Juby said, not moving.

"I mean," Alice said, "if you found this address, surely the police did, too?"

Neither of them said anything, only looked with big eyes toward the cute house where a kidnapper might live.

She was back in charge of her Doe.

Alice took a deep breath and opened the car door. The air was clear and damp, as though it had just rained, or would soon. Alice got out and started up the drive. They had been in the car long enough that her legs needed the stretch of long strides. She shortened them, giving herself time.

He wouldn't be here. The police could have found him otherwise.

Behind her, Alice heard a noise. Juby and Lillian climbed from the car, stretching. Positioning themselves to witness whatever might happen.

Her body carried her to the door. She was a passenger in this body, couldn't stop it if she tried. Alice saw her own hand reach for the doorbell. She heard the beating of her own blood in her ears. The doorbell rang, distant. She had not come up with a single thing to say.

Alice turned to look at Juby again, who made an impatient gesture. The door was opening.

A woman stood there, short and plump, pretty and tanned, with a lot of dark hair tumbling around her face. Her smile was timid, but it was a smile. "Yes," she said through the screen, looking up at Alice. "Can I help you?" She had a gentle lisp of an accent.

"Um," Alice said. "This is going to seem like a weird question . . ."

The woman's eyes flicked past Alice, then back, wary now.

"Did a man named Richard Mi—Richard Kisel used to live here?"

There was a noise from inside the house, but the woman didn't pay any attention. She unlocked the door between them and emerged, barefoot, onto the porch. She pulled the internal door behind her and let the screen door slap. It was a fast and practiced movement, from inside to outside, aggressive.

"Who are you?" the woman said. "Who wants to know?"

"I'm . . . Alice," she said.

It sounded helpless, even to her. She had no claim, only a story, and a complicated one. The woman checked over Alice's shoulder again. "And who are they, then?"

"My friends. We don't want any trouble—"

"Then you are looking for the wrong man," the woman said. "Take your friends back to the place you come from and forget about that . . . *impossible* man."

"You know him."

"You're not listening to me," the woman said.

"Who are *you*?" Alice said, grown bold.

The woman seemed to see her for the first time. Her mouth opened, but no sound came out. She swore under her breath, Spanish maybe. She seemed even smaller now, tucking her arms around herself, a set of bracelets on her arm chiming against one another. "Go back home," the woman said. "Please go, and don't come back."

She turned and was on the other side of the screen door before Alice could think what to do. In the moment before the door closed, Alice saw a face there, waiting. Dark wavy hair, sharp features—and she knew who it was.

CHAPTER SIXTEEN

MERRILY

Merrily's mom closed the door and pressed her back against it. "What was that about?" Merrily said. She thought she'd heard—

"Nothing," her mom said, but her accent was thicker than normal. Her accent got thick when she was nervous or sad, whenever she had to talk to someone on the phone she didn't know, whenever she was sure someone was looking at her and dismissing her as a foreigner, questioning her right to stand on this ground. Then the accent became impenetrable, until it might as well be Spanish, and then it was. "Is nothing but some door-to-door salesman—"

"She said Rick's name," Merrily said.

"Saleswoman," her mom said smoothly. "They thought he lived here still. They sell to him . . . magazines."

When she lied, too, the accent. "Mamá, who was that lady?"

Lady? Merrily went to the window and watched as the tall woman crossed their yard back to her car. She walked as though injured, with one hand held across her stomach. She was only someone her own age. She started for the door, but her mom wouldn't move. She curved her spine and ducked her head, compressing herself. Protecting herself as though from an attack.

"Mamá, stop it," Merrily said. "What if she knows about Rick?"

"Knows what?"

"Knows— Move! Knows where he is, what's happened to him."

"She won't know anything," her mom said, but stepped away. "She won't know as much as you, even." Merrily flung the door open and yelled through the screen. The woman in the yard turned. The two regarded one another.

I know who you are.

"Come back," Merrily yelled.

THE WOMAN'S FRIENDS came with her, and that was too much to put her mom through, so Merrily took them around to the backyard. Now the woman who'd come to the door—*Alice*, she'd said—stood looking at her mom's garden. Merrily found herself protective of it, though she hadn't planned or planted it, had never dug a hand in its soil. It needed weeding. *This bitch better not say so.*

Now Merrily considered staying on with her mom another night, tidying the garden, helping with the yard. But she'd already stayed two nights this week, curled up in her old single bed. There was something in that, how easily she let herself be talked into sleeping in her childhood bed. She didn't want to think about it.

The older woman caught up with them, breathing heavy, and helped herself to the garden bench, filling it. The last woman, who had kindly shuffled along with her friend, now held out her hand and smiled, warm. Merrily didn't need to be invited to like her; she just did. "I'm Juby," she said. "Thanks for talking with us."

"I'm not sure I can be much help," Merrily said, looking toward Alice. "But you said his name. You said 'Rick Kisel.' Didn't you?"

"Rick," Juby said softly, trying it out. "You're friends with him?"

"He was my— It's hard to explain," Merrily said. "My mom dated him for a while when I was young, and he's always, you know, been around."

Alice turned stiffly. "Around? Around you, as you grew up?"

"Well, not actually *around*," Merrily said. "I only met him once when I was old enough to remember. But he texts and stuff, to say hi, happy birthday . . . stuff like that."

The women glanced among themselves.

"What?" Merrily said. "Where is he?"

"You haven't seen him?" the older woman said. Her voice was thin, almost a whistle.

"I thought that's why you were here." Would she know him? He was a stranger to her, really. Would she recognize him if he walked into the yard right now, his arms open to her? If he said, *Hey, kid*, and wrapped her in a hug? They were not the affectionate sorts, she and her mom. She couldn't imagine making room in her life for someone who might be.

The other women hadn't filled the silence.

Merrily took a deep breath. "I haven't seen him in twenty years. I don't even know what he looks like now. I have mostly old photos, him, my mom. Some of his old girlfriends." She looked at Alice for a long moment. There were things she could tell them about Rick—the three kids with three different wives, the burned-out house. How much did they already know, though? "Are you— Why are you looking for him?"

Juby and the older woman seemed to retreat into themselves. Alice stepped toward Merrily. "I knew him when I was a kid," she said, "and then this week I heard he was missing— I guess I wanted to help. We're volunteers for a website that helps find missing people."

It was a breezy, rehearsed story that smelled like a lie in every way. There was more to it, Merrily didn't have to be told. "Family friend?"

"Yeah," Alice said, without much conviction. "Family friend."

Merrily rolled her eyes at the grass at her feet. She was still wearing the short pants from her old closet, the cast-off T-shirt, no shoes. She'd slept in them and hadn't yet changed back into her clothes from yesterday, now clean. Every time it mattered, she was wearing someone else's clothes, a costume. They thought she was some bumpkin, some kid. She folded her arms across her chest. "I met someone who thinks Rick's been buried as a John Doe in their local cemetery for the last two decades. Who do you think *that* is?"

No one moved.

If you could see your faces, Merrily thought. "A fire. The guy who lived there died."

Juby broke the spell. "Do *you* think it's Richard—Rick?"

"My mother says no way," Merrily said. Over Juby's shoulder she saw movement at the kitchen curtains. "And all those texts he sent me—"

"They could have been sent. By someone else," said the wheezing woman.

"Your mother, in fact," Juby said.

"She wouldn't go to the trouble," Merrily said. "Not for Rick."

"But for you," Alice said, her voice strained.

Merrily had to look away from the raw ache on Alice's face and the feeling in her own gut. Her mom would do anything for her, it was true. "I got the feeling she regretted giving Rick my number," Merrily said to her toes. "If someone offered her the chance to kill him off to get him to stop texting me, she would have taken it."

The silence was thick. Merrily looked up. "I didn't mean *really* kill him. I meant, tell me he died in a fire to get out of having to deal with him."

At everything she said, the other women exchanged glances. It was tiring.

"Where was this cemetery?" Alice asked.

They sat on the deck and compared notes. After a few minutes, Merrily knocked at the back door. When her mom opened it—after a brief delay, Merrily noticed, as though she hadn't been right there watching them—she slid inside and reached for the drawer under the phone.

"What now?" her mom demanded.

"Looking for a pen that works," she said. "And a notepad."

Her mom brushed past her and opened a different drawer roughly. "Don't bring those people inside the house."

"What if they—"

"Make them go to the gas station, or *home*," her mother spat. "It's a long drive. She's not welcome here."

Merrily dug out a notepad and pen and returned to the deck, listening to the click of the lock behind her. She wondered if the inn was closed to her, as well. Disobedience punishable by withheld access to her clean clothes, her birthday cake.

Outside, Juby sat on the edge of the deck, hunched over her phone and swinging her brown legs in the sunshine. Alice sat at the café table on the deck, where Merrily and her mother often had dinner in warm weather. The umbrella hadn't been put up yet, though. *Maybe I should visit more often,* she thought, remembering the ache on Alice's face when they'd touched on the topic of mothers. She sometimes forgot how lucky she was to have a mom who would fight for her, who *had* fought for them when no one else would.

Merrily realized too late she should have brought out some

cake. Maybe some lemonade. But then they'd have needed the gas station bathroom sooner, and she wasn't ready for them to leave.

"We need a timeline," the older woman said. "Juby, what's our first dot on the map?"

Juby started to speak but Alice rushed in. "When did your mother date Rick, Merrily? Let's start there."

Merrily almost didn't hear her. She was back in the kitchen, even as she sat in the chair next to Alice on the deck, the notebook and pen slipping from her hand, the idea of lemonade fading. Her mom had said—

"What?" Merrily said. But she wasn't calculating the year she'd had a father figure. She was calculating which "she" her mother meant wasn't allowed in the house. There were three women, and yet only one of them needed to get home, a long distance away. Merrily knew which one was meant, felt herself agreeing that Alice shouldn't be allowed to get too comfortable here, shouldn't be allowed to take everything she wanted without offering anything in return. Merrily thought of the box of mementos back at her apartment, like a nest of treasure she had made for herself. For *her*self, not these women.

But most of all Merrily wondered, before she settled in to share information: How had her mom known how far Alice was from home?

CHAPTER SEVENTEEN
ALICE

This was the woman who loved Richard Kisel.

Alice could barely look at her. Merrily Cruz was a collection of parts that wouldn't come together: a wild childlike smatter of freckles across her nose but the guarded eyes of a much older woman, long legs and arms jutting out from clothes that didn't fit. She was like a doll dressed in a costume she hadn't been sold with. In fact, the woman had seemed like a ventriloquist's dummy until she'd come out with the thing about the fire and the cemetery, which was when Alice started to pay real attention to Merrily Cruz.

It hurt to do so. Merrily's hope that Rick—*Rick*! He had a *nickname!*—would be OK? That this would all end up with Rick Kisel being returned to her life? It made her sick. *Returned to Merrily as a number in her cell phone, really.* The guy hadn't really been in her life. Not that the dumb girl could tell the difference.

In this way, pity crept in.

How long could they go along in this conversation before Juby or Lillian said something damning, or Alice herself had to tell the truth?

"We need a timeline," Lillian said. "Juby, what's our first dot on the map?"

Alice jumped in before Juby could mention the kidnapping. "Merrily, when did your mother date Rick? Let's start there."

"I was so young," Merrily said. She closed her eyes. "He was gone by the time I was two, for sure, maybe earlier. I just turned thirty this week, so . . ."

When Merrily opened her eyes, Alice realized she'd been staring.

"What?" Merrily said.

Alice didn't look in Juby or Lillian's direction but she knew they'd done the math alongside her. This woman could be the baby from Alice's memories. "How long did they date?"

"No idea." She laughed. "They met after my dad died. My mom was already pregnant with me, so less than two years and nine months."

Are you sure? But Alice wouldn't ask questions she didn't know the answer to. If the timing lined up, did everything else? Could they place infant Merrily in the high chair in the house to which Alice had been taken? Had she lived there? There was no reason to think she had been kidnapped, too, was there?

The curtains twitched at one of the windows of Merrily's house.

"When did *you* meet Rick?" Merrily said.

Alice could tell by her tone that Merrily didn't believe them about helping find Rick for the Doe Pages. She wasn't completely dumb, then.

"I met Rick right around the same time you did," Alice said. "Actually, he and my dad met. I was just a kid."

Merrily leaned in. "Who's your dad?"

She might have lied. She might have given his name, his current occupation—what did it matter? It was better, Alice decided, if they began to zero in on the thing. "At the time, he was a police officer."

Merrily nodded solemnly and leaned back with a sigh. "Was Rick in trouble?"

"Was he often in trouble?"

"Sometimes, I think," Merrily said. "From the way my mom talks about him, he is sometimes in trouble and sometimes causing it."

"What kind of trouble does he cause?" Juby said from her perch on the deck's edge. She managed somehow to make the question sound casual.

"I should know, right?" Merrily said. "I should have looked him up. I'm not sure how to look him up, though, to be honest."

"Lil?" Juby said.

"Bring me your phone, Jubilee."

"Lillian knows her way around the darkest corners of the web," Juby said, sliding off the deck.

"The darkest what?" Merrily glanced toward the house.

"Not sure about this," Lillian murmured over the phone once it was placed in her hands. "Tiny rocket launcher."

"That's one of its selling points, Lil."

"Eyesight too bad, fingers too fat." She and Juby put their heads together over the screen.

Alice listened to a bird far up in the maple next door, noting the shadow the tree canopy threw across the Cruzes' yard and then the silver sky to the west: rain. They should go, but she didn't say so. "What else do we know?" Alice said. "The fire—when was this, exactly?"

Juby brought the notepad up to Alice with a meaningful look—*Be cool*—then returned to Lillian. Alice looked over the spare notes and passed the notepad on to Merrily, who filled in a few dates: the fire and the last day Merrily had seen Rick in person, the date of the last text she'd received.

"That's a long time," Alice said. "Since seeing him, I mean. What did he say in his last text? Or is that too—"

"He sent me a weird see-you-in-another-life text instead of—"

Merrily turn her head. Alice regretted she'd asked.

The other woman hadn't had the advantages Alice had enjoyed, the embarrassment of riches in her upbringing, her luck of birth to a mother who'd desperately wanted a brood, and a father who had not been able to give her one. A father who had happily spent his life making the world a safe place for his only child.

Alice couldn't explain it to anyone, how much her parents had stored up for the large family they meant to have. And, with only Alice to carry it all, how much their worry weighed, how the home they'd built around her had been almost too comfortable. So comfortable, she might never have left. So comfortable as to become a padded room.

As soon as she thought it, she was ashamed.

She had no complaints. Or—she did, but it felt disloyal to want something other than what she'd had, which was everything.

She was sorry she'd compared Merrily's fatherless life to her own, but then, she knew something about Rick that would eventually make Merrily glad she was not tied to him. "Why did you keep texting him, even though you didn't really know him?"

The other woman shrugged. "He was there, I guess. And he was fun. Funny. Goofy, I guess, is a better word. Sometimes I got so mad at him—"

Over on the bench, Lillian and Juby got quiet.

"It's dumb," Merrily said, looking toward the house again. "He doesn't owe me anything. He had—a lot of other things going on. I just wished sometimes he would decide who he wanted to be . . ."

"To you?"

"To my mom," she said quietly. "My mom's been single a long time, and you saw her, she's a knockout. The way he left things— well, she's still mad. She never got over it."

"You think your mom's still in love with Rick," Alice said flatly.

Merrily leaned forward quickly and shushed her. "Maybe," she whispered. "I don't know."

Maybe, Alice thought. Maybe it was Merrily who was still in love, with the idea of a family that had never fully formed. This guy Rick—how many hearts would he eventually break?

"I can't operate," Lillian huffed. "Under these circumstances."

"Lillian is being an old lady," Juby said.

"News flash, Jubilee," Lillian said. "I *am* an old lady. A hundred years from now. Some young bint will try to make you—" She coughed until her lips were wet with spittle. "Use some technology not fit for human—"

"Just give me your password and I'll do it for you—"

"My passwords are worth more than your life," Lillian rasped. "No offense."

Alice sighed. "What's going on?"

"Having trouble seeing the details," Lillian said. "But I don't think Richard Kisel exists." She passed the phone back to Juby. "Do we know that's his real name?"

"You think his real name is Miller?" Juby said.

"No, she means his real name might be something other than Miller, other than Kisel," Alice said so Lillian wouldn't have to. "If he changed it once, why couldn't he change it twice? Or more than twice."

Lillian nodded her thanks.

Merrily glanced among them. "But . . . why?"

"In trouble, causer of trouble," Alice said. "This is thirty years we're talking about. How many lives could one guy live in thirty years?"

None of them said anything for a long moment, until Merrily said, "If he had to keep changing his name, how can we say he's lived even one?"

She was starting to get the idea. Finally.

CHAPTER EIGHTEEN
ALICE

Juby had to pee. Merrily tried to explain why they couldn't use the bathroom in the house, but it went awkwardly.

"Go get your shoes," Alice said to her. They were not done with Merrily.

Merrily came out wearing an entirely different outfit—nicer stuff that fit, and red sandals Juby gushed over. They all piled into Alice's car and drove into town, watching the residential street turn into commercial, many of the buildings shuttered, signs turned around, paper in the windows.

"What I wouldn't give for a functioning fast-food joint right now," Juby whispered.

"I'm so sorry," Merrily said again.

"Stop," Lillian said.

"No, I mean it. It's ridiculous—"

"Stop the *car*," Lillian gasped, pointing. "Library. Chinese restaurant."

"We can make use of these things," Juby said. "Nothing goes with a background check like chow mein."

"Background check?" Merrily said.

"Egg foo young first," Lillian said.

"*Library* first," Alice said. "Because it will close early."

"But my MSG levels," Lillian said. "They're too low."

"*Toilet* first," Juby said.

Settling in at a microfilm viewer with a solicitous librarian bringing her reels of thirty-year-old newspaper pages, though, cheered Lillian right up. She listened to the woman detailing the library's holdings as though a menu had been placed before her.

"*Indianapolis Star,*" Lillian mused. Alice knew she was showing off for Merrily because Lillian did not waste breath. She didn't muse. "Where did Richard Whoever live when you were—" She looked at Alice, then spun in her chair to find Merrily. "When you were a baby?"

"Um," Merrily said. "Here, I think."

"Oh, I doubt that," Juby said, back from the bathroom.

"Why?" Alice said.

"Because he's a runner," Lillian said. "He gets out of burning buildings. He gets a new name. Again." They waited while she took a gulp of air. "And again. He doesn't stay in one place. Not this guy."

Lillian solicited Merrily's birth date and then requested the local county paper for that day and eighteen months following it. Merrily watched the trays of film arriving with concern. "What are you looking for?"

"Just fishing," Lillian said.

Behind Merrily's back, Alice exchanged a glance with Juby. Lillian was a step ahead of what they were willing to say aloud. They were looking for news of a missing baby in front of the likely candidate herself.

Lillian asked about the town with the burned-out house, but the library didn't have an archive for any newspaper near it.

"Indianapolis it is," Lillian said. "What other papers . . . big ones?"

Alice stepped in to translate Lillian's breathlessness for the librarian. "What were the other major papers in this part of the state thirty years ago? Do you have any of those?"

The librarian was tired of them already. "You won't be able to get through all this." She checked her watch pointedly. The place was open another forty-five minutes, and they would need every single one.

There were two microfilm viewers. Lillian was already zooming with a practiced hand through the film for the *Indianapolis Star*. Alice loaded the other machine for herself with the local paper and scrolled, though more slowly. Much more slowly. The *Morning Daily* covered a lot of ground, including news from the surrounding small towns and beyond, and she didn't have an exact date, even a month. They really were fishing, and the lake was wide.

Juby leaned over Lillian's shoulder. "You can't possibly find anything reading that fast."

"Microfilm whisperer," Lillian said. "Headlines and the state news roundups. Skim, skim. Float like a butterfly. Sting like . . . a research librarian."

Time raced away from them. As the march of news rolled past, Alice glanced occasionally toward the clock over the librarian's head in the next room. They needed some kind of hint, something to narrow the rest of the search. And then she scrolled right past Richard Miller Kisel's face.

"Stop," Merrily said. She leaned in, pale in the light of the screen.

"Hold on." Alice reversed the machine and framed the article. "Lillian."

"Read it," Lillian said.

"Richard *Banks*." She was nauseated to say it. "Richard A. *Banks*

is wanted for questioning regarding the disappearance of his—"
Alice shifted her eyes out of range of Merrily's.

"Wife," Merrily read.

"He was married?" Juby said.

"The part to pay attention to is *wanted for questioning*," Alice said.

"I guess that explains a few things," Merrily said. "Richard
Banks Kisel Miller, or was it Miller Kisel?" She sat down heavily
on the edge of a chair, her hand to her forehead. "I'm starting to
lose track of . . . "

Of the man she thought she'd known, Alice knew. He was
being torn into so much confetti before Merrily's eyes. And she
didn't even know he was a kidnapper yet.

"What's the dateline?" Juby said. "The town where the news is
being reported from, the first line of the article."

Alice rolled the page back to the top. "Victor—" She swallowed
hard. "Victorville." If *Banks* made her sick, *Victorville* was a kick
to the gut. Alice knew the name. She *felt* the name. This was it.
Victorville, Indiana, was where it had all started.

"Print it, Alice," Lillian said. "Is there a . . . Victorville paper?
Jubilee, go ask—"

"We close in ten minutes," the librarian called from the desk.
"No more materials can be pulled out. Please start placing what
you have on the cart."

"We'll go to Victorville," Juby said to Lillian. "We'll just have
to go there."

Alice turned back to the page on her machine and hit the print
button. The old machine clunked and whirred, then spat out a
sheet of paper. *Skim, skim*, Alice thought as she read the page, trying not to think about the proprietary way Juby and Lillian talked
over the case next to her. *Her* case. No, *her* life. She was not a fucking Doe. She was not a Pages pet project. Was she even invited on

this trip they were taking all of a sudden? She had heard stories about volunteers who had gone all-in on a case, bending rules, stomping all over delicate relationships with victim families, with law enforcement. They policed themselves harder now. Scofflaws got banished. She hadn't been a volunteer long enough to have witnessed a real dustup, but they happened. Most often because someone got ahead of themselves before they were sure.

Alice glanced at Merrily, who was staring at the screen, dazed. She had to be sure.

On the page still on the screen, there was a grainy, blackened photo of the missing woman. Her features were lost to low technology. It was even worse on the printout Alice had made. She could be anyone.

At the bottom of the page, the article ended abruptly and sent readers to page nine. Alice maneuvered the machine toward page nine, slowing down as she got closer, wondering and dreading. Merrily watched the pages spin by.

Alice stopped at page eight. "Merrily, could you take these reels back to the librarian? Please?"

As soon as the other woman's back was turned, Alice flicked the lever to bring page nine into view. It was full of text, a gray-lady page of tiny newsprint and one small dark photo. Without reading the page, Alice hit the button to print it and then brought the lever back full force to reverse the film to the beginning. She folded her two pages and shoved them into her backpack while the filmstrip rewound to its end and began flapping for her attention.

She extracted the film, slipped it into the small box it had come from, and held it out just as Merrily returned. Merrily, good sport, turned and took another trip to the desk. When Alice turned back to the viewer, she found Juby watching her. Juby nodded. These pages were for later, when they were on their own again. Better to keep some things contained until they knew what the deal was, until they knew Merrily better. If there was any reason to know her better.

Alice tidied the film rolls she hadn't gotten to, handed them over as Merrily approached again. Merrily, who only laughed and turned on her heel. Merrily, who thought they were helping her. Who thought they were in this together.

CHAPTER NINETEEN
ALICE

At the Chinese restaurant next door, they ordered a tableful of food to share over the top of the timeline notes, chopsticks reaching. A little soy sauce puddle stained a corner of a page. It didn't matter at the moment. Alice slurped a noodle and looked up to find herself at a table of women laughing and joking. She was enjoying herself. When a noodle slipped off her sticks into her lap, she barely minded, only excused herself for the ladies'.

At the sink, she dabbed at the oily spot on her blouse until it might be saved, taking in the woman in the mirror with surprise. Out in the red lacquer dining room she had turned into someone else, someone carefree and fun-loving, someone much more like Juby, smiles and cheekbones and a bit of baby fat at the wrist—

She didn't look like her mother in the slightest, but there she was in the mirror. They had the fine lines in common, the cracks and fissures, the failing luster. Alice smoothed her hair as best she could until she couldn't stand the sight of herself any longer and swung open the door to the hall.

"... going to be *fine*," a voice said.

Alice stopped, waited. The voice was Merrily's, assertive, impatient, and it was coming from just beyond her view, near the restaurant entrance.

"Soon, I promise," Merrily said. There must be another half of this conversation. Alice sat on a bench outside the ladies' room to listen. "Talking, you know? Girl talk, like—Mamá, we're not—"

The mother, then. The woman who'd blocked them out of concern for herself and her daughter. None to spare for the missing man. The mother was clearly accustomed to the man being missing, one way or another.

It couldn't have been easy for Merrily, no dad. It obviously wasn't—not the way Merrily forced Rick into the shape of father, no matter how bad the fit and against her mother's wishes.

Merrily came around the corner, startling at the sight of Alice. "Oh, hey."

"Your mom worried we've kidnapped you?" The words jumped from Alice's lips before she realized. She turned her face down, fussed at the spot on her shirt. It might not be saved after all.

"Something like that," Merrily said. "I should grab a ride back home, if you're—"

"We'll take you," Alice said. "It's not a problem." It was not a problem for her, not for Juby or Lillian. It was only a problem for Mrs. Cruz, wasn't it? For the woman's animosity that felt like old-growth hatred. But why? To keep away who, or what? "Not a problem at all."

⋆　　⋆　　⋆

THE THREE OF them let out a collective breath and watched Merrily walk up to the door of her mother's house. Alice waited a polite amount of time for the woman to get to the door. She had Merrily's number in her phone now but no intention of using it. Juby had it, too, and it was Juby that Merrily would want to hear from. It was not difficult to prefer Juby.

Before she pulled away from the house, Alice noticed a light on in the window upstairs and a figure there at the curtains. Mrs. Cruz on watch. Alice pictured her imperious, looking far down her nose at her, as though Alice were something stuck to the bottom of her shoe.

The other two were quiet, sated with dumplings and noodles. Or so Alice thought. As soon as Juby's crisp-voiced GPS system got them back to the interstate, Lillian cleared her throat and Juby took the cue. "So do we think that's the other kid? Was she kidnapped, too, or what?"

"Can't be," Lillian said. "I mean, yes. Her. But not kidnapped."

"Her mother . . ." Juby said.

"She looks just like her," Alice said. "Except—" She decided not to say what she had noticed. She wasn't *sure.*

What came to mind were Merrily's mother's haughty eyes, black and burning with something Alice couldn't name.

"Except she's tall and skinny, lucky bitch," Juby said. Juby had nothing to complain about. Was she short? Everyone was shorter than Alice. She didn't often notice variances between shorter than her and even shorter than that. Though Mrs. Cruz was the tiniest person she'd encountered in some time.

Alice felt the presence of some connection. Like a black bird flushed from its hiding place and darting from view. She steadied herself. She felt fine, really, but if she reached—

"Is that . . . the woman?" Lillian said. "From the house?"

"Wait," Alice said.

"Are you OK?" Lillian said.

"I'm fine," she said. "But let me . . ." If she stretched, her fingers brushed feathers.

"Oh," Juby said. "Oh, wow. You think Merrily's mom was your kidnapper?"

"Stop," Alice said. She took her own advice, pulling to the side of the dark road. A fat raindrop hit the windshield.

"Continue on route," said the snotty GPS voice.

"Sorry," Juby mumbled, and fretted over the screen to silence it.

"You all right?" Lillian said.

"Please."

Mrs. Cruz's imperious look, the hot eyes bearing down on her from above. Had she given her that look today? But how? Merrily's mother was small—she could only have looked down her nose at Alice if—if she had done it while Alice was a child.

Now Alice caught a glimpse of her, full glory, hair waving and long, like flames pouring from a volcanic seam, red and dark. Thinner, younger. A face shaped into rage and glaring down her nose. At Alice. At *her.* "She was there," Alice said.

"Knew it," Lillian breathed.

"Merrily is the baby," Juby said. "And her mother was the other kidnapper? You said it was a couple, right?"

"I don't know." She signaled and pulled back out onto the road, wishing she could have the car to herself, to talk it out. She needed to hear herself think to know what she really thought.

"Did you want?" Lillian said. "Juby to drive?"

"She was there," Alice said. She wasn't going to hand over control. "She yelled at him, I think? Maybe she wasn't in on it. There might have been another woman there, maybe this wife who went missing. Sketchy, right? I think—I think he brought me to Merrily's mom, or she showed up and, and—she wasn't happy about something. About me."

Her. That's what Merrily's mother had called Alice. *Her,* like she was a stray scratching at the back door and not someone there against her will.

"This is why we can't talk to Merrily about this stuff just yet," Alice said. "OK?"

"Agreed," Juby said.

Heavy raindrops splatted against the windshield. Alice reached for the wipers, sighing. This would only slow their trip home.

"You never said," Lillian said.

"Hm?"

"How did you? Get snatched? In a public place?"

She didn't know, didn't want to say so. "The yard, I think."

"You *think*?" Juby said. "You don't know? What about when you got saved? By your dad, you said. But how?"

"I don't remember much. He somehow got me back."

Lillian looked confused. "Anonymous tip?"

"Ohh," Juby said. "Maybe Merrily's mom told on them?"

Lillian wasn't wasting her breath on guesses.

Alice said nothing. She didn't know. They drove in silence.

"Hey," Juby said after a while. In the rearview mirror, Juby's chin was lit by the glow of her phone screen. "Why would a missing person's profile come down from the Pages? List the reasons."

"Found," Lillian said. "Found alive, found dead."

"Found? That's the only reason an Empty would suddenly be gone from the site?" Juby held her phone over the seat for Lillian to see. "Because Richard Whatever is no longer listed as a Doe."

"What?" Alice yelped. She looked over, the car swerving in answer.

"Hey!" Juby cried. "There's plenty of time to talk about dead people without killing us all."

Alice committed herself to the steering wheel, fists tight. She watched the dotted white lines disappear alongside them, concentrated on the gray road she could see, the dark road beyond that, wishing for the city lights.

Found. Found meant everything was about to change. For better or worse.

CooooKIES: Did I miss something? That MP that got added from Milwaukee this week is gone from the site. I was going to look into that one!

SparkleSoo RE: @CooooKIES Maybe they found him!

MrJonesToYou RE: RE: @SparkleSoo Obvious answer.

SparkleSoo RE: RE: RE: @MrJonesToYou No one was talking to you.

JennDoePagesMOD RE: @CooooKIES There's an administrative reason that listing was pulled.

SparkleSoo RE: RE: @JennDoePagesMOD Good news, I hope!

MrJonesToYou RE: RE: @SparkleSoo I guess @JennDoePagesMOD isn't answering that one. Does that mean it's classified or what?

JennDoePagesMOD RE: RE: RE: @MrJonesToYou It means I'm going to pull down this thread in about two seconds. Let's just say that guy has enough people looking for him and we have plenty to keep us all busy.

CHAPTER TWENTY

MERRILY

When Merrily arrived back at her apartment, Justyce was still up, eating an oatmeal cream snack pie over the sink. A lit joint rested on the edge of the counter.

"You're not starting another fire, right?" Merrily said.

"I thought you moved out." Justyce's eyes were on springs, like a child's toy. She gestured to the joint. "Where have you been?"

Merrily waved her off. "I might have to move out."

"Oh, man. Layoffs are a drag."

She let it go. They weren't great friends, or even good ones. They were basically business associates, a financial arrangement personified, an understanding that paid the rent, brought home milk and bread in rotation. But she wasn't being a good fiscal partner, either, leaving a decent job for no good reason. The first pang of regret hit her. "Yeah."

"Your friend make it through?"

"What?" *Layoffs, right.* "Uh, yeah. Kath is still there. Lucky bitch." She would have to make sure Justyce and Kath never met. Shouldn't be a problem. If she really did move out, maybe she'd never see either of them again. They were just people, and people moved in and out of your life. It wasn't the end of the world.

Merrily grabbed the box of oatmeal cream pies off the counter. Empty.

Justyce was looking her up and down. "Where were you? At your mom's again?"

And now she felt a different kind of pang. When she'd arrived back to her mom's house, the doors were locked. She'd seen the light in her mom's room from outside, but by the time she let herself in and got upstairs it was dark under the door. She might have stayed, forced the issue the next morning over juice and toast. Except Mamá Cruz was often better behaved when she'd had time to claim her victories. Merrily wasn't sure, though: What kind of victory was this? Those women who'd come to the house were taking the search for Rick so seriously. It worried her. Was Rick's life in danger?

That last text he'd sent her, distancing her. The breakup text. Had Rick done something crazy?

"So are you really moving home then? Aw, shit." Justyce used a set of tongs to oh-so-carefully pick up the butt of the joint. "I cannot face another open call for sublets. All the creepers come out."

Merrily went to the living room, plopped down on the couch. "Like me?"

"Creepers and loose women."

"Shut up."

Justyce joked too much about how many guys Merrily brought home, how many times she stayed out—and she had definitely said she'd been at her mom's once or twice when she hadn't been. Envy. Justyce was thick, like the trunk of a tree. Out dancing, she was a sturdy wing-girl, slapping men off Merrily left and right. But she'd been left to catch a ride home alone too many times, and now that was who they were to each other. One went home with someone, the other went home. Except, plenty of times, Merrily caught the ride home along with her and they sat up watching reality-type shows about fixer-uppers and bridezillas.

She couldn't shake the person Justyce pretended Merrily was. Luckily she'd never told Justyce about the chats.

Her little conventional world, Merrily thought, grabbing the remote and flipping through the channels, *would be blown all over the wall.*

"Hey, I was watching that." Justyce stood in the doorway, pie in hand.

"You were not. You were burning one down in the sink."

"I was, too—"

"What show was it?"

Justyce collapsed onto the other side of the couch. "Cooking?"

"Nope." Merrily churned through a few more channels, dissatisfied. So many channels and nothing worth the trouble of staying up late. They'd have to cancel the cable, first thing.

"House-swapping fixer-upper?"

"No way."

"Bad plastic surgery," Justyce said.

"I would watch that. What channel?"

Justyce's eyes were glassy, staring. She pointed. On the TV, a woman with the smoothest jawline in human history and wide-awake eyes talked into the camera. A little logo in the corner of the screen said *Crime Time Tonight with Jen Minarik*. Nice. Merrily turned up the volume to hear the commentator talking about a missing person, a woman gone for more than twenty years. Laura Schmidt, drug addict. As though that were her profession.

"Why are missing white chicks always named *Laura*?" Justyce said.

"Hush."

"They are, though."

"Maybe they just play this show all the time."

"Oh, they do," Justyce said. "I've seen this episode already. I've seen all the episodes: Laura and *Amy*. Susie, Nadine, Jessica . . . like Terri Ann and shit."

The commentator was saying something about the woman's kid—

"She's *totally* dead," Justyce said over the TV, shoving the last of the pie into her mouth and talking around it. "If Jen Minarik from *Crime Time Tonight* is talking about you, you're dead."

When they finally broadcast a photo of the missing woman, the image was jarring. She was all bones, gaunt cheeks, with lank hair hanging over a pair of haunted, hunted eyes. It was a mug shot, and the woman was seriously juiced. Or angry. "Is that an *after* shot?" Justyce brayed, licking her fingers individually, noisily. "That is going to make me paranoid as fuck."

The photo disappeared from the screen. "You're fried." Merrily clicked off the TV and started for her room.

"Hey," Justyce called after her. "I was watching that."

IN HER ROOM, Merrily paced across the messy floor, kicking shoes and purse straps as she had to, tripping over the corner of her mattress on the floor. She looked out the smudged glass of her window at the grim view of a tiny bit of rooftop and sky, now mostly invisible in the darkness. She was wound tight. Maybe a hit of Justyce's good stuff was in order, if she had any left to share. But no, that wasn't going to help here.

She stopped. What did she need help with? What was the actual problem? Rick?

Rick was an old problem, decades old. He wasn't worth pacing over. Except. Except he was *her* decades-old problem, and her mom's. Why? Why did her mom keep in touch with the guy, even though he was bad news? And then to give her teen daughter the guy's phone number and say, sure, right, text this old man, no problem. That was—that was—she had no words for how weird it was, now that she was thinking it through. And she knew weird. Even if her mom was in love with Rick, why was it Merrily's job to keep the lines of communication open? Was she being pimped out in some way?

Sorry, Mamá.

That was what being Mamá Cruz's kid got you—thirty years old and crossing yourself, saying Hail Marys not to a priest but your mom, who wasn't even in the room, even though no one witnessed your evil, even though no one could witness your evil, because it happened inside your own head.

Merrily couldn't even fault her mom much. She was exactly as she should be, loving, protective. But also smart, independent. Mamá Cruz hadn't needed a man in almost thirty years. And yet. And yet, Rick lived just outside their inner circle, hovering, privileged, texting in his *Hey, kid.* An impossible man, her mom had called him, and yet he was allowed to stay.

Merrily pulled out her phone. She had three notifications from ChatX. Michaelangelo24 again. She probably owed him for the birthday bonus, but that could wait. He'd like her knees even more if she put him off a day or two. Another one of her regulars had checked in, but he was one of those who wanted to hang out with her as she went about her life, not a talker, not a listener. An inefficient use of her time right now, and not worth what he usually gave her.

She had a note from Searcher, though. Perfect timing.

But she also had notifications from PhotoSocial, far more than she normally got. She pulled down the notifications to see what was happening. *Link doesn't work*, one of the messages complained. *Your post is broken*, another one said. *You're cute tho.*

She clicked over to the site, and sure enough, the link under the photo she'd posted didn't work. *Cannot display.*

She threw her phone at her bed and went to the laptop, navigating to her post and clicking through. The link failed there, too, leaving her stranded on the newspaper's site. *Error 404.*

Whatever the fuck?

Merrily searched for the site the women had mentioned, Doe something, and found it quickly.

Yikes, she thought. This website was *fucked up*, a real horror show, so she moved quickly, using the search bar there to look for Rick's profile. She hesitated over the last name, but in the end tried them all as each version of Rick failed to produce a single mention of him. Finally, she went to the main page for missing people and scrolled to the bottom, ignoring the sea of misery and loss, where Rick was one of the last—

He was gone.

She startled into movement, standing up from her desk, but then there was nowhere to go, no one to see, not at this hour. No one to call. She reached for her phone, found it gone, then tracked it to her bed among the covers, and opened the contacts. *Alice, *Juby. The stars before their names made sure their numbers stayed at the top of the list so she could find them—but for what? For this? They were the only people she might bother right now. They'd said they worked with the site, didn't they? Or was that the first lie of many those three had told her?

Across the room, her laptop chimed. Her phone joined in. One of her guys wanted to chat.

Her thumb hovered over Juby's number on her phone screen. Merrily knew without having to wonder that Juby would get to the bottom of things, and make her feel OK for asking.

But then, it had seemed to Merrily that the problem of Rick hadn't mattered much to Juby, even with all that we'll-just-go-there business, whatever that meant. Alice. Alice was the one with eyes like open wounds, whose every movement and breath seemed focused on what Merrily might say. Alice was the beating heart of this, this—what was this?

That was what was bothering her tonight—not Rick being missing. That wasn't news. It was that the women who'd come to her mom's house were after something more than they would admit to and they hadn't included her. That was the day's headline, in addition to which, her mom was lying, hiding in her room, rising to full-on drama queen.

Merrily crossed the room and sat down in front of her laptop again. Another alert from Searcher6, wanting to talk, if she had time. Most of the guys wanted to direct the interaction, to dominate it. If she had time. She liked that.

It was Alice she would need to talk to, wasn't it? She couldn't quite bring herself to dial. Tomorrow. Tomorrow she might call Alice. Or. Or maybe she would go to the library on her own and see what she could find about that website and the people who worked for it, if they even did.

Below Juby's number on her phone was another entry. *9–1–1 Vasquez*, she'd labeled it, the numerals in the listing also keeping the number high in the list. Maybe it was time to call the police. She was known for her excellent phone manner, after all.

More simultaneous chimes from her laptop and phone. Searcher6, persistent tonight. Sometimes persistence was a bad sign, just as in real life.

Thinking about you, the message said. *Been a while. What's new? Check your account.*

When she did, she knew she would give Searcher6 any time he wanted. She had the time, oh, yes. Alice and the others forgotten, she relaxed, opened up a chat, and tapped out a playful response. *Hello to you, too. Ask me anything. I am an open book.*

CHAPTER TWENTY-ONE

ALICE

On Sunday afternoon, Alice drove out past the confines of Chicago, past the farthest suburbs, past Fell Creek, the town where her mail was still collected along with her dad's, past the last neighbors they had never met—out to the woods where he'd built their home, like a pioneer clearing acres in the New World. It was as inconvenient a place to live as any he might have found, a quiet place for her mother to rest.

She squinted into the setting sun all the way there, realizing far too late that she had forgotten her spare key. She could get through the security gate with the electronic doodad on her windshield but she'd have to ring the doorbell like someone who hadn't had to grow up there.

At the door, the trees around the house swayed, the leaves fluttered. She could hear him pausing on the other side of the door, checking the peephole just as he'd always taught her. Harrison Fine, always a cop.

She stuck her tongue out. He went through the locks and opened the door.

"Where's your key?" He wore a smeared apron. Her apron.

The sense memories rushed at her: the smell of the pantry, the sound of her mother's voice, all of it, the taste of it a sweet and awful ache. It was a gale, over as soon as it began, but it must have passed over her face. He looked down at himself and winced. "I'm sorry, sweetheart." Behind him, a talk radio station prattled, *stocks, trading floor.* "I didn't think. It was close to hand, and I wanted to keep sauce off my shirt."

She nodded and cleared her throat. "Spaghetti."

"Only the finest for special guests." His bachelor cooking was unrefined, uninteresting, disinterested. She'd never learned, either. No one had been teaching. Well, they hadn't starved.

"I love your bottled sauce better than anyone else's."

"I've got to put the noodles in. Come on in, keep me company."

"Actually," she said, "I was looking for something recently and I think maybe I left it in my room. Going to go dig around for a minute."

"You'll definitely need a shovel. Grab a box of stuff or seven while you're in there."

"You're a comedian tonight."

She walked through the house. Nice to see him cheerful, but she also recognized how it put her back up. As though one of them had to be on misery duty at all times. No—as though he'd been in such a bad mood lately that a good one was suspect.

In her room, she flicked the light. The room was tidy, really, despite the jokes, and she knew he didn't really want her to move it all out. What he wanted was for her to move back in. At the least, he didn't mind a few boxes left behind. He already had enough empty rooms. What use was another?

That was the problem with visiting, noticing how unlived-in the place felt. Not dusty, since he had someone driving out once a week to take care of the details. But since her mother's death, the house had seemed to contract on itself. He'd been giving things away, maybe. She'd noticed a few small pieces of furniture missing, as though he were clearing a wider path through the house. Tidying up, but was he letting grief out or giving it room to grow?

Her room had been spared. She sifted through a stack of magazines on the desk. Home improvement, decorating, design. Maybe she'd been born for the family business, after all, if they ever got to do anything other than parking decks.

Alice opened the drawers of her old dresser one by one, finding linens for the rest of the house, an old umbrella. In the bottom drawer, T-shirts she hadn't taken and wouldn't take now.

It was a fabric-covered box she was looking for. The box had always held life's bits and pieces, old paperwork they wanted to keep nearby, things that had no other home. Her mother had moved the box from room to room, closet to closet, trying to find the proper place for it. Filled with things that rejected classification, the box couldn't help but be in the way.

She thought her dad's notes from the kidnapping might be found there. She needed them. She'd been through the article from the newspaper, and she hadn't learned much. Surely transcriptions of her own memories when she could still recall detail would be more helpful.

No sign of the box in her bedroom closet. Not in the hall closet, either.

At the end of the hall was the bedroom her mother had lived in, alone for the last year of her life. Alice's stomach dropped. It was always dark at this corner of the house, with windows that faced into the quiet woods. Alice's footsteps were lost in the thick plush carpet they'd had installed for her mother's comfort and warmth.

Opening the door, Alice felt a sad sense of relief. The curtains were pulled back, light filtering in on a room that was strangely bright and clean. She had lived in this room right alongside her mother, really, but now the pall was gone. It smelled like lemon, like a furniture store.

She hurried across the room. The box was covered in a black fabric, maybe, with tiny pink buds? The back of a top shelf? Maybe on the floor, among her shoes? Alice braced herself for the shoes.

The closet door opened to emptiness.

Alice jumped back, stung. Only a few bare dry cleaner's hangers lined the bar.

The same taste rose in the back of Alice's throat—pantry, history, unease. *He couldn't have. He wouldn't—*

She stepped backward and looked toward the corner shelf. It was gone. The carved wooden figure—a feather, a flame, some shape that had meaning only to Beth Ann Fine—was missing from the high shelf on the wall opposite the bed. The piece had sat there for years so her mother could gaze upon it. In a fire, her mother would have grabbed it first. At her funeral, it had stood near the closed casket, the rising phoenix of a woman who had fallen. And then it was restored to the shelf, some bit of her still in the room.

Now Alice noticed that the bedroom was not simply clean—it was a stage. The scenes that had played out here, pushed out.

Time was not universal, then, but personal. Alice had expected a museum. Meanwhile, her father had at some point opened the closet and, instead of sniffing for the last of his wife's scent, had reached for her favorite object off the wall, had taken out all that was left of her—a box or seven—and moved it to the garage. The garage if Alice was *lucky*. Maybe he had moved it all to the porch and called for a charity van pickup. Maybe he had put everything out at the bins, from which the trash service picked up twice a month. Maybe he had lit a fire in the barrel out behind the garage and tossed in the lot to smolder and smoke.

Alice closed the closet door as gently as if her mother were still asleep in the bed.

No one slept there. That was clear. Was he still sleeping in the guest room?

That left one possibility for the fabric box.

But in the guest room, there was no change on the bedside table, no dirty clothes in the laundry bin, no beloved statuette anywhere. No alarm clock? Was he not sleeping at all? She imagined her dad living somewhere between the two bare rooms, nesting wherever comfort might be found.

In this room's closet, she easily spotted the tiny pink buds on black she remembered. She pulled it out, sat it on the bed, pulled off the lid.

Inside sat a gun.

She dropped the box and the gun tumbled out, heavy and obscene on the comforter. Her hand reached for it before she even knew what she was doing—*bad idea*—and then let it fall—*worse idea*. She stood up and backed away.

Alice listened for her dad, her heart pounding in her throat. It was his old service weapon. He had a safe for it somewhere, and yet here it was stowed in the odds-and-ends bin, unsecured. Maybe even *loaded* and unsecured. It was against everything he believed.

Had there been trouble? Did it make him feel safe to have it—

Close to hand.

She sat gently on the edge of the bed. She had to worry about him, too? With everything they'd lived through?

Her dad was calling from down the hall.

"Coming!" she said.

Alice dumped the contents of the box on the bed, threw back

the paper clips and rubber bands and other loose ends. She pulled the papers aside. A piece of fabric fluttered to the floor. She reached for it.

The scrap was soft, satin-cornered, with a ragged fabric tag. Handwritten on the tag in faded marker was the name "Blanksy," but it needn't have been. She remembered. Someone had tried to preserve the name. The letters, clumsy and crowded, were not all faded to the same degree.

She used the blanket scrap to pick up the gun and place it carefully back into the box, then tucked the scrap into her jeans pocket. Alice returned the box back to the closet and, pages in hand, raced to get out of the room and close the door.

From the kitchen, her dad called out again. "OK?"

She'd taken every page from the bin, not just the notes she'd hoped to find. Clutched to her, the patter of her own pulse against the pages. "Fine," she said.

She wasn't sure either of them was fine.

CHAPTER TWENTY-TWO

ALICE

By the time Alice arrived in the kitchen, the spaghetti was over-cooked, almost to the point of disintegration. "I didn't know pasta would do that," her dad said apologetically. "I'm hopeless."

"You should practice more often," she said. "Have people over."

He looked up. "Like who, exactly?"

Alice flicked at the noodles with her fork, unable to eat. The gun. The gun. It was like a black, beating heart under the floor-boards. "Uncle Jim could probably use the company."

"I get to see enough of JimBig King, trust me. And before you suggest Jim Junior, no. You and I have always been happy in our own company."

That's what he'd said to reassure her about the wedding being called off. Maybe it was true. Maybe she should move back in.

"Matt's doing well," her dad said. As though he'd been listening to her thoughts. "He'll be back on his feet in no time."

She looked up from her plate. "You don't have to protect me from reality. I was there Friday."

"Fine. Reality it is."

"Great. Is Uncle Jim OK?"

He chewed thoughtfully. "Why? Did Jimmy say something?"

She didn't want to move back in. "Are *you* doing OK, Dad?"

"What's this all about?"

"Have you ever thought about selling this house? Moving closer to the city, maybe?" *Getting a girlfriend?* "Maybe *into* the city? Jennifer says the 1799 penthouse is taken, bad news."

He was staring at her. "I thought I was the one nagging *you* about getting out—"

"I'm worried about you."

The smile slid from his face. He dug into his plate. "Why would you think you have to worry about me?"

"You don't know why?"

He set his fork down. "It's not contagious, you know."

She wouldn't bring up the gun. She couldn't. Where had all her mother's pills gone? Were they still here? *Close to hand.*

"I do think about selling the house sometimes," he said. "I'm not sure I can part with it. But I think you might have me wrong, Al. You don't have to worry about . . . me. Not in that way, I mean, I'm fine."

Fine. The not-much she had come to accept. *Fine.* Juby pulling a face, mocking.

But it was Lillian she thought of now. Lillian's questions, digging deeper than Alice had ever thought to.

"Can I ask you a question?"

"Anything."

"How was I taken?"

Her dad's expression morphed from earnest amusement to serious concern, his eyes passing through a stage Alice couldn't identify, dark and fleeting. Impatience? "Do we have to do this tonight?" he said. "Haven't we talked this to—into the ground?"

He'd almost said *death*. "We haven't talked about it in years."

"Well, the last few years have been a little busy."

The last few years had been empty and sad, but before that they'd had plenty of time to bring it up. No one had.

"I have time now," she said.

"This is more of that Doe shit, isn't it?"

"Dad, it's not hurting anyone. This is easy stuff. Like, how did I actually get kidnapped? How did he get me away from you?"

"He," her dad said.

"The . . . couple, I mean."

"You're being squirrelly," he said. "Did something happen?"

"No." He meant like before, like the first—and only—time she and Jimmy had gone out, some guy had grabbed her arm in the street. Jimmy pushed him off, and nothing came of it—except that she'd been shipped off to boarding school in Montana the *second* her dad had found out. Was it in response to a grabby panhandler or the fumbling hands of Jimmy Junior? She never found out which had set him off. All she knew was: It took four years of horseback riding lessons and reading the classics to get another chance to go on a date. "No, nothing like that."

"No?" His jaw, set. "You would tell me if someone was bothering you?"

"No one is bothering me, Dad." When was the right time to tell him about the Doe?

"You can always come back here until—"

"Until when?" she snapped. "Exactly how long is long enough until the coast is clear?"

He squinted down at his plate of cold spaghetti. "I only want you to be safe. You have to admit we've had . . . more than our share. Of trouble."

"You mean *me*. I'm the one—"

"Don't say that," he said fiercely. "You're not the trouble. It's— I made you a target, that's what. A cop's kid? I left us open to that kind of thing as long as I was on the force." He stood, began clearing the plates.

What about after that?

She'd always thought he'd left the force because he hadn't been able to save that baby. The misery over it, the shame, even. Now it sure seemed as though he'd left because of her. Her safety, which always seemed to be in question? "I always wondered why they would attempt it, with who you were. Or maybe they didn't know? How did they—"

"They knew." Behind her, a scrape into the garbage can, water running in the sink. "I wasn't there," he said. "You were taken from the yard. Your mom was watching you, and—well, she must have looked away. No time at all, you were gone."

Alice watched her dad's back, slumped shoulders, lazy strokes of a dishcloth on the plate. Her mother. *Of course.* Pieces slid into place. "And he grabbed me and put me in . . . a car?"

He sighed. "We always assumed so."

"No one saw it? We had neighbors—"

"No one saw it," he said. "No one came forward, at least. We didn't have good neighbors then."

And none since.

"And then they took me to their home—"

"That's what you said." Almost defensive. Alice thought it over, pushed her plate away.

"And then you got me back."

"Right."

"But how?" She had been too incurious about her own life. She would accuse her dad of hiding from the real world out here in the woods behind the security measures, but she was the one whose life had always been folded inward, a tiny origami shape of a bird that would not fly.

His head was lowered over the sink, his spine stretched. Some kind of evasion yoga.

"I mean, how did you know how to get me back?"

"An anonymous tip," he said. "Probably from someone living nearby."

"Better neighbors than we had."

"One of the reasons we got out of there," he said. "I couldn't forgive them. It's supposed to take a village, isn't that the phrase?"

If it took a village, why had they moved out to the literal sticks? "But the guy—I mean the *couple*. If you got me back from their house, why did you need me to tell you how to get back to it?"

He turned at the sink. "What's that?"

"You used to ask me what I remembered, things about the house—"

"You were a witness," he said. "A material witness, no matter how old you were. And there was that baby to think about." He came for her plate, looking pointedly at how little she'd eaten.

"I thought you couldn't find the house again, that you were trying to get me to tell you how to find it."

He turned away, dumped her plate, went back to the sink. "Well, no. I'd been to the house. To get you."

"So why—"

"To hear any details you'd picked up," he said. "Maybe they'd talked about where they were from or where they were going. On the third telling, maybe you'd come up with a name for that baby."

"Merrily."

Her dad froze. "What did you say?"

She shouldn't have said it. She hadn't meant to bother him with it, not with all the stuff going on with Matt. Surely the lawyers were involved by now.

But he deserved to know that the baby they'd both worried about all these years was safe, always had been. "Merrily Cruz," she said. "I'm pretty sure that's who it was, and that her mother was there, too, yelling at the—at the couple. The guy, really."

Her dad slumped against the sink. He turned a dish towel over in his hands. "I don't know where to start, Al. You think you know the name—I can't—how in the world—"

"It's a long story."

"I have time now," he said. "You wanted to talk about it, right?"

"A few days ago I was working on the Pages—"

"The dead people site?"

"Dad, don't call it that—"

"I don't know what else you would call it." He threw the dish towel onto the counter and pulled his chair out at the table. "I'm sorry," he said, when he had settled in and leaned forward over clasped hands. "I'll keep my thoughts to myself. I'll *try*, how's that?"

"I was working on the Doe Pages a few days ago when I saw a photo that I recognized. I mean, not at first. I just noticed it, but later in the day when I was having lunch with, uh, some friends, I realized how I knew the guy's face."

"You recognized the guy who snatched you? On that site?" Her dad frowned at his hands. "You mean one of the dead bodies?"

"Dad, no. It's—there are missing people on that site, too. He's missing. At least, he was."

"What do you mean?"

"His missing person report disappeared," she said. Not just from the Doe Pages, but everywhere, including NamUs, the national database. She wouldn't bother him with the details. If he got confused about what the Does were, he couldn't handle NamUs.

"So he was found," he said.

"Maybe."

He had a way of looking at her askance, setting up another attack at a new angle. "You sound disappointed."

Was she? She'd set her sights on finding the guy herself. Finally discovering curiosity only to realize that it came with a gut-dread apprehension of success. She was disappointed—in herself.

It would be so easy to let her dad talk her out of further involvement. "A kidnapping thirty years ago might not be his only problem," she said.

Her dad folded his arms. "Tell me."

"Some nasty people are after him, from what I can gather."

"Gather? You're *gathering*? You're not— I don't even know the words to ask you what *the fuck* you think you're doing."

He might as well have struck her. He was red in the face, the scar at his jaw white in contrast. "Dad—"

"Are you turning into one of those homebound conspiracy theorists? If you are getting yourself mixed up with the likes of—of—"

He ran out of steam.

"Richard Kisel," she said. "I wanted to, I don't know, *hand* him to you."

"You know his *name*."

"Richard Kisel. Banks, I mean—I have no idea. He was going by Miller at the last."

He put his hands flat on the table. "That *piece of shit*. You're talking about him like he's otherwise a cheerful guy, like he's someone people have walk their dogs and babysit their kids."

Alice kept her mouth shut.

"This guy," her dad said, his voice tight. "Miller? You didn't contact him, right?"

"No, of course not—"

"You didn't try to reach him, right? You didn't call him. They can track calls, these guys."

"No." She wouldn't bring up last known addresses. She shouldn't have gone there.

"Then the girl. Who? Mary Lee?"

She nodded.

"Last name?"

She didn't want him showing up at Merrily's mother's house, *always a cop.* "Cross." That wasn't a lie; it was a translation.

His eyes flicked to her. "And you found her how?"

"The internet." He didn't understand it that well, wouldn't get far if he tried.

"And she—I don't know what to ask. She's OK? Grew up fine?"

Fine. Grew up better than *fine*, in some ways. "Present and loving mother," Alice said icily. He had the decency to look away.

"What's this girl's story? Is she in touch with the guy, or what?"

He was getting lost in the details. "I don't *know* her," she said. Split hairs, left and right. "Anyway, I need to get home. My boss won't cut me a break if I'm late again. Five minutes, even."

Not the hint of a smile. "You're the one who brought this up."

"My mistake."

He sighed. "I'm sorry I got carried away. I want you to be able to tell me anything. I have a few more days away from the site—"

"You do?"

"Last-minute addition to the calendar," he said.

Matt's fall. It would cost them, and he didn't want to worry her with reality.

"When I'm back in town, let's grab a proper dinner, where the chef knows what he's doing."

She wouldn't smile, though.

"Promise me," he said. "Promise me you will stay away from this. This guy is trouble. You might as well stay away from that kid and her mom, too."

Alice found herself wanting to fight him, even if she'd led him here. It was what everyone wanted of her, to leave Merrily alone. To leave well enough alone. An easy enough promise to make. She nodded.

"Good," he said. "I worry, OK? If I lost you again, I don't know what I would do. I don't know if I could—"

Survive it. Alice thought of the gun, let him wrap her in his arms. She was forgiven.

He walked her to the door, where she zipped her backpack to hide the papers she'd taken. Which reminded her—

She pulled the little scrap of comfort blanket from her pocket.

He stared at it. "That's not what you were looking for."

"Nah, just found it."

"What do you need that dirty thing for? Let me wash it for you."

"It'll fall to pieces!"

"We can only hope," he said. "You're a grown woman."

Maybe not entirely forgiven. She shouldered the backpack. "If I hadn't remembered being kidnapped," she said, "would you have ever told me?"

Impatience, for sure, this time. "Honestly, no. What good has it ever done you?"

Alice walked out to her car, listening to the dark woods whir and chirp with night creatures. Her dad watched from the doorway, a square of light in the vast blackness. She hurried.

She unlocked the car with the fob, the headlights lighting up the trees. All around her, the night noises cut to silence. She imagined everything hiding there, birds, bats, frogs and things, all of them cowering and waiting for the danger to pass.

She was the danger. This time, it was her.

CHAPTER TWENTY-THREE
MERRILY

A slim finger of streetlight from Merrily's bedroom window reached across her mattress and her knee. Merrily rocked back and forth over the naked form of Officer G. Vasquez, his hands gripping her hips. He made such cute, self-conscious noises when she sat back on him, quiet noises, as though she cared one damn about the neighbors hearing or Justyce. She wanted him to cry out, weep, speak in tongues. She'd once made an unassuming white boy she'd met clubbing start to speak forgotten high school Russian, fifteen years gone, all the dirty words he'd learned outside class.

G. Vasquez, though, was a sturdier sort. Graciano was his name—he'd have to be sturdy to carry that his whole life. His friends called him Gonzo, like he was some kind of children's toy. She wasn't ready to be friends with him, though. *Graciano*: graced by God, pleasing. Graciano, a benediction, and she was newly devout.

Afterward, Merrily collapsed next to him, one of her legs still thrown over his. The finger of streetlight pointed at her across his chest.

"What the hell just happened?" he asked, panting.

"Oh," she said, fake sympathy. "First time?"

"First time I ever met with a person of interest and then ended up in her bed."

"Boy Scout," Merrily said. First time a person of interest had stalked the station until Vasquez arrived on duty, more like. First time a person of interest had made Vasquez a person of interest.

She'd called and made an appointment to get an update on the case. That's what she'd said, those words, like she was on *Crime Time Tonight*. She didn't normally seek out the attention of cops—but she was impatient. She shouldn't have had to go to them. If they'd kept her updated, or if Alice and her friends hadn't just run off in the night without her, she wouldn't have to go shopping through the police station. Not that she minded what she'd picked up.

"Do you do this . . . often?" he said.

"Don't get prudish on me now, not after you got yours," Merrily said. *Graciano.* She should have known he'd have a pious mother in there somewhere. She pulled her leg off him. "No, I don't do this *often.*" She did it *sometimes.* She did *this* when she fucking *wanted* to, OK? It wasn't usually because she wanted to talk afterward, though. Now that he was good and warmed up—

"Was there something you wanted to know?" he said.

Pretty *and* smart. "You said you hadn't found Rick yet, but are you looking?"

He sniffed. "I'm going to try not to be offended by that."

"I meant, where are you looking? His apartment. The casino. Have you talked to anyone in Victorville, Indiana—"

"Whoa, whoa, what about Victorville, Indiana?"

We'll just have to go there, Juby had said, but she hadn't been talking to her.

"He might have lived there," Merrily said meekly.

He sat up, Officer G. Vasquez suddenly on duty. "Suppose you tell me what you want to tell me and ask me what you want to ask. To start with." He noticed a glass of water on her nightstand, and helped himself.

She told him about the three women who'd come to Port Beth, leaving out her mom's confounding reaction. She told him about the library, the little boxes of film. At the moment when she could have told him about the burned-out house, she took a breath instead, reconsidered. She wasn't sure yet how much was the right amount to share. Her mom had been there the day of the fire. Was Mamá above burning a place to the ground?

"What dates were they looking at?" Vasquez said. "How did they know where to start?"

"My birthday—birth date, I mean. I was super-young when Rick was in my life, so I guess it was around then that—" She didn't know, actually. Alice and her friends had used her birth date as the basis to search the newspapers, but why? "They found him, actually. Something about his wife. I didn't get to read the full story—the library was closing."

And then they'd gone for Chinese, and the pages Alice had printed hadn't been offered for her inspection.

Vasquez sat up on one elbow, frowning down at her. "They *found* him—what do you mean? *What* about his wife? Wait, which wife was this?"

Right. Those three children by three women. Rick, the stud horse. "The picture was really bad, so it was hard to tell. His wife at the time I was born, I guess? Almost perfectly thirty years ago. My birthday was this week."

She closed her eyes, braced herself for a lame belated wish.

"Which paper was it?" He was up and into his pants.

"Wait, you're going?"

He pulled his shirt over his head and tucked it in, lost in thought. "That would have been another name."

She sat up. "You knew Rick Kisel wasn't his real name. Why didn't you—"

"Open investigation. I'm sorry—there are things I can't divulge. Even if I want to. Which name was in the article you saw?"

She stared at him. He had a lot of demands. This was her info-gathering, not his. She was missing prime Sunday-night lonely chats for this. "How many names are there?"

He smiled. "Nice try."

"Banks," she spat. "Richard, of course. Not very imaginative."

"Well, they let you keep your first name sometimes," he said sweetly. He leaned down and kissed the top of her head like a toddler after a bedtime story. "So that you answer to it when you're waiting for your tire change or the doctor. You get me?"

She grabbed his arm and pulled him back down. "They?"

He pulled away. "Even nicer try. Think about it."

"Are you saying—"

"I'm not saying anything, OK? Not a word was uttered by me."

She frowned into the hills and valleys of her comforter, peeled it away from her, and grabbed a T-shirt from the floor. It was his. She threw it at him and pulled on another one.

"So you're *not* saying that he was in . . ." She didn't quite know the phrase, even from *Crime Time Tonight*. "Protection?"

"Yes, I am *not* saying that." Socks, shoes. T-shirt thrown over his shoulder. "Let myself out?"

She led him out and through the living room. "Witness protection," she said. *Rick?*

"I've heard of it."

"Protection from who?" she said.

"Many things I'm not saying here. Many, many things."

Was that why she'd only seen Rick that one time? He was living under a different name for a reason? For his safety? For *theirs*? It was like a spy story, the kind she might have made up about her real dad at one point. He's not dead—he had to go undercover. He's not dead—he's behind enemy territory. He's not dead.

Rick's kids had the story. "Wait," she hissed after Vasquez, halfway down the stairwell. "What about his kids? Three kids, three women. I know that's what my mom said once."

He held up a finger to his lips and came back. He folded her into his arms, pressed her against him. Merrily felt her T-shirt rise above decency. Who cared? Against her ear, he whispered. "He cut all ties, part of his protection agreement. As far as the law is concerned, he has no kids."

He released her and headed for the stairs again. Over his shoulder, he said, "I did *not* say that. I'll call you."

Merrily crept back inside, hoping Justyce would stay in bed, if that's where she was. Of course that's where she was. *Stay*, Merrily prayed. *Don't come out and judge the T-shirt, the ass hanging out.*

In the shower, Merrily put her head under the stream of the hottest water she could stand. What did it mean to be in witness protection? Having to give up everything you'd owned or been, everyone you'd ever known. The life left behind must have been a dangerous one. A life of risk. An impossible life. She thought of the kids Rick didn't have anymore. His crimes, whatever they were, had spared them having a dad like Rick. In legal terms.

Was that why he texted *her*? He could reach out to her, when he couldn't with his own children? *Hey, kid.*

The messages from him seemed wretched now, and the time she'd given to them miserly. Merrily imagined Rick sitting on some lumpy couch somewhere, address unknown, address protected, name changed, life upended, no one to call, no one to trust, a loneliness like rage rising through him with no end. He chose her name from his short list of phone contacts, again and again, reaching out for human contact when all others had been taken away. Or, like her mom's attention, withheld.

She'd always been able to imagine what others felt, maybe because she had to, maybe because she was an only child, because she'd always needed to tune in to which way Mamá's mood swings might fly. She could taste Rick's desperation, reaching out and finding only the almost-stepdaughter he might have raised, if things had gone differently.

A lonely life. A life completely hollowed. Merrily let her chin fall to her chest and cried. Cried for all of them and the family they might have made.

CHAPTER TWENTY-FOUR

ALICE

Alice spent some time on Jane Doe Anaho before work Monday morning. Jane and her little remnant of orange fabric, which suddenly reminded Alice of her scrap of baby blanket. Jane Anaho had been a regular person, with regular person problems, maybe a boyfriend who wasn't quite good enough, a job that wasn't good enough by far. And now she was gone.

When Alice next looked up from her laptop, she was late for work again. Actual late, actual had-to-text-the-Jims late. When she arrived at the site, the crew was already having their morning break. Some of the guys sat at the base of the structure. She walked toward them, trying to discern the morning's progress overhead.

"Hard hat," one of them called, and Brody, the youngest guy on payroll, hustled in with an extra for her. She hadn't meant to put them to the trouble, but rules were rules. An example to be made.

"Hey, guys," she said. A few of the others who had been taking their ten elsewhere, smoking where they shouldn't, came out and gathered around.

"What's up, Al?"

"Didn't get a chance to tell you I went to visit Matt Friday. He's doing . . ."

But she couldn't say how he was doing. The guys exchanged glances among themselves.

"He's not doing great," Gus said. She'd known Gus most of her life. He was like a pillar that kept her life upright, and now he looked at her with an expression she couldn't name.

"Not great," she admitted. "I took over some flowers from all of us." The flowers seemed an empty gesture, now that she'd announced them. "But if you think of anything we could do to be helpful to Lita, I hope you'll suggest it."

The break seemed to be over, the men drifting away from her, the noise starting back up. Brody stood at her elbow. When the rest of them were gone, he turned at an angle to her, away from the others, and spoke out toward the gate. "He's going to die, is that what you think?"

"I hope not," she said, and doffed the hard hat to hand it back.

He studied the hat, then looked up at her, squinting. "He's a good buddy. I was—I *am* hoping for a miracle."

"Two stories is a long way to fall," she said, looking toward the structure.

"Three," Brody said, pulling a long strand of her hair from the hat and smiling at her as he let it go in the breeze. "I was on the west end that day. He fell right past me, Al. It was horrible."

She hadn't imagined how hard it would be for the rest of the crew, had only swallowed her own grief, was full with it. "Did he yell out?"

"Oh, yeah." Alice watched his Adam's apple bob in his thin neck. Such delicate machinery. "He yelled the whole way, Al. Screamed." He wouldn't look at her now. "It was fast, at least. I haven't been able to stop thinking about it. It was—" He stopped, swallowed.

"If you ever need to talk with anyone, I hope you know you can call me, OK?"

He wouldn't look at her, and his neck splotched red as she watched. "He's a real good buddy of mine."

"Oh, no. I just meant—"

"Ten's over," said a voice coming across the lot. It was JimBig, hard hat sitting high on his head like a tea cozy. He approached them slowly. It was a power move to keep people waiting.

"Yes, sir," Brody said, turning away.

"I'll text you," Alice said.

"Hard hat area, kid," Uncle Jim said to her. "You know that."

"I had one," she said.

"Your noggin is one we got to protect." He stood back and gazed up at the structure. "Over the halfway hump. Maybe this won't be the one to do us in, after all."

"When did we finish the third deck, do you remember?"

"Well," he said, chewing the side of his mouth. "We're ten days behind, Jimmy says, maybe more now with all the— But you know where to look it up proper in the shed."

"Ballpark," she said. "How far along were we on the day Matt fell, for instance?"

He pushed his hard hat back, swiped at the sweat at his temple. "I know you're hurting, but let's not keep time that way."

"I just remember which day of the week it was."

"I don't remember if we'd cleared the third deck by then. All the concrete's starting to run together in my memory."

"How far up did you take the tour?"

"You OK, kid? That tour was canceled, remember? Now, you get back out of the hard hat zone before someone sees you. If you get us cited while Harris is gone, I never knew you."

She walked across the gravel to the trailer and opened the door.

Jimmy Junior sat in her chair with his dusty black shoes on the corner of her desk, his phone to his face. He had wedged open the small window behind her computer, which created a cross-breeze with the open door. Sticky notes peeled off her computer screen. Loose sheets of paper on her desk fluttered. She closed the door quickly.

"Finally decided to come earn your one percent?" Jimmy said.

"I texted you I would be late," she said. "As a courtesy. You're not my supervisor."

"Matter of time. Texting that you're going to be late isn't the level of professionalism King Construction expects."

She looked pointedly at his shoes, which were leaving dried mud on the paperwork on her desk. "King and Fine. And now you'll tell me that's just a matter of time, too."

"Or have you changed your mind? We could make it King and King."

After a morning of trying to match the unidentified remains of a dead girl with a list of missing women, Alice didn't feel playful or even angry about his pestering. Only tired.

"I don't know why you bother," she said. "You don't even like me."

He blinked. "I like you." The innuendo and attitude fell away. "I mean, I think . . . I think I'd like to get to know you better."

They'd known each other their entire lives, grown up side by side. What was left to know?

"Again, I mean." He was blushing now. And then so was she, remembering.

"Well, that's a much nicer approach."

A slow and hopeful smile spread across Jimmy's face. "Yeah?"

Alice held out her hand, a stop sign. "But we work together. That's a real problem because, like you said, one of these days we'll be business partners. King and Fine, all over again. Or something like that, whatever the lawyers say."

She thought of Lita's face when she'd brought up the company attorneys. What kind of document was Lita expecting Uncle Jim to send her? And why had Matt been on the third level of the garage before they'd cleared it? He should have been on the second deck, which was why her dad had assumed he'd fallen from there. Maybe it was an insurance thing. If they hadn't safely cleared deck three and Matt had been up there anyway, they'd be in trouble. Insurance trouble, financial trouble.

"What lawyers?" Jimmy said, his feet finally on the floor.

"From the papers we signed," she said. "I didn't really read them."

"Yeah, you're going to make a great business partner."

"Well, did you?"

"Did I read the thing before I signed it? Sure I did." He blinked at her. "I don't remember what it said *exactly*." He slipped past her and waved the desk over to her possession. "It was a while ago."

She didn't have the luxury of misplacing the timing. "The day you went off to college. Afterward I went home and kept my mom from harm. For a while anyway."

He looked away. "We could check what it says, right?"

"What? Why?" Alice went to her desk, dumped her backpack in the drawer. None of it made any difference until the unthinkable happened. "Is your dad OK? You can't wait to get hold of his portion?"

"I'm not a jerk, Alice," he said. "I mean, yeah, sometimes I am. This is thinking ahead, which is what a good businessman—a good business*person*—does. Not that either of us have great models for that."

"That's a jerk thing to say."

"This place could be so much more, and you know it." Jimmy went to the photo over the safe and popped it off the wall in a practiced move. He stared at the dial.

"Twenty-two right . . ." she said.

"I know."

He had the thing open quickly, smug, pulling out the pair of ledgers and setting them aside. He brought out a stack of files and held them aloft. "Where would we keep that?"

Helpless. Honestly, the best reason to leave this cush job was that if she didn't, someday she would have to run it alongside Jimmy King.

She went and took the folders, sorted out the one he wanted from the stack, and handed it to him. He sat in the guest chair in front of her desk and started flipping through it while she returned the rest of the stuff to the safe. She noticed no one had bothered to start the coffee.

"Huh," Jimmy said.

"What?"

He made appreciative noises over the papers, turning one over, reading.

"*What?*" she said.

He pulled his head up from the paperwork, laughing. "I'm not sure how they got this through, but we're considered a woman-owned business. A goddamned woman-owned business. That explains your one percent."

"Shut up." Alice went to the door and looked out. She could see Uncle Jim out on the site, gesturing angrily toward some aspect of the project to Gus, Brody, and some of the others. "My one share is enough to make us woman-owned? That's . . . well, that's a scam."

"Oh, absolutely," he murmured approvingly. "But Chicago sets up the rules, not us, and if we can get lucrative city contracts because— Wait. How many shares? Just one?"

"Isn't that what you got?"

"One share, yeah, but then who . . ." He went back to the pages, flipped through them. "No. That can't be right."

Now she was concerned. Her share in the company was her inheritance, her fallback. What if it was just, *poof*, gone? She hadn't planned for *poof*. She hadn't planned for anything. "What is it?"

Jimmy looked up from the pages, all the color drained from his face. "I need—" He stood, papers in an array in his arms. "I need to talk to my dad."

"He's— What is it? What's wrong?"

He tossed everything in his hands toward her desk and raced out of the trailer, the door left hanging. The suction between door and window opened up again, pages lifting, starting to circulate. Alice gathered them against her as best she could and ran to the door. Jimmy was kicking up dust crossing the site to the spot where JimBig stood.

Alice pulled the door closed. Back at her desk, she smoothed pages, found page numbers, and put them in order. There. Tidy again. She stared down at the top page, wondering. It didn't matter if she peeked. She wouldn't understand it anyway.

She was still reading when Jimmy stormed back inside, JimBig filling the doorway behind him. Alice looked up, stunned.

"It wasn't a joke," she said. "All these years. I'm really the boss?"

CHAPTER TWENTY-FIVE

ALICE

Uncle Jim couldn't explain it. Wouldn't. He sat in the chair across from Alice and avoided making eye contact.

They'd been up and down the list of questions he wouldn't answer. He wouldn't budge. "Look, it was a business decision, that's all I can tell you. Ask your dad—he might have understood the lawyer-speak better than I did. There was a good reason, sweetheart. It's just been a long time since I heard it. And it's worked out so far, hasn't it?"

Jimmy watched his dad from the door, his face contorting from one emotion to another. He still had his one share of the company, but now that the dish had been divided with a larger portion for her, Alice knew he was dissatisfied, hungry. She kept catching him staring at her.

"Dad, why in the world would you put the company into the hands of the one person on site who doesn't care about—"

"James," JimBig bellowed. When he turned back to her, she flinched.

She had watched her dad look to JimBig King for a nod her

entire life: a nod before he spoke, a nod before he acted. And now she knew why. To act against Big's wishes might draw out this monster. She could barely look at him.

And then just as quickly he was Uncle Jim again. "I'm sorry, kid. I'm not the accountant."

"Is that all it is?" she said. "Accounting?"

"It's a gift. Think of it that way."

It felt more like a weight, something to pin her in place. Another way her dad had built the fortress around her: the job, her apartment, even her car. Now her entire future. He'd negotiated the deal. *Every* deal.

Once, she would like to make her own way and see what it felt like.

"So is this just so we get hired by the city of Chicago, or is it to safeguard the company from—oh, God, is this tax fraud? Is this illegal?"

"What could be illegal about sharing ownership of the company with your kids?" Not mentioning the uneven split.

"What was illegal about last time?" Jimmy said, moving on his dad a couple of steps.

"Jimmy, shut it."

"What?" Alice said. "Which last time?"

"He went to *jail*," Jimmy said. "When I was a kid—"

"I said don't, didn't I?" his dad thundered. No sign of the guy who'd come back from vacation looking weary. JimBig waved Jimmy off. "Made no difference to you whether I was there or not."

Jimmy didn't blink at his dad's rage. He'd seen it before. "I remember—"

"You don't remember shit. What you got in your head is what your mother put there."

Alice felt small between them. She might as well not be here.

"I remember plenty," Jimmy said. "I wasn't some little kid, not while you were being sent up, and not when you were gone."

"When was this?" Alice said.

"You were away at finishing school, Barbie Doll," Jimmy said. "Sent off so you wouldn't notice a thing, if I had to guess. They didn't bother to send *me* away. I thought that meant . . ."

That he was somehow the chosen one. But he'd been cut out of the deal.

Rn, rnn. Her phone, buzzing against her hip. She drew it out.

Text from Juby. *Lil wants to dump some info on you. Sneak out for lunch?*

Did she even need to sneak? She owned the fucking place.

News? she typed. "What did you go to jail for, Uncle Jim?"

"*Prison.* Stop calling him that. He is not your—"

"Shut up, Jimmy," JimBig said. "Not everything is up to you—"

"Clearly," Jimmy said.

"—and thank God for it," his dad finished. "You've been in your mother's damned pocketbook like a toy poodle your whole life. You'd never get more than a single share of this place, even if it was all mine to give."

Jimmy froze, but not quickly enough. Alice felt the stab of pain that flashed across his face. "Uncle Jim," she said gently.

"No," JimBig said. "He was supposed to learn the business to learn the business, not to run it, but to start his own when the time came, or to be a good right hand to you."

"Me?" Alice had been assuming the ownership percentages were just temporary, skewed to maneuver around a barrier, to hold something in trust, to protect. To hide. "I'm actually supposed to own this place someday?"

"You own it now," Jimmy mumbled.

"But that's—"

"It makes business sense," Uncle Jim said. "Like I said, from what I understand—"

"Maybe if you understood more, you wouldn't have done the time. Did you ever think—"

"I did wrong," Uncle Jim said, turning to Alice, "and your dad was the one who saved me. He gave me a chance to be a better man this time around. Ask him about it. He'll tell you why the lawyers set things up the way we did. It was no accident, I can tell you that."

Accident. That made Alice think of Matt. *It's been X days since our last health and safety violation— Oh, God.* Was that her responsibility now? The lawyers and the hospital and the insurance? She had no idea how to run things, really—that joke about being the boss was . . . a joke.

Her phone revved again. In the silence, the sound was huge.

"We keeping you from important business, *boss*?" Jimmy couldn't even sneer through it anymore. He was a kid, trying on bravado, as scared as she was. While their fathers were busy growing old and turning over the company to them, they hadn't been paying attention. They were the fucking grown-ups?

Rnn.

Jimmy rolled his eyes as she reached for her phone.

The problem of Richard Whatever is being Slapdashed.
Lil is on the case. Come pick up what she's got?

Alice glanced at the time on her phone. Sure, why not? She'd put in a good hour of mind-blowing revelations here. Time for a break. She stood up and grabbed her backpack from the drawer. Time for a *drink*. She might not come back today, actually. There had to be perks to holding the controlling share, and to having Warden Harris Fine gone for a day or two.

"Wait, seriously?" Jimmy said. "You're going?"

"I have to run an errand," she said, wondering what would happen if she told him he was fired. "And frankly—"

"Take the day," Uncle Jim said. "This can wait. When your dad's back, we'll talk it out. It's all fine, OK? This doesn't have to change a thing. It's only paper."

Alice wouldn't look at him now. He'd been to prison? She'd always been a little afraid of JimBig King. She didn't know that it was going to be fine. Maybe it never had been.

She made it down the steps before Jimmy came bursting out of the trailer behind her. The door bounced against the frame, hanging open behind him as he rushed across the gravel.

"What the fuck, Alice? Is this how you're going to run the place?"

"I can't deal with you right now."

"Oh, sure, another day we have to feel sorry for little Alice from Wonderland. Because your mom died when you were an adult, you *poor* thing."

His mother had died when they were in high school. "Your mother had cancer, Jimmy, God. It's not the same— OK, you want to know why I'm rushing off? I'm *this* close to finding the guy who kidnapped me."

"What? I thought you didn't know— Wasn't it a couple?"

"Right, it's a long story, but we found that baby." This was the good Doe Pages had done her. She could hand this guy's guts over to the police and show Jimmy King she was capable of more than cleaning up after him. "The baby my dad didn't have a chance to rescue? She's fine. She's OK. Her name is Merrily Cruz, and we had Chinese food with her last week."

He looked at her sharply. "Who's we?"

"My friends. They're really good with, you know, finding out stuff."

"From that crazy website? The dead people site?"

"Don't—" She sighed. "Yes, through the site. We think we might be able to find him, and—"

"And then what? What will it accomplish?"

She didn't like his tone. This was one thing she had that he had zero share in. "I'm seeing something through, OK? It's the first time I've ever had the chance to— I don't know . . ."

"Own something?" He laughed. "Yeah, I know what you mean. I *really* do."

"Jimmy," she said. "I'll talk to my dad, figure out what's going on. You put in a lot of work here. You deserve to understand, and if I'm in charge—*fuck*, right? I'm going to need you."

His gaze was searching. "Merrily Cruz, huh? That's good, I guess, that she's OK."

"Yeah, and she's cute, too. Maybe I'll set you up."

He smiled, tried not to. "Only if she's like you." He turned to go.

"Hey, Jimmy," she said. "Were you on the site the day Matt fell?"

"Yeah," he said, frowning. "Of course I was."

She remembered the ring across his forehead from the hard hat. "With the tour?"

He shook his head. "Just one investor. Dad said he could handle it. Why?"

"Which investor?"

"Didn't recognize him. Prospect, maybe, or scouting for someone else? He seemed younger than the regular Scrooge McDucks we get."

She thought of the man she'd pointed the pepper spray at outside the gate that day. An investor? That guy had been right; she *was* curious. "Matt fell from the third floor, right?"

"Second," he said. "Luckily. Three floors would have killed him."

"Yeah," she said. "Lucky."

CHAPTER TWENTY-SIX

MERRILY

Merrily drove past the town sign—VICTORVILLE, POPULATION 12,358, HOME OF INDIANA HIGH SCHOOL FOOTBALL CHAMPIONS, a long list of years in which the news was true—and smiled to herself. *We'll just have to go there*, Juby had said—but when? They were held back by their jobs, their rule-following, their mild curiosity. *By the long-ass drive through an absolute wasteland of nothing but farms.* But this was a matter of life and death for Rick, and she was the only one who understood that. Who *cared*. It couldn't wait.

Once in town, though, Merrily wished she had asked Juby what she would do once they got there. Library again, she supposed, and drove into the town, looking out for the kind of flat and faceless buildings committeemen built. She found a domed county courthouse on a pleasant square, and at the last minute turned and followed the road around, left turn, left turn. Feeling her way like a diviner. But that wasn't quite right, because she knew where to find the library—suddenly, violently. She knew she had been to this town before.

She parked in front of the library and sat, unnerved. Down the street was a park with a creek running through it, with a stone bridge. She would drop a pebble in, watch the ripples, try to skip a stone, though the angle was bad. She knew that bridge. Behind her, a storefront that had once sold ice cream. Merrily could have any flavor she wanted but only one scoop, and it would run down to her elbow, melting, before she could finish.

These were fleeting memories at best, laced through with stories she'd probably only heard, but she'd been to this place. No. She'd lived here. She knew this down to her shaking bones, down to her knocking knees.

The librarian in the research room frowned at her request. Her name tag said *Ask me, I'm a librarian*, and under that, *Devin Abraham*.

"I know how to use the machine," Merrily said, best behavior.

"The machine's broken is the problem. Maybe I can help you find what you're looking for another way?"

Merrily had to catalogue what she was looking for. Her past, and Rick's, somehow leading her to the spot Rick would be now. It was a lot to ask for, and she had no idea where to begin. "This would be information from thirty years ago," she began. "I'm not sure—"

"The missing woman?" The librarian gave her a tight look.

"Yes, that's it. You've only had one person go missing from this town?"

The librarian led her to the front desk and brought out a thin binder. "Two," she said. "But thirty years ago, that has to be Laura Banks. Local woman who disappeared and never turned up."

Justyce was right. They were all named Laura. "How did you know I wanted to know about . . . something like this? I could have been looking for, I don't know, old football scores."

The tight look again. "No one comes looking for thirty-year-old football scores." She opened the booklet to plastic-sleeve pages that held photocopied news articles. A few pages in, she stopped. "The ones who come looking for something like this, they always have the same . . . manner."

"Oh." Merrily hadn't realized she had a manner. She leaned over the open binder on folded arms.

The photocopy was grainy, the photos dark. She glanced longingly at the microfilm station, then back at the photo of the woman. Something about the shape of her face—all she could see, really—caught her eye. The photocopied face was mostly shadow. The highlights of her cheeks, blown out. She was probably white. Laura and all. "Did you know this woman?"

"Oh, no," the woman said, showing real emotion for the first time: horror. "She was—well, they say she was a drug addict. She had her child taken away from her, you know, and some boyfriend of hers turned up dead—"

"Dead?" Too loud.

The librarian pursed her lips. "Not around here, and much later. I think. Maybe I'm not remembering it right." She flipped through a few pages until she landed on one Merrily recognized as the article the four of them had found in her town's library: Rick, way back when he was Richard Banks, sought for information.

"This one," the librarian said. "Her husband, I guess. I don't know why I thought it was a boyfriend."

"This guy is the guy you think died?"

"In a fire, maybe?" the librarian said. Merrily took a breath. The fire, of course. The woman was flipping through the pages of the binder idly. "No clipping for that. Must have happened in another county."

"Is this, like, your crime scrapbook?"

The woman's face returned to a mask. "It's a collection of the stories we get asked to track down over and over—by experts and researchers, reporters. And lookie-loos."

She was the latter, obviously. Merrily wondered about the others. Who else came asking? Crime . . . tourists? Who were they, and why would they want to know about this particular missing woman, this particular town's sadness? Maybe they were all like Alice and her friends, trying to put pieces together, but caring more for the puzzle than the people missing or dead. They couldn't all be like her, could they? All looking for a person they themselves missed from their lives?

If she was already a tourist . . . "Who's the other one?" she said.

"Who? Oh, you mean the other—" The woman paged through to the end of the binder, backed up a page, and turned the book around for Merrily to see another copied article, another grainy photo. "This guy disappeared from town, too, and I can tell you, he was no dropout. He had a family, a job. I can't believe they never found a hair from this guy's head."

Before she saw the page, Merrily thought, *I'll know him.* But she didn't. His face, though just as hard to see as the other's, was a stranger's. Someone's husband, someone's dad. If she went to that website Alice said they all worked for, maybe she'd find him there. Missing person, last seen—

The date leapt from the page.

"Are you OK?" the librarian said.

"No, I— Is there, uh, water?"

The woman hustled away. As soon as she was gone, Merrily pulled the page out of the binder, turned to the pages for the missing woman, too, and pulled those. She took a dollar from her wallet and left it on the binder. They were just copies, right? When the machine was fixed, they could replace them. It wasn't stealing. It *wasn't* stealing. Best behavior.

She dropped another dollar, hearing her mom's voice in her head, and was gone.

CHAPTER TWENTY-SEVEN
ALICE

Talking about Merrily with Jimmy, Alice had lost track of everything she'd had to absorb, but then, while walking to the restaurant to meet Juby and Lillian again, each piece washed over her until she was walking uphill through it. JimBig King, in prison. The business, entrusted to her, thrust at her. She wished Jimmy had never gone looking through the files. Three stories instead of two. Did it matter? Prison for what, had he ever said? Her dad had given JimBig a fresh start, but—what was her dad willing to forgive?

She arrived at the restaurant and sat in the same booth, a window to the parking lot at her shoulder. She ordered a drink, something indulgent and alcoholic, but then when it came, like a flamingo standing on the table, she took one cloying sip and set it aside.

She sat for a long time, sorry she'd stormed out of the trailer only to have to fend off the waitress three, four times. At last she remembered the notes from the fabric box and pulled her backpack up next to her. She remembered the gun, too, and shuddered. There was no reason it should have been there. *Close to hand.*

She should text her dad more often, check in. Right now.

She couldn't bring herself to. He was busy, traveling again, and she had too many questions even to start.

Instead Alice started sorting the paperwork she'd grabbed. The notes were easily found, small stenographer-pad pages filled with cramped handwriting she'd recognize anywhere, ruffled edges from being ripped from the notebook.

House, baby.

She dug in. The pages were a sort of log, multiple entries with dates that moved through time and through an array of pen ink colors and integrity. That fit the occasional sessions Alice remembered, her dad checking in to see if she remembered anything new. She never had, and the notes played this out. Some of it was difficult to figure out, but she could tell that the entries started robust and grew thinner as time passed. She never came up with new information. The log was better at keeping track of what she *forgot*.

That would have been frustrating for her dad, on top of everything else he was dealing with, to watch the details—and hope—fall away. She had to find this guy.

Alice paged through, catching a word here and there.

Sunshine, singing.

The black bird flew at her face. She dropped the notes and grasped the edge of her bench seat until the darkness passed and she could see the people around her, hear the jangling music. A little boy a few tables away stared at her, but no one else had paid her any attention. She gathered the pages back to the table and grabbed for her water glass.

The last time she'd talked to a doctor about her spells, he'd wanted to talk stress tests, Vitamin D. A psychiatrist. Maybe it was time. Was this what her mother suffered? Is this what she couldn't withstand anymore?

Alice sat back and looked out the restaurant window.

A different shining window, another time.

She allowed the memory to come at her gently.

Her mother, barefoot in the kitchen. Swaying, dancing. Singing, *You are my sunshine.*

Proof that her mother had been happy once. She didn't want to forget it. *My only sunshine.*

Alice looked back at her dad's notes. She'd shuffled early memories of her mother into his questions about the kidnapping, getting it all mixed up. No wonder she'd been absolutely no help.

Alice caught movement from the corner of her eye. Outside the window, Juby and Lillian faced one another, both talking at once, Lillian thumping a cane in the air like a drum major. Juby shifted an armful of paper against herself. Alice had never seen them say a disagreeable word to one another, had she?

She leaned out of view and waited for them to arrive inside.

At the table Juby let her stack of paper thump down in front of Alice. "Lil made you something pretty."

"I didn't bring her anything," Alice said.

Lillian was still catching up. Juby stuck her thumbnail between her teeth and then dropped it. "Gotta pee. Back in a second."

Lillian made herself comfortable, letting her cane rest against the table's edge. She caught Alice watching. "I don't want to talk about it," she said.

"Fine."

"Look, Jubilee and I disagree. Some of the interpretations." She wheezed for a few seconds, coughed, started again. "You should dig in. Make your own calls."

"Calls?"

"Your own opinions." Her coffee-stale breath reached Alice across the table. "And decisions."

"I'm not sure what you mean."

"Well," Lillian said. "When you do."

Alice put her pages on top of what Juby had set down, and then pulled it all to her. A lot of reading. Cramming for another exam, but the exam mattered this time.

"What's that?" Lillian said, raising her chin to look through the bottom of her glasses.

"My dad's interviews with me after the kidnapping. I wasn't much of a witness." She slipped the notes off the stack and into her backpack. She didn't need help from Slapdash on this one.

Lillian tilted her head at the stack. A page left over from the stuff Alice had taken from the house was still there, some kind of legal document with tiny print. "I bet you remembered plenty," Lillian said. "For a while."

Alice grabbed the rest of the stack and stowed it just as Juby came back to the table. She nudged Alice into the interior of the booth.

"Did Lil go through what she found? There's a lot—"

"I suggested. She read it for herself."

The waitress arrived. Juby reached in quickly and asked for their orders to go.

"Busy at work," Juby said. "Month closing and all."

"Oh," Alice said. "I thought—"

"Sorry," Juby said. "It turned into an interesting day right as we were leaving. We need to get back."

"I had an interesting day, too," Alice said. *This is what friendship is.* "Apparently I own the company I thought I only worked for."

Juby and Lillian glanced at each other. "One surprise revealed," Lillian said to Juby, as though she were granting her a wish.

Alice looked from one to the other. "You knew?"

"Catch up. On your reading."

"Give me the CliffsNotes."

"Why did you start? With the Does?" Lillian said. "To find the guy?"

"Of course not," Alice said. "I wanted to help out, if I could. So many missing people, and they don't all get returned to their families the same day, I know that. I was the lucky one. I thought I could do some good with it."

"It?"

"The experience. The . . ."

"Anger?" Juby said.

Lillian looked away. Alice could see that Juby was the angry one. "Not anger, exactly. In my case, not anger. It's disbelief, I guess, and gratitude."

"Gratitude?" A blade had sneaked into Juby's voice. "For what?"

"Jubilee," Lillian said.

"For—for my dad, I guess," Alice said.

Juby picked up her phone and fumed at it.

"Volunteers show up. For all different reasons," Lillian said. "You're inspired by your own happy ending. Others, by—"

"By no ending at all," Juby said, not looking up.

Alice had never bothered to ask. The Does weren't all driven by personal loss, but many were. Was she supposed to ask? Was this the Doe Pages secret handshake, and she'd screwed it up?

"Juby's older sister," Lillian said simply. "Missing. Age twelve."

"I'm so sorry—"

"I don't want to talk about it," Juby said.

"And," Lillian said. "And my baby brother. Christopher."

"Oh, no. Christopher," Alice said, remembering that Lillian liked to hear the names spoken aloud. "And . . ."

"Shadira," Juby said. She had put down her phone. "I hope she's dead."

"What?" Alice's yelp turned a few heads.

"If she's not," Lillian said. "Juby has the imagination. To give her a hundred fates."

"A thousand," Juby said. "Each one worse than the last."

"Christopher could be dead," Lillian said. "But he might have lived out his life." Lillian was almost pleading with Juby, but Alice couldn't imagine why. "Loved, cared-for. It's not the worst outcome."

Their food came, Juby and Lillian's in bags. Lillian nudged them toward Juby, who took them, stood, and walked toward the exit without looking back.

"Is Juby mad at me for something?"

"It's Shadira's birthday soon. Things get hard." Lillian picked up her cane and dug in to stand. "That's too easy, though. Sometimes we need to resist tidy answers. Doing what we do." She caught her breath. "Life is far more complicated."

Alice had always resisted *questions*, but now she knew curiosity fed on itself. "I want to know everything."

Lillian nodded sadly. "Everything is there. Or maybe you already have everything. That's for you to decide."

She clattered away on her cane, careful, methodical. Slapdash. It made her sound fast and invincible, and maybe that was how she liked to be seen. Otherwise it was all irony. She couldn't believe Lillian could be all irony.

Christopher. Shadira.

Alice called over the waitress and sat silently until the bill came. She got her food to go, too, not touching a crumb. Curiosity fed on itself, and it fed her until she was sick.

CHAPTER TWENTY-EIGHT

ALICE

When she got back from lunch, Alice found the trailer locked. A few of the crew paused in their work high up in the top deck of the parking structure to wave. She waved back, shamed to be returning to the site so late. She'd finished that flamingo drink, too, on an empty stomach.

She opened the door. The wind started up at once, the papers on her desk rising and starting to dance. She slammed the door behind her, found the trailer empty. She could hear Jimmy and Gus talking as they walked past on the way to the fence, but neither came in.

She locked the door, closed the window behind her desk at last, threw the to-go container in the trash.

On the table, the ledgers from the safe still sat out where Jimmy had left them, though the safe had been closed and covered. He expected her to pick up after him? *Christ, I might* as well *marry him.* Oh, except she could just hire better help, now that she was in charge.

Alice moved the ledgers to her desk and dumped her backpack

in the empty spot on the table. She pulled out the pages she'd taken from her dad's closet, the articles she'd printed in the library, and the work Lillian and Juby had generated. It was a lot. Pages and pages of material, and some of it just as indecipherable as the cryptic handwriting of her dad's interview notes.

Where to start?

She was reminded of the Doe Pages themselves, the world's most horrifying deck of cards, shuffled and cut, shuffled and cut, to sort the information through different lenses.

She had already seen the article from the library and had studied the notes her dad had taken as best she could, so she put these aside and started paging through what Lillian had found. Slapdash! She'd heard Lillian was the best among the Does for digging out the primary sources on any subject and for the pure heft of information she delivered, and now Alice believed it. She just . . . couldn't find the thread to pull, the place to start that would lead methodically through the pile. Her sorting stacks took up the entire table. She moved to the floor. She couldn't seem to find a beginning, to make sense of it.

The materials weren't slapped together at all, but the accumulation was somehow a disaster. On purpose? What had they been fighting about? *We disagree on some of the interpretations.*

If they had interpretations, though, she couldn't make any. What she needed was Juby's talent for divining the river of truth that flowed through the pages. Alice didn't have it. She sat back on her heels.

Why couldn't they have talked her through it? Instead, she was supposed to wade through faxed documents, printed-out spreadsheets that went for twenty pages, copies of handwritten forms, and—what was this?—U.S. census records, newspaper articles, and obituaries for people she'd never heard of.

She dug further: Newspaper articles about drug busts and small crimes, public records requests in Juby's round hand, some formal documents that looked like property records, a page scanned out of a phone book, another scan from a high school yearbook, and various printouts from the Pages and its like: Doe Network, NamUs, Porchlight, the NCIC, the Charley Project, and more.

A thorough, maddening display of information in the twenty-first century. By the time she got to the bottom of the pile, Alice could almost forget who she was looking for, and why.

Richard Banks. *Are you in here?*

The last documents were certificates, marriage, birth. Alice held these to the light but realized she still couldn't read them. She looked up. The trailer had started to go dark around her, and the site outside was still and quiet.

Alice went to the desk and turned on the small lamp there. She didn't want to turn on the overhead light, in case Uncle Jim or Jimmy were still on site and came to investigate. She'd have to explain, and she couldn't.

She sat at the guest chair at her desk and read the certificates, one after the other, and then over again.

Richard Alistair Banks, married to Karolyn Steele, Victor County, Indiana. Victorville. Alice checked the date, which was written out in long form. Years before he had kidnapped her. And then a daughter, Natallie, born to Richard and Karolyn. So, this could be the couple who'd taken her—except she didn't remember an older child, only the younger one that might be Merrily.

Alice sat with the certificates. Her kidnapper was a father. There was something, again, unfair about it, that someone like this man could be allowed to go about a normal life. Until he decided to nab a cop's kid, of course.

Alice sat back in her seat. Why *would* someone take a cop's kid, of all the kids playing in their yards in Victorville, Indiana? For ransom? For leverage? Or was it simply dumb luck, finding her unsupervised?

The thought beat around her skull like a trapped bird until she had to let it fly.

Not unsupervised. Supervised badly by the wrong parent.

Because it was her mother's fault, as so many things were. Beth Ann Fine was a woman who sang "You Are My Sunshine" barefoot in the kitchen and then she was a woman who gouged the thin skin of her own wrists, and in between she'd lost track of her own child.

Alice leaned over the research, not in the mood to forgive. Another birth certificate clung to the first. She pulled them apart. Daughter born to Celia Cruz, father unnamed: Merrily Ana.

What was Lillian saying by including Merrily here? Merrily had been kidnapped, too? Or she wasn't the child in that house at all. Or she was there, only a child Rick had known. She could have used one of those interpretations Lillian had mentioned.

Alice took in the mess in front of her. Lillian was laying down every stone, but it wasn't building toward anything. Probably half of this was of that sort: background info, dead ends. But which half?

Alice carried the certificates back to the table and started gathering up the pages she'd spread out, packing them into type, if she could figure out what they were. A few stood out to her now. The obituary of Karolyn Steele, survived by daughter and two grandchildren, made more sense. A name-change form, decades old, Karolyn Banks to Karolyn Steele. Alice looked twice at this until she understood the woman had reverted to her birth name. Probably after her marriage to Richard broke up. There were also property records for the house where she and Juby and Lillian had met Merrily, in northern Indiana. Paperwork for the relinquishing of parental rights for Natallie Banks. Pages and pages of legalese. Paperwork relinquishing—

There was a clang outside, nearby. Alice stood up and went to the door, checked it was locked, and peered out the window. The site was dark except one floodlight that the guys had forgotten, which lit the face of the parking garage. Nothing moved. Outside the fence, a car revved its engine and drove away. A group of people walked along the sidewalk on the other side of the fence. She couldn't see them through the dust screen but could hear them laughing, making plans. Was the padlock secured? The chain was pulled through, at least. Alice waited a long while, watching for someone to be where they shouldn't, before going back to the papers.

She found an article about the friend of her dad's who'd gone missing several years back. Twenty years? That poor family. She scanned over it, wondering what it had to do with any of the rest of this. Travis Malayter had gone missing years after they'd already moved away from Victorville, but she remembered it happening. When she'd first found the Doe Pages, she'd made sure he was included in the Empty database.

Whenever she thought of Victorville, she felt an odd pang, like homesickness for a place she didn't actually know. If she hadn't been grabbed, they might still live there. She imagined herself a small-town girl. What would she have done for work? Who would she be?

Lillian was not at all slapdash. The article they'd printed in Port Beth about Laura Banks was replicated, another bad copy with dark photos. Alice hadn't seen a second marriage certificate, though, only the one to Karolyn and then the form when Karolyn ditched Rick's last name.

Alice sorted through the loose pages again and pulled out the obituary. Karolyn's obituary didn't name Richard Banks at all—

not that he'd preceded her in death or that he'd survived her. Just: omitted, as though he had never existed.

She had a headache. She pressed the heels of her hands to her eyes and calculated it out: marriage to one woman, child, second marriage possibly in name only, and then where did Mrs. Cruz fit in? Well, she had a theory.

More information slapdashed together: A copied page from a newspaper column that listed police calls and activities. Warrants and DUIs; domestic disturbances, solicitation. All Victorville. Alice read through them but didn't recognize any names. The next page was a small notice framed in the center of a wide, white page that announced the arrest of a local woman, Laura Schmidt, for possession of drugs. Alice turned back to the police blotter and found Schmidt's name—three times in one month. Did she know Laura Schmidt? Laura Banks? Was it the same person?

Dammit, Lil. I give up. She would have to ask for their help.

But then she saw the xeroxed yearbook page. Richard Banks, captioned. He was slim, sharp-featured, not even a hint of a smile but an expression that made it seem like he was taking direction. *Am I doing this right?* She skimmed the page until she was reminded of the faces lined up on the e-cemetery of the Doe Pages.

It was late, and she'd strained her eyes reading in the near dark. She'd have to be here again in the morning, and on time, in case her dad was back. She both hoped and dreaded he would be. They had a lot to talk about.

She was kneeling on the floor, returning the research to her backpack, when she heard the doorknob on the trailer rattle.

She jumped.

Someone had left the padlock undone. *And now some rando was wandering the site—*

But then a key pushed into the lock.

Alice didn't think. She dove quickly for the hollow spot under her desk and wedged herself there. The door swung open and a flashlight swept over the floor. That's when she saw she'd left her backpack across the room. She forced herself into a fist.

A beam of light swung past, and footfall crossed the floor toward her.

In the dim light, she could see dark pants, black boots. She remembered the man with the silver car who had only wanted to ask her a question. The boots walked toward the desk and stopped.

Above her, the lamplight turned, a spotlight toward the middle of the trailer, and then a figure appeared in the glow—a dark ball cap obscuring the face, gloves covering the hands that reached for the photo frame. Jimmy had warned her not to talk about the safe—

The man raised his flashlight to the dial.

Jimmy.

Alice swallowed a gasp. She was paralyzed, could only watch as Jimmy emptied the safe and pawed through the contents. He held the flashlight in the crook of his neck, mumbling to himself as he searched through folders and paperwork, then went back to the safe.

"Dammit, where—"

His boot connected with her backpack. He reached for it, dropped it on the table, seemed to consider it. He unzipped the pack's compartments, sorted through her belongings, fanned through Lillian's research.

"What are *you* up to?" But he was only talking to himself.

She should crawl out and face him. But she couldn't.

This was not the Jimmy she knew.

She could only watch as he shoved everything back into her backpack, zipped it up, and hitched it over his shoulder. Her laptop. All the information Lillian wanted her to have.

The flashlight arced across the floor toward her, and his boots followed, approaching the desk again. She breathed shallowly.

Above her, Jimmy made a triumphant noise. Papers rustled. A zipper sounded, then again. He was putting things into *her* backpack to carry them out.

He left the doors to the safe and the trailer hanging open, the things he'd taken out and rooted through on the table. The dim lamp was left, too, turned on the scene of the crime.

Alice, under the desk, waited until she was sure he wasn't coming back. And then she waited some more.

CHAPTER TWENTY-NINE

MERRILY

Merrily's key was still in the lock when Justyce opened their door, her eyes dancing.

"What?" Merrily said. Traffic had been bad on the way back from Victorville, and she hadn't learned much, anyway. *We'll just have to go there.* But what was so important about that place? She'd lived there, and so had Rick and her mom. It was probably where they met. Big deal. The back of her shirt was damp from sweat. She wasn't in the mood.

"Your mom's here," Justyce said cheerfully. "She's currently doing your laundry."

"*What?*"

"Oh, yeah. Something about your *sheets* being a little on the stale side?"

Shit. "Why did you let her in there?"

"I am not on security duty for your crusty sheets," she said. "I'm also not the hired help. The guy they sent about the leak in the bathroom says it's fixed now, I guess? So don't take any of your free time to bother about it."

Justyce stomped away.

"There's something between friendship and hired help, you know," Merrily mumbled. She hadn't even noticed a leak in the bathroom, so how was this *her* problem?

Standing outside the open door of her room, she could hear her mother humming. Fucking Mary Poppins, dusting while she waited? Except the tune was nervous, warbling. "Mamá?" she said. Justyce wouldn't have noticed the look on her mom's face, but Merrily couldn't miss it. "What's wrong?"

"Nothing," her mom said. "I—" They could both hear Justyce in the kitchen. "Let's go for a walk or—have you had dinner?"

On the sidewalk outside the building, her mom looked around helplessly. "Why don't you live in one of those neighborhoods with cute stores and coffee shops?"

"We have cute places."

"Very cute tattoo parlor over there."

"There's a decent taco joint down a block," Merrily said, and led the way, hoping her mom wouldn't mention the body shops, the high fences with razor wire at the top, the graffiti. Wouldn't notice that "down the block" was more like two blocks. "Why are you here?"

"A mother can't stop in to see her daughter? To see where she lives? To clean up a little after some kind of sex party she has?"

"Mamá! Don't nose around if you don't want to know."

"I want to know." A dark figure walked toward them, hoodie pulled up, face obscured. Her mom moved in closer and clutched at Merrily's arm. When the man passed by, she fell away as though nothing had happened. "I want you to tell me, though, so I don't have to discover things like they are secrets."

Hypocrisy. Merrily couldn't say so. Her mom's accent was thick, upset.

"I don't have secrets." Merrily pictured the grainy, copied pages from the library's scrapbook, resting now inside the purse on her shoulder. She could almost hear them, the missing man, the missing woman, jumbled together and not getting along. She an addict, maybe worse, gone thirty years. And then him, upstanding citizen with a life and family, gone twenty. They had nothing in common other than the afterlife of that scrapbook—or was that wrong? Now that she had seen the date the guy had gone missing, she couldn't be sure. Merrily couldn't hold it all in her head.

"You don't have secrets, but where were you today? Your phone went to the recording a million times. You know I don't like that."

Her mom didn't like to leave messages, didn't like the sound of her voice and didn't want anyone to have to listen, to translate, to get it wrong, to make fun. She didn't want to leave a record, Merrily realized. She lived her life so lightly, sweeping the road behind her. Someday she wouldn't be here any longer. Would it seem as though she had never existed? Only Merrily would remember. Merrily pulled out her phone and ducked her head over it to hide her wet eyes. No messages. No notifications at all? Well, that was odd. She pressed and held down the power button to restart the phone. "I went to . . . to work on a project, and I lost track of time. None of your calls came through."

Restarted, Merrily's phone buzzed, plink-plinked, and sang for a full minute with all the messages it had been keeping to itself. Calls missed from her mom, notifications from social media, from ChatX, all of it. Merrily shielded the screen. No calls from G. Vasquez, not that she expected one. No calls from Juby or Alice. "I was out of range, I guess. Some kind of electronic road jam. No big deal."

"Out of range? Where did you go, that none of my calls came through? My texts, even? Merrily, where in God's green pasture—

No. Tell me you weren't out there messing about with all this . . . *Rick*." The way she said his name sounded like *reek*. Of scents and disgust.

"Like I said, Mamá." They had reached the taqueria, a shack of sorts with only outdoor patio seating, with Christmas lights strung overhead, all colors. She saw her mom notice them, notice the picnic benches where they were meant to eat. She knew what she would be thinking. It was too Mexican. *Well, too bad.* Merrily thought it was the right amount of Mexican. "If you don't want to know, don't come around. Don't ask."

They ordered at the window and carried their drinks to a table, her mother as elegant as possible as she hiked a leg over the bench seat. Merrily poked the lime wedge into her beer and tapped the bottle against her mom's water glass while she was fussing with paper napkins for them both. When there was nothing else to fold, place, tidy, or bother with, her mom arranged herself on the bench and looked up at the lights. "What do you think about going to Florida for a while?"

Merrily choked on her beer. "What? Why? Who do we know there?"

"Or anywhere. A few months in the sun would be nice."

It had been sunny today, all week. "What's happened?"

Her mom looked up at her. "Someone broke into the house."

"*What?* Mamá— Are you hurt?"

"I was gone," she said. "Nothing taken, I think. They barely disturbed a thing. But I could smell them."

This was the strangest thing her mom had ever said, in Merrily's memory. "You could smell them."

"Oh, yes. He used that awful green soap that only unmarried men use—"

"Should we call the police?" Officer Vasquez would know what to do, though she wasn't sure she wanted to let him loose on her mom. Or her on him.

"Nothing's gone. In fact, I wonder if— It's fine."

"We should call the police."

"It's just Rick."

Merrily sat up straight. "You think *Rick* broke in—"

"No, no. Not him. It's Rick they were looking for. Someone is always looking for Rick. Why do you think he's only at the end of a phone?"

Merrily looked her mom over, thinking about the things Vasquez shouldn't have told her. How much did her mom know? "Uhhh, because he's bad news?"

"There is worse news than Rick," her mom said. She sighed and dug out her wallet. "Go get another beer. And one for me. I need a drink."

CHAPTER THIRTY

MERRILY

The tacos arrived and were pushed to the side.

"Tell me," Merrily said.

Her mom sipped at her beer. When she put the bottle back on the table, her hands trembled, shaking the collection of bracelets at her wrists. She hid them under the table.

"You always used to tell me the truth," Merrily said. "You treated me like a real person, not a kid. All my friends envied that, you know. I probably never told you."

"I told you the truth when it was safe for you to know."

"The more I know, the safer I should be, right?" Maybe that was the part that wasn't true. "How did you meet Rick? Start there."

Her mom shrugged. "We lived in the same town, not so big a place. We knew some people in common. I met him at a party, I think. He had—"

Merrily leaned forward. "What?"

"A way to make me laugh," she said. The deep frowning line that seemed always to be between her eyes was gone.

"He's goofy," Merrily said.

"Yes, this. Goofy. An easy person to talk . . . talk, talk, that man."

"He didn't mind that you had me?"

Her mom looked at her for a long moment, her gaze turning from uncertain to loving. She reached out and placed her hand on Merrily's arm. Merrily admired the rings there, one on each finger, even the thumb, and the jangling metal bangles. "He didn't mind a thing about you." She stared at the table, then pulled her hand back. "I should have been worried about that."

"What do you mean?"

"He wasn't—he wasn't what I hoped he would be, and I couldn't have him around you."

"But you did," Merrily said. "You let him around me. The phone messages, texts. If he wasn't safe for me to be around—"

"Phone messages," her mom said, waving the phrase away with the chime of bracelets.

At her old job with Kath, they'd used a phrase for documents with a flaw of logic—*internally inconsistent*. This was what she thought of now. Something inside the stories her mom told was broken, some necessary gear stripped and spinning in place, not connecting. "You're not making any sense."

"Merrily, he kidnapped that girl."

"What? What are you *talking* about? Which girl?" But then she understood. Her mom had recognized her immediately. But— Merrily thought it through. She'd thought she'd known her immediately, too, knew in an instant who Alice was, would turn out to be. She'd been wrong. "Alice."

"Is that what they call her?"

There was a flavor to her mom's tone, a spice Merrily couldn't identify.

"You're saying that Rick kidnapped a child? First of all, I don't believe that Rick would do something like that, and second, I'm pretty sure Alice's dad used to be a cop. Why in the world would Rick kidnap—"

"Not smart," her mom said.

"—a cop's kid? And third, if he had, why would you give him my phone number, and—"

"You're getting hung up in some innocent phone messages, who cares?" The hand flip again, the bangles clanging together in a noise that made a table of young men behind them look over.

"*You*," Merrily said, "are getting hung up in your lies."

Her mom could have feigned shock, but she didn't. She peeled at the label on her beer bottle, no fight left in her. The deep divot between her eyes was back.

"This time, the truth is not safe," her mom said, her accent thick. "You need to be careful, Merrily. There are bigger things going on than you can see and . . . *stubborn* your way through."

Merrily picked up a corn chip from her plate, dropped it. "Mamá," she whispered. "Was Rick in . . . witness protection?"

Her mom's eyes rolled back. "Is that a guess? Are we stabbing the dark now?"

"Let's say I had a reliable source." *Reliable* was still up for grabs. "Someone suggested Rick might have been put into protection and swept away."

Her mom pulled her plate in front of her as though they were finished with the difficult tasks. She took a bite. "Mmmm," she murmured. "So *authentic*, this taco, just the way the white people like it."

"But he's not in protection anymore, or he would never have shown up on that missing persons site," Merrily said. That really was a guess, but some form of chaos had made Rick's disappearance public and then just as quickly pulled it down, and all while he was still missing. The bulldog and Vasquez. Shouldn't they know where he was? Was he missing from his *protectors*?

Her mom's mouth was full. She mimed at her distended cheeks like a child, like a brat, when she didn't get her way. Merrily had always wished for a baby brother or sister, but she needn't have bothered. Her own mother provided all the mischief she could handle. Her mom and Rick, of course. Why were the grown-ups in her life so damaged and needy?

Her mom was still chewing in a pantomime of effort.

Merrily felt her patience snap in two.

"He might have been in protection for a while," Merrily said. "Until someone went to visit him when they shouldn't have known where he was. Visited him where he was safe and led the exact wrong person right to him."

Across the table, her mom stopped chewing.

"Rick would have defended himself, and maybe it was helpful for people to think he was dead." The truth wasn't safe, but how bad could it be? Was Rick really the goofy guy who sent her kitten emojis, bad puns, and a *Hey, kid*? Merrily, telling herself the story, could almost justify who Rick might have become. To cover a death that couldn't be helped, to cover a life that might still be lived, to distract, if possible, those who might ask questions. A fire and, in the ashes, the body of the man who had come to kill him. Merrily reached into her bag and pulled out the pages she'd taken from the library. She dropped the article about the missing man on the table.

Her mom, pale, her mouth still full, her lips greasy, glanced from the paper, to Merrily, and to the other page in Merrily's hand, then reached for a napkin and furtively spit her mouthful of food into it.

Merrily held down the man's grainy photo with her finger. "This man," she said, "disappeared from Victorville, Indiana, too. Only . . . he was last seen the same day you and I went to see Rick. It was a *very* busy week, because that was also the day Dora, Indiana, had to get the fire engines out."

"I don't know anything about him."

"But you and I know that the body in that fire wasn't the guy living there. We've been in touch with Rick—I assume it's been Rick?—all this time. And so . . . this guy. Still missing. He left behind a family." Merrily turned the article around and found the details. "Yes, a teen son. He'd be an adult now, of course, maybe have kids himself. Think of all the things that guy missed: seeing his kid graduate, reading stories to the grandkids—"

"Stop!" Behind Merrily, the chatter at the taco shack window quieted. The occupants of the other table stared. In a lower voice, her mom said, "What do you want me to do about it? There's nothing."

"There's a body to exhume."

"Desecration."

This was as close as Merrily knew she would get to hearing the truth from her mom. "Not for his son," she said. "Not for his widow. Not for the closure they might have." She was getting near the mumbo jumbo from that website Alice supposedly worked with.

Merrily brought the other sheet of paper up and placed it next to the first. "Let's talk about her."

Her mom's eyes opened innocently. "Her who?"

"Rick's wife—"

"*She* was never his wife."

"The paper says wife."

"The paper is wrong. He was already—" Her mother stopped talking, clamped her jaw.

"He was already married to someone else."

She waggled her head, fluffed out her wild curls. The bangles at her wrists rattled together, back and forth with the motion, then again as she put her hands back down. Noise, noise, nothing but distraction.

"Not to you?" Merrily said.

"Ha!"

So there was a woman out there who still might call herself Rick's wife, and then this woman, Laura Banks, Laura Not-Banks, missing. Merrily turned the article about her around, found the date, stared at it. Just over thirty years. She knew what she'd been doing at the time: teething. "Mamá, did you know this woman?"

"No."

Not enough words to hear the accent, to know if there was a lie. But it felt like one. "Mamá, help me out here. Rick was dating you and then ditched us for her?"

"He was with her, and *then* me." This time Merrily caught the precise tone, one of triumph.

"You stole him away?"

The head waggle again, so pleased with herself she couldn't help but gloat.

"So when he left the area, when he was—" Merrily looked around, suddenly aware of how candidly they'd been talking. She lowered her voice. "When he was *whisked away*, he was leaving her? Or you?"

"He didn't leave *me*," she said. "He never left *me*."

Aha. Merrily understood. She dug for her wallet, threw a few ones on the table, weighed them down with her empty beer bottle, and stood up, taking her copied pages with her. She was down the sidewalk when she finally heard the scurrying of someone following, someone much shorter and trying to catch up, someone with jangling jewelry.

"Merrily, stop. You with your long legs. Take pity on me—"

Merrily whirled on her, as angry as she had ever been. "Take pity? Do you know what you did? Did he ever explain it to you?"

"Why do you defend him so much? Over your own mother. You don't even know him!"

"I do know him, though. For some reason, you made sure of it, and now I have to wonder why you risked it."

"Risked . . ."

"He was in hiding, Mamá. From dangerous people, or he wouldn't have agreed to it. But you took the people looking for him right to his front door! He could have died, and someone did—"

"But not a good man."

Merrily opened her mouth to shout something but then swallowed it. Her mom was right. The person who had come to that house and been killed in it, burned, would not have been a good man. He would have been trying to silence Rick, silence whatever it was Rick might be willing to tell. He would have been someone dangerous. But people were still looking for Rick. They were still looking, and they had broken into her mom's home. These people still wanted something and knew where her mom lived. Knew where to find them now.

"Mamá," she murmured, and pulled her mom into her arms. She was small, like a child, fragile. And yet she had survived something she couldn't yet talk about. "Come on, let's go. Let's find somewhere better to stay the night."

Back at her apartment, they packed Merrily's clothes and the things she had borrowed from her mom, now that they'd been laundered. The sheets, forgotten. While her mom's back was turned, Merrily reached into her closet and pulled down the box with the photos Rick had left behind and dumped them, loose, into her overnight bag. In her doorway, she gazed around to see

if she'd missed anything important. She felt as though she were
leaving for a long time.

Her mom waited in the hall while Merrily left a note for Justyce:
Gone to Mamá's for a while. That was not where they were going. She struggled with whether to give Justyce a warning. But
what could she say? The less Justyce knew, the better. She held her
phone in her hand, her thumb hovering over G. Vasquez's number, and then Juby's. They didn't need to go as far away as Florida,
did they? They only needed to be surrounded by people. They only
needed friends.

Later, in the dark of her car, Merrily said, "You thought she
went with Rick into hiding. Laura."

"I never thought that." Thick tongue, the spice of untruth.

But Merrily remembered the two of them arguing in the playground in Dora. He had never left Mamá Cruz. She hadn't let him.
For some strange reason, her mom had forced Rick to stay in their
lives when she could have let him go to hell. And now they all might.

CHAPTER THIRTY-ONE

ALICE

Hers was the last car in the lot. Alice fumbled with the key fob and then the door, threw herself inside. Doors locked, she grasped her phone with both hands, putting all her thoughts on the other side. *Please.*

"Hello?" Juby answered with real curiosity but also a stiffness Alice recognized from their last conversation.

"I have another favor to ask," Alice said. "I'm sorry, but—I—could I—"

"Are you OK? I can't hear you."

"Someone broke into the trailer. My work." She had managed to get out of the shed and the site, leaving the broken padlock hanging. Jimmy had broken the padlock, like a common burglar. She was shaking. "I managed to hide, but—"

"You were there? OK, wow. Do you need to call the cops?"

The cop she needed to call was her dad. But—Jimmy. She didn't know what to do. The truth made no sense. But to tell her dad anything other than the truth—it was better not to call until she knew more. She didn't want him running home, not on her account.

She couldn't face her dark apartment, though, security cameras or no. "Can I come over? I—I need to go where someone else is."

Juby didn't say anything at first. "Don't get mad."

She'd had the sense that Juby was mad at her, and it was a relief to be offered a scrap. "Why would I get mad?"

"Hold on."

When Juby came back on the line, she had an address.

"Is this . . . where is this?" The address was near the posh building in the south Loop that King and Fine had constructed. "That's tourist country."

"It's a hotel," Juby said meekly. "I'm meeting Merrily there in an hour."

Alice looked out at the parking lot dreamily. That was her hand gripping the steering wheel. Her other hand, holding her phone in her lap, Juby's name and number displayed. That was Juby's voice calling to her from the end of her arm. "Hello? Hello? Alice?"

They were doing it. They were going on with the search for her Doe without her.

She put the phone back to her ear. "Why is Merrily *here*?"

"Well, she lives on the *South Side*. It's not like she's driving in from Mars. Something about her mom—"

"Her mom lives in *Indiana*."

"An hour away, Alice. I guess they got broken into, too—"

"When?" Could Jimmy be making trouble out there? Why? She'd told him, she realized. She'd told him that she knew Merrily, that they were getting to know one another. Given him a name he could chase down.

She shivered. Jimmy King? Her childhood playmate, her first crush? Why was he doing this to them? To what end?

"What does it matter, when?" Juby said. "Tonight, I guess. You can ask her. They're checking into a cheaper place down the street and then she's coming out for a drink."

"And the plan is to what? Talk about her poor, poor sainted not-even-stepdad, who happens—"

"I get it," Juby said. "No one owns all the shit here, though. Plenty to go around. Come have a drink with us, talk about stuff, don't talk about stuff. If you still need a place to crash, you can come to my house afterward."

Alice thought about hanging up. She never had to speak to Juby again. They might show up on the same thread on the Doe Pages' chat, but they didn't have to interact. It would be so easy, no good-byes, just the simple snip of Juby's number from her phone. *Beep boop.*

"Just a heads-up," Juby said. "My house is actually my parents' house. No *jokes.* Also, fair warning that my mom will definitely force-feed you before you can go to bed. Remember how her oldest kid went missing? She'll—she might *adopt* you."

Alice made an appreciative noise in her throat. She could sever ties with Juby—but she didn't want to. *This is what friendship is.* It was a lot of hard work, is what it was.

For a Monday night this late, traffic into the city was heavy, and then the dark sky above opened up. Alice hit the windshield wipers and inched along, hunched over the steering wheel. An accident, maybe. She tuned the radio to soothing music but it didn't help.

Jimmy the thief.

Was he teaching her some kind of lesson?

Gathering intel to hold the company hostage? To mess with them, feed their competitors?

Was he so mad the company wouldn't someday be his that he

was willing to rob it blind? But what that slick-haired man-child had stolen were mostly files that were backed up elsewhere. But *her* computer, *her* wallet. He hadn't laid waste to King and Fine, but he was giving her a bad day.

If she hadn't had her phone in her pocket and her keys tossed on her desk, she'd be marooned back at the site, filing a police report.

Her fingers tapped on the steering wheel. She should be at the site, filing a police report. Or—

Alice pressed a few buttons on the steering wheel and asked the onboard system to call her dad's cell number. It rang out for a while. She was composing a calm voice mail she'd leave when her dad picked up the phone. "Hey, Al, what's up?"

It was such a relief to hear his voice she almost sobbed. "Nothing," she said, gaining control. "Missing you. Are you ever coming home?"

"I'll assume this is from love and not because of some new mess the Jims have gotten us into."

She listened to his laugh. "Not a new mess, no."

"Oh, boy, what's going on?"

"Hold on." Her car was creeping past the accident. The highway was six lanes wide a mile or so outside of downtown, a parking lot of red taillights up to the site of the wreck, a crumple of machinery at the median. She wouldn't look. She wouldn't.

Quickly, the traffic broke up, gained speed.

"Are you in the car?" her dad said. "You know how I feel about you on the phone while driving . . ."

"It was all backed up—"

"But now it's not." Harris Fine, always a cop. "I have to run, anyway. You get home safe, that's all I care about."

She had to say something about the break-in. And Jimmy. "Dad—"

"Whatever it is, we can fix it up tomorrow, OK? I'll be in early."

She let out the breath she was holding. "Love you."

"Love you more."

When he hung up, the radio came back on, news, something about a protest staged in D.C. that day. She noted the time. She shouldn't have even called him, it was so late, and who knew how late it was in—

She couldn't remember where he'd traveled this week, and she hadn't asked.

She hadn't asked him anything. The ownership thing. The discrepancy in how far Matt had fallen. The break-in. She should have led with the break-in. She was complicit, for some reason letting Jimmy get away with whatever he was up to. She traced her feelings to their source, and discovered she was amused. Jimmy King thought he was smarter than the rest of them. More than wanting to stop him, Alice wanted to see him lose. She wanted to watch what would happen.

Curiosity fed on itself, never sated.

Alice let the highway split toward Wisconsin, toward Indiana, holding steady east toward the skyline and onto city streets still busy with cabs and ride shares, with late-nighters and the late-shifters. She drove straight toward the hotel address Juby had provided, but at the last minute, instead of turning toward the hotel, she hung a right on Michigan Avenue.

Down the block, the high-rise at 1799 South Michigan, King and Fine's grand masterpiece, rose high above its neighbors. A beacon, calling her home.

She took too much pride in it. Her satisfaction had nothing to do with who owned the company, who put in the last rivet, who smoothed the concrete, who would cut the big ribbon with ceremonial scissors on Friday. She wasn't responsible for any of it.

Her sense of ownership had been earned, though. She'd driven this route every day for almost two years, worked the phones, headed off the problems, stayed late. They'd built this cathedral, and her role—

She didn't just sweep the trailer floor. What she truly did was absorb all the trouble that occurred among the crew and between JimBig, Jimmy, and her dad, all the discontent above and below, witnessing and listening, accepting all the worry and letting it live inside her. She had always served that role, at home as well as at the site and inside the shed. She absorbed free-floating conflict. She kept the dust down.

So if she took a little pride in their south Loop jewel, she thought she was allowed.

In the last block, she slowed to let the building slide up to her. She pulled over to the opposite curb. The city had installed raised medians to keep pedestrians from crossing except at crosswalks, planters with thin trees and hardy ornamental grasses. Overhead, the building glowed like something out of an old-time movie, like something King Kong had climbed. The shops on the first floor were dark at this hour, but above, some of the offices burned the midnight oil. The next twenty-five floors were condos, lit up like a game board, a light here, there, a guessing game of who had insomnia, who had too much work from the office, who was up binge-watching TV.

And then the cherry on top, the top floor, lit like a parade float. The rest of the block was quiet, dark, caught in a lull between L trains passing through. A few blocks away, Roosevelt Avenue still roared with traffic. Another night, this might be a busy thorough-fare after the final inning of a White Sox game, but tonight the sidewalks were rolled up.

The radio murmured: stock prices and the NASDAQ, a little

tune to transition from national news to local. Alice put the car into park, rolled down the window, and leaned her head against the frame. She might like finished projects more than the grime of construction and progress. In this, she was not her father's daughter. He loved to build, but the second the project was over, he itched for the next. Alice liked the build, too, but she loved the details of living, of home. Home was everything. Maybe that's why the Doe Pages had drawn her in. Matching an Empty had everything to do with the details of a life that, once noticed, could only lead home. That crooked tooth, the birthmark on the back of the neck, that scar from a childhood fall. Set dressing that turned out to be structural.

". . . body found this morning in the Indiana Dunes National Park, within three miles of Lake Michigan," the murmuring radio said.

Alice reached for the volume.

Only because she'd been thinking of the Doe Pages, only because she was on her way to see Merrily, did it occur to her. The body could be Richard Banks. It wouldn't be, would it? But in all his lives, he'd never wandered too far from the area, even with his life in danger—*Why was that? A detail of living*—not far from where he'd kidnapped her and disappeared, not far from where he'd been some kind of father figure for Merrily, not far from the casino and Rebekah and her daughter.

It wouldn't be him. The sad fact was that the area saw more than its share of bodies.

". . . a Caucasian male of approximately forty-five to sixty-five years old. The man has scarring on an upper arm, from an injury or tattoo removal. Tonight, police are seeking anyone who may . . ."

The *scarring.* She recognized the detail from his Doe profile.

He was dead, then.

She was strangely frustrated, even a little sad. There was nothing left to do, no way to understand. It would be an untidy ending. Lillian had warned her.

Alice had a fleeting thought for Merrily. Well, she'd have to live with it, the way you had to. She was only lucky Rick wasn't her dad, hadn't taken out his proclivities on her. Merrily was a lucky one, too.

Alice heard the announcer give the time, checked the dash. She put the car into gear and pulled into the center lane to find a break in the median and make a U-turn. No traffic was coming either way, so the U was an easy maneuver, until a large, dark SUV rushed out of the parking garage in the sub-level of 1799 South Michigan like a tank.

She pulled hard into the median, barely missing the corner of a concrete planter. She laid on the horn. An oversized hulk of a machine, the SUV still moved so quickly that it was halfway down the block before Alice could think anything other than prayers and foul phrases. Before she could consider how much the SUV had looked like one of the two King and Fine company vehicles, and wonder if Jimmy hadn't stolen one of them, too.

CHAPTER THIRTY-TWO

MERRILY

Merrily walked down Michigan Avenue toward the bar Juby had selected. It would be a hotel bar, nothing special, but that didn't matter. Her mom was calmed and tucked up in the room they'd booked, and she was downtown, walking the Magnificent Mile like a red carpet. Midnight, a Monday. Her old life was like a movie she'd watched once, something she would have fallen asleep to. Unless one of her guys had been looking for her to chat, she'd be in her pajamas by now, maybe making dinner out of a single bag of microwave popcorn, savoring the butter and salt on her fingers. One of her guys would have paid a premium to watch that.

Actually, one of them might throw some ChatX coin for a pic of her now. She'd gone to the trouble of putting on a pair of high-heeled booties and a short, silver trench coat with a belt, pieces that she'd never had quite the occasion to wear. She hadn't had the kind of life that required them.

Merrily stopped, opened the trench, arranged the neck of her blouse to show a bit of cleavage, pulled out her phone to snap a shot to send to the guys later, the tall buildings of the skyline over her shoulder. Maybe she'd send it to Vasquez, too.

She had a notification from ChatX. Searcher6. *You busy?* it said. The message was from within the last hour. They had talked for an hour the last time he'd reached out, but she didn't have that kind of time now. Still, it was Searcher.

Only a little, she messaged. *Visiting the Magnificent Mile!*

He got back right away. Logged in again, or still? Sometimes she wondered what these guys did for a living, that they were so available every time she showed up.

His message read: *I live in Chicago!*

She hadn't remembered that, and clearly she'd never mentioned to him that she also lived there. *Great city!* she texted. *Luckily, a big one.*

A split second later came his response: *What are you in town for?*

What was she in town for? Sanctuary. A long story, and one she wouldn't tell. She sent him an enthusiastic lie about visiting friends and shopping. She sort of hated Mer-Maid, if she was honest.

A group of men in red and black sportswear, yelling and laughing, were coming down the street toward her. She tucked herself against the stone wall of the nearest building but looked up as they passed, noticing them noticing her. A transaction of appraisal and appreciation. In real life, peeping was free. Though sometimes looks were so disgustingly physical, she should be allowed to charge.

Searcher's next message appeared. *Sounds fun . . .*

Dot, dot, dot. Merrily waited, impatient. She'd never wished Searcher6 away before. He was always good for an airdrop into her account and not too much bother. A nice guy who probably traveled for work, needed someone on tap, and if he was getting off on anything she did or said, then he was memorizing her for activities performed decidedly off-line. He didn't waste her time.

She swiped through the photos she'd just taken and sent him one. What did Searcher6 need tonight? Real girl? Fantasy? One photo, could go either way. He already knew she was in Chicago, so . . . Dot, dot, dot.

His immediate response: *Damn.*

She smiled. That should tide him over. But her phone buzzed in her hand again immediately, three texts, one right after the other.

Would you ever see me in person, Mer-Maid?
You asked me what I wanted.
I would make it worth your time.

A car horn blared out in the street. Merrily looked up from the phone. She had a sick-gut feeling, sour. She'd never met any of her guys in the flesh, but she knew some of the girls used ChatX that way and made a living. Made more than a living. Student loans, paid. Cars bought for cash. Down payments for high-end apartments. She'd heard the stories of the lucky ones.

What she thought of, however, were the pages and pages of missing girls on that website Juby and the others worked with. Girls unlucky in birth, in love, in career, in timing. How many corners could you turn and run into your own death? It was already a dangerous world; she didn't need to go increasing her chances by becoming an actual . . .

She couldn't think the word, couldn't let it in. Once it took up residence, she might not resist the next opportunity.

Merrily pulled her trench coat tight around her.

This was Searcher6, though. She moved her thumb over his avatar photo: the line of his jaw, the fine golden hairs across an excellent wrist. She had her own fantasies, a couple of months of daydreams built around this one man.

He hadn't sent any other messages. She liked that, liked that he wasn't explaining himself away, backpedaling out of shame. He was a real man, and he wanted her. He wouldn't apologize for that.

At last, she typed: *Let me think about it.*

Merrily put her phone into her pocket and moved down the street, more aware of dark doorways, of people passing her in the other direction. She was freaked out, actually, suddenly alert to being a woman walking down a street in a hard town, alone.

She pulled the phone back out of her pocket and held it to her, hurrying a bit around the corner toward the well-lit front doors of the hotel. It was not just some hotel bar. She let the doorman open the door for her into the ornate, gilded entrance and stood looking around at the opulence of the lobby until her phone buzzed in her hand.

Searcher *again.*

Think about it. I am. As she read it, a second notification alerted her that a cool thousand dollars had been deposited into her account. A thousand, simply to think about it, to entertain the idea of meeting him, maybe in a hotel like this one, claw-foot tub, bubble bath, champagne, *Pretty Woman* rescue into a new life.

While she was staring at the deposit message, another notification came in. *Send me another pic. I like to see you enjoying my city.*

That was easy enough. She held up her camera, framing herself against a bronzed stair railing and a darkened shop window. People brushed past her as she positioned the phone just so, curled her lips into flirtation. Not too sexy. He was already hungry.

Merrily sent the photo and then wandered up the stairs into a central court, the ceiling soaring and golden-gorgeous. Like the Sistine Chapel. Was that what a fresco was? Juby waved to her from a small table tucked away in the corner of the room with a squat palm tree throwing fronds out in defense, shielding them. "Alice is coming, too," Juby said, first thing.

"Oh," Merrily said.

"Is that OK?"

"Why wouldn't it be OK?" But she was a little disappointed not to have Juby's undivided attention.

The waiter had the sullen look of someone who had not expected a life of service. He placed a menu of shockingly expensive cocktails into their hands and departed. Juby turned her attention to the drinks. Merrily nudged a palm frond away from her shoulder, thinking wistfully of Searcher6's ability to drop a thousand dollars on a whim. How badly did he want to meet her? Ten thousand dollars' worth? Twenty? She forced herself back to the menu. She could afford a drink, at least. "So how did Alice—why is she—?" Most of the phrasings that came to mind sounded too possessive of Juby.

"She's had a little life experience tonight and wanted some company." Juby tapped her teeth. "Life experience calls for a sweet cocktail or two."

"What about your other friend?"

"Lillian needs her rest," Juby said. "But she'll yell at me tomorrow when she hears I let her have some."

Merrily wondered at the list of drinks. "Is she your . . . grandma?"

"What? No, we work together. God. Good thing I didn't invite her, or she'd be over the table at your throat."

"Sorry, it's just you said you'd see her tomorrow, and I know you saw her—"

"Colleagues," Juby said, putting her menu up, a barrier. "And we both help at the Doe Pages, too."

"How did you start doing that, if you don't mind me asking?"

"I mind," Juby said pleasantly.

They ordered lavish drinks and then sat waiting for them. Without the others there, Juby was less vibrant than Merrily remembered. Or maybe she was having a bad day, too.

"I brought some photos," Merrily said. She'd sorted them while her mom was in the shower, looking for those that would help Juby understand that Rick was a real person. King Richard! He had been someone's little boy. But she hadn't found the photo of Rick as a tiny guy. She remembered propping it up on her desk back at her apartment, but then had missed it somehow when she packed her bag. She brought others instead, a few snapshots of Rick as a young and virile guy. He was someone. He mattered.

She pulled the photos out of her purse. It was a cute purse, and she was glad, given her surroundings, that she'd carried it and worn the booties. She let her long hair wave over her shoulder, imagining her photo was being taken in this decadent room, imagining someone watching, admiring. "I just wanted—I don't know. To show you that—"

"That he's a real person and that people loved him, but not you."

"Did I do something to piss you off?"

Juby grabbed the photos and sorted through them. "No, you didn't."

Merrily watched. "Did Alice?"

Juby had paused on one of the photos. "That's Richard, right?" She turned it around. It was a shot of young, handsome, letter-jacket Rick laughing, his date turned in profile toward him. "I've seen his high school yearbook photo, but he wasn't smiling."

"You've seen his *yearbook*?"

Juby glanced over. "Well, yeah. We've seen everything by now. Maybe. Most everything. Who's this woman with him?"

"One of his girlfriends, I guess." Merrily paused as the waiter returned and set down the two tall glasses, pale pink and yellow.

"I'm only lucky my mom didn't tear up all the photos of him with other women."

"He had a lot of other women?"

"Well." Merrily didn't like this line of inquiry. It made Rick seem like a boar, not like little King Richard at all. Not worth rescuing. "He was married, we established that. And then . . . I have it on pretty good authority that he had some kids, but severed all ties to them. But not because he wanted to." She left out the witness protection thing—this was a public relations battle.

"We found one of them," Juby said. She was going through the photos again, sorting them into piles. "Daughter. Natallie. If Lillian were here, she could track Natallie through public records before the ice melts in this drink."

"Natallie." Merrily's mouth was dry.

"He seems to like this beach a lot," Juby said.

Merrily turned her attention to the array of photos on the table in front of them. Juby had sorted them into a solitaire-like arrangement: young Rick, dating Rick, family Rick. Not all the divisions were immediately clear to her. "Beach?"

"Look, he's fishing here. He's camping, I guess, here. He's got a bonfire going in that one. See this house in the corner?" Juby pointed to a photo with Rick in a camp chair sitting in front of a firepit with a hot dog on a two-pronged barbecue fork, his head turned as he talked to someone off-camera. In the background sat a wood-slatted building with Swiss chalet windows crisscrossed with white lattice. "It's the same one here, I'd wager." Juby pointed again. The second photo was black-and-white, but the house, the same windows, loomed in the background. In the foreground, a slip of campfire and Rick, cross-legged in a folding chair. A woman embraced him from behind, standing, her long black hair sweeping across her face and over his shoulder, almost in motion. They were both smiling, laughing. "Where is this beach?"

She didn't know. Merrily reached for one of the fishing photos—there were many, once you sorted them out—and found in the reflection of Rick's aviator sunglasses the distended view of the same house, crisscross chalet windows. "I'm not sure. I don't think I've ever been there. Maybe my mom would know."

"Would she tell us, though?" Juby sat back, reached for her phone.

Merrily grabbed for her drink. It was as though Juby had reached into her chest for her still-beating heart. She knew right where to punch through, how deep to dig, how hard to pull. Merrily's mom was all she had, but she was also a brat, a kicking, screaming child monarch who could demand anything—

"King Richard," Merrily said. "King Richard conquers the dunes."

"*What* are you talking about?"

"The Indiana Dunes—that's a beach, isn't it? He was a kid there. Maybe that's a place he returned to—" She picked up the photos one after another. "Again and again. Maybe that's where he is *now*. That's not far from where we lived, or where he lived when—" She couldn't remember if she'd told them about the fire or not, couldn't keep track of who knew what.

Juby already had her nose to her phone.

Yes, she'd told them about the fire. She plunged back in. "When the fire burned down that house. Dora, Indiana, isn't that far from the dunes."

"It's not far from Milwaukee, either," Juby murmured to herself. "It's not a great place to hide, though, is it?"

"Anywhere people don't expect you to be is a good place to hide."

Alice was suddenly standing at their table. "You guys—"

"The dunes," Merrily said triumphantly. Juby swept the photos of Rick off the table.

"I know—"

"We know where he is," Merrily said. Juby handed the photos to Merrily, gesturing toward her purse. Merrily tucked them away impatiently. "We have to go—"

"That's what I'm trying to say," Alice said. "I heard on the radio on the way in—"

"Oh, no," Juby said into her phone screen.

Alice sank into the seat between them. "A body," she said. "There's been a body found, with the tattoo scarring on his arm. I think it's Richard."

C0000KIES: Shit, you guys. I think that Empty who dropped off the site just got found. Dead.

SparkleSoo RE: @C0000KIES Oh noooooo. Was hoping it was good news for him.

MrJonesToYou RE: RE: @SparkleSoo Have you noticed how little good news there is around here?

Dreaming312 RE: RE: RE: @MrJonesToYou It really depends on your perspective.

MrJonesToYou RE: RE: RE: . . . @Dreaming312 You're kind of a creep, you know that?

Audrey89: RE: RE: RE: . . . @MrJonesToYou SAYS THE ORIGINAL CREEP.

MrJonesToYou RE: RE: RE: . . . @Audrey89 I may be a creep but I'm YOUR creep. Who is this guy with his weird self-portrait? If you use your own photo but won't show anything but your WRIST, there is something going on with your FACE or with your INTENTIONS.

Audrey89: RE: RE: RE: . . . @MrJonesToYou AND MR JONES HAS SPOKEN.

JennDoePagesMOD: Let's settle down over here. @MrJonesToYou, please be our creep with a little less all-caps, OK?

SparkleSoo: Oh, that's weird. That Dreaming312 guy's account just disappeared.

MrJonesToYou: RE: @SparkleSoo Good riddance to lurkers.

CHAPTER THIRTY-THREE

MERRILY

Merrily flicked palm fronds away from her neck and reached for her silly drink. Her hand shook. She pulled it back.

"I'm sorry," Alice said to her.

"We don't know it's him." It wasn't him. It couldn't be. Not Rick. She took out her phone, pulled up Officer Vasquez's number, and tapped out a text: *Body found in the Dunes not him right?* "It's not."

Her mom. What could she say to her? Nothing. Nothing for now. She held the phone to her chest and tried to breathe. Not him. It couldn't be.

"I think we need to accept the possibility—"

"No!" It was a big room, and everyone in it turned to look their way. She'd wanted to be watched, hadn't she? In a lowered voice, she said, "I don't need to accept it. It's not him. It won't be him. Remember the fire? The body that wasn't him? It won't be him."

"It was *someone* in that fire. Do you think it's weird that you're hoping he leaves another dead human being in his wake?" Juby said.

"That's not what I meant," Merrily said.

"But if it's not him, then it's someone else," Alice said. "Someone's dead." She glanced toward the nearest table. "Maybe we should go somewhere else to talk."

Merrily stood up. "I don't want to talk." She had no idea where she was going. If she saw her mom right now, she would break down and her mom would call Rick some disparaging word and then she'd have to feel pathetic for liking the guy, for wanting him to be alive. Not that he was dead. It wouldn't be him.

"Come on, Merrily," Juby said. "It's not him, OK? It could be some other person found dead in the dunes, right? Someone drowned, maybe." Alice turned toward the awkward hope in her voice.

"Then let's go to the dunes right now," Merrily said. "I'll drive."

The other two women didn't move, wouldn't look at her. Juby said, "I don't think that's a great idea. Stay in town with your mom, go shopping or something, take your mind off—"

"I'm not *shopping*." She couldn't make herself understood. It wasn't him, but what if it was? She couldn't walk up and down the Mag Mile having the time of her life. In her hand, her phone buzzed. G. Vasquez.

I am not your cop boyfriend, Nancy Drew.

Fine for him. This was why she didn't waste her time with—*with real men*. "I'm going."

Alice put a hand out before Juby could jump in. "Is that a great idea? If it's him or if it's not him—is it better to go there and be frustrated and kept away, or is it better to wait and see?"

At some point, without Lillian, Alice had decided she was the leader, the big sister, that she got to be the voice of reason. Merrily didn't have to listen to them. Who were they to her? She wanted to leave. The destination didn't have to be the dunes. She didn't know where to look, anyway, and the beach would be closed off with this body—this other person, this stranger—found. The dunes weren't a single beach. They were miles of sand, miles of places to hide, to be found, not to be found. Miles and miles of sand and lakeshore. She'd been once or twice, her mom bursting from a bikini and the men turning to watch as the two of them carried their picnic basket. She needed to be somewhere else, though, to be someone else, right now.

Merrily pressed the heel of her hand to her eye. She was going to lose it.

Her phone *plink-plinked* the news she had a ChatX notification. Searcher6, *again*, with something else to say. She was tired of men. Exhausted. Weary of them, always wanting, wanting. Even with the tips into her account, it wasn't worth it, to give so much of her time away. To give so much of *herself*, and then have to cover for the missing pieces. She had hollowed herself out and draped the gaps with secrets, and for what? She pulled up his latest messages.

I recognized the hotel from your photo, the first said. *Forgive me.*

The penthouse suite is ours. Now.

Merrily's stomach fell to her feet. He was breaking every rule, online and otherwise. What was that *now* about?

But she knew she would go, even as she thought of all the ways she should scold him, take back the power she held. She was in charge. She called the shots. It wasn't seedy or sad—she was queen of this board, all moves were hers. And she was going to remind him of that, upstairs in the penthouse, with a glass of real champagne in her hand. Away from here and these people, in any case.

"What's going on?" Juby said.

"I'm meeting a friend." Merrily tried to sound calm.

"I thought you were having a drink with us," Alice said, picking up the drinks menu.

Merrily reached for her glass and threw back the last of it, set the glass down harder than she'd meant to. Then she went for her wallet, reaching into her purse past the photos of Rick, steeling herself for his youthful grin, for that hot dog *ploinked* onto the roasting fork, and threw a fistful of bills onto the table, as much cash as she had on her.

"Whoa," Juby said. "I think a twenty should do it." She pawed through the bills and Merrily knew she would try to hand back the rest, a gesture so cheap and degrading that she turned and stalked away to avoid it. She didn't look back when Juby called to her, only located the registration desk and directed her attention there. Every move was her move, and if she believed it, if she convinced herself, then she might convince everyone else.

CHAPTER THIRTY-FOUR
ALICE

Alice and Juby watched Merrily stalk away.

"That was weird," Alice said.

Juby glared at her. "It depends on your definition of *weird*. The bar is high."

Speaking of bars. Alice hailed the waiter. Things might be clearer with a gin and tonic in her hand.

"Did we have a fight at some point?" Alice said.

Juby sighed. "You and me? No."

"You and Lillian?"

Juby looked away.

"*About* me," Alice said.

Juby leaned over her elbows on the table between them. "Sometimes you're able to see clearly through the garbage to the finest sliver of truth, and sometimes you're a fucking brick, you know that?"

"Me? Specifically me?"

"Total brick."

"Tell me, then. What am I such an idiot about?"

Juby stirred her drink with her finger, sucked at it. "Let me tell you a story—"

"I would love nothing more—"

"And you shut it while I do." Juby sat back, crossed her legs. A man at a nearby table turned to admire her. Alice made a face at him. "When I first started helping out at the Doe Pages, I was so excited. I was too excited. I thought I was going to solve every case, that all I had to do was pick up a little slack and I'd get match after match. You probably felt the same way."

Alice knew better than to answer. The waiter returned and put down her drink.

"I made a mistake," Juby said, when they were alone again. "I got really into this Empty case out of California and decided I had found the UID match, some remains in Oregon. The timing of the woman going missing was right, the age, the racial makeup, the clothes. She had the mole, right here, on her upper arm. My first match. I thought. You know Don and Jenn's strict rules about what happens next. You submit to the site managers. They decide if they agree. *They* reach out to the family of the missing—"

"Oh, no," Alice breathed.

Juby raised an imperious finger. "Right. I went around that. I reached out to the family because I was so sure. And you can imagine the rest. It was not a match. The body I was convinced was their mother, sister, aunt—that UID had already been considered and ruled out. It was not her, and I broke their hearts all over again. I inserted myself into a situation without knowing enough, and all I did was hurt people. Left, right, center, I hurt people."

"You were only trying—"

She raised the finger again. "I went about it thinking only of my own feelings, my own goals. I didn't think about the people who had the most to lose. I didn't think. I was impatient. I flouted the rules put in place by people with far more experience than I had, than I have now. I was too busy trying to tell people how and what and when and why, instead of letting the information rest its own case."

Juby reached for her drink, the finger now put to use stirring again. Alice waited. "And?"

"And so that is what I'm doing right now, even though it is not my style."

Alice thought of the impervious stack of pages she'd gained and then lost. "It's Lillian's."

"After much *discussion*, we're going with the Slapdash model. 'Slapdash' is sarcasm, if you haven't figured that out by now. Lillian's style is to collect information, all information, too much information, until you think you'll drown in it. And then we surf it, we sort, we swim in it until we know . . . everything. She makes me crazy, but it's the way she does it, and it works. She's had how many matches?"

"Two," Alice said.

"'Two matches in *fifteen years*.'" Juby shook her head. "I don't think I have it in me. But that's how Lil does it. That's how Don and Jenn do it. The people who caught the Golden State Killer, the guy who matched that body in Kentucky thirty years after she was found. Tent Girl. Do you think Todd Matthews woke up one day thirty years in and just matched Tent Girl out of the blue? This is a *marathon*."

Alice pictured Lillian, always breathless. In her pocket, her phone buzzed. *Rnn.* She ignored it. "This reminds me of a story my dad tells about construction," she said. "You know, how the little daily projects that don't seem like much still add up to the cathedral. You're putting down the stones or you're building a cathedral, it's all in your perspective. The skyscraper—or the six-story parking structure, I suppose. Either way, you have to put down the foundation."

Juby looked at Alice over the rim of her glass, then crunched on an ice cube. "And if the foundation is rotten?"

"Oh, you're totally fucked."

Juby nodded. "Did you get a chance to look at the information Lil put together?"

Alice sucked in a shaky breath. "It was stolen."

"It was—" Juby stuttered but found no further words.

"That's the break-in I told you about."

"Your office was burglarized and they took three inches of Doe research?"

"And my wallet." Alice's phone buzzed again. She took it out to silence it and saw a text from a number she didn't know. When she clicked on it, she saw it was not the first message from this secret admirer but the third, at least. She'd block it later. "And my laptop. And some stuff from our vault."

"Vault? Like black velvet bags of diamonds or what?"

"Just company information, nothing valuable."

"Then why take it?" Juby said.

The very question. "I don't know."

"Corporate espionage?"

"From competitors, you mean? Maybe." Alice didn't want to incriminate Jimmy yet, not until she understood it better.

But without admitting she knew the thief, Juby didn't get her anxiety. "He got an old computer and your wallet," she said. "It sucks, but it doesn't seem like anything to be scared about." Juby yawned into the back of her hand. "Just call the cops."

"I will." She sounded defensive. "I didn't want to face it all on my own. I guess I got worked up over nothing. I'm more calm now."

"So . . . place to crash tonight or no?"

Juby's mother feeding her and tutting over her, finding the clean sheets for the couch—it was tempting, to be fed real food. *Adopted*, Juby's word. What would that feel like? To be mothered by someone who wanted the job? *My kidnapper wanted more than my own mother*— But this was the darkest thing Alice had ever allowed herself to think. The black wings were beating at her peripheral vision. That fucking bird. She drowned it with her drink.

"I'm fine," Alice said. "You should go home to bed."

After Juby left, Alice stayed at the table, waving the waiter off a second drink. She would have to drive home to Glen Park, the safest suburb in the world, where the security cameras didn't need to feed anywhere. She had a few bucks from her emergency stash in her car, but Merrily had thrown down enough for all of them. When Alice's phone buzzed in her pocket again, she took it out and gazed at the texts, all from the unknown number. *Caller Unk.*, she thought.

The first message: *Some pleasure reading?*

The second message was blank, but had an attachment. The third was another attachment. Dick pics? While she tried to decide if she ought to click—*were viruses spread this way?*—she got another one and chanced it. The attachment was one of the articles from the teetering stack Lillian had pulled together.

Jimmy King, taunting her.

But why? Why bother using a burner phone to send her the things he could have simply returned? All this to make her life miserable?

Jimmy, she typed. She stopped herself, deleted the draft, stood, and headed for the exit.

Yeah, she wasn't scared anymore. She was mad. Let him play his little game. It was Fine versus King, and he was losing. And he had no idea.

CHAPTER THIRTY-FIVE
MERRILY

The bellhop led Merrily to the elevator and offered to see her to the top floor. She wished she'd kept a few dollars for him, for the quiet way he took in that she had no luggage. Discretion. She might have had him take her up and then had Searcher tip the man, but she didn't want money exchanging hands just yet. Didn't want the scale to start so low.

The bellman inserted a key card into the elevator panel, pushed the button for her, and stepped back for the doors to close. She pretended he wasn't there, and then he wasn't.

Eighth floor. Did it make sense that the penthouse suite was on the eighth floor, though there were floors above that? How was it a penthouse, then? *If you have enough money*, she thought, *you could call anything what you damn well pleased.*

In the elevator, she leaned into the mirrored wall and checked her teeth, her breath, her hair, her cleavage. She was glad again of the coat, the cute shoes and bag, but also her long legs, her height. She imagined walking into the room, projecting the authority that Searcher had stolen.

The elevator opened up to a small entry, tastefully decorated. It seemed a shame, a waste of effort that so few people would ever experience. But maybe that was the point of wealth. Merrily admired the white marbled floor. How few people had ever stood in this place?

The door to the suite stood open a few inches. She pulled the handle, walked through, clamping down on the urge to gaze around in wonder, to covet the lavish room and everything in it, until she'd been properly introduced. She'd enjoy every inch of the suite once she'd been invited to.

He wasn't there.

A fleeting relief washed over her. Maybe she'd get the room for the night without having to figure out who he needed her to be. Was it possible?

She got out her phone. *The room is ours.* That's what he'd said.

Merrily's plan for coolness, for remove, started to fade.

She stood at the top of three steps that led into a sunken seating area, where two couches faced one another. In the corner, a gas fireplace sat cold. The room was dark, lit only by a few lamps turned low. The fine details of the room glittered and gleamed. Everywhere she looked, something had been carefully placed, layered. She allowed herself to take it all in, a feast, knowing that it had all been arranged for the viewing pleasure she now took, accepted. It was her job to taste it, to appreciate it, to appraise it, though she had no idea what such a place must cost, either to furnish it with that vase or that lacquer dish or to rent it for the night.

That's how he must have seen her, her eyes ravaging the room and her feet in the silly booties turned inward like a child. She had only found herself in a mirror across the room and seen the same vision, not at all how she had planned the moment, when he cleared his throat in the doorway from the next room.

"Good evening," he said. Even in the dark room, she could

tell he was handsome. She'd known he would be. He had always comported himself as a handsome man would—not needing anything, not asking for anything. With the confidence of a man who could have what he wanted, if he ever decided he didn't already have it. Or maybe that was his age. He was old enough to be her father, at least. The light behind him gave him a sort of halo. In his hands—Merrily noted his hands and wrists, the fine, light hairs there, the only feature of him she'd ever seen—he held aloft two flutes of sparkling wine. He raised them in a welcoming gesture.

"Hi." Nothing else occurred to her.

"I've made you nervous," he said. "That was not my aim. I only wanted to meet you, and this seemed the most likely way to make it happen. A young woman like yourself probably wouldn't come to a stranger's apartment."

He was right. But she'd come here, to territory that was far from neutral. She remembered the stoic face of the bellman as the elevator doors closed. Someone knew where she was, at least. She should have tipped him.

"I hadn't pictured you this shy," he said.

Merrily felt a prick to her professional pride. Not only hadn't she regained the upper hand, she was disappointing him. "Not shy," she said, her voice betraying her. She paused and tried again. "Admiring the room."

"It's actually six rooms, three bedrooms, all with private baths, a powder room, a dressing room, a living room, a dining room, a study. But it impresses." He smiled, held out one of the glasses.

She got control of her legs and stepped down into the room and crossed the thick carpet. She took the glass, her hand trembling only a bit. "Take my coat?"

She used the minute he was gone to store the coat to pinch herself. *Game face.*

"But to your point," he said, arriving back, "yes, this room is in fact lovely." He gestured toward one of the couches and took the other for himself. He took a phone from his pocket and checked it briefly.

It's like a job interview. But she wanted the job. She crossed her long legs, letting him take a look. He did, his eyebrows shooting up in admiration. When his eyes traveled back up to hers, he seemed less turned on than—was this weird?—proud.

"I imagine you don't stay here often, if you live nearby in your own penthouse."

He blinked once too many times, a frown resting lightly on his features. Had she gotten something wrong?

"I didn't realize I'd told you that I lived in a penthouse," he said. He thought it over. "No, you're right. I don't stay here often. No need. But, as neutral ground for our meeting, I thought it fit the bill."

"Indeed." She had never said *indeed* in her life, for the love of God. Who was she supposed to be? He had never given her any hints. She had no idea which version of Mer-Maid she should lean into. "You've never asked me for a treat before. It would've been rude to turn you down."

"Treat? Oh. I suppose they must ask you . . . for all kinds of nasty things. Tell me. What brought you to this line of work?"

Something in the question stung a bit. It wasn't her *career*. Well. She supposed it was, now. For the moment. "I don't really see it that way," she said, sipping at her drink. She already had a headache from the sugary cocktail she'd downed earlier, and now she remembered the drink and everything about it with regret. The body in the dunes rushed up to her. It couldn't be Rick. It couldn't— *Be here*, she scolded herself. *Be here now.*

"I've insulted you," he said.

She re-crossed her legs, letting her dress ride up on her thighs. He watched. "Not yet," she said, trying to make an invitation from it. She wasn't going to get where she wanted to go without making some promises.

"What if I meant to insult you?"

She hadn't heard that correctly. "What?"

"If I paid you enough, does it matter what transpires?" He gestured around the room. "Does it matter to you what happens here? I'm trying to understand it."

She pawed the couch cushion for her phone. It was in her jacket pocket, she realized, tucked away. The hairs on the back of her neck were standing up. She should have told Juby where she was going. Alice. This was a mistake. She set the drink down on a nearby table.

"Of course it matters," she said. "It matters to me that you get what you want."

"For a price." He glanced at his phone again. "You might be worth top dollar, if I was in the market. And I might have been, if I hadn't already got exactly what I wanted today. All the devils are now back in hell. If they weren't, tonight would have worked out differently, I think, and not in your favor." He checked his phone again. It was like a compulsion.

"What are you talking about?" She glanced toward the door.

He stood up and reached for his wallet. An array of bills peeked out, and he made a show of looking her over while he counted them out. "What's your rate?"

"I don't have— What did you say about devils?"

"I would have enjoyed divulging what you've turned into, and what a fun night I had taking you up on it. It's almost worth taking you into the master suite to say it happened that way, if I had the time. If I didn't worry for the venereal disease."

"*Fuck* you, I don't—"

"You can't decide who you are. Are you the innocent lamb who's never done this before or are you the harlot who might, for the right dollar amount? Your brand, sweetheart. It's a little wobbly." He checked his phone, smiled. "Excellent, coast clear. Here—take this and think twice next time before you skip up to a stranger's room. Some of them might treat you worse than I have."

He held out an array of the bills. All hundreds. She would have to lean forward, reach for it. She would have to beg for it, get on her knees for it. She turned her head. "I'll take my coat now."

"Ah, too proud. That's nice, isn't it? Keep your pride and your twenty-dollar coat. You're still a bargain, even with the room. Here's your finder's fee." He flung the money at her and walked off.

Hundred-dollar bills slapped her shoulder, landed on her lap, and on her hand on the couch. She flicked them away and stood up. If her phone hadn't been in her jacket pocket, she might have left without it. She waited at the door and tried not to count the number of bills lying back at the couch. Thousands of dollars. She was walking away from it and couldn't even feel like the better person. When he came back, he was holding the jacket out from him, as though it smelled. She ripped it from his hand. "What was the point of all this? Is this your kink? We've been talking on ChatX for . . . *months*."

"You wouldn't believe the long game I've played, but don't take it personally. It was never about you." He opened the door. "And it was you doing all the talking. I'm just an excellent listener. A really patient, excellent listener."

She reached into her pocket for her phone, but it was gone.

He held it up. "You should take some of that money to get a new one. A nicer model. Here." He took out the wallet again, doled out several more bills, and leaned in to tuck them into the pocket of the coat. His breath was hot on her neck. "By the time you try to tell anyone anything, this room will be empty, and that chat pro-file will have never existed. Go home to Port Bethlehem, and take your mamá with you. Plan your party."

Merrily stared at him, trying to understand. Mamá. Was he threatening them? But wait—

The man led her to the door by the elbow and pushed the eleva-tor button. She snapped her arm out of his grasp. "You leave my mom out of this."

"She can go home now. We were only cleaning up behind our-selves."

The elevator was slow. "If I see you anywhere near her—"

"Does she know what you do for a living? Would she want to?" The doors opened, and Merrily stepped forward without having to be invited or guided. She blinked tears away while he pushed the button for the lobby and used the edge of his own shirt to wipe the button. "How's her heart? She's not a young woman anymore."

Smiling as the doors closed.

Merrily pressed her back to the corner of the elevator. *Mamá.* What party? She reached back through the hot shame of the thirty minutes she'd spent in the man's company. *All the devils are in hell.* He'd already gotten exactly what he wanted, which wasn't her.

When she reached the lobby, Merrily hobbled out of the eleva-tor on baby-deer legs. At the desk, she waited for someone to pay attention to her, but no one did until the bellman came along and she reached for his sleeve. His name tag said *Thomas.* "Ma'am?" he said, but stiffly, the things he imagined she'd had done to her written on his sanctimonious, punchable face.

Merrily reached into her coat and pulled out the fistful of bills, peeled off a Benjamin Franklin, and shoved the rest back into her pocket. "The man in the penthouse. What's his name?"

"We don't give out details like that, I'm sorry." His eyes took in the money, the pocket, and then drifted to the desk.

She pulled out a second bill.

"Let me show you where that is, miss," he said loudly, and led her back toward the elevator. "You're going to get me fired," Thomas hissed.

When they were out of sight of the desk, she placed the money in his gloved hand.

"It's a matter of life and death." Mostly death.

"He paid in cash, OK? The penthouse suite, in cash. We don't ask a lot of questions in a situation like that."

"You don't ask for ID? Is that legal?"

"It's illegal to have a fake ID, but we're not the cops." He glanced around nervously. "He showed up here, like, an hour ago, paid my manager in cash, with a huge tip, and had the bottle sent up."

"Did he sign for the wine?"

"Just a big swish, nothing you can read. It would be a fake name, anyway."

She reached for the pocket of her coat, watching the bellman's gaze follow along. "I will give you the rest of what I have in this pocket if you can get that champagne bottle from the room. And the glasses."

"I can *try*."

"How hard would you try?"

Now his eyes were on her, and he'd started considering the other currencies. "Really hard."

She folded the second bill into his glove and shoved it away from her. "I'll be in the lobby behind the palm tree."

He licked his lips. "There are a lot of palm trees."

"Put a little effort into it, Thomas."

Slapdash: Have we ever considered the case of 973MPIN Laura Schmidt AKA Laura Banks?

MrJonesToYou: RE: @Slapdash Jen Minarik had a thing on _ CrimeTimeTonight_, like, last week.

JealousTypist: RE: @Slapdash Give us the details?

JuJuBee95: RE: @Slapdash Lil, what are you doing?

MrJonesToYou: RE: RE: @JealousTypist She was a drug addict in some crappy small town in Indiana, arrested a million times, had her kid taken away, her boyfriend bails and she's missing. Open, shut. It was the boyfriend.

JealousTypist: RE: RE: RE: @MrJonesToYou I didn't mean YOU. @Slapdash, what's the deal with this one?

Slapdash: RE: RE: RE: . . . @JealousTypist Actually @MrJonesToYou gave a pretty good wrap-up, though we only have her arrest records as proof she had a drug problem, and the boyfriend bailed *before* she lost her kid. The kid was taken away after she was busted for drugs a third or fourth time. She disappeared almost 30 years ago.

Audrey89: RE: RE: RE: . . . @ Slapdash Dead.

Slapdash: RE: RE: RE: . . . @ Audrey89 Maybe.

JennDoePagesMOD: Let's be a little more generous here. @Slapdash, has there been renewed interest in this case?

Slapdash RE: @JennDoePagesMOD The boyfriend might have been in some kind of protection program. He resurfaced long enough to get himself murdered this week. Laura is still unaccounted for. I'm posting some documents in the discussion board if you want to try and crowdsource this. There are approximately 158 UID profiles in the region that could fit, given her age, racial makeup, and the timing of her disappearance. Anyone want to help sort some bodies?

JuJuBee95: RE: @Slapdash Is this a good idea?

Slapdash: RE: RE: @JuJuBee95 I guess we'll find out.

CHAPTER THIRTY-SIX

ALICE

By the time Alice arrived at the site the day after the break-in, Jimmy's burglary had shifted in her mind to complete absurdity. It couldn't have happened.

Inside the site trailer, the safe hung open, empty, and her backpack was still gone. She called the police and waited for them outside the fence, watching the crew methodically build up the next parking deck.

When her dad arrived, she was sitting at her desk going over the details with the officer who had shown up, a middle-aged lump in no hurry.

Her dad took the news calmly, checking the safe himself as though they all might have missed a clue. His only show of anger was a swipe at the framed photo of 1799 South Michigan Avenue, still resting on the floor. The frame rattled against the wall. JimBig appeared in the doorway. "What happened?" he said.

No one rushed to tell the story. "Someone . . . helped themselves to a few things," Alice said.

"Why would a thief want our old ledgers?" her dad said.

"The ledgers? What else?" JimBig's eyes raked the room, pausing at the computer on Alice's desk. As though anyone would steal that anchor.

"I had some things here," she said. "They're gone."

"Like what?" her dad said.

"I forgot my backpack and it had my wallet in it."

He frowned. "How did you forget your backpack?"

"Did you lose any cash? A wallet at least makes sense." JimBig sat on the edge of the table.

"And my laptop," she said.

"We'll cover your losses, kid."

"You will need to cancel your credit cards immediately," the police officer said.

"I already did." They all looked at her. "Right after I called 911," she said. Actually, she'd done it the night before. She should have waited. What was Jimmy going to do with her credit cards? Nothing.

He wouldn't do anything with any of it. He was creating chaos.

Alice tidied her desk while her dad and JimBig determined which files were missing for the police report. As the officer was ready to leave, he ripped a layer off the triplicate form and handed it to Alice. Yellow, with his business card stapled to it. She looked up at him.

"You can use that for identification until you get your license replaced."

JimBig escorted the police officer out. Alice listened to the crackle of her dad's sour mood gaining ground. "How was your trip?" she said.

"Well, it's a hell of a thing to come back to this."

She wasn't going to apologize, though the empty air seemed to require it.

"What do thieves want with those old books?" he said.

Their accounting was backed up on her computer and probably in three other places. He wasn't moaning about her lost laptop, the time it would take to rebuild her wallet of IDs and cards. She would need her Social Security card to get a new license, and she hadn't had her hands on that in years. It wasn't about a real loss to him—only that some minor villain had gotten it over on Harris Fine. *Always a cop.* She tried to think of something else to say. "When did you get back?"

He was distracted, pacing slowly past the safe one way, then the other. "This morning, early." He stopped, his hands at his hips. "I talked to you last night, didn't I? Did you think I sneaked into town?"

"I thought I saw a K&F truck pulling out of the garage at 1799 right after I talked to you. Almost ran into me, actually. Must have been Jim." Maybe it hadn't been one of their trucks after all. "The trucks are accounted for, right?"

"Why were you downtown?"

Oh. "I went to meet a friend for a drink last night."

"Why were you out so late? Which friend is this?"

"I didn't say I was out late," she said. "Just out."

"Well, you look tired."

"Thanks."

"Which friend?"

"No one you know." She wouldn't apologize for having a friend, either.

He was still watching, peeling away layers of skin for the lie. "Is payroll done?"

Alice sat back and directed her attention toward her computer. "It will be."

"Good," he said. She could still hear the electricity of his anger.

He grabbed his hard hat from the peg on the wall and went out. At the last minute, he looked back. "I'm sorry."

She wondered which part he was sorry for but didn't look his way.

"Your stuff. We'll get you a new laptop. Maybe it's time to upgrade the tech in here, too."

When the door closed behind him, Alice's hands faltered on the keys. She wasn't sure why. Something stood between them. Maybe if she'd told him about Jimmy, she could have cleared the air. Or maybe the tinderbox of the trailer might have gone up in flames.

She took a deep breath and got to payroll. At least she had actual work to do.

ALICE HEARD THE men breaking for lunch—the repeated slamming of the Porta-John door was the giveaway—and grabbed an extra hard hat off the wall. She found Brody sitting with a few of them in the shady east corner of the project's ground floor. As she approached, she heard the others ribbing him.

"You got a date," one of them mumbled. Brody hopped up to meet her halfway across the deck.

"Hey," Brody said. "You didn't text me."

"What? Oh, sorry." She hadn't given him another thought. She'd barely had time to think of Matt. "It's just been . . . yeah. You know this isn't—you know."

The guy's neck was pink again. "No, I know. Of course not. How's . . ."

He couldn't think of a single thing to ask her about.

"I'm working on payroll this morning," she said. "Except that you don't have any hours down for last Thursday. You clocked in, and I clocked you out with everyone else, but now it's zeroed out, so I was wondering if I missed—"

"No, I called in sick that day. Migraines." He waved a hand over his head vaguely. "Had them since I was a kid. Nearly go blind with them, if I'm honest."

Alice noted his watery eyes, hazel, nearly golden, the kind of eyes you might see on a cat, except Brody had none of the qualities: no sleekness, no stealth. His expression was startled, and his movements mechanical as he seemed to decide to cross his arms. His attention was split between her and the men behind him.

"You were here that day," she said, quiet and even. "That's the day Matt fell three stories. Right past you, screaming. Remember? That's why I offered to text you."

"You misunderstood," he said. "I'm definitely having the heebies about it, just from what I've heard. The guys who were there . . . man, I wish they would keep the details to themselves, but they like to mess with me. I'm sorry if I— I was home in bed. Hell of a headache."

Alice let the lie hang between them until Brody grew uncomfortable. "Have you heard any news from Matt?"

"Not recent."

"Well," he said. "I guess I'd better go finish my lunch before break's over. Good to see you, Al."

He walked away and she stood stunned, even as she realized what it must look like. She'd had enough on-site arguments with Matt to know what it looked like.

She turned and started back to the trailer but then swerved toward the other end of the parking structure, entered the stairwell, and climbed.

She skipped the second floor, glancing out the window cavity on the way past, and ascended to the third, where yellow caution tape stretched across the door opening. Behind her, wind blew up the stairwell, blowing her hair forward. She tucked it behind her ears and looked out. Above, the fourth deck was coming into shape, steel, frame, concrete, steel, frame, concrete.

Alice tapped her toe under the tape. Solid now, of course, but it wouldn't have been last Thursday.

Matt might have been helping with the structural frame for the fourth floor, but there wouldn't have been much to balance on up there. Protocol was to allow essential crew only, until they cleared the new deck. It was too dangerous. The third deck would have been taped off, just as it was now. *How could he have fallen from here?*

Alice gazed out at the smooth floor of the third deck. It was a miracle, in a way, all this concrete fighting against gravity. She'd watched a thousand times as a patch of uneven land was leveled and improved upon, made useful. Not that she was against open spaces, but parking garages made sense in a high-density zone. She was her father's daughter there. Maybe she could run this business, when the time came.

She couldn't think of it; she wouldn't. She wasn't Jimmy King.

The wind cut across her face, dust in her eyes. She turned and reached for the window cavity to blink away a speck. When she could open her eyes again, she was standing at the high slab of the window shelf, the view wide, dusty, hot. She could see their trucks and her little car lined up in the lot down the street, and through the avenue of nearby buildings, the chunky spires of what she would always call the Sears Tower. If she leaned into the deep ledge of the window and looked down—

Below, the patch of ground that from all reports had caught Matt's fall.

Why was Brody covering his ass? He didn't want to choose

sides, didn't want to stick his skinny Adam's apple out for his buddy?

Alice leaned farther into the window well. Forward, forward, tiptoes, waiting for the pull of gravity, for nature to take her at her offer. She could army-crawl both elbows up into the cavity, stretch—

Her hard hat tipped off. Alice fell back on her feet, heard the crash below, and then leaned back into the window to make sure no one had been hit. She heard the guys reacting, calling out, racing from all directions. "Al? Alice?" someone called from below, then again up the stairwell, echoing. She could hear the footsteps coming up to her. A herd of them.

"Sorry," she called, waving out the window. "Everything's fine."

High in the frame of the window, a thin blue thread clung to a rough seam.

She turned her back to the concrete and slid to the floor, her feet splayed out in front of her. When the first of the crew reached her, they approached uneasily. In construction you never wanted to see the bottoms of someone's boots, and here she was, boots out, hard hat gone. "I'm fine. I'm sorry."

But she was shaking. She waited until the word got back down to the rest of the crew, until she could stand again on weak legs, until she could convince them she'd slipped, that's all. No need to call an ambulance. No need to bother her dad. When she came down the stairs on Gus's sturdy arm, Brody stood at the wide entrance of the garage, his lone figure thin and frail within the frame of sunlight, his hands red and chapped as he held out her hard hat.

The plastic had split up the back, cleaved in two like something out of stories she'd liked at school. The cracked skull of Zeus, birth of Athena.

Without looking at Brody, she took the hat and turned toward the trailer. Safety. It was all she could think of. Safety, quickly, before someone asked her what had happened, how she was, and what was the matter. She hadn't fainted, hadn't flown away on black wings. But something was definitely wrong.

Matt hadn't gone off the deck. He'd gone out the window. And he couldn't have done it by accident. He would have to be pushed.

CHAPTER THIRTY-SEVEN
ALICE

Alice hurried across the site, kicking up pale dust. Behind her, the wind moaned up the empty stairwell.

No, Matt hadn't been pushed. He'd been *thrown*.

Alice forced herself to stop. Stop. She put the busted hard hat on her head and walked toward the trailer. At the last minute, she veered toward the fence and let herself out. She walked around the perimeter of the site until she could see the elevator tower's bank of windows. Six floors of blank cinder block, six empty eye-holes, all facing west. The spot where Matt landed was directly below.

She was being ridiculous. That blue thread was a coincidence. The cops had been on the site to check things over, anyway.

Of course, they might have been looking at the second floor instead of the third. And at the deck's ledge instead of the window wells.

That blue thread caught high in the window frame was just confirmation. The window was built high on purpose, idiot-proof, too high for people to tumble through by accident. It had been too high for her, and Matt was several inches shorter than she was. Idiot-proof, and Matt was no idiot.

Alice pulled off her hard hat and turned it over to study the fracture. Sonofabitching Matt.

IN THE TRAILER, Alice hid the cracked hard hat in the bottom drawer of her desk and sat with her hands at her temples.

She wasn't sure how much time had passed when the door opened and Jimmy came in. Outside, lunch break was over. The crane was back at work, lifting materials up to the fourth deck.

"Robbed, they said." Jimmy, smug, swept into the office. "What will we ever do without those dusty tomes?" He was striking for his usual mix of flirtation and harassment, but she could sense the difference. It was hollow.

"And a laptop and wallet." She opened up the payroll file and finalized Brody's zero hours for the previous Thursday. If he didn't want to get paid. . . . While she was in the file, she put his phone number into her phone and texted him. *It's Alice. I want to talk to you.*

"What was your backpack even doing in the trailer?" he asked innocently.

Some nerve. If he only knew why her stuff had been lying around for him to take, she'd own him.

She had bigger fish at the moment. And also, something inside the King and Fine shed seemed delicate and off-kilter. One wrong move might split the tension like the back of that hard hat.

"The burglar didn't seem to have any trouble *jimmy*ing his way inside," she said.

He blinked. "Maybe you didn't lock up properly."

"So this is my fault."

Something in his face relented. He went to the guest chair and sat down, stretched his legs. "It's no one's fault," he said. "Maybe it was our turn. I mean, how many times have we been robbed in the thirty years King and Fine has been in business? Zero. Those odds are almost supernatural, when you think about it. Are we protected by voodoo curse? By a junkyard dog?"

By JimBig King's reputation, maybe. "During the day we are."

Jimmy and Alice stared at each other.

"Did you need something, Jimmy, or are you just here to shift blame?"

"Shift?" He leaned forward on his knees, looking away. He seemed different. Younger. He didn't have that gunk in his hair and instead of his dumb suit he wore jeans, a checked shirt. He could be someone's brother, someone's boyfriend, instead of the shark he always tried to be. He wouldn't look at her. Instead his gaze landed on the framed photo of 1799 South Michigan, still leaning against the filing cabinet. He stood and approached the frame, picked it up, studied it. "You know, I thought this was it for us. The sky is the limit and all that. After we did 1799, we'd never have to do another parking garage again."

"What's wrong with parking garages? They're useful." She would rather have one more shot at a building like 1799 South Michigan, just once, than build a parking structure ever again. She felt like a fight, though.

"They're dull."

"They pay the bills."

"Now," he said. "Now you're talking like the business partner I'll need."

Baiting her, daring her. He wanted her to play her role. If only she played along, if she made a face over the word *partner*, if she turned down whatever proposal he came up with, the balance held. Everything was fine.

Everything was not fine. She just didn't know yet where the rifts were.

She stood up, grabbed the yellow copy of the police report, and stuffed it into her pocket. Her phone and keys. She walked to the door.

"Hey," Jimmy said. "I wanted to say—" She didn't stop.

AT THE HOSPITAL, Alice bypassed the gift shop and went straight to the elevator. A crowd waited for the next car. Instead of taking her turn, she helped herself to the first car she could wedge herself into.

A uniformed police officer strolled the hallway outside the critical care unit. Alice glanced his way but hurried down the hall, pausing briefly at the door of the family room. A line of chairs sat haphazardly in the center of the room, but the man who'd made them his bed was gone. Bad news? Good news? The sunflowers drooped in their vase in the corner.

The white of the CCU surprised her all over again. The only splash of color was a red sweater curled on the seat of the chair near Matt's bed.

He'd been removed from the complicated spread-wing contraptions, no longer strung up, ready to be drawn and quartered. His face seemed a better color.

Alice glanced around, but no one paid her any attention. She slid open the glass door and closed it gently behind her. At his bed, she reached out for his hand. Wires and tubes traced the contours of his limbs, all the way from his fingertips, up his arm, to his nostrils. His lips were dry, cracked.

Alice lifted the edge of his gown sleeve and found the spot on his shoulder with the tattoo, the same black-winged bird in flight she'd had put on her hip, when the future had seemed so certain. She pulled the chair up and sat on its edge. She hadn't had the chance to see Matt, to look at him with such care, since he'd called off the wedding.

"Probably a good thing you canceled," she said. "I'm too young to be a widow."

His eyelids fluttered.

"Matt?" She stood and peered at his face. His eyelids twitched again, twice. "Can you hear me?"

His lips moved. She leaned down to hear, her hair dragging across his chest, but could only detect a hum, his lips trying to part.

The door opened. "Don't you dare touch him," Lita said.

"Lita, he can hear me. Is he—"

"You're not supposed to be in here. It's family only."

Alice couldn't take her eyes off Matt to argue that she might have been family, that she had meant to be. He was King and Fine family, if nothing else.

"Has he been talking? He's trying to say something to me."

Lita was gone from the doorway and when she came back, the officer from the hall followed. He took Alice's elbow. "Hey."

"You can't be here," the officer said.

Germs and stuff? She should have thought of that. She let him lead her out, taking a last look over her shoulder at Matt as the door closed. In the hall, Alice snatched her arm away and turned to Lita.

"I'm sorry. I only wanted to—actually, I'm not sure why I'm here. I wanted to make sure you knew I hadn't— I mean, just be- cause we're not—"

Lita said to the floor, "We appreciate it."

"Did he wake up?"

"He's not out of the woods yet." This was directed toward a nearby doorframe.

"Can he tell you what happened?"

Lita finally looked up. "He doesn't need to."

"I went up there, Lita, to the third deck where no one should have been, and I wonder if he might have been . . ." The other woman concentrated on Alice's mouth, as though she had to read her lips. "Pushed."

Lita took a breath, blinking away tears. She stepped back. "I shouldn't be talking to you. You own the company, Alice. Fine and King money won't save him."

"It's just a paperwork thing." The ownership issue, she meant. But it was all paperwork, wasn't it? Insurance and all that, the lawyers sorting the thing out, Matt getting the care he needed, workers' comp, their entire lives boiled down to what was left at the bottom of a stack of pages. Even marriage, when you thought about it, was a matter of paperwork.

If he'd been pushed, though, it should be a matter of justice.

In her pocket, Alice's phone buzzed. She ignored it. "Which money won't save him? We're bonded and insured, and I'm sure JimBig and Dad will—"

"Not that money. Let's call it the brideless dowry—I don't want to call it what it is."

"I don't understand."

"His accounts flush, the new truck." Lita searched her face. "There's nowhere else it could have come from." She seemed to remember herself. "I'm sorry I brought it up. Can you just—"

"Is that guy guarding Matt? Is he protecting Matt from *us*? From King and Fine? From—"

"I only have time to save Matt right now," Lita said. "You're going to have to sort yourself out." She turned and walked away.

Alice had to wait for the elevator, stretching her sleeves down over her wrists.

Protecting Matt from her? Was *she* the enemy?

In the parking garage elevator, this time going up, Alice watched the numbers rise, numb. Third floor. At her car, she went to the barrier wall of the parking deck and looked over. What happened if Matt died?

What if he lived?

Alice was almost home before she heard what Lita had said. *You own the company, Alice.* Not: *You work there.* Not: *Your dad owns the company.* Not: *Someday it will all be yours.* How had Lita, stuck in the CCU, heard about that?

Jimmy King. It had to be. He wasn't stealing info for the competition. He was taking Uncle Jim at his word; he was *becoming* the competition.

When she finally checked her phone, she had two messages from the number she'd added for Brody earlier in the day.

Find out who was on the tour.
Don't use this number again.

CHAPTER THIRTY-EIGHT

ALICE

Alice parked in front of her apartment to find her neighbor Patricia standing at the bottom of a ladder by the front door. She chattered upward at the boots of a man standing on a high step. *The security cameras, God.*

Alice put the car back into gear and pulled away. She drove, not knowing where she would go. She needed to think. Brody's message, the back-channel discussions between Lita and Jimmy. *Dowry?*

The traffic was as bad as it ever was, and after being honked at twice for not pulling forward quickly enough on green, Alice drove into a shopping center and parked near a chain restaurant. King and Fine had built the place a few years back. Bad lighting, fake antiques on the walls. The kind of place no one liked, but went to anyway. They had a bar.

Inside, gin and tonic in her fist, Alice logged into the Doe Pages app on her phone and read through the notifications she'd missed in the last few days. When she reached the post about Laura Schmidt, she sat up straight.

"Anyone sitting here?"

The man was good-looking, tanned skin, dark eyes. He was already smiling at her, too many teeth for a casual question. "Yes," she said. "My fiancé is meeting me."

"Lucky guy."

He wasn't. Where would she be now, if the wedding had gone ahead? Not alone at the Nighthawks' Bar of a family-friendly steakhouse in Glen Park, Illinois, not admiring the muscular shoulders of a stranger as he moved to the empty seat on her other side and sat down.

"Get you another drink?" He ordered a beer, gesturing for her to jump on his tab. She turned back to her phone.

A few minutes later the guy reached across her elbow for a napkin. He had the outline of a holster under his jacket, the bulge of a weapon at his hip.

"Are you a cop?"

"Yes." He thought it over for a second. "Did you need a cop?"

She'd spent too much time with police today, had resorted to showing the police report to the bartender as ID. "Not at the moment. My dad is police, if I need one. Used to be."

"So you trust the police."

Was he flirting? "Maybe."

"You said 'used to.' "

Was it any of his business?

"OK," he said. "What do *you* do?"

She threw back her drink, thought it over before answering. "I work for him."

He nodded and waved the bartender toward her empty glass. "You don't sound happy about it."

"I'm fine with it." *Fine.* She had to stop saying it. "I probably should have built something for myself by now, that's all."

"Well," the man said, grinning. "You will, right? After the wedding."

"What? Oh, the—yeah." The fresh drink appeared in front of her.

"Very modern," the guy said. "No engagement ring."

She let that sit, sipped her drink. The first had been too strong. So was the second. "I'll be honest with you . . ."

"If you like."

"The wedding isn't happening," she said.

"Sorry to hear that. I'm sure the groom was broken up over it."

The way he said *broken up*—

Alice slid off the stool, feeling the liquor in her knees. "I'm going to sit somewhere else."

"Didn't mean to offend. Look, I'll leave you alone. You need to wait out those drinks before heading home. I only wanted you to have this." He held out his hand. "Never hurts to have a spare cop, right?"

It was a business card. Officer So and So. She took it. *G. Vasquez, Chicago Police Department.*

Chicago PD? This suburb wasn't his beat, then. He couldn't even live here, with a city job.

Alice focused on the sharp corners of the card. "Who are you?"

"Someone keeping an eye on things."

He looked familiar. "For King and Fine?"

The man squinted at her. "That's interesting. You're a company girl."

"No, I'm not."

"I guess we'll see." He knocked on the bar to catch the bartender's attention. "Coffee for this lady, please? I'm buying."

Suddenly she knew who he was. The guy from outside the gate who'd almost taken a friendly spritz of pepper spray. He'd been at the site the day of Matt's fall, the big-shouldered shadow playing against the screen of the fence.

"You," she said.

"Me."

A police officer, talking with JimBig, long after the action had died down that day. Or long *before*, if he was also the investor, so-called, who'd taken a canceled tour. "What do you want?"

"Nothing. I thought you might want something from me. If not yet, then someday."

"Am I in trouble?"

Raised eyebrows. "Why would you think so?"

King and Fine like a weight around her neck. Matt. Jimmy. Lita. And now a police officer trailing her from the city. "I feel like things are coming apart."

"Maybe when they do, you can put them back together better than they were before."

The guy had never worked construction. You built it right the first time, or it fell down around you.

"Let me do you a favor," he said, and gestured to her cell phone. "May I?"

Her phone was in her hand and then it was in his. He dropped it to the floor and, before she could reach for it, crushed a bootheel down on the screen.

"What are you doing?" she cried.

He stamped it again, then stood back and swept a lock of hair back into place. "Get a new one—and don't let anyone else touch it. Anyone."

He dropped money on the bar and headed for the exit.

"Hey!" she yelled to his back. The other patrons were staring. "What the hell was that about?"

*   *   *

ALICE ARRIVED TO work Wednesday late again, a good hour wasted replacing her phone. New phone, transferred number, astronomical fees stacked on her emergencies-only credit card, dug out of her freezer. Was that how much phones *cost*?

At the door of the trailer, she was met with a stampede of muddy boot prints. She flicked on the lights to find her dad sitting silently in the back, reclining in the chair he and JimBig used, hands knotted in front of him.

"Dad? You OK?"

"Hey, Stretch," he said, sitting up. He might have called her "sunshine," as her mother had, but he never did. She would never suggest it. "I'm fine. Just peeved at JimBig. The usual."

She hadn't even told him about Jimmy or the cop. What business did JimBig have with a shady cop? "What's he done now?"

"Cracking the whip on the crew for slipping on the timeline when he's fresh off a week of mai tais in the Keys."

"I don't think he really went to Florida."

He raised his head. "Why not?"

"Doesn't he seem more run-down than ever?" She sat at her desk heavily. Were they all feeling this weight? "Did you get any rest on your trip?"

"My—oh. Not even close. No new deals, either, but . . . you put in the hours, eventually something breaks through."

She launched the old computer. Braced herself. "Are you going to teach me that part of the business at some point?"

"You're interested in learning the business?"

"Come on, Dad," she said. "I'm sure Uncle Jim told you."

"Big and I are giving each other some room right now."

"The ownership thing. King and Fine, woman-owned."

"Oh." He turned in his chair. "How did you— Well, it's just a paperwork thing," he said. "Don't let it scare you."

It was what she'd hoped to hear, but also a disappointment. Putting the company in her name might have meant she wasn't the fuckup, the bad example. The ornament. "You don't think I can run the business someday?"

"I didn't realize your interests ran in that direction," he said.

"I haven't had much of a chance to decide where my interests are."

"Since Monday? Of course—"

"I meant . . . ever. I haven't had the chance to decide for myself who I want to be."

"Is this somehow my fault? Oh, for cutting you some breaks?" He couldn't seem to decide if he wanted to joke about it or fold this into his annoyance with JimBig. "We have to take care of each other, Al. Nobody out there will do it."

"I'd like to be able to take care of myself, too. You want me to be able to stand on my own two feet, right?"

"You do," he said. "You *are*. It's just like building. I'm only giving you a solid foundation—"

"How much?"

"What?"

"How much do you want me to be able to stand on my own two feet?"

He sighed. "Not sure where we are, Alice. What's going on?"

She took a steadying breath. "Did you pay Matt to break up with me?"

"What? Of *course* not. Who said that I—"

"No one," she said quickly. No need to send him Lita's way. "Some gossip's going around about how he paid for that new truck."

"I guess we pay our crew well enough to let them splurge once in a while," he said thoughtfully. "He's a young guy, good job, no—" *No commitments.* She watched him stumble over it. "Or maybe he borrowed himself into a bad financial place. I never thought he was good enough for you, I won't lie. But—no. Either way, it's a lucky thing you don't have to worry about him anymore."

She was going to worry. Not as the apparent owner of King and Fine, but as the woman who had harbored all the hope in the world. It was an ugly thing, hope. It wasn't a valve you could shut off. The thing with feathers, she'd learned back in school. The thing that flapped at the periphery, trying to get in where it wasn't wanted.

"Yeah, lucky."

Her phone pinged loudly in her pocket. Her dad looked up.

"Sorry, I need to . . ." She pulled the phone out and changed the setting to vibrate.

The text was from Juby: *Funeral Thursday. We're going.*

Funeral for who? she typed. She had a feeling she knew. *No way.*

Yes, ma'am, we are all going.

At the same time another text came in, this one from the same unknown number that had been plaguing her. Jimmy again.

Friend of yours? With an attachment. She put the phone away. He was too much. It was all too much. What did they all want from her? "Would you mind if I took a couple of days off?" she said, almost before she knew she would.

"What's up?"

"I need to clear my head, take care of some errands."

"Anything I can—"

"Dad!"

"Everybody take a damned vacation, we're only twelve days behind, nothing to get worked up about—"

"*Dad.*"

"Fine, sure. But you are cheating me out of my self-righteous indignation over Big's mai tais, whether he drank them or not. I'll never forgive you for that." He was smiling.

"You can save your indignation for something else next week."

"You know how I'm always running out of indignation."

Rnn.

Another message from Juby. *U are going. And u have to drive.*

To: Rajul@dotnet.net
From: Patricia.Gussin@securenet.org
Subject: EMERGENCY TENANT MEETING NEEDED!!!

Rahul! We HAVE to get the tenants ALL OF THEM!
to meet immediately to discuss the problem with the
SECURITY CAMERAS!! The guy who was out yesterday
says the video feed is being uploaded (???) to a website
and he has no idea which one or who put the cameras in.
WE HAVE NO IDEA WHO IS MONITORING US AND
WHY. Did you bring up my petition? It's the worst kind of
breach of security for EVERYONE WHO LIVES IN THIS
BUILDING!!! We demand action IMMEDIATELY!!

To: Patricia.Gussin@securenet.org
From: Rajul@dotnet.net
RE: Subject: EMERGENCY TENANT MEETING NEEDED!!!

You know I just live here, right? No one cares about a
petition signed by six people, Patricia. You can contact the
management company yourself, same company you write
rent checks to. Top Floor Management. Stop emailing me.

CHAPTER THIRTY-NINE
MERRILY

What are they doing here?" Merrily's mom hissed into her shoulder, her breath hot.

Merrily looked up from her shoes. It had rained the day before. Her heels had poked into some mud at the edge of the grass on the way to the grave, and now they were caked in dirt. She had missed some important instructions on how to go about this, burying someone. What to wear, what to say. She'd done what she could, spending the last twenty minutes fending off various strangers who'd come to take part in the proceedings. They were not mourners. They were colleagues from her mom's last job, a few people who knew Rick way back in Victorville, they said. At least one cop, hiding his eyes behind sunglasses, but thankfully not G. Vasquez or the bulldog.

One woman stood nearby but apart, her head lowered and a large-brimmed black hat hiding her face. *Auditioning for the role of widow.* Besides her mom, Justyce, who had insisted on coming, and herself, this woman was the only other brown-skinned person there, her thick, dark arms slipping out of flowing sleeves when she raised the most impossibly white handkerchief to her face.

And now Alice, Juby, and Lillian shuffled across the grass from the gravel path at Lillian's pace.

Another tricky interaction, then. Should she go greet them? Her mom had been less than helpful on protocol, throwing up her hands at decisions, at expenses. She didn't give Merrily any clues as to what Rick might have wanted or how to get in touch with his children. Maybe he'd relinquished his rights, but whatever. They were not in attendance. They wouldn't hear about his death in time to pay respects or to spit on the grave, as her mom threatened.

Justyce leaned in, her own fist of tissues ready in case Merrily should need one. She was here for the gossip, in Merrily's opinion. "Who are they?" she whispered.

"Trouble," Merrily's mom said, not whispering.

"Mamá. They're my friends." Her voice betrayed her. Were they? They'd thrown up their hands, too, in a way. She hadn't seen them since Monday, since that night when she'd gone off to meet Searcher, only to be returned, shamed, to the hotel bar to sit in the shelter of palm fronds. Remembering it now, she was embarrassed all over again. The bellman had come back without the glasses, without the bottle. "Smashed," he'd said, and he'd walked away so easily from the money in her coat pocket that she had to wonder if money hadn't passed hands on the eighth floor, too. She'd been outbid.

Days had passed with only a couple of logistical texts about the services from Juby. Silence from Alice. It shouldn't have mattered. She hardly knew them and she'd had a funeral to plan. Merrily crossed her arms as the women took places among the sparse showing.

The minister called them all to begin and somehow Merrily took the steps required to duck under the tarp stretched over the grave site and take a seat in the single row of chairs. Her mom sat on one side and one of her mom's former office mates, an older woman Merrily didn't know, sat on the other. The woman just wanted to sit down, which was fine with Merrily. But then the stranger was determined to earn her position. She put her arm around the back of Merrily's chair and patted awkwardly at her arm.

The minister said a few words, something about lambs and a lost flock. *Wayward*, he said. Merrily tried to pay attention, tried not to think about Rick's goofy texts, his *Hey, kid*. She'd had him cremated, but bought a plot anyway. *You had to have a plot, right? A stone?* Her mom had done this before—for her father, buried somewhere down South. But she had been no help. Now Rick's urn sat on a stage in front of them, only in need of a spotlight and they'd be having themselves a show. What would he have thought of this circus?

In a flash, she knew she'd done it wrong. She might have taken his ashes to the dunes and the house he'd apparently owned all this time, hidden among his many identities, which she'd learned from Vasquez after Rick's body had been found. He'd loved that house and that area and had left behind the pictures to prove it. She might have released his ashes to the lake, into the sand, treating herself and her mom to a campfire to burn away any words that weren't necessary. She hadn't needed to turn his already public death into this performance.

But instead: this shallow pit, this grassy sea of strangers' graves, this mumbling man reading from a book Merrily wasn't certain Rick cared about. It was wrong. She'd gotten it wrong.

She didn't realize she was crying until the woman to her left started patting at her shoulder again, pat pat, pause, pat pat, rhythmically, incessantly. *There, there. There, there.* Someone behind her was humming something vaguely churchish under her breath, but off-tune. Merrily sniffled to silence, wiping her eyes and hoping she wouldn't start laughing instead. She glanced behind her to find Justyce, to share the moment so they could compare notes later, and found Alice. Alice stood outside the reach of the blue rain cover in the sun, her eyes turned away from the ceremony and toward the horizon, as though the whole thing bored her.

Something in Alice's far-off gaze reminded Merrily of something else, maybe a painting she'd seen in a textbook or something, some actress from a movie she liked.

But then it was gone and it was her own ChatX avatar she pictured. She'd sold her knees and her attention to pay for this funeral. Her mom had a *lot* of questions. She'd told her the funeral director gave her a break.

Merrily had the feeling her mom didn't believe her but any lie was better than trying to explain. Her mom wouldn't understand that it was nothing. It was only that her legs went on for miles. For the nicer headstone she was ordering, she'd shopped a snapshot of cleavage among a few of her regulars. Searcher, gone as promised.

Merrily lifted away from the graveside, to a lush sofa not meant for comfort, peeling hundred-dollar bills off her shoulder, off her lap. He'd made her what she'd always said she wasn't, without laying a hand on her. And what had he meant—

The minister made some change in the tenor of his voice, bringing her back. Alice was frowning at someone Merrily couldn't see. Merrily turned back toward the urn, the stage, as though someone might break out into warbling song any minute. She let the stranger to her left pat at her shoulder all she wanted. She would take the comfort. Little had been offered.

After a few more words of scripture closed the program, a silence reigned. Merrily heard it begin and knew that no one would know when to stop it. No one was humming now, and the woman next to her had pulled her arm away. She should stand up, say a few words, invite people back to the house. She should. Her mom should. Someone should do something.

Finally the people behind her started to shuffle away, out from under the tarp and toward their cars or to a nearby spot to await further instruction. Merrily looked up and saw Alice, Juby, and Lillian waiting. Lillian could have used a chair, but she hadn't taken it. Juby raised her hand from her side in a small wave. Merrily turned her head.

In the other direction, the woman in the hat considered a nearby grave, her white handkerchief put away. Merrily stood, felt her mom's hand reach for her. The woman in the hat looked up as Merrily approached, then turned and started walking toward the drive, where their cars were lined up.

Out in the sun, it was hot. Merrily squinted after the woman, who glanced back but didn't stop until she reached a car that had been parked askew, pointed out toward an easy exit. This was a car not going to anyone's home for coffee and more polite condolences. It was a rattletrap, rusted along the bottom of the doors, the hubcaps missing. Merrily studied the brim of the hat until the woman raised her chin and she could study the square brown face streaked with tears.

"OK," Merrily said in a low voice. "That was some noir shit, getting me out here. What do you want?"

The woman removed her hat, exposing sleek black hair, and

threw it into the open window of the car. "I have something for you."

"Who are you, exactly?"

"I was a friend of his." The woman's eyes roved over Merrily's shoulder. Merrily turned to see what had caught her attention. Alice, Juby, and Lillian had come to stand in view of the meeting several yards away, but present. Witnessing. Being nosy.

"What kind of friend?"

"Not a great one," the woman said. "Or I could have figured out a way to help him. But, that's the kind of friends he had. If he'd had a better one—"

"I was his friend." Merrily felt like starting something.

The woman looked her up and down, but gently, almost lovingly. "You were his best friend, I think." She shook her head. "It's a shame he had to rely on a little girl."

Shades of Searcher6, calling her names as he peeled off money to make her something she wouldn't be. "I'm not—"

"Not now, but you were." The woman reached into her car, stretching for something in the passenger seat, her round butt framed in the window and her muscular legs ending in church shoes. She emerged with an envelope and took the three steps between them. "He just wanted to know you. I don't know what he left you but I suppose he wanted to shore up against something happening." She looked past Merrily again as the envelope exchanged hands. "Against something like this."

The envelope had her name written in a hesitant hand, the loop of the *y* reaching around with a flourish, like a monkey's tail. "When did he do this?"

"He gave it to me for safekeeping about two years ago. Something was worrying him, and he wasn't sure . . . But then, should any of us be *sure*?"

Merrily felt her patience nose-dive. The envelope shook in her outstretched hand. "He thought someone might stab him twelve times?"

The woman winced. Her eyes filled up. "I hadn't heard that."

"It's hard to forget once you do."

The woman's lip trembled.

"Were you his girlfriend?" Merrily said, thinking of her mom's jealousies. Her mom. She looked back toward the grave. A few of the gathered had wandered away, but everyone was blocked in by the lead car, which would take her and her mom back to the church. They were all in this together, like it or not. She was keeping them here. No—this woman was. She was holding them all hostage.

"Nothing like that," the woman said. "Ask your friends. They'll tell you." She used her chin to point over Merrily's shoulder, and then her eyes shifted to the envelope. "And who knows? Maybe he'll tell you."

Merrily finally pulled the envelope to her. *Hey, kid.*

The woman opened her car door and got in.

"Wait," Merrily said, and walked to the window. "What's your name? In case he says something about you."

"Rebekah," the woman said, her voice thick. "And my daughter is Mira."

"Mira," Merrily said, licking her lips. "Is she—is she one of his kids?"

Tears had spilled over Rebekah's cheeks, but now she smiled. "Nothing like that, I said. He helped me out of a jam once, stood up for us when no one else would. He was all right, no matter what you hear. He was all right. He never should have ended up—"

Stabbed twelve times.

Rebekah's face shuttered. "I'll tell you that story another time." She nodded goodbye and got the car started and moving, the gravel under the tires crunching all the way to the road.

Another time? Merrily turned to Alice and the rest, the envelope held to her like a shield. She couldn't imagine another minute.

CHAPTER FORTY

ALICE

How had it come to this?

Alice stood at the edge of the blue tarp covering her kidnapper's grave. Rain had been predicted but the sun was out, hot. The mourners fanned themselves. They wore a bluish cast to their faces from the tarp overhead.

Bluer than he deserved.

She'd taken the temperature of this small gathering. Obligation, pity. Or outright manipulation, the tool that Juby had used. One of her texts had said: *Think how u would feel if it was ur dad.* That wasn't fair, was it? Richard Banks—*Rick*—wasn't even Merrily's. He was a stranger, and so was Merrily, actually. Merrily, who was a stranger she had promised her *actual dad* she wouldn't see anymore.

U might as well be kind, Juby had finally said, as though she knew exactly where to strike. People had been kind to Alice when her mother died. She didn't mind paying it forward.

But really? What was she *doing* here? "Maybe you'll be glad someday you were there," Juby said in the car.

To top off her mood, she'd spent the morning before picking them up at Juby's parents' house searching for her Social Security card, unsuccessfully. To get a replacement of *that*, she'd need her birth certificate, which she wasn't sure she'd ever seen.

At the grave, the minister sweated through his vestments and invoked some forgiving passages. *Lost sheep, my ass.* Alice fidgeted until Juby turned a stern jaw in her direction.

She would never be glad to have been here. She was only glad to see how few people suffered Rick's loss. Other than Merrily, only one person bothered to cry, a woman hidden under a giant Royal Ascot hat on the other side of the gathering. Alice wondered at her, frowning, and kept herself outside the shelter of the tarp.

The minister stopped talking. A heavy silence took over. Time stretched on, thin, until Merrily jumped up and hurried out from under the shade. Juby grabbed Alice's wrist and dragged her in the wake of Merrily's long strides.

"What are you doing?" Alice hissed.

"You don't recognize her?" Juby said. She released Alice's arm. Lillian caught up after a moment, a little more breathless than usual from the heat. She took a seat on the nearest gravestone.

"Lil," Juby whispered. "That's someone's nani."

"They don't seem to mind."

Merrily stood at the side of a junker car, talking to the woman in the derby hat. Recognize who? And then she did. *Rebekah.* "What's she doing here?"

"Mourning, I imagine," Juby said.

"But Rick was—"

"You're going to have to get this eventually," Juby said. "Sometimes people get loved, whether you think they should or not. People are more than one thing, OK?"

Alice started making a list of the many things Juby had turned out to be but she kept silent until the woman at the car had handed Merrily something and driven off. "Well?"

"You have somewhere to be?"

Alice stretched her neck to see Merrily's hand. "It's an envelope. What do you think it is?"

"She'll tell us. When she wants to," Lillian said.

It seemed for a few minutes that Merrily wouldn't even open the envelope. If she'd had a pocket, she might have hidden it. When she looked their way, she seemed to decide, tearing at the missive with both hands until the envelope skittered across the lawn, a white bird with broken wings.

Merrily walked toward them, the letter in both hands. Juby darted between stones to snatch the envelope out of the wind and brought it back.

"Is it OK, Mer?" Juby said, glancing nervously at Lillian.

Alice looked between the two and then back at Merrily, feeling as though she'd been left out.

" 'Hey, kid,' " Merrily read, her voice thick and wobbling. " 'If you're reading this, it's because I didn't make it. It's OK for me. I'm tired of the chase. But I wish I'd had more time with you. Thanks to your mom, I got more chances than I deserved. Sorry for the cloak and dagger shit, kid. She'll have to explain it better but I'm worried she won't explain it at all, so here it goes. I'm your . . . dad.' "

Lillian made a breathless sound, like she'd been kicked, and said something under her breath. She and Juby compared shocked faces, then Juby looked Alice's way.

Alice wasn't that surprised, not Lillian's kicked-in-the-gut surprise, not Juby's openmouthed awe. She felt strangely empty of emotion about it. She'd had a theory. The first time she'd seen Merrily, she'd had a feeling she knew her face, and not just from the avatar from the site where the younger woman had posted the plaintive message about Rick being missing. She looked like him a bit, when you paid attention. Sharp features, thin and awkward shape. Alice hadn't *known*, exactly, but now it seemed like maybe she might have. Merrily had been in the kidnapper's house as a baby, so where was the mystery there? *Congratulations, it's a girl.*

" 'Yes, the real one,' " Merrily continued, choking through the words. " 'The things she told you or didn't tell you were to protect you. If you're reading this and I'm gone, then there's no reason to protect you anymore. I love you more—' " Merrily's voice broke and fat tears ran down her cheeks, left, right. " '—more than you can know. I hope you have had a good life despite me being the worst father in the world. You were the one—' " Merrily stopped.

"What?" Juby said.

Merrily sniffled. "It's scribbled out a bit there. 'Tried to' something. 'The one I tried to keep in touch with,' maybe? And then it's signed, 'Love, Rick.' "

They all waited. Behind them, some of the mourners talked loudly, impatient to get going.

"Love," she breathed. "I wish he'd signed it *Dad*, just once. But I guess he didn't think he had a right to. Or maybe he . . . I don't know if I should guess what he was thinking."

"I'm so sorry," Juby said. "I was sorry before, but now I'm really sorry."

"Thanks," Merrily said. She squinted toward the grave. "I can't believe she kept this from me my whole life."

"It seems like. They were trying to keep you safe," Lillian said. She spiked her cane into the ground to drag herself off the headstone and shuffled a few steps toward them. "Considering . . ."

"Yeah," Juby said. "I think we can agree there might have been something to protect you from."

Some of the bereaved had chosen open revolt, pulling their cars around the lead car. The driver for the Cruzes' car leaned against its trunk, smoking a cigarette.

"I think it's time to go, you guys," Alice said.

Juby gave her a look. "It's time to go when Merrily says it is."

Alice sniffed. She was far more impatient with the scene than any of these so-called mourners. All this way, to stand at the grave site of the man who might have ruined her life, or ended it. How much time was the right amount to spend on such a person, out of respect? She had none, not for Richard Banks. *Think how you'd feel.* Yes, fine, she had respect for Merrily. A little. And it had turned out that Rick was indeed Merrily's father, so . . . she got credit for doing the kind thing.

Alice knew the sting of that kind of loss, anyway. It was like no other pain in the world. She could relate—except she'd actually known her mother, hadn't she? Had loved her, had been loved by her as well as she'd been capable.

No point in competing. *All grief, open-ended.* That was the thing Merrily really mourned, whether she knew it or not. The father he might have been, not the one he was. The trouble was, they were both buried in the same grave.

"I need a minute, I think," Merrily said. "Can you . . ."

"Of course," Juby said. She turned toward Alice.

"What?"

"Let's give Merrily *a few minutes.*"

The three of them shuffled toward the grave, toward Mrs. Cruz's folded arms and the small crowd who hadn't managed to get out, all of them sour faced, even for a funeral.

"Tell me again," Lillian said, her voice gruff with exertion. "Stolen why?"

Alice sighed. Juby had broken the news to Lillian about all the research swiped from the trailer, but Lillian still had questions. "It wasn't stolen for a reason," she said. "The thief used my backpack to carry stuff from the safe, and it was all in there. Along with all my IDs and money, by the way."

"All your IDs?" Lillian said.

"You'll need to get that replaced," Juby said. "Do you have the right paperwork?"

"They're very strict. About the paperwork," Lillian agreed.

"You guys are so hot for paperwork," Alice said. "I don't have the right stuff but surely I can get it. Where do you get a copy of your birth certificate? I think the hospital where I was born is closed."

"The county clerk where you were born." Juby tilted her chin. "I'll go with you, if you want."

"I would have to go all the way to— Is there no other way?"

"You should go in person," Juby said. "Since you don't have a driver's license, you'll need to take your police report. They'll want the original of that. And you don't want to mail it. What if it gets lost?"

It was a long drive, three, four hours, probably. She hadn't been to Victorville since she was three and had no interest in seeing it now. The town that had tried to seize her. She glanced toward the urn of Richard Banks's ashes, a tarnished bullet of an urn.

"I'll go tomorrow," she said, as though it were no big deal. She didn't want Juby to go with her. She had an idea that she might visit the library there and see if she could retrieve some of the lost research on her own. If there was any point to it. Richard Banks was dead.

She was tired of the glances Juby and Lillian kept sharing when they thought she couldn't see. Every time they passed a secret look, she resolved more deeply to become the right kind of Doe Pages volunteer—sharper, more attention paid. She'd *demand* their respect. She'd found Richard Banks, hadn't she? In a way? There he was, dammit. Mission accomplished.

She needed a new Doe. Maybe Jane Doe Anaho was beyond her abilities, but she could select another case to make her own. She didn't need Lillian's log-ins. She only needed the inspiration of the right case—

Alice was reminded of the grainy photo of Laura Schmidt, her slim neck and jawline almost visible in a low-quality image. A mug shot? Laura *Banks*, the news story had called her, except that they'd never married. Still, it was the couple of them who'd held her at that house. Laura Banks might be just as guilty, and she'd never been found? But Lillian was playing around with that Doe on the site, wasn't she?

Then Alice remembered the other guy, her dad's friend who had been missing twenty years from Victorville. A newer case, totally unrelated to Richard Banks, for once. Or was he unrelated? There had been a page about him in the frustratingly robust materials from Lillian. She hadn't been able to bring her kidnapper to justice in quite the way she meant to. His death was unsatisfying, in a way, and would never make her dad see why the Doe Pages mattered. But maybe she could find closure for his friend's family.

"When you go . . ." Lillian said. They all watched Merrily stumbling in from the cemetery lawn on heels, the letter flapping in her hand and then folded and tucked into the neckline of her dress. "You'll want the certified version. Of your certificate. Raised seal. That's what they call it."

"Raised seal," Juby said. "No matter what else they offer you."

"Raised seal," Alice repeated. She pictured circus animals, fish thrown.

"There's an application to fill out," Juby said. "And a fee. Take the checkbook or cash—"

"I think I can figure it out."

Merrily took her mother's arm and steered her toward the waiting car. At the last moment, Mrs. Cruz glanced back at the urn, her mouth a straight line.

On the way to her car, Alice passed the urn and resisted the urge to tip it over with a clang into the well that had been dug for it. She would never be glad she'd been here. It was a betrayal to her dad, to her mother, the entire family this man ruined.

She would never forgive herself for standing at his grave when she could have been at her mother's. When she could have been anywhere else at all.

CHAPTER FORTY-ONE
MERRILY

Merrily couldn't see. Her eyes were swollen from crying, and she'd scraped an ankle on the low flat memorial slab of Mr. and Mrs. Clive and Rowenna Buckle as she passed. She kept walking, her mom clutching at her. At the car, the driver threw his cigarette toward the Buckles and opened the door.

Inside, it was dark and almost cold. Like a tomb. Merrily was glad she'd chosen cremation. "What happens now?" her mom said.

"We should have invited people to the house." She'd planned to, but didn't really regret not doing it. She didn't care if anyone came over and ate cold cuts from small plates, helped themselves to the good coffee. The cold cuts she'd ordered just in case would decay in the fridge, funeral meats in every sense. They would say a little prayer over the trash can when the time came and it would all be fine. She held a fist to her mouth to keep the sob in her throat.

"I don't mean . . ."

Merrily knew what she meant. She really knew. What happens now that Daddy was never coming home? The sob escaped.

"Oh, Mer." Her mom reached for her, the bangles at her wrists clattering together. She'd chosen a demure number rather than her usual. The car started to roll toward the gates of the cemetery. Merrily watched the arch of the entrance as they passed under it, through it. Like they were being swallowed.

"Why didn't you tell me?"

"Tell you." It wasn't a question.

"You could have told me. I could have known him."

"You did know him."

Her mom had claimed the texts were nothing before, and now they would have to be enough for always. "I could have known him as my father."

The bangles clanged together, a sour note, as her mom's hand lowered back into her own lap. "How— I couldn't."

"You could have—"

"I mean that I wasn't allowed to," her mom said, a little more forceful than was warranted, in Merrily's opinion. Her mom had gone straight from mournful to rage, as though they'd been having this argument for years. Maybe they had. Maybe she'd only been having it with herself. "He was in secret," her mom whispered, eyes darting toward the back of the driver's head. "Hiding. We weren't supposed to be in touch."

"We were, though."

"I needed his help." She brushed at something invisible on her skirt. "I lost my job, and he was swanning about, protected and paid by the U.S. government—"

"I hardly think you can call living under protection *swanning.*"

"He disappeared practically the moment you were born. He owed us. He owed *you.* Maybe he signed away his rights, how nice for him, while I was left—"

Merrily heard the accusation. *He* escaped. *She* was stuck. Was she truly saying Rick had given up his life, his kids, his freedom, and he was the lucky one? Because he had escaped child support? Child support for—

"Three," Merrily said, wonderingly. "You said he had three kids with three women—"

Her mom's eyes shifted to the window. "When did I say that?"

"And if I'm one of the three, that means I have sisters or brothers—"

"You're an only child with some half-siblings not worth bothering with."

"*What?*"

"It's a can of worms," her mom muttered into the window. Cornfields rolled past. "It's better to leave it."

"Better for you, you mean. Have you ever said anything to me that wasn't in your own best self-interest?" Merrily said.

"How dare you?" Her mom folded her hands, stuck out her chin. Her accent, thick.

"Think about it, Mamá. Are the cans full of worms because you'd rather have me all to yourself? Is that why you told me Rick was a kidnapper? Even the little bit of Rick I had, I couldn't keep? You had to ruin it?"

Her mom fiddled with her bracelets. "That was true. He kidnapped that girl."

Merry stared. "I don't believe you. You're so worried I might want to have a relationship with his other kids, you would stick to that crazy story."

"Those kids do not have the same *blood*—"

"When did you pick up an interest in genetics? Half-siblings are still siblings. I want to know them. I want to meet them, at least."

Her mom's head bounced on her neck. *We'll just see about that*, that bobble said.

"What?"

Mamá Cruz could keep something to herself when she wanted to.

"You know who they are," Merrily said.

"No."

"Sons or daughters?"

Her mom thought about it. "Sons. That's all I'll say."

"You know *where* they are, too, don't you?"

"That's all," her mom said.

Merrily placed her hand over her heart, felt the letter crinkling there inside her bra. "He was right."

Her mom glanced over. "Who?"

"Rick. He thought you'd never tell me, so he had to."

"*What?*" She crossed herself.

"A letter, Mamá. He left behind a letter."

Her mom was more worried about the letter than any ghost. Her eyelids fluttered. "Can I see it?"

Merrily made a big show of brushing something invisible from the skirt of her dress and pulling a snooty face. "I don't think so."

"Don't be childish."

Merrily snorted, watched out the window as the town of Port Bethlehem welcomed them back. Merrily had always thought buildings here at the outskirts were held together by rust, that rust was somehow the glue, not the signal of decline.

"I didn't raise you this way—"

"You raised me to be the adult while you got to be the baby. Congratulations. You're the child. But this part of the conversation is for grown-ups. And don't try tears," she said, as her mom sank her head into her hands. "They won't work."

Merrily's eyes watered, even so.

"I loved him," her mom said hoarsely. "He left anyway. And then we needed his help. To eat. To survive! I wish I could've done it without him. That's who you wanted me to be, the woman who didn't need a husband—but that is not who I was." If she didn't calm down soon, she would slip into Spanish. "I had to have his help so that they wouldn't take you away from me." Her mom sniffled into the back of her hand, bracelets sliding away to her elbow. "They could have taken you away. It scared me more than anything."

Merrily kept her face to the window. "More than being killed? You could have gotten us both killed, going to visit him in Dora."

Her mom's eyes darted to the driver. "He said they didn't know about us."

"They? They followed you to the place he was hiding, Mamá. *They* knew."

Her mom blinked at her. "They were watching."

"Probably listening, too." They sat in silence as the car drove through the familiar streets of Port Beth, where regular life continued, children playing on the sidewalks, a man washing his car. Another day unspiraling from the clock, as though nothing had happened. Their car pulled into the small parking lot behind the church. Merrily's car was parked in the back corner, alone. They'd come together from the house, house to church to grave. Now Merrily wished she could leave directly for her apartment. She'd been away too long.

She listened to the driver humming as he got out of the car and waited until he had closed his door. "Did you ever figure out what was stolen from the house the other night?"

"Nothing."

"Nothing."

The door opened and they slid out into the too-bright sun. A few niceties exchanged, and Merrily slipped the driver a twenty while her mom watched, mouth twitching with questions she would ask later.

In her own car, the doors closed, Merrily looked all around, ran her fingers over the face of the radio. She put her hands on the wheel. "I wonder if they only stole what shouldn't have been there."

A hand shot to her mom's mouth. "What do you mean?"

"Turn off your phone." Her own phone was factory-fresh, thanks to Searcher.

Watching. Listening. Waiting for her and her mom to make contact with Rick. And hadn't they? Mamá, letting Merrily text a man she hardly knew, her father. They'd known? The bulldog? Vasquez? They'd known that Rick was her dad, even when she hadn't?

"So the guy who was supposed to be my dad who died—that guy was, what? Fiction?" She felt a pang for him. He had been someone to her, dead, and now, faked, dead again.

"Just a story I could tell you. A nice man with a regular life."

"Until it ended."

"It was all going to end sometime," her mom said.

CHAPTER FORTY-TWO

MERRILY

Merrily dropped her mom off at her house and drove back to the city. She crept back into her apartment like a thief, crossing the spot of sun coming through Justyce's open door before sighing with relief. Alone. She hadn't been alone more than a few minutes since her mom showed up Monday night. In her room, she paused to appreciate the scene. Justyce had finished the laundry her mom had started and put the folded sheets on the corner of her bed.

Above her desk, the photo of the man she'd been told was her father, a man in uniform, sharp-shouldered and squinting into the sun. Who was that, then? A photo from a flea market or a freebie with the frame?

She turned the frame over on its face, let her overnight bag fall to the floor. Home. She kicked off her sandals and dove for the bed. She curled on her side and pulled the comforter over her, a cocoon. The last time she'd been in this room seemed a million years ago. The last time she'd been in this room, her father was dead, and now that man was a story and her actual father was dead, too. Double prizes.

Merrily opened her eyes. The overnight bag hadn't been zipped, and some of her stuff had burst out. Some underpants, the hem of a dress that hung out like a tongue. She reached into the side pocket and grabbed a handful of the photos she'd stowed there. Young Rick, dating Rick, family Rick. She shuffled the edges into a square and dealt them like a casino dealer, stopping on one of him in the leather jacket she might have saved from the dumpster. If only she had.

Her *dad*.

She could see it now, actually. Sometimes, when his head was turned at the right angle, she saw her own nose. She reached for her new phone. Thank fuck for auto-uploading apps, or she would have lost all the photos she'd ever snapped. The last photo she'd taken was the selfie from the hotel lobby before she'd met Searcher. It made her sick, her in her sad little jacket. Now she looked at her own face for Rick's nose. Rick's nose, which had become hers. And he was tall and long-limbed. Her mile-long legs, right from the source. How had she not seen?

Because she hadn't been looking. No—she'd been looking right at it, but she hadn't been *searching* because her mom had managed the world's greatest magician's trick of misdirection. Don't look at the father over there! Look at the father *here*.

She couldn't even feel bad for that kid she was, that sucker born three minutes ago. She didn't even have to be gullible. She trusted. She had no reason not to.

She was less trusting now.

Merrily didn't buy for a second that Rick had kidnapped someone. It was ridiculous. Maybe he wasn't perfect, maybe he was an *actual* skeeze, she didn't really know. *You don't get to choose who taught you to ride a bike*, she thought.

Rick hadn't taught her to ride a bike. Everything Rick had to teach her she was learning right now.

She was definitely getting to the bottom of this story, this supposed kidnapping. Those brothers she'd never met—

Merrily sat up. Juby said they'd found one of Rick's kids, a *daughter.*

Mamá Cruz strikes again.

She would not accept another lie as long as she lived. She'd just assume everyone lied all the time. Never again *I'll call you.* Never again *Just this once.* Never again a scammer like Searcher6. Fuck that guy. Her coat was *cute.* She held up the photo on her phone again. She made that nose work.

One minute she was admiring the cascade fall of her own hair in the image, and the next she could only see the face that appeared over her shoulder, a ghost. It was him. Searcher6.

Merrily sat up, her hand to her mouth. *How in the—*

She cast her mind back. She'd been standing with her back to a darkened store window in the hotel lobby that night. In the photo, Searcher is reflected, indistinct and blurry, caught in movement. And exceedingly close to her. Was that why he'd snatched her phone?

Her arms goosefleshed. He'd walked right past her as she posed. He'd said he recognized the background of her photo and known where she was, but that was another lie. He'd followed her into the lobby.

Had he somehow tracked her phone to be right where she was?

"*Seriously* messed up," Merrily murmured.

She saved the image to her phone and, thinking of those listening devices, of the phone he'd taken, she made sure the photo was still saved to the cloud. And then sent a copy to herself by email. And to her mom. In case. And then in a text to Juby, in extraordinary case. *Thanks for coming today,* she typed, though she knew the photo and text had nothing to do with one another. Mostly she just wanted to talk to Juby.

Of course, came the reply. *I'm so sorry. Cute jacket.*

Then Juby sent another message. *Did u talk to your mom about the letter?*

She didn't want to tell me, Merrily tapped out. *Just like Rick said. She never would have.*

Are you glad u know?

Merrily sat with it a minute, to allow herself the chance of feeling whatever it was she could feel: Sad. Stuck. Scared. But she could feel a tiny light down deep, under the rest. *Deep, deep down.* Something hopeful, below everything else. Something that had to do with how messed up things were, had always been. Nothing had ever been normal. If she couldn't seem to find normal easy to pull off or at all appealing now, then whose fault was that?

Yes. She tried to think of what else to say, but there was nothing. *Yes, I'm glad.*

Good, Juby wrote. *When things calm down . . .*

She sent three wineglass emojis in a row.

Merrily sent a smiley face in return. *Holy shit yes.*

Hey, Merrily typed after a moment. *Where did Alice live when she was kidnapped?*

Supposedly?

There was a long pause. Merrily began to wonder if Juby would ignore her. She flicked through the photos of Rick while she waited. Young Rick, dating Rick, family Rick. She found that she sought more detail from the photos now. This was her family, her loose-leaf family album. Who was the woman who'd written *King Richard*? Her grandmother? She pawed through the photos looking for little Rick and his stuffed toy. Who was that woman with Rick at the campfire? And the girl admiring his leather jacket, her face turned from the camera and only the curve of her jaw visible behind a sheet of long, dark hair—who was that? Merrily paused over this one.

Her phone buzzed.

You heard?

Several messages arrived quickly. *Ugh I'm sorry.*

Victorville.

Why?

This time Merrily was the one letting time lapse. She went through the photos again, digging a few stragglers out of her bag on the floor. She sorted them into a timeline, based on Rick's approximate age from boyish cheeks to bushy beard, his hair, his weight. In this order, the photo of the girl with her jaw turned to the camera and the photo of the woman at the campfire with her hair over her face were back-to-back, one, two. The same woman? The same woman from the newspaper, too? The woman from whom her mom had proudly stolen Rick?

Merrily chewed on her bottom lip, looking up from the photos only to see King Richard himself, jaunty little boy of the dunes with a toy at his feet, resting against the computer speaker on her desk. She stood up and went to it, touching it as though it couldn't really be there. It couldn't. It hadn't been there when she'd packed, her mom waiting at the door. Had Justyce found it and put it on her desk?

She opened the door. "Justyce, did you—"

Justyce wasn't home. The bathroom door stood open. The bathroom. Hadn't Justyce said something about someone coming to fix a leak?

She'd never seen a leak, hadn't reported one to the super.

Merrily closed the door, then slammed down the screen of her laptop and picked up her new phone.

She was just paranoid. Probably.

No reason, she typed to Juby. *It's too crazy right?*

She added an emoji: round yellow face, pink tongue sticking out.

Crazy.

And that was exactly what she might be, if she did what she thought she might.

Unknown Caller: Friend of yours?

Attached pdf.

Former Steelworker, Family Man Missing

Victorville, Ind.—Police are looking for any leads on the whereabouts of Travis Allen Malayter, missing since Tuesday. Malayter was last seen dropping off his son at Victorville East Elementary School Tuesday around 8:15 a.m.

Malayter was most recently employed at Van Iden–Calloughway Steel Works in Indianapolis, though his wife, Eileen Ryan Malayter, says he had also been working odd jobs. Travis Malayter is the father of one, Shawn, age 9. He is an alumnus of Victorville High School and a member of the Steel Workers United Local 908 and the Victorville Christian Church.

Those who have any information to help locate the missing man are encouraged to contact the Victor County Sheriff's Office immediately.

CHAPTER FORTY-THREE

ALICE

At the gas station north of Victorville, Alice leaned on the counter, pointed. "Pack of lights," she said. The guy behind the counter reached automatically, not looking at her or the racks of cigarettes above his head. He named his price but she hesitated until he looked up. He stood up straighter, sucked in his gut.

There was only one gas station at the exit, prices sky-high. Alice slid her dethawed credit card across the counter. This was not an emergency. She didn't smoke.

"Alice Fine," he read from the card.

He was a big guy, doughy as well as tall, with an undercut that revealed an unattractive scalp under long greasy strands. He had a lot of holes in his earlobes now empty. Other than that, he could have been anyone. No tattoos or scars she could see. Anyone.

"Shawn Malayter," he said, holding out a hand. "I think our parents are—were—*are* friends."

She shook his clammy hand, took her time pretending to place the name. She'd planned the trip to get her birth certificate sorted for her new license, but then she'd finally read Jimmy's last text. A few clicks online—*beep boop*—and she'd found Shawn hashtagging through a woodworking hobby and dull days at the gas station. Easy enough to find the place based on his photos, and luck was on her side to find him on shift. "Malayter," she said. "As in Travis Malayter?"

"Hey, Mia," the guy called toward the back of the store. "I'm taking my break."

A muffled voice hollered agreement.

Alice followed him out the door to the back of the station, found some shade. The drive had been long, hot. A trickle of sweat rolled down her back. "Not a word? Still?"

"Fatherless these twenty years."

"I'm so sorry." She was determined not to play this intense, like the Does had always seemed to her. *Casual* curiosity. "And in all these years, did they ever get even a . . . lead? Any idea at all?"

He scuffed his bootheel against the ground. "Once in a while they'd come and talk to my mom. This or that. Questions they hadn't thought to ask, or can you look at this photo, that kind of thing."

"Do you remember the day he went missing?"

"You serious? Of course I fucking remember it."

Could you forget a detail if you wanted? "There was another person who went missing from here, too," she said. "Someone named Laura Banks. Or Laura Schmidt?"

His attention sharpened. "Have people been saying he ran off with her?"

"She disappeared long before your dad did. And she was—well, she was a mess, showing up in the news . . . drug charges and stuff. Your dad didn't have a drug probl—"

"No." He reached for the pack of cigarettes she'd just bought and started slapping one end against his palm. "If you're going to buy shit so you can talk to me, buy the full tar, for Christ's sake." He didn't say anything else until he had a cigarette lit. "He was a lot of things but not that."

"Do you mind talking about him?"

"I don't. But why would *you* be interested?"

The villain of her childhood was now a canister of dust dropped into a hole. Everything else was a fucking mess, but maybe Travis Malayer's family might like a quiet spot to visit, too, if that's all they could have. "I work with this website that helps find missing people."

"Seriously?" His nose wrinkled. "For fun?"

"Intellectual exercise. For a sad and lonely life."

"That's going around." He took another drag. "So you think you could find him?"

"I'd like to try."

"In what condition?"

She stuttered to answer. "Well—uh. *Found—*"

"Sorry, I'm rusty with social graces. It's been a while since anyone asked about him."

Alice was reminded of Lillian, wanting the chance to say her missing brother's name. "Tell me about Travis."

Shawn frowned, turned the bootheel on the ground again. "He worked random hours, slept a lot when he was home, yelled at us for being too loud. Ready to whoop someone's butt, given the chance. Still. He was my dad. I think he loved me. I know he loved her. He wouldn't walk away from my mom."

"That's the theory? He just left?" At his hard look, she amended, "I mean, *their* theory, not yours."

"If by *theory* you mean the idea they burrowed into so deep they didn't consider any others, then *yeah*. All that *Travis Ma-layter, family man*, bullshit, but they didn't believe it. They didn't look that hard for him."

"What do you think happened?"

On the other side of the gas station, cars rushed by. The high-way had a certain noise to it on a hot day, and Alice wondered what it was about the sound that made her feel a little sick. The sound of everyone racing away, the sound of time passing while she stood still.

"He wouldn't have left us."

"You think he was killed," she said.

"This is the part I'd rather not *theorize* about." He started back toward the door.

Inside, the air-conditioning was cranked. Shawn let himself in behind the register.

"What was his job?"

"Factory welder. He got laid off a few months before . . . before." He glanced around. "Mom said he paid the rent doing this and that, but I heard them talking once when I wasn't supposed to. He said he was a driver."

"Like over-the-road? Big rig? Or, like, taxi?"

"More like . . ." A customer approached, an old man in glasses thick enough Alice hoped he wasn't driving. He was, though, pay-ing for his seven dollars' worth of gasoline in soft bills. Seven dol-lars wouldn't get anyone far.

Shawn leaned over the counter and spoke more quietly. "More like chauffeur? But like not really? A guy who . . . you know. The one who makes things happen, for a guy who *really* makes things happen."

"Wait, like—"

"All I know is after my dad had been gone awhile, the guy he worked for sent us money. A lot of money. I'm not sure what to think about that, but as far as I know, even my mom doesn't know who he is. We needed the money. She never told the cops *any* of this, so don't tell your dad."

"My dad's not a cop anymore," she said. *Always a cop.*

"I know, but she wouldn't want your dad to think less of her. They're still in touch. I thought maybe someday they might . . ." Shawn blinked at her. "But maybe not. I don't think she wanted to accept the money. The night I heard my parents talking, she sounded like she was not in favor of, like, anything having to do with that guy. 'His Highness' this and 'His Highness' that."

"His . . . Highness?" Alice smiled, unsure. "What is that?"

"Because whoever it was treated my dad like a servant, I guess, making him do his bidding? That's what they called him, to each other. His Highness."

"Like . . ." Alice licked her lips. "Like a king?"

"Just like a king. Hold on." Another customer approached, and this one wanted to chat about some product the station had once carried and no longer did. "This is a real problem," the woman said, her voice going shrill. Alice let herself be pushed aside and turned to the exit.

"Wait," Shawn called after her. "We could, uh, do you want to—"

She was outside, gulping at the dusty air before he could get the question out.

Just like a king. Just like.

ALICE SAT IN her car, the keys useless in her hand.

It didn't mean anything, only a thing people might say.

JimBig King was *family.* He couldn't be . . .

Could he?

She remembered her dad always looking to JimBig for the nod, for the go-ahead. *Jesus.* That look JimBig could give that would stop a train had always felt like a physical threat, but she'd never realized he meant it. Never realized he might deliver.

Had delivered, and how many times? How many people standing in his way? No, it was too cliché. Construction? All that concrete—

Alice gagged. She threw open the door and leaned out, caught her breath.

All those foundations, rotten, and the business in her name to protect the big men. Jimmy saved for bigger things.

Oh, God, what to make of him stealing the books in the dead of night, and just as the business was vulnerable with Matt's accident—

She leapt from the car and retched onto the asphalt.

The Kings would be looking to assign blame. All that cash in Matt's bank account, the dowry, another strike against. But why push someone off the third story when you'd already bought him? Was the money Lita mentioned from after the fall? A payment for a life, as the Malayter family had received?

Alice sat sideways on the driver's seat, her feet on the pavement, her head in her hands.

If JimBig was calling shots and making payments, what did that make Harris Fine, his right hand and left?

Her dad couldn't know about this. He never would have dragged her into this, or her mother. He'd only given JimBig a leg up, second chance after his stint in prison—one he didn't deserve—and had drawn them too close, bound the families too tightly.

A strange sound drew Alice's attention toward the highway. Two cars were stopped, one spun nose-to-nose with the other, at cross lengths to the flow of traffic. As she watched, another car plowed into one of the stalled ones, then another. Another. The roads were dry, and yet tires kept screeching, metal kept crunch-ing. Alice watched until she thought of what it meant to be a wit-ness. She couldn't stop it, could she?

She turned back to the station, where Shawn and others had come outside to see the commotion.

Alice met Shawn's eyes, then looked away. She was tired of wars raging over her head, the decisions being made without her having a say. She owned the company. She was the boss.

But she wasn't the king. Only one man was.

CHAPTER FORTY-FOUR

ALICE

I would know you anywhere," a woman's voice said.

Alice, impatient, looked up from the county clerk's form, half filled in. She'd broken two of those dumb little golf pencils. Address. Email address. Parents' information. She might have to give a vial of blood and promise her firstborn child to get this birth certificate. She could barely concentrate. *Just like a king.* She needed to get home and talk with her dad.

The woman leaned against the counter, waiting for the clerk who had already looked askance at the police report Alice was using as identification. It was Friday. No one in the building seemed to want that yellow form or her story.

The stranger waiting at the desk had a bad haircut but a pleasant face, as though she were in the process of doing someone a favor.

Alice tipped her head over the application again. "Oh, yes?" she said, more sound than words.

"I thought she went off," the woman said. "Haven't seen her in years."

Went off. Her mother, she meant, as though her mother were a ticking bomb. As far as comparisons went, it wasn't bad—though her mother had always treated *her* as carefully as an unexploded mine. Something to hold at arm's length.

"Is she back in town?" the woman said.

The third pencil snapped. Alice sighed and slammed it down. "Yes? What?"

"Your mother? Did she move back?"

"I'm sorry to report that my mother died two years ago," Alice said.

"Oh, I hadn't heard." The way the woman's face sank, Alice almost offered her condolences.

"I'm not sure the obituary made it this far," Alice said more kindly. "We haven't lived in the area for a long time."

"I was at school with her," the woman said. "She struggled to find her way, didn't she? I thought that Harris Fine could have gone easier on her."

Alice's memory called up the image of her dad at her mother's bedside, gently tucking the corner of a sheet or getting up to turn the blinds so that the light was softer on her face.

"I'm not sure what you mean," Alice said. "He was absolutely devoted."

An odd expression passed over the woman's face. She started to say something, but then folded the words and swallowed them. "My mistake . . ."

The clerk appeared behind the counter, which distracted the other woman. Alice turned back to her form, confirming she had divulged every scrap of information requested. She didn't want to have to make another trip to Victorville because of some checklist. She didn't want to make another trip to Victorville *ever.*

The chatty woman left with a glance in Alice's direction. Alice regained the counter position and slid the paperwork across.

"You're seeking your original birth certificate, raised seal," the clerk said. Her glasses were too big for her face. Someone must have told her once that glasses made her look smart.

"Raised seal," Alice said, pleased to have the lingo. "That's right."

A computer almost as old as the one Alice used at work sat on the counter. The clerk tapped away at the keyboard while Alice watched a scar on the woman's knuckles. Had she punched something? People could surprise you.

"You were born in this county? You're sure?"

"I was born at Victorville Memorial, before it closed. That's this county, isn't it?"

The keyboard took the brunt of this information. Alice leaned on the counter.

"Oh, *there* you are." The clerk considered the screen thoughtfully. "You needed a new driver's license? You'll need the amended to get the Social Security card and then a new license."

"I definitely need a new license." How much was this going to cost her? "That's the only reason I'm here."

"But original and the amended? Both?"

She'd need a little firesafe to keep them, so she'd never had to do this again. Another fifty bucks, but the idea of that flat metal box under her bed appealed to her. "Yeah, how long does that take?"

"Three weeks. Could be sooner. You'll get it in the mail at this address." The clerk's finger found the specific location on the form. "The P.O. box in . . . Fell Creek, Illinois?"

"Wait," Alice said. "Let me give you my street address. I don't want to drive out there." She grabbed another pencil.

"The *traffic*, right? I can't imagine living up there."

"Well, we can't all live in God's empty acre, can we?" Alice said cheerfully.

"I'm sorry?"

"What do I owe you?"

The clerk pushed up her glasses. "Forty-four, cash or money order. And let me make a copy of that police report, too."

Alice kept her eye on the yellow square of paper, into machine, out of machine, carried back to the counter, and placed into her hand. Until she touched it again, she couldn't think of anything else. The police report was the only tangible proof in the world that she existed.

For a moment she wondered what would happen if the form got sucked into the copier and shredded. What was left? How easy was it to throw off an identity?

What if you wanted to? What if you *needed* to?

Outside the clerk's office, she stopped. People sighed and went around her.

JimBig was a dangerous man. Jimmy Junior, court jester, did his father's bidding. They even had a dirty cop in their pocket.

We can't win.

In the game of Kings against Fines, there was no contest.

Alice pushed her way to the wall and sank her shoulder against it. She closed her eyes, fumbled for her new phone. Who could they trust?

She got voice mail. She hung up, dialed again. This time when her dad's voice offered her a chance to leave a message, she did. "Dad, I need to talk to you. Something is . . . I don't even know what's going on. Please call me."

She hung up, thought about trying again and again until he picked up. Who cared about another parking garage right now?

Who cared about King and Fine? The company was a front, their work only a monument to the ego and crimes of one man.

Monument.

Yes.

Tonight was the grand opening reception for 1799 South Michigan. They'd all be there, a public space. Several hundred witnesses to keep things civil. Alice hurried toward the exit. Tonight. Tonight the Fines broke from the family business.

CHAPTER FORTY-FIVE
MERRILY

The Victor County Sheriff's Office could have been a dentist's office. It reminded Merrily a bit of the cube farm she'd so recently worked in, and she thought suddenly of the messages on her phone from Kath, left unread.

She'll think I'm dead.

"Help you?"

Merrily wasn't sure which man behind the counter had spoken, since neither of them looked in her direction. She focused on the younger man, tender-aged, with a scrawny look about him. An intern? Or did people just look that young to her now? He finally glanced over, did a double take, then hopped up to be of service. He was several inches shorter than she was, but he didn't seem to mind looking up.

He had a name tag. "Zachary, hi. I could use your help. How can I get a copy of a police report from . . ." She sucked her teeth to show it was a big ask. "Thirty years ago?"

Zachary cleared his throat and answered a spot over her shoulder. "Well, that's not too difficult. All you need to do is fill out a request for public information and there's a small fee once we know how many pages we need to copy, but then you'd get a response within thirty days."

"Thirty days?" It came out sounding harsh, unfriendly. She turned on her ChatX charm. "Thirty days is too long for my . . . needs. Is there any other option? Is there anything *you* could do, perhaps?"

The stress she put on the word was almost a physical stroke, like a hand reaching to pet a cat. The cat, arching its back to meet the touch.

His voice lowered. "I could—"

"What's going on, Zach?" The other man had finally looked her way. "Freedom of Information Act forms are right there on the counter."

"Thank you," she said. Some people you didn't need to bother with. This guy had a fat gold band on his left ring finger and a scowl. His wife was cutting back on treats in his lunch bag. His shoes pinched. Whatever it was, she could sense it like a cloud, an aura, around him. She reached for one of the forms. "Thank *you*, Zachary," she whispered. "I'll just take this and be going. Where's the ladies' room, please?"

Zachary's neck was pink. "Down the hall to the right."

She winked at him, rotated, walked away. When she was sure he could see the length of her, she glanced back over her shoulder.

Down the hall to the right, she waited outside the ladies', checking her phone. She messaged Kath and heard back immediately, with a panting message about Billy, their old boss. *He's accused of sexual harassment*, Kath wrote. *No one is shocked.*

Who turned him in? she typed but didn't care. It was like another life. It was like a prehistoric time, something out of a history book. Billy? Dinosaur. If she'd stayed, it might have been her, and all the women on fourth would be burning up their data plans trying to figure out what she'd worn, what she'd said, how much she had asked for it.

She felt someone at her shoulder and turned. "Hey, Zachary," she purred.

No POLICE REPORT. None. The kidnapping might not have ever happened, for how much the local law knew about it. But Zachary went back and looked up Rick's name, too, all of them, just in case. Under his last name of Banks, Rick showed up in the system as a string of moving violations—failing to stop at a stop sign, speeding—and one outstanding ticket he'd never paid. Headlight out. Merrily looked over the handwritten list Zachary had brought her. Bad driver. Bad *luck*. But then there was one last notation: B&E.

"Breaking and entering? What happened after that?" she asked, the paper gently shaking in her hands.

"Nothing," Zachary said. "No more traffic stops, nothing."

"When was this?"

Zachary had to go back and look. When he came back out, he looked less hopeful. He gave a date. Thirty years.

"So he's ticketed, ticketed, ticketed . . . is that normal?"

Zachary dragged his eyes away from her chest. "And then nothing for thirty years. That's probably the abnormal part."

That part she could explain. Zachary had thought to jot down an address, current at the time of Rick's last arrest. Merrily entered the address into her phone's search bar. It was only a couple of blocks away.

Breaking and entering . . . where? "I can't," Zachary said. "My boss just asked if I have an upset stomach, I'm visiting the john so much. I better get back to work."

His tone begged for an excuse not to, but she had what she'd come for and another lead or two. He passed her one last slip of paper, a phone number. From the lobby she texted him an emoji kiss. *Hashtag thankYOU.* She didn't wait around for him to consider it an invitation.

She was standing on the steps, the map to Rick's old house on her phone, when a shadow fell across her hand. Merrily jumped back.

Alice Fine stood in front of her. "What are you doing here?"

Her face was a fierce, hot white, long strands of hair flying outward in the wind. Merrily stared, captivated by the sight of human combustion in process.

"What. Are. You. Doing. Here?"

"What? What are *you*— I just wanted to see the place." She wouldn't say this was her second trip. "Rick used to live here."

Alice dismissed her and the town with a wave, a piece of yellow paper flapping in her hands. "This shithole. Well, I wouldn't want to stand in the way of you getting to know *Daddy*." She brushed past Merrily, down the stairs.

What was her *problem?* "Not everyone gets raised as royalty."

Alice whipped around. "What do you mean by that?"

"You act like you're somehow better than everyone else. Juby says—"

"Juby!"

"She says you're not the absolute lunatic I think you are, that I should give you a chance."

"A chance to what?"

Merrily put her phone away. "She said you were fun."

"I'm not that fun."

Merrily felt a smile twitch at her lips. "What's fun to Alice

Fine? What do you do for hobbies, besides hanging out with dead people?"

Alice flinched. "I don't fucking knit, OK? I'm only here because I have to be."

"So we have that in common," Merrily said. "We're just a couple of . . ." She couldn't think of the right way to say it.

"Blank slates?"

She practices mean lines in the mirror. "I wasn't going to go that far."

"How far would you go?"

Alice was still in the conversation they were having, but Merrily pictured Searcher's hundred-dollar bills flying at her. She could taste those bills in the back of her throat. The ones he'd forced her to take, shoved into her pocket with his hot hand, grazing her hip through her coat—those were folded up and hidden in her purse. She should have taken them all. "I have somewhere to be."

Merrily pulled out her phone again and held it up. She took the steps down and followed the blue arrow down the block.

Alice fell into step with her. "And where is that?"

"Nowhere you'd care about."

"I used to live in this town, too, you know."

"This *shithole*?" Merrily said.

They walked in silence for a block, turned up a street lined with houses left to fight off nature and time. Merrily checked her phone, faltered.

"Where are we going?" Alice said.

Merrily continued down the street. Within a few steps, Alice caught up again. "Is your mom doing OK?" Alice said.

Merrily glanced her way. "The guy she loved died but outed her as a liar on his way to the grave. She's great. Oh, and we think our house might have been bugged."

"Bugged? Why would your place be *bugged*?"

"Rick was in witness protection. That's federal shit. They can do anything they want. Bugging a little casita in Port Beth, Indiana, that's probably a ten-minute job. Our phones? No problem."

Alice stared. "Witness—"

"Shh!"

"If your house was bugged and your phone, who do you think we're keeping secrets from at this point?"

Merrily stopped. "That's the problem, Alice. I don't know. Maybe it's you I should be scared of. Maybe you're the enemy."

Alice looked away. "I might be."

Merrily checked the map on her phone screen. Alice leaned in. "Is that the phone you think is—"

"New phone, untouched by human hands other than mine. Are you coming?"

Alice followed, feet scuffing the sidewalk. But Merrily knew that trick, one of her mom's favorites, and it wasn't going to slow her down.

CHAPTER FORTY-SIX

ALICE

The kidnapper's daughter, of all people. If not for bad luck, Alice would have none at all.

She followed Merrily away from the county courthouse, knowing she was being petty, knowing she couldn't stop.

"Bugging a little casita in Port Beth, Indiana, that's probably a ten-minute job," Merrily said. "Our phones? No problem."

"Witness—"

But she was thinking of the security cameras trained on the only door she used, the feed going fuck-knows-where. Her old phone, smashed under a cop's boot. *A favor.*

"Maybe you're the enemy," Merrily said.

She'd told Jimmy King about Merrily. On the steps of the trailer, just before the Cruzes' house got broken into. "I might be," she said. How had one family of problems transmitted to another, if not through her?

When she next looked up, they'd stopped in front of a house with a flat gray face, yellowed newspaper in window eyes, front stoop mouth with boards missing. Alice checked up and down the street. Merrily had taken a stack of photos out of her purse and was sorting them thoughtfully, like a meditation.

"What are those?"

"Nothing." Merrily tucked the photos away and held up her phone, framing a shot of the house.

"What are you doing?" Alice hissed.

"Rick lived here."

Alice pivoted away from the house. With the letter to Merrily, all Rick's sins were washed away. A baptism of sorts. He was sainted, no longer in the realm of man or mistake. And now they would walk the sites like pilgrims? "This is—you brought me to the house—"

"I didn't bring you," Merrily said, smug-faced. "You invited yourself."

Alice wheeled on the house as though facing down a foe. But it was just a house. Faded brown paint, weathered and peeling. In the right light, with some tender attention, it might be cute, a home for a family. A wave of nausea passed over her, and she sensed the soft stretch of black wings somewhere near the base of her skull. "Did you ever ask your mother about this house, about me?"

Merrily's self-satisfied twist of smile slid away.

"She confirmed it, didn't she?" Alice said.

"My mom has fed me nothing but lies and birthday cake for a week." Merrily sighed at the house. "Let's go get a drink and you can tell me."

"Convince you, you mean. Aren't you going to knock on the door?"

Merrily gazed up at the house. "What does it matter who lives there now? Not every lead needs to be hunted down to its end."

"But—" Tidy endings. Maybe she couldn't resist them. Merrily started walking back the way they'd come.

Alice didn't hurry to catch up, but watched from behind the swing of Merrily's arms. "Witness protection from what?"

"No one will tell me. I don't think he stayed in it. I mean, if you're in witness protection, they know where you are, right? But they lost him."

"*They* who?"

"The FBI shouldn't have to come to my job and ask *me* where he is."

"Why did they come see you and not your mom?"

"Right? They knew she wouldn't tell them. Or maybe she really didn't know. I was the one he texted all those years. Other than us, who else could they have asked?"

"Rebekah," Alice said.

Merrily turned on her. "How do you know *Rebekah*?"

They needed to share information. Maybe that's what Juby meant to say to Merrily, that they should work together. Except they weren't really looking for the same man. They never had been. Rick, Richard—he'd been at least three different people.

And I'm not looking for any of them anymore.

No more lost causes. No more dead ends. Alice stuffed away the memory of Shawn Malayter's hopeful face. She was only saving her own family from here on out.

They found a lit neon beer sign in the window of a pizzeria on the courthouse square. Alice hesitated, checked her phone for messages from her dad. There were none. She should go home anyway. Richard Banks was a closed case, and Merrily Cruz was no use to her.

"Come on," Merrily said. "One drink with the likes of me won't kill you."

They sat down across from one another over a sticky table.

"So Rebekah probably reported him missing," Merrily said.

"And submitted his info to the Doe Pages, I guess. Her or his landlord."

"But then his info came down from the site."

Alice tried wiping the table with a paper napkin. "It's possible it was ordered down, by whatever agency had him in protection. He would have been in danger, from whatever he was hiding from in the first place."

Their eyes met. "I wish I knew what that was about," Merrily said. "I only know the last time he was arrested—"

"The *last* time?"

"Mostly speeding tickets, actually," Merrily said. "But he was arrested for breaking and entering, and then, poof, nothing."

"Nothing."

"Nothing about *you.*" Merrily stared at her. "No police report on that supposed kidnapping. Are you *sure* he—"

"I'm sure," Alice said.

Merrily caught the waitress's attention. "Two Lites? OK, give me the facts, Alice in Wonderland."

"Don't—please don't call me that."

Merrily rolled her eyes. "What do you remember?"

"I remember that house," Alice said. "The inside, I mean. My room was off the living room, a mattress on the floor. There were two people there. At first two people, a man *and* a woman, and then another woman and a baby. Your mom and you, I'm pretty sure. You were crying and she was yelling—"

"She's an *excellent* yeller," Merrily said, smiling. Alice noticed her hands were shaking, though.

"—and she didn't like me being there at all. I suppose she felt—"

"Stop," Merrily said. "No supposing. Facts."

She doesn't want the truth. She wants a story she can live with.

Their beers arrived, and they took a minute to sip them. "OK, facts. I was scared and crying and clutching my blanket and I remember my dad holding me. I felt absolutely safe." She closed her eyes, letting a shadow of something like grief pass over her. She reached for the memory, testing. The great black wings stretched but did not take flight.

Merrily sighed. Alice opened her eyes to find the other woman sorting the stack of photos from her purse again. She slapped them down into piles like a strange hand of solitaire. It must be self-soothing, like the worn satin edge of her old blanket as she tried to sleep. "How long were you missing?" Merrily said.

"Why does it matter?" Alice looked out the window. "An afternoon."

Merrily paused over her array of photos. "Only an afternoon?"

"My parents would have been frantic."

"Of course, I'm not saying it's nothing. It's just—you said 'my room.' "

"What?"

" 'My room,' " Merrily said. "You said *my* room."

Alice put down her beer. "No, I didn't."

"You did," Merrily said. "You said *your room* was off the living room. You make it sound like you lived there." She returned her attention to the photos, then plucked one, stared at it. Finally she held it out. "Do you know this house?"

The black-and-white photo shook a bit in Merrily's hand. Alice took it from her. The photo showed a young man in a leather jacket, thin and tall. *Rick.* He grinned down at a woman, her long, straight hair a shiny curtain drawn across one corner of the frame. The photo revealed little about the room or surroundings. The photographer had only meant to capture the interaction of the couple.

Alice traced the curve of the woman's jaw in profile. "Who is this? Is this . . ." It made no sense.

Merrily slid another photo across the table in answer. The same couple, a lakeside cabin. The man sat in a camp chair and the woman grasped at him playfully from behind, the length of her hair swinging across her face. The same curve of jaw, barely visible.

I know who you are, Alice thought.

But she didn't. She didn't want to know. She only wished the woman could turn more fully into the frame of the photo, could reveal herself to be a stranger. But from this angle, she was all too familiar. Her cheek, her face—

"Is she—"

"I think she's Laura Schmidt," Merrily said gently.

"I don't understand." Alice could only muster a whisper.

"You don't know her?"

Alice's stomach hurt, and her head felt like it might blow apart. The beating of black wings was like distant thunder, closing in. "No, I— Is this some kind of joke?"

"On the day I met you, I thought you looked like someone I knew. But it's this woman I was thinking of." Merrily held up the other photo, gazed at it lovingly. "I've had these photos a long time, you know? They're almost like—well, it's sad to say *friends* and now it turns out they're family."

"What is this? What is this about?"

"I don't know, but—" Merrily met her eyes, looked away. "I thought you must know her. Your mother maybe—"

"My mother—" Alice's voice was stronger, louder, but then it strangled into nothing. She couldn't breathe, though the great black wings beat the air. She tasted the dust they stirred.

"Alice?"

The clippings Lillian had collected, the ones Jimmy had been spoon-feeding her like an infant. The woman at the county clerk's office. *I would know you anywhere.* The bad xeroxes of Laura Schmidt's face. An *amended* birth certificate? "No." The word was a wheeze. She sounded like Lillian. How could this woman be her mother? She could think of a way. "I can't—" she choked. "I have to—"

"Are you—"

"I have to talk to my dad." Her dad hadn't wanted her to know. "My dad or . . ."

Not Uncle Jim.

Merrily looked down at the photos, then started collecting them, one by one, searching. "I used to have a photo of Rick with two buddies at the beach. I wonder if your dad was one of the guys."

"They weren't *friends*." Were they? How had her dad known how to find her when she'd gone missing? Why had it been kept out of the papers, exactly? What precise *arrangements* had been made?

Alice grasped the photo of Laura Schmidt. *That Harris Fine could have gone easier on her.* She was the product of some dalliance? And then what? She remembered the clipping from Lillian's pile of research, the child sent to family services from the scene of an overdose. *You are my sunshine*, sung in a bright kitchen. A memory that had never matched the woman Alice knew as her mother. She had always blamed the change in their relationship on the isolation, the depression, herself. She was no one's fucking sunshine.

Why not tell her? She was an adult! He had to stop protecting her, shielding her. He'd had plenty of opportunity to explain it to her when he'd taken his notes—

Alice stared at the photo in her hand.

What had Lillian said? Something about how the notes showed how much she remembered—*for a while.* She'd even noticed herself that the interview notes documented the loss of memory, not the gain. Was she supposed to forget something—or someone?

In her pocket, her phone buzzed. *Rnn.* Jimmy. She couldn't look. "This doesn't make any sense. My dad wouldn't cheat on my mom and then—I don't believe any of it. It's crazy."

"Hey, I already live in the funhouse," Merrily said, cornering the photos together, tidy. She darted a look at the photo clutched in Alice's hand. "But still."

Alice took out the last of her emergency cash and threw it on the table. She needed to see her dad. He could sort this all out. "What? But still what?"

Merrily shrugged, threw down her own money. It was a hundred-dollar bill. "Even if it's the worst thing you can imagine, it might still be true."

CHAPTER FORTY-SEVEN
MERRILY

Alice stared at the hundred-dollar bill like she'd seen something dirty. Merrily put her handful of photos down on the table and yanked the money back. She dug through her purse for a smaller bill. She'd be trying to break one of these bitches for the rest of her life. That asshole.

She finally found a wad of ones and held them out. "This is what I have, and beers should be dead cheap here—"

Alice was reaching for the money, then past it. She dove instead for one of the photos on the table, grabbing and holding it between them, a wall. Above the print's scalloped edges, her face was stark. Merrily almost couldn't stop herself from snatching it back. Instead, she stood and moved to see which one it was.

Young Rick. Jam jar with some dark liquid, cigarettes rolled into the sleeve of his T-shirt, a shoulder turned to the camera. Slicked hair, trying to be Elvis. Just a guy with his life ahead of him, and what a mess he'd make of it, and hers. "What?" Merrily said.

"His tattoo. What is—is that a crow?"

Merrily took the photo and peered at it. "Maybe? A black bird, in any case. Why does it matter if it's a— Hey!" Alice stumbled away from the table, her eyes wild. "Are you sick?"

Alice used the backs of chairs to steady herself toward the door. "I'm fi—oh, God. I have to—" She bolted for the door.

"Hey," Merrily called after her.

Alice yanked the door open and was gone.

Merrily looked down at the photo in her hand. The waitress appeared at her elbow and eyed the hundred-dollar bill sticking out from Merrily's purse. "Black birds, yeah," she said. "You don't want to mess with those. They're major bad luck."

ON THE WAY back to Chicago, radio turned nearly to silence, Merrily played the conversation with Alice back through. Like a stage play. She said, and then *she* said. She hadn't set out to smash Alice's entire sense of self or whatever, but . . . how was it different from having a new dead dad foisted on you? Foundational damage. Maybe there was more long-lost truth to be had, and it didn't all have to be for her. Something had transpired at the end of their meeting that she hadn't understood.

"*My* room," Merrily muttered.

A billboard rising up on the side of the road read LOOKING FOR A SIGN? THIS IS IT. She knew it was just a lame sales tactic, but it offended her, struck her like a slap. This was not it.

This couldn't be it.

What would she do now? Get a job? A real one, a job she would have to be on time for and good at, would have to care about. Some office? She'd have to go to interviews and pretend as though she cared about whatever their widget was. Smiling like an idiot, living to serve some empty corporate cause.

Her phone made the *plink-plink* sound of a notification from ChatX. Even the notification exhausted her. It didn't even matter who it was. It didn't matter to them who *she* was. A pair of knees, a pair of legs, a pair of—a piece of something to someone, a piece of shit to Searcher, apparently. She wasn't even real. Had she ever been real? Constructed by everyone else, anyone else, jagged, broken pieces formed into the shape of a woman.

She was crying, and then she was sobbing, the road obscured. Merrily pulled her car to the side of the road and rested her head on the steering wheel. When she got her breath back, she reached for her phone. The notification from ChatX waited, but then so did a text she hadn't heard come in. Her mom. *Come home*, the message said. *Now.*

"Mamá?" Merrily rushed through the house, banging a shin against a couch she should have predicted, same couch, same spot for nearly thirty years. She found her mother in the dim kitchen, alone, her phone in her hand. Nearby sat a cup of hot tea gone cold. "Mamá, are you OK? You scared me."

"*Me* asustaste. *You* scare *me*."

The Spanish. Not a good sign. Merrily went to the refrigerator, pulled out juice. "What did I do now?"

"What did you do? I don't even know. This." She waved her phone. "This, you send with no explanation."

Merrily poured a glass, sipped. The last thing she had sent her mom . . . she couldn't remember, and then she did. The selfie in the lobby of that hotel, sent for safekeeping. "The photo of me looking cute?"

"A photo of you looking like lamb led to slaughter."

Merrily froze. *Are you the innocent lamb who's never done this before?* What did her mom know?

How could she know?

"This man," her mom said. "He is not good."

On the screen was the photo and Searcher's face, like a ghost rising out of the black window at her shoulder. Merrily sat down to keep from losing her legs out from beneath her. "You know him?"

Her mom, ashen, looking older than Merrily had ever seen her, reached across the corner of the table, no bracelets to clack together, practically naked without the music of her jewelry, and gripped Merrily's arm. "*You* know him. This is the problem. I was hoping it was a mistake—but no, there he is, looking where he has no business. Are you—" Her mom's throat caught on a word she didn't want to say. "Is he your—"

"Mamá, no." He was her nothing now. Never mind that it might have gone the other way. So easily might have gone some other way. What had he said? *Tonight would have worked out differently, and not in your favor.* The threat seemed darker to her now. "I knew him online."

"On the computer only?" Hope.

"I met him one time, and . . . he's no friend of mine."

Her mom looked as though she might cry with relief. If only she didn't ask how Merrily had met him online, which site, to what purpose. "And you won't see him again? Never, OK? Or talk to him on the computer."

"Never." An easy promise.

Her mom closed her eyes briefly, a little prayer, and reached for her mug. She made a face and rose to start the kettle.

Merrily watched her stretch to put the tin of tea bags back into the cabinet. She hadn't thought about the confusing things Searcher had said. About her mom? About a party to be planned? *All the devils are back in hell.*

She gasped and stood. "Did he know Rick?"

The tin fell with a clang to the floor, the lid rolling into a corner.

"Mamá, who is he?" Months she had played with him on ChatX.

Or he had played with her. For what? To lure her, to taunt her, to make her feel dirty and small. But he'd turned her down when he might have humiliated her, might have violated her in a million ways she had only asked for. Why bother with any of it? Why bother with *her*? "Did he know I was Rick's daughter?"

Her mom let out a shaking breath. "I guess it's time to show you where the devil lives. So you stop knocking on his door."

MrJonestoYou: @Slapdash I re-watched that Jen Minarik _ CrimeTimeTonight_ episode and it seems to me that we can narrow the timing down further for that MP, Laura Schmidt, you're asking about. This is just a hypothesis, but what if she missed that custody hearing because she was already dead? The new timeline (from overdose/arrest to the missed court date) really only leaves us with 18 viable UIDS (see list below). With all the other factors, I think 973MPIN Laura Schmidt AKA Laura Banks might make a match with 226UFIL (link to profile also below). The timing is right, the hair, height, racial makeup. There's a reference to dental records . . . DNA would be trickier; she'd have to be exhumed. (Gravesite.com has a photo of the donated marker where UID was buried as, "Jane Doe O'Donohue Park." Link below.)

Slapdash: RE: @MrJonesToYou I'm going to call you Mr. Genius Jones from now on.

JennDoePagesMOD: RE: RE: @Slapdash. This is an excellent theory. Well done, @MrJonesToYou! Will get the team on it ASAP and if the committee agrees, we'll get in touch with local PD immediately. Crossed fingers, everyone. More soon.

CHAPTER FORTY-EIGHT
ALICE

An orange parking ticket flapped under Alice's windshield wiper. Victorville's welcome, officially overstayed.

She threw it to the ground and got in. She started the car, but could only sit inside and gasp for breath. She felt like Lillian, except her breathlessness wouldn't end. She couldn't breathe. She couldn't sort her thoughts. She couldn't find her way through it.

A Victorville junkie who looked just like her?

The tattoo she'd put on her own hip, a crow, the bird that holds grudges, appearing on the arm of—

I bet you remembered plenty. For a while.

No. She just had to get to her dad and clear this up. It was ridiculous to think—

Why was her birth certificate amended?

Her phone buzzed in the passenger seat. *Rnn.* Alice grabbed at it, but it was only a text from Jimmy. Actually Jimmy, not secret Jimmy. *Is this thing black tie or what?*

The reception. She'd forgotten all about it, again. Had lingered here in Victorville and incurred the wrath of Jennifer York-Niemann from Top Floor Management for missing the setup, as if it mattered at all.

But.

The reception was where she could intercept her dad and figure out what was real, what was true. What wasn't true. What couldn't be true.

She put the car in gear. She tried not to think ahead. Black wings opened, stretched. Alice fought them off and concentrated. She drove.

A FIRE-ORANGE SUNSET colored the high windows of 1799 South Michigan. Below, the lobby lights leaked onto the street. They'd hired a valet team for the event but Alice pulled up, jumped out, kept her keys even as they shouted after her. Someone held the door and she swept by. The party under way, a roar of noise, women's shoulders, glasses in hands.

Jennifer stood behind the lobby counter. "Where have you been?"

"Have you seen my dad?"

"The caterers you suggested were *two* hours late."

Alice searched the fringes of the crowd. "Jennifer, I need to talk—"

"Is that what you're wearing?"

She had no idea what she was wearing. She glanced down. "My dad?"

"I saw him come in earlier, but . . ." Jennifer gestured grandly to the counter between them. "That was a million name tags ago. We've had *several* walk-ins, I have to tell you, including at least two—"

But Alice was already walking away, into elbows and chitchat, laughter. A three-piece jazz combo played in the corner, too loud for the high ceilings and marble floors. Sound bounced all around the room, so that people had to shout to be heard, and then louder still, to be heard over the shouting. A few people reached out for her, called out, but Alice hurried through as quickly as she could, eyes only for Harris Fine.

Black suit, back to the room, far windows. She battered through, spilled a drink. "Sorry," she said.

The man at the window turned.

It was JimBig. Alice spun to avoid him, but he threw back his drink and pursued.

"Alice? You OK?"

She put the catering table between them. Canapés and crudités and *God*, she hated it all. The blue cheese smelled like rot. "Have you seen my dad?"

"He's here somewhere."

A platter of champagne flutes appeared in her vision, and she grabbed one.

"What's going on?" he said. "You look like someone stepped on your grave."

Alice shot the drink, wouldn't look his way. She didn't care what he was, only that she and her dad had a chance to escape his pull. She put down the empty glass and pulled out her phone. Another text from Jimmy waited. *Are you here yet? Don't make me walk into this thing alone.*

"Jimmy's here." She had a bunch of missed calls. No time for that now. She tucked the phone away, reached for a wedge of Gouda. Alice in Wonderland eats the cake to make herself smaller. Smaller and smaller until she can slip away.

"You take good care of him," JimBig said. "Better than he deserves. Better than I ever have, until lately." He looked at her, his eyes almost sad. "He loves you, did you know that? I don't suppose there's any chance . . . He would treat you like royalty."

Her mouth went dry. She reached for a napkin and spit the cheese into it.

"No," he said. "No, I don't suppose so. Look, maybe don't blame him for what's going to happen."

JimBig had almost suggested . . . what? That she take care of Jimmy, I do, for the rest of her life? "What's going to happen?"

"Just. Forgive him, OK? If nobody else." He was talking to her, but his attention shot over her shoulder. She turned her head. Beyond the party, a couple of men stood near the elevator doors, backs to the room. Giving off less-than-festive vibes.

She sensed him easing away. "What do I need to forgive you for, Uncle Jim?"

He set down his glass, reached for another. "You'll never forgive me."

The list of his crimes was long, but there was one—

"Did you bribe Matt to cancel the wedding?"

His eyes shifted around, trying not to touch her. "Don't hate me, kid. I only wanted what was best for, well . . . both of you. I hope."

"Did you think I would marry Jimmy if only Matt fell out a window?"

"Now, I had nothing to do with that," he said gruffly, taking a step around the table, looking to see who might have heard. "As far as I know, that kid was trying to fly. All I did was incentivize his cold feet—and yours. I knew Harris would happily take care of the tab, the caterers and whatnot, but one of you needed to yell *uncle* and you weren't doing it. He should have got a new job afterward, but he didn't have the sense God gave a rock."

So it was JimBig King who had saved her from a bad marriage. Or a good one, who knew? Other people were allowed to live it out and see. She had a thousand questions and accusations, and all of them felt dangerous.

"That day," she said. Her jaw was tight. "Who did you meet up with on the third deck?"

"Oh, kid." He was pale, wretched. An old man. "They were supposed to save us."

"*They* who? Who's . . . *us*?"

"Some of us. I'm sorry."

Without a goodbye, JimBig walked off. Alice felt weak-kneed. She backed out of the crowd feeling for the wall and pressed herself to the cool stone. She had confirmed the material for this wall, had observed the installation of every panel. Her cathedral.

She heard a familiar laugh and looked up. Her dad held court near the back bar, a handsome man commanding attention, the women enthralled, the husbands starting to rattle the ice in their glasses.

"There she is," he said as she approached. He and the women looked her up and down. "Working so hard she forgot to put on her finery. Al, wouldn't you like to—"

"My God," one of the women brayed. "She's a tall one, Harris."

"Enough of that," the man at her elbow said, pulling the glass from her hand.

Alice didn't look in her direction. "Dad, I need to talk to you."

"And the beauty in the family," her dad said. He was flushed, working the hot room in a tux jacket, probably a double scotch into the proceedings. Having a good night, showing off their masterpiece.

"I just need a minute," Alice said. The group around him broke up easily at her suggestion. In her back pocket, her phone revved. "Five minutes."

"Fine." His eyes scraped the room and then he led her a few

feet out of the frenzy and under the staircase that led to the mez-
zanine. "What's so important as to interrupt this celebration we
so richly deserve?"

She didn't know how to ask. What to ask, where to start. "I had
to replace my driver's license from the break-in, and I couldn't
find my Social Security card or my birth certificate—"

He gazed out at the crowd. "Is this urgent? I can lay my hands
on all that by Monday. Let me take care of it for you."

"I went to request it in person. In Victorville."

He sipped the last of his drink. "I didn't realize you knew that
name."

"Were you hoping I would forget it?" Even in the din of the
party, she was loud. A few guests pivoted to see if the speeches had
begun, or trouble. She was like a bird that had gotten inside, bat-
tering against the window. Out of place, wild. "Also, there's something going on with Uncle Jim."

"Let's go somewhere quieter," he said, and led her away from
the crowd to the elevators, JimBig and his friends nowhere to be
seen. He had a key card, pushed a button. Her ears were popping
before she realized they were in the residential elevator, rising past
the management offices to the penthouse.

"Somebody bought it," she said, to end the silence. "The penthouse. Jennifer said—"

"Pending. In the meantime, we might be able to hear ourselves
there."

The elevator opened to a wide room with floor-to-ceiling
windows that overlooked Michigan Avenue and the west Loop.
Across the room, Lake Michigan. It was like being at the helm of
a great ship. It was staged as sparse, nothing extra. A few pieces
of elegance were tastefully displayed. The minimalist language of

wealth, others need not apply. To Alice, it felt cold and empty, like their house in the Fell Creek woods had since her mother died.

The woman she had thought was her—

She had to start someplace.

"Dad, am I adopted?"

He waited, as though she might have a two-part question, then stood back. "Oh, Alice. They gave you the original birth certificate? Is that how it happened?"

He seemed only distracted, as though this conversation were just a barrier to getting back downstairs to the party.

"Does it matter how I found out?" It stung. Her throat hurt from keeping tears at bay, her head. Young Rick, young Laura. Her parents? She'd been hoping against all evidence that it wouldn't be true. She stumbled farther into the apartment and found a couch to catch her before her legs gave out.

"It got away from us," he said. "The right time to tell you—"

"Surely some point before *now*."

"I'm so sorry. I wanted to, and then your mom . . ." He gazed down at her. "When she was sick, it didn't make sense to break your heart."

"Except she was sick all the time," Alice snapped.

He didn't take the bait. "And then we lost her, and you were all I had. So it didn't make sense to break mine."

He stood between her and the west windows, a figure carved out of the glow of city lights. "So they were—the people I remember, they weren't kidnappers. I wasn't kidnapped. They were my—"

"No. You were never kidnapped. You were abandoned."

"I'm—" She could barely choke the words out. "Rick's daughter."

"You're *my* daughter."

"And I remember them. I remember her singing to me. 'You are my sunshine—' " Warbling, out of tune, on the edge of hysteria. "She *called* me Sunshine, didn't she?"

He sighed. "Your birth name was Allison. They might have called you something like that."

"Allison." It was just a sound, deadened. A throwaway name. Another version of herself sprung up alongside the person she'd been. She didn't know who the hell she was.

"You were—you remembered too much at the time to change it entirely," he muttered, shaking the ice in his glass. "We should have changed it."

She remembered too much *now*. "He had a crow on his arm." She stood up, so that he was forced to glower upward.

He'd hated her tattoo the second he'd seen it. Because it was low-class, trashy, she'd thought, because it branded her, because it matched Matt's—

Because it matched Rick's.

He knew where the crow had come from. He *knew*.

"All this to avoid telling me I was adopted?" she heard herself say. Her mind flitted ahead. Lillian's research, Jimmy's texts, conversations she'd had with Juby and that cop—that cop from the bar! That's who'd drawn JimBig's attention downstairs. Was JimBig somehow on the side of justice? Something was happening. Something had already happened.

Alice turned to the west-facing windows. Towers like bookends to the city, and all the life between. Below them, the grid of the city was a comfort. All those streets in perfect parallel, all those cars and people crossing and intersecting without hazard. If everyone stayed in their lane, if everyone stopped at the red light. She recalled the crunch and skid of cars colliding outside of Victorville, of lines crossed. Of collision after collision.

It wasn't—it couldn't be. But only this morning, she never

would have guessed, couldn't have foreseen the world stretched to madness. She was in Wonderland. And there was more to it. This wasn't the end. She could feel the presence of how it would end, somewhere. It was in the room with them. This wasn't it.

She turned, but the words flew from her lips.

On a shelf over her dad's shoulder stood the slim wooden flame of her mother's favorite object, the holy artifact missing from the Fell Creek house in the woods and now centerpiece to a million-dollar home, a bandit's home, a thief's. A killer's, a king's.

"You live here," she said, and thought: *I know who you are.*

CHAPTER FORTY-NINE
MERRILY

T his story is about a woman," Mamá Cruz said.

"Me? You?" Merrily perched on the edge of her chair. "Alice?"

"Laura. Stories are not always about ruin, but this one is." Her mom was making tea, her round shoulders moving as she talked. As the story unfurled, her mom's voice seemed to be separate from her, coming from far away. Through time. Her mom had been working on this story for a long time. Merrily only hoped it would be, at last, true.

"But it starts way back, with Richard. He is a speeding train. He is only looking for the wreckage." Teacups assigned, poured. "He is always hungry for a better deal, a better chance. Which is fine, only . . . you can't take your better deal from what others earned rightfully. He caught the attention of the police in town and after that, every little thing he did, they were right there to catch him."

The speeding tickets, failing to stop, one after the other. "He broke the law—"

"And then the law broke him. There are men in power who like to stay that way, at any cost. At anyone else's cost. Rick had a wife and a child at this point, but he chose the wrong side. He chased that woman off." Her mom waved her hand, fingers fluttering, goodbye. "Then another woman, who he didn't marry, couldn't, because of the wife already. And another child. He loved his woman, his little girl, but not enough, never enough."

Her mom looked at her. "The rich and powerful men got away with things, you see, and Rick was not rich or powerful. But he knew he would be, someday, if he went along, did what he was told. He had faith in this, like a disciple. Small job, small piece of the pie. You want more pie, you have to do more work. You have to stretch your neck out. But Rick was impatient, losing faith. He thought he was starving. So he took a big bite from another man's plate. The wrong man. *That* man."

"Searcher."

"What?"

"Nothing." Rick had been arrested for breaking and entering, but was that the crime that had gotten him noticed or the one that had gotten him killed? She didn't want to slow down the story. "Then what?"

"Richard has another woman, another child." She might have been talking about characters in one of her telenovelas, but Merrily had heard the entrance of the characters she cared about, the subtle shift in tone. "But the ground, it shakes under his feet. He knows he is in danger. All his women, all his little children, they are in danger. He finds people who want to know what the rich and powerful men have been doing, and he turns himself in, in exchange for protection."

Merrily let the silence drag on until she realized her mom thought she was done. "He turned himself in to the police?"

"The man, he *is* the police. Rick goes higher than that, but they do not protect the women, the children."

"Rick signed away his parental rights—"

"Fly away, Peter Pan." The fingers fluttered again. "This paper and that paper, who cares? He should feed his children, clothe them."

So she and her mom hadn't gone to see Rick in hiding because her mom still loved him or even needed him, but because he still owed them.

"He gets word to me when he shouldn't. And yes, someone follows us. Another man, who is doing the small jobs now, only now the job is . . . kill Rick. Rick got out of there, but he's less use against his old boss now, you see. He is a killer now, too, and they know it. He's stuck between one life and the next, between one name and another. He can't settle down. He makes mistakes, and all the while this devil man is looking. Isn't satisfied with what he has, what he's gotten away with. He wants Rick's head on a platter. And Rick is . . ."

"What?"

"Lonely. But I wouldn't allow him to tell you—what good would it do you to know what sort of man your father is? A few years ago, something happened, I don't know. He begged, and I—I wouldn't let him. I told him I would move you far away, give you a new phone, no number for him. I dangled you, like a toy over a dog's head." Her eyes darted in Merrily's direction. "I regret many of my decisions."

"About two years ago, right?" Rick, giving valedictory speeches and life lessons by text. The temperature of the water around him must have jacked up a few degrees. "He got so . . ." All the words hurt her to say. "Anxious. What about the other daughters?"

"The first one, she thinks he is dead. I mean, she thought he was, already."

Merrily reached for her purse, for the deck of photos, and held out the last image she had of Rick and Laura together. "And the second one is Alice."

"Oh!" Her mom reached for the photo. "I thought these were all lost."

They might have been. "What happened to Alice's mom?"

"You know how some people say, 'Whatever it is, we'll get through it'? Well, we don't. Not all of us. Laura is the one who did not get through it. His other women moved on, and his children grew up without him. Laura fought it, and she was ruined for it. He badgered her. He badgered her, ruined her reputation, said she was something she was not, and then . . . she disappeared. He *took* that child."

Merrily's head snapped up. "Rick? I thought—"

"*This* man," her mom said, gesturing toward her phone and the photo there. "He used his high-and-mighty friends. He used his standing, his position, his money. And he took that child, wrapped her in a pretty bow for his barren wife, took her *prisoner*, so that Rick could no more make a case against him than . . . than *fly*."

"Wait. The man who took Alice—"

"The worst insult. She calls him her father."

"That man," Merrily said. "That man is Alice's dad?" *Oh, holy, holy, holy, holy shit.* Her face burned with the memory of the way she had offered herself up, plump dumpling on a plate, how he had treated her. She was such an idiot. He'd stalked her for months— to find Rick. Longer than months. Years. Her entire life.

And she'd led him right to him. *King Richard conquers the Dunes.*

All the devils were *definitely* not yet in hell. Not by a long shot. "Mamá, Alice is in danger."

Her mom waved her hand. "She's lived with him since she was a child."

"But she knows now. Alice *knows* Rick's her real dad, which means she's no longer any use to this guy. He could hurt her."

"He could."

"He could kill her."

Her mom looked sick. "He might."

MERRILY TRIED ALICE, got voice mail. G. Vasquez, voice mail. She called over and over, texted Alice, texted Graciano, thought about calling 911. Texted Juby. There was a text from a number she didn't recognize.

> *Hi, it's Zach. That B&E was the address below. House owned by Harrison and Beth Ann Fine. Mean anything to you?*

Hell, yeah, it did, but too late. Rick wouldn't have broken into any cop's house, but who's to say he didn't?

> *Anyway if you're ever in Vville again . . .*

Poor kid. Delete.

Juby finally answered, but she didn't know where Alice lived, where she might be.

What's going ON??? she sent.

> *Too long a story but shit is going DOWN.*

Are you guys . . . friends now? Juby sent. Smiley face.

If she lives through it, Merrily sent. *This is serious.*

> *Oh, THAT shit is going down? Hold on.*

A few minutes later, Merrily received another message and a link: *Lillian says Cinderella's ball . . . tonight! 1799 South Michigan. Be careful.*

Merrily started to dial Juby and give her an earful. Her phone buzzed again.

Meet you there.

Mamá Cruz barely let her out of the door. Merrily bought her freedom by playing the ace: she had a police officer friend who would meet her there, too. "I'll call him," she promised, and she did, repeatedly, but his phone went again and again to voice mail. She had to put down the phone and drive, an hour door-to-door, but with traffic, this time of night on a Friday, who knew? She went over the story her mom had told until the details were singing to her in rounds, tumbling over and over. *She calls him her father. She calls him her father.*

So Searcher had seen King Richard conquering the dunes during the chat with her and known where he could find Rick—hunted him and killed him, and then invited her up to a perch with an expensive view to lord it over the city and her, to celebrate a thirty-year victory.

To gloat? Was that all there was to it? Why bother? He'd pulled her out of that argument with Juby and Alice, and—

He'd pulled her from a conversation with *Alice*. All his stalking, all his phone-tracking and home-bugging, hadn't kept her from converging on the same spot as Alice. He couldn't have that. She hadn't been there as a sexual plaything, or as a witness to his power, though that might have been a bonus. He'd been keeping her hostage until Alice left the hotel, checking and checking his phone until she did. And then he'd spanked Merrily with a threat about her mom so she might stay home for a while, nabbing her phone for safekeeping. But what if he'd decided it wasn't enough, that he had to do more to keep her and Alice apart.

Tonight would have worked out differently, and not in your favor.
Merrily's foot came off the gas.

The car behind her immediately jumped into punitive honking. She sat up, kept driving, just a car, just a link in the chain that would get them all where they were going.

If things had gone differently, if he hadn't already found Rick and killed him, he might have banged her for the sport, for something to plague Rick. He might have held her captive.

He might have killed her.

Oh, holy.

Good night, Michaelangelo24. Goodbye to avatars and chats. Her knees belonged to her alone. She'd have to make her own way, go back to school, get a job. Move home. Whatever it took. Maybe Alice needed a roommate, or a personal assistant . . .

All her hopes leapt toward Alice.

She inched into the city, a tiny scale on the spine of a dragon's tail of traffic curving around Lake Michigan and into downtown. The city streets were clogged with people going about their lives. Every second was an eternity.

As soon as she could, Merrily abandoned her car in a parking lot, placed one of those hundred-dollar bills into the hand of a surprised lot attendant, and ran. She had legs for *miles*, and she used them.

CHAPTER FIFTY

ALICE

The graceful feather, her mother's beloved treasure, looked like a blade over Harris Fine's shoulder. "You live here," Alice said. *I know who you are.*

She knew who she was, too, what he'd made her.

"You don't understand," he said, reaching for her. She stepped back. Her skin crawled. She had never understood that phrase, but now—

"Yes. I live here."

The house boxed up, her mother's things missing. Bachelor dinners at his house with old saucepans, all to make her think nothing had changed. He was the same guy he'd always been. She gazed around in wonder. Everything new, except for her mother's sleek flame. "How do you *live* here? How do you live *here*?"

He took a breath, seemed to consider. "I wanted to bring you here, but I couldn't find a way."

"I'm sure you considered kidnapping." A joke, but then she was reaching beyond the fog of memory to the sheer terror of the stranger reaching for her. The homesickness, the fist of herself in a room she didn't know. The baby crying and the woman looking down at her. The warm safety of her father's arms.

The wings of the black bird beat the air.

The terror of the stranger. The safety of the father. She'd gotten everything wrong. She hadn't been returned to loving arms. She'd been ripped from them.

"I *was* kidnapped." She could barely say the words, and felt what little power she had over herself and the situation slip away. She focused on the bright circle of the elevator button across the room. "Legally, through the courts. Held *hostage*, for spite—"

"For *control* over a *situation*—"

"For *money* and control over everything you could grab—"

"For a lot of reasons you'll never appreciate."

"And you never minded that a few people's lives were destroyed. How could you do it?"

He put a hand to his forehead and pulled it over his eyes like a blindfold. "It wasn't about you. Can't you understand? You weren't even—you weren't *you*. You were just—"

"An insurance policy. Collateral."

"I'm sorry." He dropped his hand, and his expression was not one of regret. It hurt to have him look at her.

"I don't think you are," she said.

"I'm sorry for what I've done to you."

"What about what you did to my *parents*—"

"Don't," he said loudly, then recovered his calm. "Don't call them that. Never. They were *trash*. They didn't deserve you."

She hadn't even reached the depths of grief they deserved, and he was already digging a thumb into the wound. They hadn't mattered. They were less than human, and if that's what they were, what was she? He hadn't denied his actions, only the value of those who had suffered from them. "Is that what you have to tell yourself? To sleep at night?"

"You should have seen the squalor, the disregard for your safety—"

"Oh, so it's my *safety* you're worried about. It's a good thing I didn't get too close to a window."

"That wasn't me," he barked. "Your idiot ex was nosing around where he shouldn't have been, watching Big sell us out, and Gus got a little carried away—"

"Gus!" But of course a kingpin would need his heavies to do his dirty work. Gus would have been the one to convince Brody he'd been home sick that day, too.

"Al, *sweetheart.* We—I—*I* took you in for the wrong reasons, but—but you'd never have had this life, raised by them. All the comforts," he said, flinging his arms wide like wings. No irony that they were standing in the middle of opulence she had never been offered. All the comforts were his. "You'd never have become the person you are."

"You have no idea what I might have been. Maybe I would have been—" She swallowed the thought that occurred to her.

"Don't dare say you'd be better off. They couldn't have loved you more than I did. Than I do."

"Not more than you did," Alice said.

He reared back. "She loved you, too," he said. "And you know it."

He reached for her again. Alice flinched away, but he kept coming. She couldn't keep stepping out of his embrace. She didn't want to. He put his arms around her, gentle and awkward. She let him but wouldn't embrace him in return. She sagged into him so that her chin hooked over his shoulder. Against her cheek, a flat weight under his jacket, the leather of a holster.

Always a cop. Except when he was the criminal.

Alice disengaged herself and walked to the elevator, pushed the button. "She could barely look at me," she said. "I disgusted her. I always thought it was because I wasn't the right kind of daughter, didn't look like either of you, wasn't delicate, graceful, wasn't . . . whatever she wanted me to be."

The elevator appeared, and Alice leapt into it.

"Alice." He rushed in with her. "Let's talk about this—"

"Do you know how much I ate my heart out over it? Because I thought it was something about me that wasn't good enough or pretty enough or smart enough or *anything* enough. I had plenty of time to wonder, packed away to Siberia for four years. And when I came back to care for her, she didn't *want me there*. I gave up everything to be there, and she didn't *want me*."

"Well, obviously she wasn't always—" He swallowed it.

"But it wasn't because of me, was it? Every time she looked at *me*, she saw—"

"Her beloved child."

"—death. *Murder.* The monster she married."

"Stop it."

"She knew who I was." Alice choked on the words. "She couldn't love me, though, because I made her realize who *you* were. Where is Laura's body? Why stab Rick twelve times? Twelve. You did those things yourself, just as sure as you killed Mom—"

"Enough! And stop calling him *Rick* like he was your fucking buddy."

The elevator doors opened to the commotion of the party. Alice stepped out, turned, and blocked him inside. His hand reached under his jacket. "Wait," he pleaded, his eyes darting behind her, left, right. "I don't want to—"

"Then don't. For once, don't do the worst thing. Do the right thing. Do the thing Harris Fine would do, the Harris Fine who was my *dad*. The one who says he loves me."

She turned. JimBig King in one direction, Jimmy in a tux in the other. Nearby, a woman who looked remarkably like Juby. And—was that *Merrily*?

But then her dad had a grip on her arm and was leading her toward the lobby. Under his jacket, a gun. He pressed the muzzle into her ribs. "Prison for the rest of my life," he said. "Is that what you want?"

"Aren't you threatening to end mine?" she said. "Either you're my dad or you're not. How many lives have you ruined to have all this, this *empire*? What's the point?"

"Walk with me," he said.

She had no choice. He was taking care of things.

Suddenly, even with a pistol shoved into her side, Alice felt the most impossible calm. They moved through the room as if through water. A path laid out, their friends and colleagues parting.

"Where will we go?" she said.

"I'll take care of it."

She looked at him. "Fine." His face creased. She hadn't seen him cry since the funeral of—

Alice caught herself. His wife. She felt such a freedom to think of the woman that way. Beth Ann Fine, just a woman who hadn't loved her as her own. She felt a force of feeling for the woman now, was almost sick with forgiveness. Richard and Laura, too. JimBig, whatever his crimes. She forgave them all, knowing they were nothing to her.

"My car is just out there at the curb, and the keys—"

"We can't." He turned them as a unit so that she could see the party was being redistributed away from the lobby. The cop who'd smashed her phone was there, trying to get Merrily to go with the crowd. Too late for a quiet exit. "I have to explain," he said.

"You don't have to explain." Her curiosity, gone.

"I need you to hear it, in case—"

"Alice?" Jennifer came out from behind the counter. "There was a— Oh, Mr. Fine, I didn't—"

"Now," Alice said. They didn't have a choice. "Let's go now."

She allowed him to lead her outside, where the night sky burned a ruined orange, too bright for stars. The valets rushed to assist.

"No," she said. "Stay back."

"I took you," he said. "For petty reasons, to control him—"

"It doesn't matter." The car was where she'd left it, one tire on the curb, the keys still in her pocket.

"—to keep what I'd built. All that, I can't help it. That's what happened. That's who I was. But then you were *ours*."

Alice glanced at him. His eyes were dark, fevered. "And then it wasn't about him anymore," he said. "It was you."

"Don't blame me!"

"It was you. You were everything, and he was the only one who could take you away," he said. He stopped, so she did, too. The street had been blocked off, squad cars parked, lights rolling. "Don't you get it? I couldn't stand to lose you. You were all I had."

That was his fault, but then she had worn her life down to a sharp point, too. "And a fortress to keep me in," she said. "Two."

"I didn't know I would lose you anyway," he said.

"What? Why?"

"To someone, eventually. Matt, someone else. To another job. To some other part of the world. I didn't know. I didn't know that letting you go was the whole point of parenting you."

"Put down the gun, Harris." From behind them, JimBig stepped out of 1799, black gun in his hand. The valets scattered.

"No," Alice cried, sagging in the knees.

Her dad pulled her up and spun them as one to face JimBig. "There's the turncoat himself."

Turncoat. JimBig was the one leaving the business, burning it down behind him and saving only Jimmy. She was collateral damage. Again.

"Mr. King," someone shouted. Behind JimBig stood the cop who had smashed her phone, weapon drawn. And behind him in the frame of the lobby window, Jimmy, palms pressed to the glass, and nearby Merrily and Juby clutching one another. Juby mouthed messages to her she couldn't understand. "King, put the gun down," the cop yelled.

"The police seem to know your name, Big," her dad said. "Did you get tired of being too rich? Of living too well?"

"That must be what it is. Certainly too late to grow some morality." Face-to-face, they no longer looked so much alike. JimBig was shrunken, wrung out. Face-to-face, they were a man and his shadow.

He's sick. Alice didn't know how she knew, but she knew. JimBig had nothing to lose.

"Morality sounds expensive," her dad said. "It might cost you everything you have." He pulled Alice backward, stepping around the bumper of her car.

"Everything," JimBig said, edging closer. He made eye contact with Alice. She shook her head at him. *No.* "But not everyone."

The two great men of her life fighting it out over her head again. She existed only to clean up the wreckage. She was the wreckage.

She imagined a way for it to end. Another. None of the eventualities she could imagine were outcomes she could live with. "Dad."

He flinched and the muzzle pressed into her dipped away.

Alice saw the way it would go. "No!" She lurched in front of him just as the air around her exploded, once, twice. Alice couldn't feel anything but noise, tasted nothing but pain. Her dad's hand on her upper arm jerked away, and he was flying from her. He flew.

Her feet weren't under her. Down, down, down. She fell and kept falling.

CHAPTER FIFTY-ONE
MERRILY

Merrily screamed. Juby held her, kept her from running into the gunfire. But then some random guy rushed past them into the center of it. "Goddammit, Junior," Vasquez yelled. "Get the fuck out of there!" Alice and Searcher, both on the sidewalk. The man who had shot at them reached down and plucked the gun from Searcher's outstretched hand.

Merrily fought off Juby and stumbled through the door, her eyes on the shooter.

He was just an old man whose shoulders didn't fill out his jacket, but he had all the guns. He slid the guns into his coat pockets but left his hands there.

"What the fuck did you do, Big?" Vasquez bellowed, edging around the front of the guy, his own gun trained.

"What I should have done," the old man said, a whisper as thin as paper, "a long time ago."

"Drop those weapons!" Vasquez yelled.

"No, no, Alice, no." The guy who'd run in, cowboy hero, running into the path of bullets, had Alice gathered in his arms. His hands were slick with blood.

Merrily couldn't wait for Vasquez to figure it out. She rushed in and fell to her knees in front of Alice, brushing her hair away. Her eyes were closed, her lips parted. "Is she breathing? Alice? Vasquez, we need an ambulance."

"Kinda busy, Mer," he called back. "Trying to keep you from getting killed. Mr. King Senior, I'm going to need those guns, sir."

Juby edged around the action uneasily and knelt next to Merrily. "My mom will kill me if I get shot. What do we do?"

Alice's lips were moving, but the guy holding on to her blubbered so loud Merrily couldn't hear her. "Dude, shut up," she said. "Is that all her blood?"

"Apply pressure, right?" Juby reached in.

Above them, voices called for backup, an ambulance. Shots fired, live shooter.

"He shot her," the guy clutching Alice said. "You shot her."

"It wasn't me, Jimmy," the old man said. "I shot Harris. Harris pulled the trigger on his way down. Harris always finds a way to pull the trigger. Is she OK?"

"She's shot, you asshole," Merrily screamed.

"Everyone, please calm down the tiniest bit, please," Vasquez said.

"She's breathing," Juby said. "It hit her arm. It went all the way through—is that good?"

"None of it is good, sweetheart," the old man said.

"King, you want to get Alice help," Vasquez said, "put those guns down and show me your hands."

"Alice," the guy they'd called Jimmy, the cowboy, was pleading. "Stay with me, OK? Fuck, now that everyone's shot each other, you have to stay. You're the boss, remember? We have to run King and Fine."

Alice was trying to speak. The guy leaned over so his ear was close to her mouth.

This guy was gone on Alice, that was clear. Merrily looked up. Vasquez still had a bead on the old man. "Gonzo, baby, can we shut this down?"

"Trying, cariño. Mr. King needs to surrender his weapons like a man who wants to live."

When she turned back, Jimmy was still crouched over Alice, his shoulders shaking. "No," Merrily said. "No, she's not—"

He sat up. He was laughing. "She said—"

"Jimmy, for *Christ's* sake," the old man said.

"She said, she said . . . '*Fine* and King,' " he said. "Not King and Fine—"

"*Fuck*," Juby whispered. "That's amazing."

"I think she's going to be fine," Jimmy said.

The older man sighed. "Jimmy, take care of her, for a change, will you? Be a good boy."

Jimmy looked up. "Dad?"

One dad left standing, then, Merrily thought. Mr. King, eyes downcast, expression lost to the dark. Sirens sang in the distance.

"Mr. King, I'm going to ask you one more time to show me both your hands, sir. Don't make me do the paperwork."

"He deserves to burn in hell," King said. "We both do."

"What?" Jimmy said. "No. This is over. Don't do anything stupid. More stupid than you've already done."

"Jimmy," his dad said, his voice gruff, "I didn't mean it about you not running King and Fine. I only wanted to keep you out of his hands—"

"Dad—"

"They'll put me away, otherwise," King said. "I know it was bad for you when I got sent up. It was to save Harris, the business—"

"Dad, I know—I'm the one who stole the old ledgers, OK? I know what you've both been up to. You've left me so much shit to clean up, this time if you go to prison I'll barely know you're gone. Come on. I need you here."

Merrily thought of her mom in the house in Port Beth. She hoped, *Oh, God, let this be over. Let her be safe and free. She is all I have.*

But that wasn't true. Jimmy gestured for Merrily, and she crawled into place, cradling Alice to her. So much blood.

"Mr. King Junior, please stay where you are."

Jimmy raised his hands to Vasquez and sidled closer to his dad. "No more pyrotechnics, OK?" Jimmy said. "This is enough broken glass and blood for one grand opening. Let me have the guns, Dad."

"Don't—" Alice said under her breath.

"Don't!" Merrily said.

"I've got this," Jimmy said. "Vasquez, please."

Jimmy eased even closer to his dad, speaking in a low voice.

Merrily watched, then looked to Vasquez. Everything slowed, quieted. She held her breath.

Finally the old man lifted his hands out of his pockets, slowly, reluctantly. Jimmy reached around and slid the jacket off his dad's back, the guns still in it.

Things went quickly. Vasquez stepped forward, weapon on Jimmy until he had the jacket by the collar. Backup rushed in, clamping handcuffs, grabbing shoulders. Jimmy, being led away, looked toward Merrily. "Take care of our friend there."

"She's not my friend," Merrily said, forming herself as a wall around Alice. "She's my sister." The fine hairs on her arms prickled. This was it, that feeling she'd had of the other universe scraping past in its own orbit. Her whole life alone, when she might have had this. "*Sister.* And, oh, God, there's another one out there! Alice, we have another sister, and I bet she won't believe a *word* of this."

CHAPTER FIFTY-TWO
ALICE

Her arm.

She could smell her own blood. Or maybe—

Her dad. But—

It was not his blood. He had flown. On black wings, beyond their reach.

The stench that hung in the air coated the insides of her nostrils, her throat, her lungs. It was her own death she breathed, the copper tang of her own makings, the fine powder of her bones, blown to dust.

She couldn't lose any of them. Jimmy. Juby. Merrily.

"Don't," she gasped. The scene around her receded, all the sharp lines blurring, and when she woke again, Merrily had her cheek against her forehead. Merrily, her sister.

Another one, another sister somewhere, Merrily was saying.

"She's tall," Alice said, hoarse. Three thin-wristed women like something from Greek myth. The three graces. Or the three furies, she couldn't remember. She sucked in her breath from the pain.

"Her pants are too short," Merrily said.

Alice wanted to laugh, though it would hurt to laugh. And to cry. She was crying. Her dad. She could not think of him any other way.

"He flew," she said. "He flew."

"What?" Merrily, shaking against her. "Did he? Gonzo, help us. I can't—"

Alice cried. For her mother, both of her mothers, and what they might have been. And for Rick. Her father. To trade one for the other, and lose both, all. Two mothers to grieve, two fathers gone.

Merrily curled around her, a barrier.

In the swap, one family for another, Alice had gained only Merrily. She didn't know. Was it enough?

Alice pressed herself into the warm curve of Merrily's arm. Her teeth chattered. She could hear the slow beat of wings, slow, slower. Was it dark? Merrily was her sunshine.

"Are you cold?" Merrily said.

"I'm scared," she whispered. *Of losing you.*

Hands reached in. "Wait! Alice, I—you're going to be fine." Merrily's breath on her neck. "I mean, you're going to be—"

She flew on black wings.

Twelve weeks later.

JennDoePagesMOD: Thanks to @Slapdash and @MrJonesToYou and to the entire Doe Pages community for this one: I just heard back that we have a confirmed DNA match between UID 226UFIL Jane Doe O'Donohue Park and 973MPIN Laura Schmidt (AKA Laura Banks). This is a 30-year match, an amazing accomplishment for this community. A family has closure. This is why we do what we do. Thank you.

Slapdash: RE: JennDoePagesMOD A great deal of the credit on this one should go to @LuckyOne, though she's not here to take it. She was really close to this case.

JuJuBee95: RE: @Slapdash REALLY close.

Audrey89: RE: RE: @JuJuBee95 Wait. Wasn't @LuckyOne credited with the 20-year match just announced? Travis Malayter/UID John Doe Dora in Indiana? What's in the water over there, @LuckyOne? You made two matches and closed four cases in, like, three weeks? You're making us all look bad.

JennDoePagesMOD: RE: RE: RE: @Audrey89 We're not in competition here, remember. What's important is that the matches were made. Laura Schmidt is going home.

Co0o0KIES: RE: RE: RE: . . . @JennDoePagesMOD So many congrats to all those involved!

Startlevision: RE: RE: RE: . . . @JennDoePagesMOD This is so rad! This community is amazing!

JealousTypist: RE: @Slapdash So . . . why isn't @LuckyOne here?

CHAPTER FIFTY-THREE

A man in paint-spattered pants tapped the glass door with the corner of a clipboard. He held a box under his arm. Merrily buzzed him in.

"All done upstairs," he said.

"Is that it?"

"As requested." He set the box down carefully. "What is it, anyway?"

"Conceptual art. I think that's what they call it."

"Bullshit, right?" He held out the clipboard, a pen. "Like one of those tests they give you, and whatever you see in it, that tells them if you're a psycho."

Merrily's signature slowed, then recovered. "I guess so. It just means something to the person who loves it. Or the person who loves it sees something in it other people can't see. I don't know. It's not mine."

The guy shook his head, unconvinced. "Is it worth anything, though?"

"Worth money? Not sure." She lifted the flaps of the box and pulled out a wrapped lump. "In case it is, now I have to call the insurance company. Again."

Jimmy came around the corner from the back. "I can do it."

The guy ripped a layer off the form, handed it to Merrily, and bolted. He waved the clipboard without a backward glance.

"I didn't break up something beautiful happening, did I?" Jimmy said.

"Shut up," Merrily said, turning the package over in her hands. "Is that it?"

"This is it." Merrily released the wrappings to reveal the graceful flume of feather or fire or airplane propeller—whatever it was—that Alice's mother had loved. *Alice's* other *mother*, Merrily thought. They hadn't found the right words. As was said in certain corners of the internet, it was complicated. "Lucky thing that Jennifer was overseeing the forfeiture, or this might have been seized, along with everything else."

"We'll get it back."

"Are you sure about that?" An optimist with a father going to prison.

"I am certain of absolutely nothing," Jimmy said.

"Liar," she said, tipping her head toward the closed door of the corner office.

He blushed. "No hope there."

"She'll choose you eventually," Merrily said. Eventually could be a long time, though. "When the dust settles."

"She already chose," Jimmy said. "She chose Harris. And you're new to construction so you don't know this, but—the dust never settles."

"Never? This place used to be a patch of empty ground, right? Look at it now." Merrily cradled the statuette in the crook of her arm like a baby and walked to the corner office.

She knocked but didn't wait to hear a command.

"Hey, sis."

Inside, Alice sat with her back to the desk. Sunlight glared through the blinds in hashes across the room.

"Sorry, what?" Alice wiped at her face, didn't turn around. The contraption on her arm kept her from moving too quickly.

Merrily realized her mistake. She should learn better manners. Professional ones. In case this family thing didn't work out. "I'm sorry," Merrily said. "I should have let you . . . Sorry."

"It's fine." Alice sucked her teeth at her own phrase.

"They sent something down from the penthouse."

THE PENTHOUSE. ALICE cleared her throat. "They're finished? It's empty?"

"Yeah."

Compared to the nearly 360-degree vista from the penthouse, the view from the second floor of 1799 wouldn't take anyone's breath away. No bird's-eye view of the city's grid. But from this vantage point she could watch the way the light moved through the streets, from sunrise through the short shadows of midday and the blaze of afternoon, then the golden glow of early evening making all things beautiful.

Not that her work kept her tied to the desk. Assignments were a little thin until JimBig came to trial and all the lawyers sorted the receipts. Recovery was slow in all ways. In the meantime, they perched upon the ruins of a once-great realm. From this desk Alice had consolidated an empire—part real, part criminal, owed and confiscated—and consigned all the broken branches of her family tree into final rest. Laura, newly recovered, placed with Rick in Indiana. Harrison interred with Beth Ann on a green hill out near Fell Creek. The arrangements were both a lot of work and not enough. She sometimes sat at her desk until she couldn't bring herself to make the trip home. Merrily's place was closer.

Now Alice swiveled in her chair to find Merrily, the statuette in her hands. Her breath caught.

"I'm sorry," Merrily said again. "I thought it would be a nice surprise."

"It is."

"Yeah, I can tell by the absolute agony on your face how excited you are." Merrily gazed at it. "Do you want me to put it away for a while? A hundred years?"

Alice held out her good hand, wincing at the stretch over her desk.

"What is it, anyway?" Merrily said.

Fallout. Captured treasure. Debris. "Does it matter? She loved it. At least when she looked at this thing I could see that she was capable of love."

"You're such a hard-ass," Merrily said. "We're giving people breaks from now on, remember? We never know what kind of crap someone's going through, and all that? Like they might be, say, secretly kidnapped?"

"God, between your seeing the bright side and the new and improved Jimmy . . ."

"The worst."

"This is altogether too much earnestness for me," Alice said.

"Well, I have good news, then. How about some sarcasm and infighting? Juby and Lillian want to meet up and go over the latest ideas on that Jane Doe in Nevada—"

"Tell them to get their own Jane Doe." She hadn't been to the Doe Pages since it had all happened and had taken the app off her phone. But she still wondered about Jane Doe Anaho. She still wanted to see her home.

"They're just trying to get you to come back," Merrily said. "You're some kind of folk hero over there, I guess? Come on, who doesn't want to hang out with corpses and missing people? Twenty minutes of blood and gore, and then we talk about *men*."

"I don't know any." She'd been rejecting any hint about Jimmy. Matt was finally getting back on his feet and off her conscience. He'd met a cute physical therapist, she'd heard. His lawyers were less attractive. Jimmy had been trying to help Lita clean out King and Fine, but it hadn't been necessary. Not under current management. Alice would make sure Matt got a fair settlement, and others were making sure Gus went to jail.

"There's one. How could you miss it? You can't be a tycoon *and* play dumb," Merrily said. "Keep your shit together three minutes while I go fetch your mail."

On the desk, Alice twirled the figure on its end. Feather. Today she was sure. She would have gone with him, forgiven him anything. She still would, to have him here. The figure, turning, became flame and then a blade. She could suddenly understand Beth Ann's fascination with it.

She could see every choice every way, both sides, all sides always, every decision splitting off into infinite directions. She was immobilized by choice. No, she was taking the deep breath before a busy new life, a new company rising from the ashes, Jimmy's acumen, Merrily's salesmanship, Alice's credit score, which was *prime*. A deep, deep breath.

Nothing would break ground until the season turned again anyway. They had the winter to make some plans and line up work for the spring.

She should travel while she had the chance. See the world. Take a class. But it scared her. Everything scared her.

She'd spent her whole life under surveillance, with video cameras trained on her front door in the building she now somehow owned, run by a management company she also somehow owned, housed in a skyscraper she might still own when this was all over. Tracking devices, her mail pre-sorted. All the precautions.

And now no one was watching. She'd always counted on the safety net, knowing her dad would catch her if she fell. That must be what every father's daughter felt, that he would be there always. The most shocking revelation was that there was so far to fall.

Was it any wonder she couldn't make a single unaided decision? Was it any wonder she put Jimmy off?

Was it any wonder she'd slept with that little square of baby blanket against her cheek for two weeks after it all happened—until she'd noticed why the name "Blanksy" on the tag seemed crowded, the letters fading at different rates? *Banks*, it had read, with the *L* and *Y* crammed in. A soothing presence three-year-old Allison must have required, turned into a prop for the story Harris Fine needed Alice to believe.

It was no longer a comfort to her. She slept with a Xanax prescription, like an adult.

In any case, she was not fit to lead. Alice wasn't sure if she ever would be. She sat frozen at her desk overlooking nothing at all but a segment of sidewalk, a cut-rate queenpin.

Merrily was in the doorway. She carried a single envelope. "I didn't realize . . ." She looked sick.

"What?"

"It's from Rebekah." The envelope wavered in her hand.

From the *casino*. Alice heard the word in Juby's stretched fake Australian accent. "You mean it's from Rick."

"Haven't you wondered? I mean, I got a letter. Natallie said she found her letter after her mom died, so of course there's a letter." Their older half-sister proved to be easy to find but not easy to crack. They had two nieces, six and four, who were far more delighted to meet them. She and Merrily had been to Natallie's suburban home for dinner a few times, where conversation spun out in fits and starts. The three of them couldn't agree on Rick. Did he deserve their forgiveness? Could he have changed the outcome for any of them if only this or if only something else?

Alice barely had an opinion. It was Harris Fine she suffered, and not one person left on earth understood.

At Natallie's house or at a meeting with Jimmy and Merrily, Alice might gaze down the table and see how she had traded everything for nothing. She was not Alice in Wonderland. She was the Mad Hatter, presiding over absurdity.

Alice put the envelope flat on the desk in front of her. A few words from a dead man that would not change anything. They couldn't. "What will it say?"

"You could just read it."

"I don't know if I can."

Merrily threw herself in the chair opposite with a groan. "You've always been the difficult one."

"What could he possibly say?"

"Only that he loved you, you idiot. Have you heard that too often in your lifetime that you can't hear it one more time and forever?"

She and Merrily had not said the words to each other. Alice balanced the envelope in her hands, as though the weight might tell her something.

"If you get a 'Love, Dad' from him, though . . ." Merrily made a sour face. "OK, what's he going to say? He's going to say it's not your fault. He's going to say he's . . . sorry that it all happened, that he wished things could have been different. He's going to say you were always his favorite, is that what you need to hear?"

As long as he was saying all that, she had no need of the note itself. Not now. She would build up to it. Alice opened the top drawer of her desk and slid the envelope inside.

Merrily shook her head. "You're really not going to read it? After all this *crap*? Are you *serious*? You're crazy, you know that? You—"

"I love you, Merrily."

Merrily's laugh was almost a cough. "Oh, we're doing this? This is it? You've decided to feel something again, finally, and it's for *me*?" She was blushing the sweetest shade of pink under her freckles. "OK, you lunatic, fine. I love you, too."

ACKNOWLEDGMENTS

I have my neighbor and friend Natallie O'Connor White to thank for the inspiration for *The Lucky One* and, in a strange coincidence twice over, for the names of her daughters.

Sincere gratitude to Todd Matthews and Donna Zorn and the real amateur sleuths of the Doe Network and NamUs.gov. Mistakes made in regards to how these organizations and their volunteers operate are definitely mine. If you want to help out with the effort to close cold cases like those discussed in *The Lucky One*, write a letter to your representatives about passing legislation to make sure all the missing and unidentified of your state are listed in the NamUs.gov database. You can find sample messaging to use at my website, www.LoriRaderDay.com.

The research for this book relied heavily on themes brought up by others, most especially Deborah Halber's *The Skeleton Crew*, Michelle McNamara's *I'll Be Gone in the Dark*, James Renner's *True Crime Addict*, and others. Late in the writing of this book, I became a Murderino, so thanks to Karen Kilgariff and Georgia Hardstark from the podcast "My Favorite Murder," too.

I also relied on Susan Hammerman's pro tips on research techniques; Lillian's log-ins are Susan's. Thanks to her, and to Adam Henkels and Justin Sparks for their patient answers to my questions about policing and public records, and to Julie Schoerke-Gallagher and Stacy Allen for tips on (spoilers!) some of their particular life experiences. Thank you to the Lebanon Indiana Public Library for their assistance with research and for their local headlines scrapbook, which I did not steal but wanted to. Well, I guess I did steal it—the idea of it, for this book.

Special thanks to early readers Yvonne Strumecki (who helped place 1799 S. Michigan), Kim Rader (who gave me some tips on writing an only child), and Robin Agnew (who gave an early, much-needed thumbs-up).

On the publishing side of this project, thank you to my agent Sharon Bowers and everyone at Folio Literary Management for their guidance.

Huge appreciation to Emily Krump, who made this book better, who makes *me* better, and also to everyone at HarperCollins William Morrow, especially Liate Stehlik, Julia Elliott, Jennifer Hart, Andrew Gibeley, Amelia Wood, Virginia Stanley, and Owen Corrigan.

A special thank-you to all the librarians and booksellers who have placed my books into the hands of readers. Thanks also to the reviewers who have done the same, especially Kristopher Zgorski, Dru Ann Love, Oline Cogdill, Lesa Holstine, Kathy Boone Reel, and Matthew Turbeville, who are part of the fabric of the mystery community. Thank you to all the volunteers who put together the readers' conferences. What would we do without Mystery Camp?

Thank you to Laura Schmidt, Patricia Gussin, Jennifer York-Niemann (through Ruth and Jon Jordan), and Rebekah Young (through Penny Halle) for allowing me to libel them inside the pages of this book, all to benefit charity.

I've had the opportunity recently to see how communities rise up to honor and support one another through a huge loss. For this

I cannot thank enough the people of Boone County, Indiana, particularly the people of Thorntown, and the writers and readers in the mystery community. Cheers especially to Susie Calkins, Jess Lourey, Terri Bischoff, and Nadine Nettmann Semerau.

And as last—but never least—thank you to Gregory Day, who makes me the luckiest.

About the author

2 Meet Lori Rader-Day

About the book

3 The Story Behind *The Lucky One*
8 Questions for Discussion

Read on . . .

10 More from Lori Rader-Day

Insights,
Interviews
& More . . .

Meet Lori Rader-Day

Iden Ford

LORI RADER-DAY is the Edgar-nominated and Anthony- and Mary Higgins Clark–winning author of *The Lucky One*, *Under a Dark Sky*, *The Day I Died*, *Little Pretty Things*, and *The Black Hour*. She lives in Chicago, where she is cochair of the mystery readers' conference Murder and Mayhem in Chicago. She serves as the national president of Sisters in Crime.

Visit her at:
LoriRaderDay.com
Twitter: @LoriRaderDay
Facebook: @loriraderdaybooks
Instagram: @loriraderday

The Story Behind *The Lucky One*

By Lori Rader-Day

I live in Chicago, where you get to know your neighbors whether you like it or not. In our case, we have a better-than-average chance of encountering the neighbors to our left, with whom we share a waist-high, chain-link fence. An ugly fence. About two years ago that house was sold, noisily re-developed, and sold again. One day a sweet young family appeared: mom, dad, toddler daughter, and a shaking terrier. The first meeting occurred over the ugly fence, Natallie introducing me to her little girl, Eden.

"Ohhhhh," I said. "Uh, I don't usually do this right away, but—"

My next novel, *Under a Dark Sky*, was due out in a few months, and it featured a protagonist named Eden.

Natallie was thrilled. But then she didn't know the kind of book I wrote— a dark story with a character getting herself into trouble. A murder book. "Yay," she said.

Hmm, I thought. *Probably not "yay."*

A few weeks later, over the fence again, I brought up the topic of replacing it. It was their fence, but we had been pricing out a taller one to put up alongside it. That would leave them with the original but would probably trap grass in between. "If you wanted to work on this together . . ." I offered. ▶

"Oh, yes," she said. "We're interested in that. I hate this fence. Someone could just lean over and grab Eden."

"Whoa," I said, stunned. It was my job to imagine the worst. "I never even thought of that."

"It's just because I was kidnapped as a child," Natallie said.

"Stop," I said. "You? You yourself were kidnapped? You just became the protagonist of my next book."

She was thrilled again. "Yay," she said.

Probably not "*yay.*"

Natallie's story, in short: Someone reached over the fence at her (inadequate) daycare and took her to their home to give her a snack, but then panicked and set her loose—*two years old*—in a public spot. She was returned within a few hours, safe. She remembered everything, but the woman was not held accountable.

Is that a novel? Not exactly. But it was the beginning of one.

When I encounter the seeds of my next novel, it's a physical response. It's not dissimilar from getting a case of nerves, which makes sense when you think about what it means to discover the project that will consume the next year of your life. It's a weird thing, when the fuse is lit. It can be only a few words—*I was kidnapped as a child*—or an article I'm reading. It's not always violent or immediate. Sometimes it's more like . . . I'm filing away some little piece of new information when my internal librarian says, *Hold up a minute, kid. You have a lot of files in that drawer already.*

When I heard Natallie's story, I realized I had a lot of files in that particular drawer.

* * *

The Lucky One is about a woman who once went missing but was safely returned. Alice Fine's childhood close call with a kidnapper who was never brought to justice has made her timid. She volunteers with an online community that looks for matches between cold-case missing persons and unidentified remains, a job that reminds her how lucky she was, until the day she spots a face on the site she recognizes—her kidnapper.

On the Doe Network, the website I used as the model for my book's online sleuth community, I discovered a face I knew. I hadn't forgotten about Debra Jean Cole, not by a long shot, but it was a surprise to see her there, still gone, still a child.

Debra Jean was twelve years old when she disappeared from my hometown, from the same small subdivision of MarLee in which my family lived. (I have in my memory that she was called "Jeanie," but that might be wrong.) She rode my school bus, but I shouldn't have known her. I was only eight. On at least one occasion, though, she and I sat together on the bus. On a day in March, about five months before she would go missing, we planned the colors for my upcoming birthday party and a shopping list.

Pink and green. Streamers.

I remember feeling a little pressured by this bossy girl, presuming that my ▶

family could afford party decorations, that I felt the same way about pink and green that she did. I didn't know that her birthday was eight days after mine, didn't understand until recently she might have been planning a party for herself that she couldn't have.

Debra Jean Cole disappeared August 29, 1981. She was considered a runaway. Someone said she could be pregnant— but none of this was reported in the newspaper.

I was shielded from most of this at the time. I know what I know now because when I decided to write about missing persons and the real amateur sleuths who track them in *The Lucky One*, I wanted to do the kind of research those sleuths might do. For practice, I went to my hometown library and researched Debra Jean.

I couldn't find a single word published at the time of her disappearance. No Amber Alert, not in 1981. Not even a notice to watch out for her. She was *twelve*.

Just over two years later, on October 7, 1983, a young woman's body was found along US 52, very near my grandparents' house. A farmer and his son made the discovery and, for some reason, called my grandfather, who worked out of his nearby garage as a farm equipment mechanic. He went down the road to advise. They called the police.

It was not Debra Jean.

It was, however, her older sister, Frances Annette Cole.

Annette had gone missing only a couple of days before, probably considered a runaway. She had been raped and shot.

At this point, Debra Jean's photo finally appeared in the newspaper, alongside news of her sister's murder. Age twelve, age sixteen.

None of this passes the sniff test, does it? Debra Jean never came home because she never *left* home.

The Coles' stepfather, Omer R. "Steve" Beebout, died of a heart attack in 1989 at the age of 49, never facing charges, never confessing a thing. Almost ten years later, authorities matched Beebout's DNA to the semen left on Annette's body. Case closed—except one little girl is still missing. She is presumed dead by most, but still listed on NamUs.gov and other sites, for when her body is discovered. If her body is ever found, it will probably be from dumb luck.

The Lucky One isn't about the Coles, but it owes a great deal to them. For that reason, the book is dedicated in part to the memory of Debra Jean Cole and Frances Annette Cole. When *The Lucky One* launches in February, I'll be throwing a big party. You can bet there will be streamers. They'll be pink and green.

At our house in Chicago, we still haven't built that fence. Instead, we've been talking over it and getting to know new friends. All of us are watching out for Eden and now her new little sister, too. Her name is Alice. ❧

Questions for Discussion

1. In *The Lucky One*, Alice realizes that some recollections from her childhood aren't what they seem. Do you think memories can ever be impartial, or are they always colored by our perceptions?

2. Alice and Merrily have led radically different lives. In what ways do you think they are similar? How did the opportunities they were afforded play a part in the women they became and the paths they take?

3. Do you think it is ever possible to fully know someone, especially the ones closest to us?

4. Lillian and Juby prove steadfast allies for Alice. Why do you think they are so determined to help?

5. When Alice grasps at old memories, she visualizes a black-winged bird. What do you think is the significance of this bird, and what other instances of birds did you find in the story?

6. Think about the power of family bonds in *The Lucky One*. How do the reveals of the secrets kept demonstrate the strengths or weaknesses of the characters' connections? Is it sometimes justifiable to tell a lie to protect someone?

7. How does your impression of Richard change throughout the novel?

8. *The Lucky One* explores secrets and corruption hiding in plain sight. Do you think we go through life every day not seeing problems? Do you think we don't notice, or choose not to?

9. What does *The Lucky One* convey to you about the power of identity? What role do our pasts, families, and friendships play in the formation of who we believe ourselves to be?

10. Do you think you could volunteer to be a "Doe" like Alice does? Why or why not? ∽

More from Lori Rader-Day

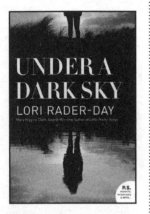

UNDER A DARK SKY

Only in the dark can she find the truth. . . .

Since her husband died, Eden Wallace's life has diminished down to a tiny pinprick, like a far-off star in the night sky. She doesn't work, has given up on her love of photography, and is so plagued by night terrors that she can't sleep without the lights on. Everyone, including her family, has grown weary of her grief. So when she finds paperwork in her husband's effects indicating that he reserved a week at a dark sky park, she goes. She's ready to shed her fear and return to the living, even if it means facing her paralyzing phobia of the dark.

But when she arrives at the park, the guest suite she thought was a private retreat is teeming with a group of twentysomethings, all stuck in the orbit of their old college friendships. Horrified that her getaway has been taken over, Eden decides to head home the next day. But then a scream wakes the house in the middle of the night. One of the friends has been murdered. Now everyone—including Eden—is a suspect.

Everyone is keeping secrets, but only one is a murderer. As mishaps continue to befall the group, Eden must make sense of the chaos and lies to evade a ruthless killer—and she'll have to do it before dark falls. . . .

"Fans of Agatha Christie's *And Then There Were None* will be riveted by Rader-Day's latest psychological thriller, which makes you question who you *really* know and trust and whether you *should* be afraid of the dark."   —*Library Journal*, (starred review)

An unforgettable tale of a mother's desperate search for a lost boy

Anna Winger can know people better than they know themselves with only a glance—at their handwriting. Hired out by companies wanting to land trustworthy employees and by the lovelorn hoping to find happiness, Anna likes to keep the real-life mess of other people at arm's length and on paper. But when she is called to use her expertise on a note left behind at a murder scene in the small town she and her son have recently moved to, the crime gets under Anna's skin and rips open her narrow life for all to see. To save her son—and herself—once and for all, Anna will face her every fear, her every mistake, and the past she thought she'd rewritten.

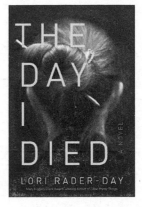

"Lori Rader-Day is so ferociously talented. . . . *The Day I Died* is a terrific novel—gripping and twisty and beautifully layered. It kept me locked up and locked in from the very first word to the very last."
—Lou Berney, Edgar Award–winning author
of *The Long and Faraway Gone*